You, Me, Forever

x

Jo Watson

HEADLINE
ETERNAL

First published in Great Britain in 2019
by HEADLINE ETERNAL
An imprint of HEADLINE PUBLISHING GROUP

First published in Great Britain in paperback in 2020
by HEADLINE ETERNAL

1

Cataloguing in Publication Data is available from the British Library

ISBN 978 1 4722 6554 8

Typeset in 11/14.5 pt Granjon LT Std by Jouve (UK), Milton Keynes

Printed and bound in Great Britain by Clays Ltd, Elcograf S.p.A.

Headline's policy is to use papers that are natural, renewable and recyclable
products and made from wood grown in sustainable forests. The logging and manufacturing
controlled processes conform to the environmental regulations of the country of origin.

www.headlineeternal.com
www.headline.co.uk
www.hachette.co.uk

Jo Wats... ...ove series,
Love to Hate You which has sold over 100,000 copies and *Love You,
Love You Not*. She's a two-time Watty Award winner with over
50 million reads on Wattpad and 85,000 followers. Jo is an
Adidas addict and a Depeche Mode devotee. She lives in
South Africa with her family.

...ore information, visit her website **www.jowatsonwrites.co.uk,**
...llow her on Twitter **@JoWatsonWrites** and Instagram
@jowatsonwrites and find her on Facebook at
www.facebook.com/jowatsonwrites

Praise for Jo Watson's unputdownable romantic comedies:

'Witty, enjoyable and unique' *Harlequin Junkie*

'...und myself frequently laughing out loud and grinning
like a fool!' *BFF Book Blog*

'...art-warming, funny, sweet, romantic and just leaves you
feeling good inside' *Bridger Bitches Book Blog*

'...ll of pure-joy romance, laugh-out-loud moments and
tear-jerkers' *Romantic Times*

By Jo Watson

You, Me, Forever

Destination Love Series
Burning Moon
Almost A Bride
Finding You
After The Rain
The Great Ex-Scape

Standalone
Love To Hate You
Love You, Love You Not

To anyone who's ever been told who they're not allowed to love!

PROLOGUE

There are a few things you should know about me before we begin this story. I think these things are important in order for you to understand why . . . *why* I did the things I did, *why* I am who I am and just *why*? Because isn't *why*? the ultimate question? *Why* is everything? *Why* is this and *why* is that and *why* am I?

So, here are the facts: my name is Becca Thorne. That's not my real name, by the way. My actual name is Pebecca Thorne, and the story of how I lost that little sloping line that magically turns a "P" into an "R" is quite a peculiar one. It involves a single drop of water that fell on just the right spot on my birth certificate to magically dissolve the ink. The stray drop of water came from my mother's eye, right around the time that she heard the news that my father had died in a car accident. If my father hadn't died at that exact moment, and my mother had received the news a mere second later, I might not have gone through my entire life being looked at strangely whenever people read my name out for the first time.

Now, you're probably wondering why I bring up my name right now—surely something as trivial as a name should have little to do with all the existential questions of *why*? But I disagree; I think my name has a lot to do with all the *whys* of my life. A name is important and being given the wrong name soon after your birth definitely gets you off on the wrong foot. Not to mention being given the wrong name under such wrong circumstances. My strange misnaming always left me feeling like some great tragedy had been etched into my story right from the very beginning. It always left me feeling that I didn't really know who I was, and, like that missing line, I too was missing something.

So that's one thing to note about me; the other thing is that I consider myself a deeply flawed human. I know what you're thinking: Everyone has flaws, and while this is true, my flaws really have led me to choose the wrong fork in the road more times than I care to remember. Dinner fork, fish fork, salad fork, dessert fork . . . *Yup*, been there, done that, got the forking T-shirt.

By now, you're probably curious about what these flaws are and why I have them. Whilst the *what* is perhaps easier to answer; the *why*, though, well, that's a little trickier, but I do suspect it has a lot to do with that single stray tear all those years ago. The tear that sealed my fate and made me who I am.

And who am I? I hear you ask. Honestly, I don't think I'm entirely sure of that either. But I am sure of a few things, and they are definitely things worth noting. I'm a person who cares far too much about what others think of me! Sometimes, I care so much about what others might think of me and what I'm doing that I land up being crippled with fear, and do nothing at all.

Let's move on to number two, now. Here it is: I work far too hard trying to prove the world "wrong" about me. I don't even know what I'm trying to prove half the time, or to whom. But I just am. I'm constantly doing things just to be able to say, "See, I did it. HA!" Honestly, it's bloody exhausting.

And here's the last one, and perhaps it's the one that's landed me in the most trouble . . . I jump before I think. I jump before I've even thought about thinking. I jump with both feet and both hands and every other limb and digit one can jump with. The problem is, I always forget to take my brain with me on these jumps. I always seem to leave it behind as I run off blindly towards a fruit fork, or— God forbid—one of those sharp, pointy, oyster forks that can definitely poke your bloody eye out.

So, like I said, I think it's important to remember these things as we embark on this story together. Because, if I think about it now, it all becomes very clear to me how I landed up in the situation I currently find myself in. I think it's rather obvious that my flaws and that tear have all played a good part in helping me choose this particularly twisty fork in the road that has found me in such a monumentally, stupendously enormous amount of . . .

CHAPTER 1

Trouble.

I was in such trouble.

Not "little trouble," like when you use a plastic straw in public these days, despite all those pics of the suffering seahorses. Or like when you swipe right instead of left and a man with a serial-killer moustache starts messaging you. Or like when you cut your own bangs because you watched a YouTube tutorial. No, I'm talking about the kind of trouble that forces you awake in the middle of the night, drenched in a layer of cold sweat and gasping from the stabbing pains in your chest.

I'd been trying to take a very spiritual approach to the "trouble" of late. This approach had me repeating phrases like, *This too shall pass*, and, *The universe will provide the answers*, blah, blah, blah! But after two months of walking around breathing into my heart chakra (which I still wasn't sure I even had) and drinking thick goopy green smoothies for so-called mental clarity, I was still Fucked. Capital F. Several exclamation marks. Screaming ghost face emoji.

Opening my heart and mind to the universe had not helped my writer's block one little bit. Neither had all that "free writing" I'd done, not to mention all that guided meditation, exercising, listening to classical music, doing a total social-media purge and, my last resort, Marie bloody Kondo-ing my entire office. Nothing had helped, and nothing changed the fact that I had exactly one month to submit my new novel to my agent and publisher, and I had exactly zero words written.

Due to the success of my first book, my publisher had signed a deal for my second one without even asking for a concept. They'd also given me a big, fat advance, which I had officially spent without thinking. So, if I didn't produce a book, I would be paying that money back until the end of my days, which, by the way, I was currently hoping would come sooner rather than later. I was so desperate that, the other night, I'd prayed that some massive, global catastrophe—like the eruption of Yellowstone Park, or an alien invasion—would wipe us all out.

I admit, I'd gotten somewhat cocky after the success of my last book. Perhaps it had all gone to my head a bit. Because, let's be honest, I don't really need the Porsche I now drive. I don't even think I like Porsches. I also don't need to be living in this huge apartment, and I certainly didn't need to fly business class on a flight that had taken all of two hours, especially since I learned that men still pee on toilet seats there. I'd become one of *those* people that my poorer self used to mock: the kind who spent R300 more for pale blue salt harvested from a babbling brook in the foothills of the Himalayas by Zen monks, for heaven's sake. But I had such a point to prove to a certain someone, that I guess I'd gotten carried away. What's new? I'm always carrying myself away, never really thinking too deeply about the consequences of such "away carrying."

It's really rather amazing how much money you can spend, and in such a short amount of time, when you're not paying attention. And then one day you go to swipe your card, and the manager of the restaurant comes over and utters those dreaded words: "I'm sorry, but your card has been declined." And they always do it in *that* voice— soft, whispered tones that somehow manage to convey both an air of sympathy and sarcasm at the same time.

I'd thought writing the second book would come easily; after all, I'd managed to write the first one in a matter of weeks. It had poured out of me like an open tap. My story had flooded the pages and filled them up until one day I'd looked up from my computer and seen that I had a full-blown novel on my hands. Sure, it had been inspired by some very painful personal experiences I'd recently had, which might have made it easier to write. I'd secured an agent very quickly and a week later had a publishing deal. "Unheard of, for a debut author," my agent had said. My book had come out, sold hundreds of thousands of copies, and had even put me on some rather prestigious bestseller lists.

Becca Thorne has written the most heartbreaking story of the year. Sad and brittle and unputdownable, the *New York Times* had said. *A truly remarkable and relatable story of love lost that had me reaching for a box of tissues more than once*, *USA Today* had said. *I can't wait to see what this author has in store for us next.*

Talk about pressure! What if there wasn't going to be a next? What if the first one had been a fluke, and there would never be a number two? I felt sick thinking about it. I looked down at my watch and felt that familiar punch in my belly again. I had a meeting with my agent in precisely forty minutes. She knew I didn't have a book. She'd already asked my publisher for three extensions and was now threatening to fire me. In fact, I think she was over threatening and today was the day I was going to be axed, and my very short-lived career as a once-bestselling author was over. My whole body constricted at the thought. I couldn't lose this. I needed this. I needed to be an author, a someone who'd done something, or else who was I? A *nothing*? A *maybe, sort-of, almost-something-once-upon-a-time, but-not-really-anything* thing.

I rummaged through my wardrobe; what does one wear for such an occasion? For one's firing? And what is the right soundtrack for it? I'm always looking for the perfect song for the moments in my life; it's something I've done since I was a little girl. I especially look for them in those quiet, anxious moments that desperately need filling. And this was one of them. I took out an old, scraggly dress and wondered, if I wore this, didn't brush my hair or remove my smudged eyeliner, and played a melancholic bluegrass song, whether she would take pity on me. Or maybe if I dressed up in an eighties power suit with shoulder pads and those pleated things called "slacks" she would find it harder to fire me. An anthemic song could be playing in the background as I stride into her office confidently . . .

"Let The River Run!"

I sighed and abandoned my *Working Girl* fantasy and grabbed a pair of jeans that were feeling rather tight around the middle, thanks to all those late-night, *very* non-keto binges, and pulled on a shirt with a smiley emoji on it—*oh, the irony*—but, honestly, it was one of the only clean things in my wardrobe. I swung my handbag over my shoulder and headed for the door, kneecaps shaking like two pathetic chihuahuas.

The strap of my handbag slipped down and I pulled it back up again. It was one of my favorite bags. I'd found it a year ago, stuffed into the corner of an old, dusty antique store in downtown Johannesburg. It was covered in a delicate, intricate beadwork that, when I felt nervous, I liked to run my fingertips over. There was something so soothing about the action, and, right now, I needed soothing.

I closed my apartment door and headed for the elevator. I lived in one of those newly refurbished downtown buildings (very cool and trendy). The kind that was part residential, part hotel, part office, part shop, part restaurant and part modern art gallery. I'd been to the art gallery once. I'd stood there sipping on a flowery, artisanal gin while pretending to understand the significance of the spray-painted iPhone hanging from the ceiling. It was on sale for R100,000.

"An expression of rebellion against our social-media obsessed society," the man with the *Pirates of the Caribbean* moustache had said to me. I'd nodded, even though I had no idea what he was talking about. Like I said, the whole place was very fancy and arty, and I *really* didn't need to live here. It was all for show, if I was truly honest with myself. The question was, *who* was I showing?

The elevator was empty when I climbed in; I liked it that way.

I fiddled with the beads on my bag as the elevator started to descend. I watched the numbers lighting up, getting smaller and smaller and smaller . . .

14 . . .

13 . . .

12 . . .

I was dreading the moment that it said "1" and I had to climb out and face my fire-breathing agent. My agent was intimidating at the best of times, what with her piercing green eyes and her uber-fancy name, *Daphne Kingsley-Hawthorne*. Every time I heard her say it out loud, I automatically mumbled, "The second esquire," in my head. The elevator gave a sudden jerk and then came to an abrupt stop. I looked up. We were on floor nine, one of the office floors.

"I'm leaving now, I'm leaving now, okay?" An agitated-looking woman walked in. "I'm walking into the elevator. I'm in the elevator. I'm pressing the button. I've pressed the button. I will be there on time." She narrated her way in and stood on the opposite side to me. I ran my eyes over her quickly before looking away. She was the kind of woman that had presence. You know the kind I'm talking about? The kind that, if she walked into a room, everyone would look up at her. She oozed professionalism with her neatly scraped-back hair, dark maroon lipstick, high-heel shoes with red soles, AND she was wearing a power suit! *Ha!* I knew I should have worn one. This woman exuded such strength and power, there was no way someone wearing *that* was getting fired today, or ever.

"Elevator doors are closing now. They've closed. I'll be there soon . . . uh, hellooooo? Losing reception, sorry . . . uh . . . See you soon." She hung up hard, as if she was pissed off, and I couldn't help but wonder who she was speaking to. I made eye contact briefly and gave a tiny smile. She didn't smile back and her eyes drifted down to my T-shirt. I crossed my arms; I could see she was silently judging my unfashionable apparel. *Wench!*

The elevator started moving and then suddenly stopped again.

Power Suit looked up and gave a long, slow sigh. As if she had no time to spare. She probably didn't; women like her were always rushing off to important things like business meetings and Pilates—*see, two can play at the judging game.* The elevator doors opened, and an even more agitated-looking woman stepped in. She pressed the ground-floor button angrily, and, when the doors didn't close immediately, she pushed the button another five times in quick succession.

"It's not going to work faster if you push it more than once," Power Suit said sarcastically.

The other woman whipped around and gave Power Suit one hell of a death stare. God, her eyebrows really were on fleek. Suddenly, the air was thick with pheromone-filled tension. Narrow-eyed stares were coupled with tight, matt-lipped scowls. I felt transported into an episode of *The Real Housewives* and wondered what was going to happen next. I was ever so grateful when the doors finally did close and the elevator started moving again. But that didn't mean the atmosphere in the elevator was any better. In fact, you could have cut the tension in that little metal box with a blunt utensil. Power Suit was tapping her phone against her palm, Fleek Brow was tapping her foot and I was fiddling with my bag. I briefly wondered why these two looked as anxious as I felt. What were their stories? Like me, did they also now find themselves standing at some great fork in the road, wondering which one they should take? Wondering who they were, why they were here and what the hell they were going to do? My mind started racing, but it quickly stopped when . . .

Disaster struck.

A loud grinding sound ripped through the silence and forced me to cover my ears. A sudden drop thrust my stomach into my mouth and made all the blood rush to my head so quickly that I saw stars behind my eyes. I grabbed on to the railing as gravity disappeared and my feet lifted off the ground. Everyone screamed as the elevator started to plummet faster and faster and faster and . . .

"I didn't mean it about Yellowstone Park!" I wailed loudly as the thing continued to fall at what felt like the speed of light. I really hoped dying in an elevator wasn't going to be painful. What the hell was I thinking? Of course it was going to be painful! I closed my eyes tightly and waited for the inevitable big bang, which would no doubt be followed by a never-ending blackness. I was going to die . . .

Now, what the hell was the right soundtrack for that?

CHAPTER 2

Pan-de-mon-i-um! It broke out.

Screams and wails and arms and legs filled the air. A sharp pain in my back alerted me to the fact that Power Suit's Louboutin had stabbed me between the shoulder blades. Another pain in my face as Fleek Brow's enormous key ring whacked me across the mouth. I tried to swat all the debris away with one hand as I clung to the railing with the other, my knuckles turning a bright white from the effort. My handbag slipped down my arm and I made a grab for it. And then the strap ripped and, like a million marbles been blasted out of a cannon, the beads shot into the air, pelting me like bullets. They bounced off the floor and the walls and ceiling with the frenetic sound of a death-metal drumming solo. *Yes*, that was the perfect soundtrack for this moment. A murderous, ear-shattering guitar riff accompanied by the violent shriek of lyrics about dying in the flames of hell.

And then, just as quickly as it had started, it stopped. The elevator ground to a halt, the death-metal song that was playing in my head concluded with a savage, growling crescendo, and then—*silence.* We all held our breath as the silence around us screamed.

Five seconds passed, six, seven, eight, and then suddenly the elevator was filled with new sounds—our desperate cries for help. I stood up, my heart banging in my throat so hard that I was worried it would shoot out. I was shaking, panting, gasping for air and wailing for help. Power Suit threw herself at the doors and tried to pry them open. *Pop*—a red-painted false nail flew off and hit the floor.

She banged her fists against the door so hard that things started to shake again.

"Careful!" I yelled at her, afraid her shaking might dislodge the elevator again, but it dislodged something else instead. I watched, my jaw dropping in horror, as the steel trapdoor in the ceiling shook and then fell. It plummeted down, picking up speed as it went, and then, to my horror, smashed into Fleek Brow's head. She stood there for a few seconds, looking stunned, and then her eyes glazed over, the blood gushed and she fell backwards with a bang.

"Oh my God." I threw myself to the floor and shook her. She moaned and gurgled. "We need to get out of here," I screamed at Power Suit. She looked at me as if her eyes were about to burst from their sockets, as if her lower jaw was about to snap off and tumble to the floor. She nodded at me, her dark lipstick smudged across her cheeks, and then she turned and hit the big red alarm button. A new sound filled the air. The siren was so loud that I had to cover my ears and bury my head between my knees.

I'm not sure how long we waited like that, alarm blaring, each one of us in our own shocked world. Time, at this stage, seemed to have taken on a whole new nebulous meaning. Seconds felt like years as men chopped at the steel doors with axes and shouted things like, "Don't worry! We're coming for you!" All I could do was sit on the floor, my knees pulled towards my chest, and try not to totally flip the fuck out. It's true what they say about having a near-death experience: your life really does flash in front of your eyes. But not the good parts. As I sat there, regret after regret, and painful memory after even more painful memory flooded me. Broken hearts, friends and family I didn't have, books with zero words in them . . .

The door finally burst open. Sweaty axe-wielding men in uniforms (which, under less life-threatening circumstances, I might have gawked at) piled into the lift. A paramedic carrying a huge first-aid bag looked around at us and then made a beeline for the woman on the floor, whose bloody brows were no longer *on fleek*. I couldn't move for a few moments, despite the men telling me it was safe to stand up. I think it was in that moment that I finally understood the meaning of the phrase "shell-shocked." I felt far away, removed from my body in some strange way, and it was only when I felt the hands beneath my arms, the gentle pull, the powerful lifting into the man's arms, that a part of me clicked back to life. He carried me out and, as he did, *applause*.

I looked around and, to my horror, realized just how many people had gathered outside to watch the spectacle—iPhones in the air, filming it. A free reality show unfolding right in front of their eyes, no Netflix subscription required. I wondered what the soundtrack for this might be.

I wiggled and jumped out of his arms, almost losing my footing as I went. His arm shot out and stopped me from falling. A few gasps rose up as I steadied myself on my feet.

"Careful there, ma'am," he said. I felt confused, nervous, and my hands reached for the beads on my bag. But it wasn't there. I looked over at my empty arm.

"My bag, my bag," I wailed loudly, as if it was the most important thing in the world. I looked around for it, and that's when I remembered all the beads. Bouncing, ricocheting, pirouetting inside the elevator. I turned and looked inside. The woman on the floor was still there; the paramedic was securing something around her neck and setting up an IV. I shuddered as the needle slipped into her arm, and then quickly looked away; I could feel the color drain from me as the white static buzz of dizziness prickled my skin.

"Sit, sit." The fireman guided me to the floor, gently putting my head between my legs as it spun like a planet on an out-of-whack orbit.

I heard a woman's voice, soft and sweet and kind. "Here," she said, reaching into her shopping bag and pulling out a Coca-Cola. She opened the can and passed it to me. I nodded gratefully and raised it to my lips. Sugar and fizz and sweetness made me feel instantly better.

"I'll get your bag," the fireman said sympathetically. "Just sit for a while." I nodded again, aware that I was in worse shape than I'd initially thought. I sipped the Coke and, with each sip, I could feel my color return, my head steady itself, and soon my legs were no longer shaking. The fireman came back with my bag and handed it to me—well, what was left of it, anyway. The strap had been ripped off and a large gaping tear in the bag rendered it useless. I looked inside to make sure all my things were still there—cell phone, wallet. And that's when I saw it.

"What the . . . ?" It looked like a secret compartment inside the bag had been ripped open. I stuck my fingers into the tear and touched something, a lot of somethings. I gripped what felt like pieces of paper between my fingers and pulled them out. I stared at them. They looked old, very old. Stained brown and dusty from time, creased as if they had been read over and over again. I scanned them briefly. They looked like they'd all been written by the same person, same handwriting. I opened the first one and started reading.

9 July, 1949
My love,
I'm sorry I couldn't get away to meet you today, but I was stopped by the police, demanding to know where I was going. We are all in such shock about what happened yesterday. It's all over the radio, it's all anyone can talk about, and I feel sick because I don't know what this new law is going to mean for us.

I turned the letter over in my hands and studied it carefully. There was no address on the back of it, nothing to tell me where it had come from or who it was for. I looked down at all the other letters and started reading them briefly. They were all love letters, that much was certain. As I skimmed them, familiar words and phrases and dates caught my attention. And, just as I was starting to piece the bits together and understand what these letters were about, my phone rang. I jumped at the loud sound; it reminded me of that alarm. I grabbed my phone and looked at the name flashing across the screen. My heart fell into my feet once again.

The phone stopped ringing and I breathed a sigh of relief, but that was quickly interrupted by the stream of WhatsApp messages pinging angrily on to my screen.

Daphne (the second esquire): Where are you?
Daphne (the second esquire): You'd better be on your way.
Daphne (the second esquire): I cancelled a lunch meeting for this!
Daphne (the second esquire): I am fast losing my patience here.

My fingers were shaking as I tried to type as quickly as possible.

Becca: I'll be there in five minutes. Was stuck in an elevator.
Daphne (the second esquire): Sure you were.

I could almost hear the sarcasm in her voice dripping from those tightly pursed lips of hers. I looked up as a gurney rushed past me; it was Fleek Brow and she was being rushed away with a great sense of urgency. I watched as the gurney raced through the hallway. I could see the flash of red and blue ambulance lights as she disappeared out of the front doors. I hoped she was going to be okay.

"I'm on my bloody way, okay! I'm up. I'm walking. I'm on my way!" I heard that familiar agitated voice and looked over to my left. Power Suit was talking into her phone again, the urgency in her voice palpable. She hung up angrily and then turned and marched away from me. Her heels clanked loudly on the marble floor as she went. And then, *it was just me.* The other two women who I'd shared this harrowing experience with were gone. And I didn't even know their names. I stood up and dusted myself off. It was time to go. Time to face the music. *Whatever the hell that music was going to be.*

CHAPTER 3

*M*y agent's office was just as intimidating as she was. Large brown leather couches were scattered across her dark-wood floored waiting room. They were the kind of couches that, if you had a sweaty ass, you would stick to. The kind that required you to peel yourself off with a spatula. I lowered myself on to the couch as one of her little minion assistants—they always looked terrified—rushed up to me with a toothy grin.

"Can I offer you some coffee?" she asked in a small, fast voice. She smiled quickly and then moved her head from side to side, like a little meerkat might do.

"No, thanks." I didn't think coffee was a good idea right now; it might be like adding petrol to a fire, since my heart was already racing like a pack of greyhounds. In fact, it felt like my heart might burst through my chest at any moment and splatter itself across her shiny wooden floor. I smiled nervously as I imagined one of her assistants having to mop up the mess. My agent would ask, "What the fuck happened here?" (she swore a lot) and her speedy meerkat assistant would reply that one of their former so-called authors, "a nobody, really," had her heart explode out of her chest.

I folded my arms across it and attempted a long, meditative in-breath. But trying to rein my emotions in was like trying to wrangle a wild, galloping horse. It was just too hard to control the nervous panic that was rushing through me, flushing and prickling my skin, dropping cold marbles into the pit of my stomach and shaking them around. Some doomsday soundtrack started playing in my head. The kind that starts as everybody drops their grocery bags in the street and stares up at the sky as the massive mothership moves in and blocks the sun . . . Duh, duh, duuuhhhh. *Do you hear that?*

"Where the fuck is she?" I heard the scream. It wasn't subtle. And I knew the "she" she was referring to was me. The meerkat who'd offered me the coffee raced across the room nervously and stuck her head around the door.

"She's here," she whispered sweetly. So sweetly it was almost bitter, like sucking on a packet of artificial sweetener.

"Send her the hell in."

I stood up and started walking towards her office. Slowly. The soles of my feet felt like they were coated in sticky gum and it was hard to move. I needed a distraction and I reached for the beads on my handbag. But it wasn't there. Shit, I felt so exposed right now. I needed my bag like a child needed its favorite blanky. I slid half my foot over the threshold of her door and paused. I couldn't do this, so I lurked in the doorway like a creepy stalker for a few seconds, until . . .

"I can fucking see you!" Her loud voice came at me like tossed daggers. "Get in here."

And so I did. I walked in and there she was. Sitting behind her huge wooden desk, leaning back in her old leather chair that looked like it had once inhabited the halls of government. Thick smoke hung in the air as she pulled on a strong Camel cigarette . . . Okay, so that last part was a lie. She wasn't smoking. But she should have been, because she was the kind of woman who looked like she gave zero fucks. The kind of woman who would use your rotting corpse as a lifeboat, who drunk petrol shots from a poisoned chalice and ate men alive after sex . . . *That's if she even had sex.*

"So, tell me," she said in her gruff, raspy voice. "Has someone figured out a way to halt and reverse global warming?" She leaned forward in her chair; it creaked loudly.

"Sorry, what?" I asked nervously.

"I don't know, or has someone discovered all the secrets to the universe?"

I shook my head. "I don't follow."

She stood up; another long, loud creak. I wondered if it was intentional. Did her chair have an "intimidating creak" setting?

"I'm asking if a miracle has suddenly occurred and you have some actual words on a page that can be made into this thing commonly referred to as a 'book.'" She gestured air quotes. It was so slimy and patronizing, and, had I been a different person, one with a much firmer backbone, I might have picked up that pompous *look-at-me-I-hunt* taxidermy pheasant that she had on her desk and stuffed it down her throat, or at least plucked its tail feathers out and poked her with the hard parts.

"I mean, to be honest, it doesn't really surprise me. I've been down this road before with other authors," she said, all sharp-tongued.

"What road?" I asked.

She sighed. "It's more common than you think."

"What is?"

"The 'one-hit wonder.' The author who's only good for one book. I suspected it, though; you didn't strike me as someone who had a lot of stories in you. I guess it's par for the course, really."

"I beg your pardon?" My jaw almost hit the floor. She was confirming my worst fear out loud: *my first book had been an accident and I didn't have another one in me.*

"I guess not everyone can be a Steve King—that reminds me . . . Natasha!" she called out loudly to one of her assistants and they came skidding in. "Please call Steve's agent and remind her of our late luncheon tomorrow." Natasha nodded and then skidded out the door again. Daphne turned back to me. "Now, Steve—he has a lot of stories in his head."

"I . . . I . . . have a lot of stories in my head, too," I stuttered defensively. It didn't sound very convincing though.

She chuckled. It was very witch-around-a-caldron-y. "It doesn't seem like it." She was as acerbic as a sulphuric-acid-soaked lemon.

"I do. I have a lot of stories and I am *not* a one-hit wonder. I have more to tell, more to say, more to . . ." I stopped talking when she rolled her eyes. This gesture was like a hot knife into my buttery gut. Her disbelief in me was evident and she wasn't even trying to hide it. Well, I was going to prove her wrong, I was going to . . . to . . .

And then her chuckle turned into a laugh.

"What?" I asked, stepping backwards as if she was about to thrust a toad at me and curse me for all eternity.

She shook her head. "I'm just having déjà vu."

"Uh . . . why?" I asked.

"So many writers have stood there—" she pointed at the floor and I looked down—"and said the exact thing you're saying now. Oh well, another one bites the dust, as they say."

"What?"

"Of course, *you*'ll be liable to pay the advance back, not me. And I'll still keep my fifteen percent, naturally," she said.

"But, but . . . wait. There's got to be a solution, a—"

"The only solution is you producing a book, which is clearly not going to happen."

"It is!" I was frantic now, even though I didn't believe what I was saying.

"Well, where is it, then?" she asked. "Where is this amazing bestseller that is going to take the world by storm?" Her eyes mocked me and judged me.

"I have it. I have it." The lie tumbled out of me.

"Where?" And then she started doing something that sent me over the edge. Pushed me too far. She started flapping through the papers on her desk. "Where could it be?" She lifted some papers and pretended to look under them. "Nope. Nothing," she said sarcastically. "What about here?" She flung open one of her drawers and looked inside. "Not there either!"

And then it hit me.

Hard! So damn hard.

A moment of pure clarity. Clarity so great I felt like I was standing on a beach looking into the depths of a tropical lagoon and seeing the tiniest shell on the bottom of the seabed. But this moment of clarity was also peppered with total and utter insanity. I folded my arms again and made eye contact with her.

"I actually *am* writing something." I stared at her, trying to look as confident as possible, even though internally I was drowning in quicksand.

She pulled her small glasses down to the tip of her pointed nose and pursed her lips together. Wrinkles appeared around her mouth, making it look just like a puckered asshole.

"And dare I ask what that is?" she asked.

"It's a book." I said the only words I could think of at that moment, because I was disintegrating under her gaze.

She scoffed. A look of vague amusement mixed with something I can only guess was disdain caused the corners of her lips to twitch.

"A book?" she repeated flatly.

I nodded. "A book."

"What book?" she asked.

"It's set in the 1940s, in South Africa." I blurted it out before I had a moment to *really* think about what I was doing. "The apartheid law and mixed marriages law have just been passed by the national government. A young couple in love are ripped apart because one of them is white and the other is not. It's *Romeo and Juliet* in apartheid South Africa." I stopped talking abruptly and then almost slapped my hand over my mouth. *Had I really just said that? Out loud?*

Something washed over her face; I wasn't sure what it was. She lowered herself into her chair once more and then placed her hands on the desk in front of her. I looked down at her nails, the kind of nails that could really rip an aorta out if you weren't careful.

"Tell me more," she said slowly, now tapping her fingers on the polished wood.

"More? Uh . . . yes," I said nervously. "Our young couple have fallen in love during a tumultuous time." My mind raced, trying to remember history class. "Tensions between white and non-white South Africans are mounting. But, amongst all this hate and animosity, and against all the odds, they've found each other. But they have to keep their love and relationship a secret from their parents, the police, society. Their story will be told through a series of intimate and beautiful love letters that they wrote each other." I stopped talking and looked at her.

She stared straight back at me for a moment, and then her eyes flicked up, as if she was looking at something on the ceiling. I waited. She looked down at her desk again and drummed her fingers loudly. And then she looked up and started nodding.

"Have you written any of it yet?" she asked.

And then I too began to nod. I nodded before I'd even had a moment to process what I was about to do. "Yes," I said feebly. I reached into my pocket and pulled out one of the letters.

"What is that?" She pointed her bony finger at the letter.

"I've been writing the letters on scraps of paper. Helps me connect with the characters more," I said, hoping she bought this.

"I see." She eyeballed me in a peculiar way. "Well, what are you waiting for? Read!"

I cleared my throat and looked down at the letter in my hand. A million thoughts tore through my mind. If she liked this idea, there was no taking it back. If she didn't like it, then I still didn't have a book. Something deep inside me started to throb.

I was about to jump straight over a line, here. A big line. But I couldn't stop myself. There was just no holding me back. I jumped! I jumped and I ran so fast that, within seconds, I couldn't even see the line anymore. The line was gone. The line was now a blurry smudge on the horizon of morality and sanity, and I was sprinting away from it.

CHAPTER 4

29 July, 1949

My love,

Last night, I dreamed of you again. I dreamed I was walking through an open field and I was looking for something. I didn't know what it was, but I could sense how important it was that I found it. As if my life depended on it. I walked for hours, going round in circles, and then I saw you. The sun was illuminating your face, as if you were an angel, divine, and I knew, unequivocally, that you were what I'd been searching for. You smiled at me as I stood in the field, and suddenly it was night-time and you were the stars and the moon and everything that made the night sky bright and brilliant. And then everything started to go dim. The moonlight and stars lost their luster and started to fade, disappearing into the darkness.

I ran. I ran as fast as I could, chasing your light as it got further and further away from me. I reached out to grab it, the light, but it was gone. It disappeared into the blackness as if it had been swallowed up by a giant mouth. Suddenly, all your light had been extinguished and everything was dark. I walked around, bumping into things, falling down, scrambling back up to my feet as I tried to find you again . . . but it was pitch black and you weren't there. And then I woke up into another nightmare.

I woke up to the news that our love has been made illegal, and now I am lost again in the darkness, even though the sun is shining.

The whole day I've felt like I've been trying to catch you again. As if you are millions of grains of sand slipping through my fingers. I feel like I've let go of a balloon and I'm watching it soar up, disappearing into the sky and, no matter how much I run, or how high I climb, it is always just out of my reach. That's how it feels today. It feels like I'm losing you, like you're being pulled away from me by something that I cannot control. I cannot stop it.

Edith, I cannot lose you. You are the best thing in my life, you are my everything, and no one can tell me that loving you is wrong. Because loving you is the most right thing I have ever done. It is the only thing that has ever made sense to me. Because, without you, my life is senseless and dark and I am lost in a starless night and I will wander around forever looking for the thing that I need in order to breathe.

I hope we see each other soon. I miss you . . .

You, me, forever.

CHAPTER 5

I looked up after reading the letter and—*oh my God*—I took a step back. What the hell was that? What the hell was happening to her face? Was that a . . . a . . . I gasped in utter shock as a tear seemed to snake out of her eye and trickle down her cheek. It carved a white line in her too-orange foundation. The tear was watery in color and I was surprised to see she didn't cry drops of blood harvested from her former clients. I heard a sniffle in the doorway and looked. Three of her meerkats were standing there, tears streaming down their faces.

PPPfffffgghhhhhh! One of Daphne's assistants took out a tissue and blew her nose loudly.

"That is . . . That is—" she stumbled and stuttered over her words—"the most beautiful thing I've ever heard."

The others all nodded in agreement.

"Read me a letter that she wrote to him," my agent said, snapping her fingers at me.

"I . . . I . . . haven't written any of those yet," I lied again. As far as I could see, all these letters had been written by the same person—him.

"Why not?" she asked.

"Uh . . . I'm writing his story first, and then I'll write hers," I added, suddenly feeling terrible for what I had just done.

"Well, they better be as good as his," she said.

I nodded. "They will be," I assured her, with a confidence that I didn't really have.

"Because if they are . . ." she trailed off and looked down at her desk again, deep in thought. "Yes! Yes!" She raised her head and started nodding. "I can see it. It's clear. Million-copy seller! *New York Times* and *USA Today* lists. Goddammit, a fucking movie deal. Netflix, even. '*Romeo and Juliet*, set in South Africa.' It will be more heart-wrenching and devastating than your first book. Becca Thorne is the queen of heartbreak. You will make the whole world weep. God, if your first book made you money, this one is going to make us a fuckload!"

I stared at my agent. Her face was red, flushed with a kind of feverish excitement. It was a strange, dangerous kind of excitement. The kind of excitement that told me there was trouble coming. *And there was . . .*

She snapped her fingers at one of her meerkats. "Get Lighthouse Books on the phone."

"Wait. Wait!" I held my hands up in panic; the gravity of what I'd just done was starting to sink in. And then the guilt. This wasn't my letter to read! "What are you doing?"

"I'm telling them what a bestseller you have on your hands. Maybe we can push them for more money. Foreign rights—this needs to be in all the languages; audio—"

"Wait!" I cut her off, a cactus of panic forming in my throat.

She looked at me blankly. "Wait, what?"

"Uh . . . well, don't you think it's a bit premature to call them . . . ? I mean, uh, I don't even have . . . I mean, it's not like I—"

She held her hand up and I stopped talking. "How many letters have you written?" she asked.

I shook my head frantically. "Not many."

"Then why is your pocket bulging?" She pointed at my jean pocket, the one the note had come out of. "Or has your one hip gotten fat?" *God, she was a bitch!* "I want Lighthouse Books on the phone . . . now!" she called out again.

"Stop! Stop!" I yelled.

Her head whipped up and she glared at me like she'd never glared before. "What is wrong with you?"

"I can't do this," I blurted out. "It's all wrong. I shouldn't have done this. It was a terrible mistake and I regret it and . . . I . . ."

Suddenly the phone rang and we both looked down at it. She started reaching for the receiver, her taloned claw moving towards it as if in slow motion. I made my move for the phone too, as quickly as I could, but I was too late. She grabbed the receiver and lifted it to her lips, and then, I was sure, she snarled at me.

"Belinda, dahhling!" she gushed into the phone. Belinda was my editor. "I've got great news for you! Really great. Terrific!"

* * *

I threw myself into my apartment and straight down on to my couch. My body ached, all the way from my toes to the hair follicles on the top of my head. Since leaving my agent's office, the enormity of the situation I now found myself in had been hitting me in steady waves. As I'd reached my building, the waves had picked up pace until a massive tidal wave almost knocked me off my feet. And by the time I was sticking my keys into my front door, the earth felt like it was shaking below my feet, as if a meteorite had crashed down. I was teetering on the precipice of total and utter mad catastrophe.

Shit! I was in such trouble.

Not "big trouble," like when you wake up in your bed in the middle of the night, drenched in a layer of cold sweat and gasping from the stabbing pains in your chest. I'm talking about the kind of trouble where you wake up in a jail cell in the middle of the night, drenched in a layer of cold sweat and gasping from the stabbing pains in your chest. Because I was breaking the law. I was officially a law breaker and I was about to commit the worst crime in the publishing industry: *plagiarism*.

As a writer, you always worry about accidentally committing such an act. You fear that one of the lines you write might actually not be your own, that perhaps you've read it somewhere else and it sank in so deeply that you thought it was yours. But this was not like that. *At all*. In fact, this was like me saying that, just because my ass was four times larger than it should be, I looked like Kim Kardashian. Let me assure you at this point in our story together that I do *not* look like Kim Kardashian—or any Kardashian, for that matter. My pale European skin, given to me by an Irish grandmother, which boasts far too many freckles when the sun comes out, and my mop of bright red hair, given to me by a very gingery uncle named Teddy, were definitely testament to this. God, my brain was rambling, my thoughts were swirling and . . .

I needed a drink. What was I saying? I needed six. I cursed the fact that I didn't consume alcohol, and wished I did in this moment.

I lay back on my couch and looked up at my ceiling. I had a real dilemma on my hands, literally. I was holding a dilemma in my sweaty, plagiarist paws right then. I raised my hands to my face and looked at the letters. *What on earth was I meant to do now?* The ball was rolling. Daphne (the second esquire) had made sure of that when she'd called my publisher and promised a literary masterpiece of epic, maybe even award-winning proportions. I'd wanted to throw up as she'd said that, but what was I meant to do? Psychically pry the phone from her claws? Tell them both I'd experienced a terrible lapse of sanity and that actually I was a liar and there was no book, and probably (definitely) wouldn't be one?

Balls were rolling alright! Like a bowling ball skidding down a slippery alley, ready to collide with the pins at the bottom and send them flying. Well, I felt like one of those pins right now, and I was just waiting for the ball to smash into me.

I sat up quickly on the couch and very shakily put the letters down on the coffee table in front of me. On my rose quartz coffee table, to be specific. Another expensive item I'd bought that I didn't really bloody need. But I'd read a book about crystals, some "woo-woo hoo-hoo" thing about mystic energies and whatnot and so forth, etcetera. It had said that rose quartz was very calming and brought love, tranquility and peace into the home. At the time, I'd needed peace. I hadn't gotten it, though. All I'd gotten was a massive dent in my credit card.

I began to fan the letters out, smoothing them down with my hands and running my fingers over them, taking in their textures, until . . .

My fingertips came into contact with something else entirely. Something smooth. I pulled it out and took a closer look. There, among all the worn and tattered letters, was a sealed envelope. I turned it over in my hands and looked at the back of it. I could see it had never been opened. I looked at the writing on the front; it was completely different to the other writing. This writing was more elaborate and feminine. Curly, calligraphic lettering and swirly hearts.

I tried to open it carefully, but my hands were sweating so profusely that I seemed to be leaving a wet, sticky stripe across it. I finally managed to open the envelope and delicately removed the letter inside. It was perfect. Like it had been trapped in a time capsule. Untouched, pristine. I unfolded it gently and looked at the frilly, cursive handwriting, and then started to read.

CHAPTER 6

20 September, 1949

Please ignore the letter I sent you last week. I didn't mean any-thing I said in it. Father forced me to write it. I tried to refuse him, but couldn't. He held me down at my desk for hours until I wrote it. It killed me to write those words. It pained me to say the things I said about our love and relationship, because none of it is true.

After we came home from the cove that day, Father ransacked my room. He found my diary under my mattress and found the paintings of you in the back of my cupboard. I'm grateful he didn't find your letters, though. I've never seen him like that before. His face went red, even the jagged white scar down his cheek went red. I was so afraid. He dragged me outside and made me build a fire; he wanted me to throw everything into it. It felt like I was digging my own grave as I piled the small sticks together and rolled the newspaper into small balls. And then he dropped the match and it all went up in flames. My heart might as well have been in that fire, it hurt so much to watch the corners of my papers curl and disintegrate, to watch the paint blacken on the canvas until there was nothing left of you. And then he dragged me back inside and told me that, if I ever saw you again, I would be dead to him. But I was already dead. A little part of me died in the fire that day.

But, when we were inside, Miriam managed to save some of my things from the fire. She kept them for me. She told me that she's known about us all along; she saw us once at night. She won't tell anyone, though; she's on our side.

The next day, Father took me to see Father McMillan because he says I have to marry Ian. He's arranging my marriage to him and I can't stop him. How can I marry him? How can I marry a man I don't love? I stood there, outside the church on the hill, and I looked out over the town. It had rained the night before and the river was overflowing, escaping its banks and running into the sea, turning it brown. The water was so fast and quick and breaking free of its confines . . . it gave me an idea.

I'm going to try to escape. I'm going to pack a bag and I'm going to meet you under our willow tree on the river. I'll be there at midnight on the last day of September—my father will be away—and I'll wait for you there, right in the place where we carved our promise to each other in the tree.

It's perfect, us meeting there, under the largest and oldest willow tree in the country, because I imagine our love is a lot like the tree itself. It's big and will stand up to gale-force winds and thunderstorms and black frost, and still it will never stop growing. No matter what my father says, the government, the world, I will never stop loving you.

I've found a better hiding spot for my letters to you. You will be able to get them there. I'm putting them inside my "favorite book." Please go and look for them as soon as you can, in case there is a change in plans. Miriam says she will deliver this one letter to you only, but she says she can't deliver any more—it's too dangerous for her. If Father found out she was helping us, who knows what he would do, and I can't put her in that kind of danger.

I love you. I love you. I love you. I love you and I cannot wait to be with you again. It's been thirteen days since I saw you. I've been making markings in the wall behind my bed, like someone in prison might do. Because that's what it feels like without you— that I'm trapped in prison.

We'll see each other soon, though. We'll run away somewhere, like we spoke about. We'll build a little house in the middle of a forest where no one can find us. And we'll live in it together, away from this cruel, cruel world . . . just like we talked about.

We'll wake up together every morning and hold each other for hours in bed, because we don't need to be away from each other. We'll spend our days swimming, and I'll paint you and you'll read to me, and we'll talk all night long if we want to, because neither of us has to run off somewhere. And we'll tell each other that we love each other, out loud. We'll say it all day and all night, until finally we've said it enough to make up for all the times that we weren't able to utter the words, and then we'll still keep saying it . . .

I love you. I love you. I love you. I love you. I love you. I love you. I love you. I love you.

Wait for me under the tree. I am coming and then we will start our life together.

You, me, forever.

CHAPTER 7

*T*ears.

This was the saddest and most beautiful thing I had ever read. This wasn't some made-up scene in a movie or a book. This was straight from someone's heart. Raw, real, beautiful, emotional . . . *and this was so wrong.* What I was doing was so, so wrong. *I knew that, but . . .*

I started opening and closing each letter, one by one, looking for more letters that had been written by her. But there was only this one, and the story ended so abruptly. *What happened next?* I was dying to know, and I also *needed* to know. I had a very incomplete story in front of me, and I'd promised my agent a complete story, from two perspectives.

I stood up and paced my room a few times. I was feeling so agitated and unsettled, like I needed to claw my way out of my skin. The letters on my coffee table seemed to be calling my name—not literally. Well, I *hoped* not literally, or I would definitely be requiring a very specific sort of help, the sort that kind doctors with clipboards handed out. The letters seemed to be calling to me in a way I didn't understand yet. This all seemed so fortuitous; only a few hours ago, I had been so desperate for a story, and now one had fallen into my lap. *Was that just a coincidence?* Or was it more? Or was I just looking for ways to justify my actions?

I turned and looked at the letters again. There were a lot of them—thirty, maybe even forty—but there certainly weren't enough to write an entire book with, and certainly not without the other side of the story, or the ending, or a setting, or more context!

I rushed back over to them and started scanning them for clues. If only I could find this place, I could fill in the blanks. I read through them, picking out small details here and there: more mentions of the willow tree and the engraving, mention of the hot summers on the beach, an old town hall, a river that ran into the sea. I gathered up clues like lost puzzle pieces, trying to fit them together to see the bigger picture.

I reached for my computer and opened Google. I didn't have much to go on—in fact, there was almost nothing. But Google usually has the answers to absolutely everything. (Although, sometimes the answers can be wrong. Turns out that rash I'd had wasn't a deadly reaction to pomegranate juice and I wasn't going into anaphylactic shock.) My fingers hovered over the keys for a while; I was deciding what to type . . . *church, Father McMillan, willow tree, river, sea*. This was like a needle in a haystack. I was never going to find this place, *or was I . . . ?*

And then, a sign. Big, bright red, flashing and screaming at me. An article about a church on a hill in Willow Bay that had been burned down, rebuilt and dedicated to Father James McMillan, who had died some thirty years ago, heroically saving a child when the river flooded and washed the boy out to sea.

What are the chances?! It was all there, as clear as daylight.

I stared at the screen and blinked a few times. I googled the name of the town, and the more I looked at pictures of it, the more I knew this was it. There it was: the river mouth that ran into the sea, making a strip of the sea a brown color; the willow tree; a church on a hill; hot, summery beaches.

Shit, it couldn't be this easy, could it? I went straight to Google Maps and entered the address. It was a five-and-a-half-hour drive away. I stood up and walked the room again, pacing back and forth. I couldn't sit still; a furnace of energy burned inside me, making me feel hot and itchy, and not the kind of itch you can scratch or the kind of hot you can douse with a cold shower. This was deeper than that.

"Crap!" I cursed and bit my nail clean off. I looked down at my nail; what the hell was I doing? I didn't bite my nails. Then again, I also didn't usually lie to my agent about having written a book that didn't exist, and I didn't usually plan to plagiarize letters I'd accidentally found in a handbag after almost plummeting to my death in an elevator.

But my career was hanging by a thread. I had no book, and if I didn't write this story, there was nothing I could write. I had been existing in a stale, lonely state of writer's block for almost an entire year now, and these letters were the first beacon of light I had seen in months. These letters were my only way out of my situation, the only way to save my career and save myself. Because, without my career, who was I? I had been nobody before it, and I didn't want to go back to being nobody again. I couldn't give *him* the satisfaction of seeing me fail, I couldn't give any of *them* that satisfaction . . .

I didn't want to go back to being the girl with the wrong name, living an ordinary life. I wanted to be Becca Thorne. That's the life I wanted. *But was I really going to steal someone else's life to get it . . .*

CHAPTER 8

The next morning, I was in my car, driving towards Willow Bay. I'd spent the whole night *not* sleeping, and I lay awake just thinking until my body and brain were unable to do so anymore. I'd plied myself with every single justification I could think of for doing this, until I almost believed them all. And then, at around three in the morning, when the fear of being caught out for doing this hit, I went off on another train of thought. It was clear that these letters were never meant to be seen, and they had been written so long ago that whoever wrote them was probably not around anymore. And if they were, it seemed unlikely that they would step forward and claim them, since they were such a secret. So, if I plagiarized them, I would (logically) get away with it. And these were the originals and I doubted any copies would exist.

Okay, don't hate me for thinking that; I hate myself enough already. But I could almost feel the pressure of the gun against my temple, forcing me to do this. *I was that desperate!*

I'd left the cold, grey buildings of Johannesburg behind about an hour ago and I was now heading into South African no man's land—those big, open spaces that exist between towns and cities that seem to stretch on forever. It was all so beautiful, the autumn sun was rising and the roads were lined with fields of pink and white cosmos flowers. Cosmos were a staple here in autumn, and as a child I always associated their pink and white spray with Easter. Easter eggs and bunnies and colorful cosmos all blurred together to form one of my favorite childhood memories—possibly the only good one. I swallowed as my throat tightened just thinking about it.

As you can imagine, the days, weeks and months following my birth were hard for my grieving mother. So hard, in fact, that my grandparents stepped in to look after me, and this is where my merry-go-round childhood all began. Being passed around from family member to family member in those moments when my mother was too depressed to look after me, and when finally my grandparents were just too old. From aunts and uncles, to cousins, and even to the neighbors on a few occasions. I was never really in one place long enough to form any kind of attachment to anyone, never at a single school for long enough to do well at anything, make any kind of a mark or make friends, never in one house long enough to be able to call it a home. I was this little lost girl with the lost sloping line, going round and round in a tumble dryer until I didn't know if I was up or down, left or right, who I was or where I belonged. I longed to be with my mother as I spun around on this never-ending carousel—until, one day, I was. Just like that, she came back into my life and we were going on holiday together.

It was a particularly warm autumn, that year. The cosmos were brighter than I'd ever seen them. The Easter eggs were sweeter, the moments spent with my mother on the beach were funnier and more joyful. The nights that she tucked me in bed and sat there reading to me, taking me away to magical worlds with her, were some of the happiest I'd ever had. And, for the first time since my birth, I felt like I belonged somewhere again and that I knew who I was. I was someone's daughter, and I thought it would stay that way. Only it didn't. After the holiday, I was back on the carousel; I reminded her too much of my father, you see. It was too painful to look at me every day, and just too hard to be a single, depressed mom, raising a daughter. I was better off with someone else, they all said. Funny thing is that no one ever bothered to ask me where I wanted to be. Perhaps I wouldn't have known, though, since I barely knew myself by then.

But what I did know—the only thing I really knew—was that I was clearly not good enough to be looked after by my mother. *I was not good enough.* In my small, childlike brain, the one that saw the world in black and white, I decided that I would need to become good enough in some way. I would need to show her, and everyone else, that I was worthy of being with her. But no matter what I did, who I became, how good I was, it was never enough. Still isn't, really.

I spent my entire childhood floating around, untethered. Like a balloon being blown around in the breeze. Being pushed and pulled around by external forces, never in control of my own destiny. One day I was here, one day there, and the next day I could be somewhere else entirely.

And I could sense that I was an imposition everywhere I went, even though they never said it directly to me. So, to be less of a burden, I tried to fit. I tried to be the person that they wanted me to be, so they would keep me. I worried about everything I did, I worried about what they thought of me constantly, always trying to be the perfect person, but never really feeling like I was. The only real constant I had in my life was the songs and stories that had always filled my head. I'd always turned to them when things got tough.

I sighed as I thought about it all. I knew I couldn't blame all that for who I had become and the wrong choices I was currently making. Those were all very much mine, no one else's.

The more I drove, the less I saw of humanity and civilization, which suited me. There was nothing here other than open grasslands that stretched to the horizon, with the odd rusty windmill to break up the monotony. I continued to drive as grasslands gave way to mountain ranges that stretched across the horizon like the backs of sleeping dragons. I'd done a bit more research on Willow Bay and discovered that it was a unique small town, situated both on the banks of a river and the coastline. The whole town seemed to sit perfectly on a small hill, which was so out of place with the rest of the flat landscape around it. One of the local folk tales tells the story of a great big turtle who liked living in the river and the sea. And, because he couldn't decide where he wanted to be, he stopped right there, so that half of his body was in the fresh water and the other half in the sea. I liked that image. I liked the idea that a whole town was built on the back of an indecisive turtle.

The small town was now a bustling tourist hub and seemed to attract a lot of artists and creatives. Small pottery studios and art galleries and craft-coffee shops seemed to line their one main road. And, when I'd tried to book a room, I discovered that most of the hotels were fully booked; I'd managed to get one of the last available places.

Because I'd set out early, I got there before lunchtime, luckily for me. My stomach was rumbling like it hadn't seen a snack in days. *Oh*, there's something else you should know about me. I can go from zero to more-starving-than-I've-ever-been-in-my-entire-life-and-I-will-eat-my-own-arm-if-necessary in a few seconds. I've always been like that. The second I get hungry, I *need* to eat. Clearly, I must have some kind of speedy metabolism, because, for the most part, I am slim. But then there's my ass. It seems that my body decided to deposit all my fat cells there. Thank God for the shift in beauty standards in the last several years, so large asses have actually become quite a hot commodity. Because, if that hadn't happened, I might not have ever gotten laid. Not that I got laid an awful lot, and not that I liked the word "laid," either. It always makes me think of a chicken on a nest. No, as far as sex went, I'd had enough to know what was good and what was bad, but not enough to truly know what I wanted yet. As far as relationships went . . . *the same*. Enough to know what a lying cheat looks like, but not enough to know what I want from a relationship yet—or, more to the point, to know what I deserve from one.

CHAPTER 9

༄

$\mathcal{I}$ pulled into the hotel parking lot and looked at it. It was a typical-looking motel in that it was built around a large parking lot—no cars in sight, though. The architecture had a very mid-century modern feel to it. You know the vibe: flat roof, those white, metal balustrades that run the length of the balconies, and, inevitably, there's always a flamingo somewhere. In this case, the flamingo was perched in a pot plant by the entrance. I climbed out of my car and walked into the reception, only to be met with an interior I was *not* expecting. Where was the wood paneling? The retro, orange wall tiles and pea-soup-colored carpet?

I looked up at the disco ball that was spewing out dancing dots of light across the black-painted floor. I looked at the tie-dye neon wall-hanging and the chandelier that seemed to be made with glow sticks.

"Right," I mumbled to myself as I rang the bell at the counter. But, when no one came after ringing it three times, I leaned over the counter and called out.

"Helloooo! Anyone there? Checking in." Suddenly, a door opened and a woman came walking through it. The first thing I noticed was her blue eyeshadow. Stretching like a great blue sea from her eyelids to her eyebrows, it was a glittery blue that shimmered when it caught the ultraviolet light in the room. Her brows were those thin, black, nineties ones that arched too high, giving a permanently surprised look. Her lips were lined with a black liner and filled in with a shimmery white pink. To top it all off, she was wearing a tie-dye neon dress with equally neon bracelets around her arm, and her blue hair was up in pigtails, with tufts sticking up like long, wild grasses.

"Hello, and what can I do for you?" she asked, leaning across the counter.

"I booked online," I said, feeling somewhat wordless.

"Sure," she said. "What room would you like? We are completely empty; the choice is yours."

I shrugged. "What rooms do you have?"

"Depends what you're looking for," she said, pulling a brochure out from behind the counter. "We have a variety of different rooms here." She tapped her bright neon fingernails on the desk as she opened the pamphlet and flattened it out in front of me. I looked at the brightly colored pictures of rooms and beds and strange decor that filled the pages.

She pointed at one of the pictures. "This is the Rave Room," she said. She looked up at me and smiled a wide, toothy grin, and then looked back down at the pamphlet. "And this is the Jungle Room." She pointed at another picture. I leaned in to get a closer look. The room looked like a chill room at a trance party. Neon mushrooms and faces of cats with the "om" symbol as their third eye were painted on the walls, *and was that a teepee over the bed?*

"Maybe something a little less . . ." I searched for the words, but couldn't find them. "Do you have any rooms with a desk?" I asked.

"Desks . . ." she repeated, very thoughtfully. As if I'd asked the world's greatest, most intriguing question. A philosophical question about the meaning of life, or why time was linear.

She finally started nodding, as if she'd silently answered the question in her head. "The House Room will be perfect for you, then." She flipped the pamphlet over and tapped on a picture. The room looked more like a dance floor in Ibiza, but it did have a desk in it.

I looked up at her and smiled. "Perfect!" I mumbled, even though I wasn't sure I wanted to use a big pink beanbag as a desk chair.

I took my wallet out slowly and pulled my credit card out. "You know, you're the only hotel in this whole town that has any openings. Everywhere else is fully booked. Is there something going on this weekend?"

She nodded again; this time, she looked somewhat forlorn, despite the fact that her pigtails were bobbing up and down, which only made her seem comic. "Yes, but the Persian crowd never seem to check in here, come the annual Persian parade."

"The what?"

"Persian cats," she qualified.

"Aahhh, I see." I nodded and then stopped abruptly. "Persian cats?"

"Once a year, PCOS comes to our town. They have a 'best in show' contest and then they parade down the main road."

"Polycystic ovaries?" I asked, in utter confusion.

"Persian Cats of the South. But they never check in to my hotel. I've even offered to put cat boxes in the rooms, but not even that tempts them. Honestly, I don't know why. It's a mystery."

I shrugged, even though this didn't seem like a big mystery to me. I passed my credit card over to her, hoping that the thing would be accepted.

"You would think that crowd would appreciate history. I am the oldest hotel in town. My grandfather built this place in the twenties and my dad renovated it in the sixties."

At that, I perked up. "Have you lived in this town for long?"

"All my life," she said, swishing my card through that dreaded machine that steals your money.

"Realllyyyy . . ." I ruminated for a while. This was perfect. "So, is it safe to say that you would know every nook and cranny in this town?" I asked.

She nodded. "And I've probably explored them all, too."

"I'm looking for the big old willow tree that this town seems to be named after. You wouldn't know where that is, would you?"

She nodded and then turned and pulled out another pamphlet. Like the previous one, she spread it out on the table. "Bane of this town's existence." She tapped her fingers on the counter again and I looked.

"*The Willow's Eco Estate*," I read out slowly.

"Bloody eco estate," she shook her head. "About ten years ago, this uptight vegan family bought the land around the willow tree and turned it into a snobby eco-estate, where everyone drives Priuses and cycles and recycles and looks down on you for not being 'off the grid.' And God forbid you use a plastic straw around them." She made some "crazy" gestures with her fingers around her temples. "Want my opinion, eating vegan just makes you angry."

I looked at the picture of the estate and the first thing I noticed was the large fence around it. "The willow tree is in there?" I asked.

She nodded. "Deep inside enemy territory."

"And how would I get to see it?" I asked casually. "If I wanted to," I quickly added, "which I'm not saying I do, but . . ." Oh, shut up, Becca. I pursed my lips together tightly.

"You can't. Unless you know someone on the inside. The security is as tight as my track on Spotify," she said, and laughed now.

"Sorry, what?" I asked.

"I make music. I just uploaded my new track to Spotify."

"Really?"

She nodded proudly. "Yeah. My name is Techno Tannie."

"Techno Granny?" I asked, translating the Afrikaans word "Tannie" to English.

"It's my nickname."

"I see." I looked her up and down. I liked her. She fascinated me. A part of me always wished I could be more like these people who clearly didn't care what the world thought of them. The kind of person that stuck out and was unapologetically themselves, not trying to blend in. I envied that quality. "So, back to the eco estate." I pointed at the pamphlet again. "This fence—is it electric?" I asked.

"God, NO! Not unless they have harnessed the power of all the elements to generate the electricity, so I doubt it," she said mockingly.

"Wouldn't want to leave a big old fat footprint on the earth; they would rather leave a trail of judgement behind them."

"Interesting," I said, half mumbling to myself. I looked up at my host again. It was clear there was no love lost between the locals and these eco-warriors.

"It's best to stay out of that place, darling. Trust me," she said, shaking her head.

I nodded. "I'll stay away." But that was the last thing I was going to do. In fact, as soon as I'd checked in, I was heading straight for that eco estate. I needed to see what was engraved on that tree. But first, lunch. Or else I would probably eat the tree in question.

CHAPTER 10

The fence was bloody enormous!

And the question was, clearly, what the hell were they trying to keep out? Free-range elephants? This thing could probably stop an army invasion, a zombie apocalypse, winter from coming in *Game of Thrones*!

I looked around. No one was there and I doubted anyone would be coming down this small dirt road that I'd found. Well, I sincerely hoped not, because I was about to break yet another law. God, I was on a roll. Becca the law breaker. That was me now.

I looked up and then clapped my hands together. I could do this. "Right!" I laced my fingers through the fence. Cue the heroic *Mission: Impossible* soundtrack. The soundtrack of a woman about to fly up a fence with the speed and agility of a vervet monkey. At least this fence wasn't electrified, or my career as a criminal would end in cardiac arrest, and that wouldn't be pleasant. I looked down at my feet. I wasn't sure I could do this with shoes on. Like a monkey, I needed my toes for added grip. I bent down, unlaced my shoes and pulled my socks off. This was all very undignified and I wouldn't have done it if I hadn't been desperate. *And I was so desperate.* And I could see it. The willow tree. Perched on the banks of the river, far off in the distance. It was taunting me with the secret it guarded. I looked up at the fence and wondered what kind of fork this was? Whatever it was, it was large!

I placed my fingers through the fence again and gripped it tightly.

And then my feet. My toes hooked around the metal and, *my God*, it bloody hurt. I cursed the fact that I had just eaten that massive pizza an hour ago! I was probably now trying to lug an extra stone up the fence.

"Ouuccch!" I winced loudly and looked down at my toes. They were turning a strange shade of purple, but I persisted. I climbed a little, a little more, more . . . The pain was unbearable. I was sure I was going to pass out from it! It felt like the wire was about to slice through all of my toes and fingers, and soon I would be completely digit-less. I gave a half-chuckle, imagining what it would look like with ten toes and ten fingers lying in the sand below. Maybe a doctor could stitch them back on if I put them in a cooler box and rushed them to hospital. But, wait—can you drive without fingers? My mind boggled, but now was really not the time for this mental tangent. The fence towered above me like a skyscraper, but I was determined, and so I pushed on through the pain and the fear of severed toes. I was concentrating so hard on the task at hand that I barely heard the noise at first. It was so subtle to begin with that I wasn't even sure I'd heard it. I was so unperturbed by it initially that I didn't even glance over my shoulder to see what it was. But, as the seconds passed, I started to become a little more concerned about it. The soft sound of tires driving up a gravel road, getting closer and closer to me.

"Crap." I looked over my shoulder and saw the cloud of dust coming towards me. I hoped it was a farmer just going about his day, someone that wouldn't care at all that I—a total stranger—was hanging on to a fence with a giant sign on it that read:

Private property. Trespassers will be prosecuted.

And then I heard the other noise and saw the other thing that struck a fairly large amount of terror into me. The siren, and then . . . *Red light. Blue light. Red light. Blue light.* Damn, what were the chances that on *this* small, dusty road, and at *this* exact moment, a cop would come past? The police car stopped below me. I heard the sound of a car door open and close, followed by the sound of feet on gravel.

Try to be casual. Try to act natural. What was I thinking? There was nothing natural and normal about a shoeless woman trying to climb a fence. I looked down as the tall man put his hands in his pockets and walked over to me. The sun was behind him and he cast a very long and imposing shadow. Like a sheriff in an old western. In my head, an old western song started playing. The kind that starts just before the sheriff draws his gun and blows the bandit to smithereens.

"Hello, officer," I said feebly, still hanging on to the fence like a chimpanzee. I tried to make casual yet purposeful eye contact with him, but his face was shaded and I couldn't see his features.

"Ma'am," he said. Why do they always say "ma'am"? It's downright intimidating! "You do know this is private property?" he asked. Clearly, the question was very, *very* rhetorical.

"Is it?" I asked innocently, with just the right amount of faux-shock in my voice. I wasn't sure it was convincing, though.

"Please can you get down from there," he said casually, taking his hands out of his pockets and folding his arms.

I nodded. "Sure, sure, I shall do that. Of course." I obliged and, with force, pushed myself off the fence and jumped. It was as I hit the ground, bending over to catch the full force of my weight, that I heard the noise. It was a noise I immediately recognized . . .

"Shit!" I quickly put my hands between my legs, where the denim had so unsubtly ripped. "Crap," I cursed again when I realized just how much of my crotch area was now exposed to the elements, and I wasn't even wearing my good panties!

"Uh, are you okay?" the man asked tentatively—and very unnecessarily, because he knew the damn answer to that question. It was clear that I was *not* alright. My poor old vagina was half-almost flapping about in the breeze! I looked up at him from my rather undignified position. He took a step forward, his face now completely illuminated by the sunlight, and . . .

A thump in my chest.

A punch in my gut.
A palpitation.
Strange queasiness.
A fuzzy buzz washing over me.
A flutter.
What the hell was *that?*

CHAPTER 11

"Are you okay?" he repeated.

"I . . . uh, yes, I'm okay . . . I just . . . I . . ." I stuttered over my words and could feel my face break out into a strange smile that I couldn't control. He looked at me; I could see he was confused by my clearly erratic behavior. Hell, I was confused. What had just come over me? An instant teenage crush on a policeman. How clichéd of me. How horrifically banal of me. But no amount of mental scolding was going to change the fact that this man was utterly gorgeous and I was feeling utterly weak in the ligaments.

"Ma'am," he said again.

Ma'am . . . ? Would he call me that in bed? Shit, what was I thinking? I placed my hands over my mouth, even though I hadn't said it out loud. He looked at me very strangely. Clearly I wasn't having the same effect on him as he was having on me, despite the fact that I was flashing my private parts at him. I tried not to perceive that as a blow to my ego.

"You do know this is private property?" he repeated, slowly and purposefully, dialing up his authoritative tone a bit. Was that the only *private* he was concerned or aware of?

This time, I couldn't lie to him. It was very inconvenient that I wasn't a more seasoned, sociopathic liar. "Yes. I know it's private," I admitted flatly.

"Well, then, the question is, why are you trying to climb the fence?" His tone of voice told me that he already knew the answer to the question. Not that one needed to be a brain surgeon to figure this one out. I'd been caught red-handed, in the act of breaking and entering.

"Good question," I said, trying to shuffle walk, my hands once again firmly between my legs. God, I hoped this didn't also constitute lewd public behavior, walking around like this, as if I was touching myself. I hoped he didn't think I was some strange pervert, jumping over a fence for God knows what. *What the hell did he think of me?*

"I'm a writer," I blurted out, without thinking. I hadn't meant to say that at all. "I was researching. For writing."

He looked at me, skepticism etched into his face . . . *his bloody gorgeous face.* The face that held *those* eyes. My God, what color were they? A brilliant green, almost emerald. Dark and shimmery and penetrating and stormy and swirly and—

"What's it about?" He broke my emerald train of thought.

"What's what about?" I asked.

"The thing you're writing. You're a writer," he said.

"Right, I'm a writer," I said, my own rather plain eyes drifting down to his mouth. "I'm writing a book. A sort of thrillery, mystery thingy," I said, examining the curves of his full mouth. He had the perfect lip shape. God, women drew that on with a pencil and pumped toxins into themselves with needles just to achieve something vaguely similar, and there he was, genetically blessed with the perfect pout.

"And what's it about?" he pressed.

"Well, um, the book revolves around a private investigator," I said, making shit up as I went. "I was just seeing how hard it was to climb a fence like this, because, in the book, she needs to break into a property, and I wanted to know how it would feel to . . . you know."

"Break and enter?" He finished my thought.

"Well, technically, I wasn't on the other side of the fence, so you can't really call it 'entering' and I certainly didn't break anything either.

It's not like I had bolt cutters with me, so perhaps that statement is not entirely accurate in describing my actions." I smiled at him.

"Why would you mention bolt cutters?" He took a step closer to me. "Do you have bolt cutters on you?"

"What? No." I burst out laughing, while my eyes drifted over his other perfect features and came to rest on the one imperfect thing on his face. A scar cut his eyebrow in half, giving it a distinctly arched appearance. My eyes followed the scar up to his forehead, where a small white line radiated outwards from the eyebrow with such perfection and precision that it looked like it might have been drawn on. It wasn't a messy scar; on the contrary, it was the most perfect scar I'd ever seen. God, even his imperfections were perfect. He'd probably gotten this from saving a starving kitten from a tree, or diving in front of oncoming traffic to save a toddler who ran across the road after her little pink ball, or maybe—

"So, when you reached the top, you were going to come straight back down?" Once again, he put a full stop to my inner monologue, which I admit was starting to run away with me a bit.

I nodded my head. "Sure. Straight back down. In fact, before you came, I'd just realized how next to impossible it is to climb a fence like this, and I was about to come down and think of another way for my character to break in."

"You were, were you?" He looked totally unconvinced, and I couldn't really blame him.

"Yes, I was thinking that maybe the character could use—oh, I don't know—maybe some kind of explosives? But I'd have to do more research into explosives, wouldn't want to hurt anyone, or myself. Maybe you know about them?" His reaction to this statement was immediate and I realized very quickly that my mouth had just gotten me into a world of trouble.

"Sorry?" He took a step forward. "Are you asking me whether explosives could be used to break into this property?"

"What? NO! No." I started laughing, a little too frantically, really, and then I stopped abruptly and looked at him again. "I mean . . . could they?"

He looked over his shoulder, as if he was searching for my hidden accomplices, or looking for clues, or he was scared. He glanced at my car and then slowly turned his head back in my direction. "Who did you say you were again?"

"A writer."

He raised that scarred brow at me. God, it was sexy. It was so Khal Drogo-ish, but without all the facial hair, and clearly I didn't have a dragon, because, if I had, I wouldn't be climbing over a fence, now, would I?

"Can I see your driver's license, please?" he asked.

"Uh-huh! Yup." I nodded and then shuffled towards my car— hands still between my legs. I opened the door, dug in my bag and pulled my license out. He took it and looked down at it, and then the usual thing happened.

He squinted and raised it to his face as if he hadn't read it correctly. Then he looked up at me, confused, looked back down, pulled it away from his face, as if he still hadn't read it correctly yet, and then looked up at me again, still confused.

"Pebecca?" he asked.

I sighed. "Pebecca," I repeated flatly.

"Not Rebecca?" he enquired.

I shook my head and he eyed me suspiciously.

"Nope," I said. This was such a familiar conversation, really; I'd had it almost every time I changed schools, every time I went to a dentist, a doctor, picked up a letter from the post office, tried to take out a credit card at my bank, or a cell-phone contract. I knew this script so well. In fact, next he would probably say, *Wow, that's an inter—*

"That's an interesting name," he said.

Aha! Told you. I sighed again, waiting for the questions about how I came to be Pebecca. Only, they didn't come.

"Can I see your ID too, please?"

"Why, does it sound made up?" I asked, half-joking.

"Can I just see your ID book, please?" He passed my driver's license back and I gave him my ID book. He flipped it open and scanned it. Once he had found the word he was clearly looking for, he stared at it for a few seconds and then started nodding.

"It was a mistake," I quickly added. "My mom was crying—there was some water, she was using that ink that feathers, you know? It was, that is to say, the line kind of disappeared and . . ." I stopped talking. I always had such a need to explain this. "It's a mission to change it. I tried once, but you know those queues at Home Affairs. And then this other time they lost the paperwork, so, you know . . . stuck with it!"

He nodded. "My uncle's name was Barnabus," he said with a small smile. "If anyone could have done with a name change, it was him."

I smiled back at him. This was also a usual response. People always tried to make me feel better by telling me about their friend or family member or someone they met that had a worse name. It always made me feel like shit. As if there was something wrong with me.

"Miss Pebecca Thorne, would you mind opening the trunk of the car for me, please?"

"What?" I asked.

"Please can you open the trunk of your vehicle, ma'am?" he repeated as he walked to the back of my car.

"This is ridiculous," I gushed. "I mean, I don't have bolt cutters or explosives in there. I'm not the bloody Unabomber, for heaven's sake."

"Unabomber? Why would you mention him?" He looked up at me again. God, I kept saying the wrong thing and I wished I could just *shut the hell up!*

"Fine. Fine." I shuffled over to the back and popped the trunk. A solitary suitcase filled the space and we both looked down at it. It was a rather expensive suitcase that I'd bought on a whim before traveling business class. I'd thought that, if I rocked up with crappy luggage, they might not allow me on the flight. It was a stupid purchase, really, and now all the big, blingy, gold *LV*s on the bag just made it look like I was heading off to star in a hip-hop video with Cardi B or Ice-T or D O double G.

"Please open your suitcase," he commanded.

"Is this really necessary?" I asked nervously.

"Please." His tone was very firm now and I did what he asked. I removed my hands from between my legs and unzipped the bag, and then watched in horror as he started riffling through it, pushing bras and panties out the way to get to the bottom. I could see he was trying not to touch them, pushing them aside with quick flicks of his wrist. But, because of this, one of them went flying out of the trunk and landed on his foot with a loud *thud*. The thud was completely silent, actually, since the panties in question were nothing more than some pink lace and elastic, but I swear I could hear it as loudly as a drum. We both looked down at the pink lace now capping his big, black boot.

"Uh . . ." He bent down quickly and hesitated before picking them up. "Sorry," he said awkwardly. I could see he didn't know how to handle them, as he picked them up with his pinkie and swung them towards me. I grabbed them from him and shoved them into my pocket. His eyes drifted down to my pocket, and that's when I realized that my hands were no longer between my legs, hiding my *other* panties. This was a disaster. Within a few moments of meeting me, this man was already an expert in my underwear. I quickly put my hands back between my legs and he looked away. He riffled through the bag again and, after a thorough search, he finally zipped it back up and closed the trunk.

"I told you you wouldn't find anything," I said, when he was done. "I'm just an author."

"Would I have read anything that you've written?"

"You might have," I said. "*The Heart is Just a Muscle*."

"Wait!" Suddenly, his entire demeanor changed. His body language relaxed and his once-stiff shoulders slumped slightly. "Becca Thorne? *The* Becca Thorne?" he asked.

"Yup, that's me," I said nervously. My cover was completely blown. Had I wanted to be incognito, that was all over now.

"Oh my God, that book was everywhere. It was huge. It was all anyone spoke about. I even bought it for a friend for Christmas. She loved it!" And now he smiled at me. He smiled at me and my insides seemed to scramble about, like eggs in a frying pan. His smile grew. So did mine. And then he leaned forward and looked me straight in the eyes. My body tensed. "Although, I must say, you look nothing like your author picture."

I felt my cheeks blush from the embarrassing memory of that awkward photo shoot. "Uh . . . yes. There was a lot of make-up and they scraped my hair back, and Photoshop, you know."

"You're not wearing your glasses, either," he noted.

I shook my head. "I don't wear glasses. My agent thought it would look better if I did wear glasses, though. Make me more intellectual, less . . . uh . . . well, I guess, *less me.*"

"I thought you were a brunette," he said, eyeing my hair.

"Black and white photos. They thought it would make me look more serious, or arty, or . . . I don't know what they were trying to do."

He looked at me for a while before speaking again. "So, what brings a famous author to our small town?" His voice had taken on a whole new quality. Gone were those stern police-y replies and steely looks. Maybe this was my lucky day; maybe he would forget that I'd tried to climb a fence.

"You know . . . writing. I wanted to get away from it all, the hustle and bustle of Jo'burg. Find some quiet little spot to write. A change of scenery for some inspiration." I was spurting out all those romanticized writer clichés. What people thought we writers did. Go off to country retreats and stay in log cabins and write by burning wood fires. The reality is that most of us are slumped over a dirty, messy desk that has a pot of yesterday's half-finished yoghurt growing fungus on it. Empty coffee cups, floss (because you eat at your desk, now, too) and more highlighters and pens than common sense.

"Do you have a new book coming out soon?" he asked. His eyes seemed to have lit up a little now. Green, like malachite—that was the color of his eyes.

"I do. Indeed," I said reticently. Just thinking about the book made me break out in a cold sweat.

"That's exciting," he said, looking even more relaxed.

"My deadline is in three weeks," I blurted out, just because I needed to get that off my chest. "Right around the corner, really. No time to lose," I said, a little more frantically this time.

"Wow! That's soon." He took his cap off and ran his hands through his hair. My knees seemed to quiver in response to this.

Okay—confession time: I've always had a thing for a man in a uniform. I don't know what it is. Maybe it's some totally anti-feminist biological predisposition we women have to being rescued. The knight, the fireman, the policeman—men in uniform, rushing in to save us. I know, I know. That's about as unfeminist as giving a woman a Hoover for Christmas. But I wasn't concerned with feminism as he looked at me with those eyes. That scruffy, ash-blonde hair, made messy by the cap, that perfect face, broad shoulders . . . My eyes drifted down to his feet . . . *Such large shoes.*

"How's it coming?" he asked, and my throat went dry.

"Sorry . . . who's coming?"

"The book. How's it coming?" he asked, with a small smile.

I cleared my throat. "Good. Just doing my research," I lied. The book wasn't coming at all. In fact, it was probably coming as little as I was at the moment. Which was not at all, since I hadn't been with a man in many, many, many moons. *Why was I thinking about this now?* Our eyes met for a split second before we both looked away quickly. *Wow.* I wasn't sure if he'd felt that, but I had: a loud buzz in my ears accompanied by a sudden dizzying sensation and an instant dry mouth, as if someone had just poured that stuff you find in that little sachet in the bottom of pill jars into my mouth. I tried to run my tongue over my teeth to wet them; it felt like it stuck.

"Well—" he looked past me and at the fence—"I guess there was no harm done, here. But, please, don't climb fences again. Even if it is just for research." He started moving towards his car and I panicked. I didn't want him to leave.

"Wait, what's your name?" I called out, taken aback by the urgency in my voice.

He smiled at me again. "I'm Mike," he said, still backing away to his car. "Mike Wooldridge."

"Cool. Captain Policeman Mike Wooldridge," I said. "I'm Becca Thorne."

He stopped walking and then let out a small chuckle. "I know." And then he was opening his car door. He stopped and looked back at me. "By the way, I expect you to drive off when I do." He looked over at my car and then back at me. "Your last book must have done really well. Congratulations." Clearly he was referring to the stupidly overpriced vehicle that I'd only really bought to show up a *certain someone I despised*. It was all rather juvenile, really. But it had always been *his* dream car, so, after what he'd done, I thought it would be a nice kick in the balls if I bought one.

"You *are* going to drive away, aren't you?" he asked again, when I didn't respond.

"Of course." I jumped, and then remembered the hole in my jeans. I shuffled sideways to my car, hands still stuck over my crotch as if I was scared something might fall out of me. "Okay. Bye." I started opening the door and looked at him.

"Bye," he said, but didn't move. And neither did I. I felt glued to the spot. I couldn't move—*didn't want to move*.

"I should really get going," he said again, still not moving.

"Me too." I nodded at him, holding the eye contact he was making.

"I hope your book goes well," he said.

"I hope your policing goes well," I replied.

And then he shot me a smile. So big, so wide, so . . . *wow!* The smile lit up his entire face, it lit up the entire world, and I'm pretty sure it made global temperatures rise by at least a degree or two. Could this smile be responsible for global warming?

"No more fences, though!" He waggled a finger at me.

I shook my head stupidly. I was slightly entranced by this man. "Uh-uh," I managed to mumble, and then we still both stood there looking at each other.

"Well . . ." he muttered, and then stopped talking.

I leaned forward, waiting for the words after the "well" to come, but nothing did.

"Well?" I asked.

"Nothing. Just . . . nothing," he said, a little strangely now. "I've really got to go," he said, after more eye contact that seemed to linger way too long.

"Sure. Me too." Wait, hadn't we already said that? This felt like one of those moments when neither of you wants to hang up the phone. But then he hung up. It felt so abrupt.

He gave me a small wave. I waved back quickly. He climbed into his car and I did the same, and then, next thing I knew, we were both driving away. Driving off in different directions and *why the hell did I feel so perturbed by that?*

CHAPTER 12

~

I drove around aimlessly in my car for a while, weaving up and down the four streets that constituted this little town on the hill. It really was beautiful here, though. It was quaint and looked completely untouched by the modern world. This was confirmed when I saw a small video store that also masqueraded as a photocopying shop that also provided internet services. The shop was squeezed between a small art gallery and a pottery studio with a coffee shop. Colorful tables spilled out on to the pavement and were filled with people sipping coffee and eating home-made cakes. I made a mental note to stop there and grab one. I drove up to the highest part of the tortoise's back, where the old church on the hill was perched. I parked my car and climbed out. I tied my jersey around my waist—to cover the giant hole in my crotch area—and walked up to the church, straight to the brass plaque by the door.

In memory of Father James McMillan. Hero and man of God.

Resting below the plaque were the remains of an old burnt cross, clearly put here to remember the fire and the original church that had once stood on this spot. I turned around and looked out over the sea and the river, just like Edith had done, so many years ago. The river was calm and so was the sea; it hadn't been calm the day she'd stood here and decided to run away. Something caught my eye and I started moving towards it. I opened the little rusty gate to the small cemetery and walked in. The cemetery looked old, some of the headstones were completely covered in a tangle of weeds, their brown stone turned green from the moss growing on them. I crouched and looked at the small, broken headstone in front of me; the name was worn off, but there was a date there: 1874.

God, this place was old. I walked up to the huge oak tree that was growing straight out of the middle of the cemetery and seemed to be the highest point here. Its leaves were beginning to fall; a golden, orange carpet has started to form on the graves closest to it. I stood under its dappled light and looked around. The small town spread out below me: little houses, colorful gardens and beach cottages. It was strange being here, looking down at the town that I knew held such a secret story. An untold story.

I sat down on the ground with my back pressed into the tree and closed my eyes to listen to the soft sounds of the wind and birds. I let out a long, slow breath and my shoulders started to relax. While most people were afraid of cemeteries, I had found them to be a kind of sanctuary—well, one in particular. The graveyard where my dad was buried was one of the only constants in my life, growing up. And, when I was feeling lost, as I did a lot, I used to go there and sit by his grave and tell him stories about my life. They were all completely made up, of course, but I used to love doing it. In winter, I would take a flask of hot chocolate and a blanket and sit there telling him all about my exotic ski trips and about all my amazing friends at school and my latest award for sport or schoolwork. With him, I could be anyone I wanted. I could imagine my life to be better than it was. Imagine that I was a better person, too. The person I wanted to be.

I've never really missed my dad or mourned him. How can you miss something that you never knew and was never yours to begin with? But I have always felt an angry injustice at having him taken away from me like that. I think I might have quite liked having a dad. Oh well, what can one do . . . ?

I opened my eyes again and looked around. I felt at home, here, at peace. I pulled a letter out of my bag at random and started to read it.

15 February, 1948

I loved spending time with you yesterday, on Valentine's Day, and I'm missing you more that I can put into words. I can't wait to see you again. The truth is, I'm still so overwhelmed by this, by us. I can't believe this is truly happening—that we are happening. You are, by far, the best thing that has ever happened to me. You. You. You. I don't know how I can express enough how much I love you and how much you mean to me. I have never felt this way before, I have never been a part of something so big, so good and this full of beautiful possibilities. You have filled my heart and soul with love and I am forever changed and forever yours. I will love and care for you as if I have been tasked with caring for the most rare and precious thing in the universe. Words aren't really doing this justice. I just wish I could express how important you are to me. You are everything and more. I can't believe you even exist. You are a dream come true and I've found everything that I've been looking for. I cannot wait to spend more time with you. I'm loving every second of getting to know you, Edith, and I cannot wait for what lies ahead.

You, me, forever.

Wow! I lowered the letter and stared straight ahead of me at the graves. Was Edith here? Could I have just walked past her? Or was she still alive? A noise made me look up, and, as soon as I saw what made it, I scrambled to my feet and worked my way around to the other side of the tree.

"Shit!" I hissed under my breath as I heard the car park and the door slam. I peered around the tree, careful not to let him see me—*again*. I watched as he stood there for a while with a confused look on his face. He looked at my car and then looked around the parking lot. He walked over to my car and my heart started beating a little faster when he took a small notebook out of his pocket and scribbled my license plate down. Then he walked up to the church and tried the door. It was locked. He turned again and I saw his eyes widen in acknowledgment. *What was he looking at?* I followed his gaze . . . I'd left the gate open! I really wasn't good at this criminal stuff, was I?

He started walking towards the cemetery and I knew he was going to find me here, and what would I tell him I was doing? *Just chilling here because I like cemeteries.* Well, that just made me sound odd. And I was sure he already thought I was odd. So, I did the only thing I could think of. I reached down and picked up a flower from the nearest grave—*God, I was going straight to hell for this*—and I casually walked towards one of the gravestones.

"Becca."

I heard my name and I swung around in pretend-surprise. I gasped for authenticity.

"Mike. Detecti . . . uh . . . Officer . . . uh . . . Captain . . . ?"

He smiled. "Mike is fine," he said, as he walked towards me. He stopped when he was a few meters away and then folded his arms and looked me straight in the eyes.

A thump in my chest.

A punch in my gut.

A palpitation.

Strange queasiness.

A fuzzy buzz washing over me.

A flutter.

What was happening . . . ? AGAIN!

I quickly looked away.

"Fancy seeing you here," he said, a strange tone in his voice.

"Mmm-hmm," I mumbled nonchalantly, trying to act natural and normal once more.

"You really seem to be getting around," he said.

I nodded. "That's me. Get-around-town Becca," I said, without thinking, and then I realized what that had sounded like when I saw him smile.

He looked down at his watch. "Twice in forty minutes," he said.

"What is?"

"That I'm bumping into you. Twice in forty minutes."

"Well, at least it's not three times," I said, looking at my car, wishing I was inside it and driving away.

"So, what are you doing here?" he asked, his eyes briefly drifting down to the jersey around my waist and then back up to mine.

"Just . . . you know." I waved the flower in the air and he looked at it suspiciously. His eyes drifted once again. They started on the flower and moved down, down, down, and then they stopped. I followed his eyeline to the vase on the grave that was now short one red rose. He looked back at the flower in my hand and then up at me again. My mind raced for an explanation, but all I managed was . . .

"This is *not* private property. It's open to the public," I gushed, way too loudly.

He studied me carefully before responding. "That is correct," he said. "I cannot stop you from being here. Or putting flowers down and paying your respects, if that is what you're doing. Is it?"

"Mmmhuh?" I mumbled, ferreting around his question. "What else would I be doing here other than paying my respects?" I tried to smile at him, but the corners of my mouth were twitching anxiously.

"You know," I declared, "I should probably go."

"Should you?" he asked.

I nodded very enthusiastically. "Yup. Yup, I should . . ." I didn't even bother finishing that sentence; I was already speed-walking towards my car.

"Becca," he called after me.

I swung around. "Yes?"

"Aren't you going to . . . ?" He pointed at the flower that was still in my hand.

I looked down at it. "Yes! Of course." I looked around the graveyard. "Let me just find the person . . ." My voice trailed off as I pretended to look around at the graves. *How had I gotten myself into this ridiculous situation?* This was some fucking fork alright. A very squiggly one.

"Maybe I could help you. Who are you looking for?" He walked towards me.

"Uh . . . It's a, um . . ." *Fuck!* "Uncle."

"Oh, what's his name?" His voice has a slight teasing quality to it.

"No worries!" I jumped. "There he is. There he is!" I rushed over to a grave and quickly dropped the flower on it and then, without thinking, did a quick sign of the cross and realized that I'd done it wrong. *I really should have paid attention in Sunday school!*

And then, suddenly, he was at my side, looking down at the grave.

"Oh, Fred Letty is your uncle. I didn't realize that," he said to me.

"What?"

"Frank Letty and the Lettys. They've been living here in Willow Bay for years. One of the oldest families around here."

I nodded as my stomach plummeted. "Mmmm," I mumbled.

"Such a tragedy, what happened to him," Mike said, looking me square in the eyes now.

I nodded. "Such a tragedy that I don't like to talk about it," I offered quickly.

"I'm sure." He continued to stare at me. "So, I take it you're staying with them, then?" he asked.

"Who?"

"The Lettys. Ruth and Samantha and . . ." He looked at me expectantly and started opening his mouth, as if he was going to say another name. He raised his eyebrows at me, opening his mouth some more. "Ssshhhhh . . ." He made the sound, still looking at me. I opened my mouth as he held the *shhhh* sound.

"Ssshhhh," I said, mirroring him.

"Shhhh," he continued, raising his brow even more.

"Shhhh . . . *aron* ?" I offered.

"Exactly!" he said. "That's the one!"

"Sharon?" I asked, almost falling backwards over my feet. "Great!

Sharon!" I laughed nervously. "Sharon. I'd better get going, then, now. Wouldn't want to keep Ruth and Samantha and SHARON—" I almost screamed that—"waiting." I turned and started marching through the cemetery towards my car.

"Goodbye, Becca," I heard him say.

"Bye, Mike!" I threw over my shoulder, and didn't look back.

"Maybe we'll make it a hat-trick," he called from behind me.

I stopped and turned. "A hat-trick?"

He smiled. "Three times in one day."

I laughed. "That's doubtful," I said, and then continued walking back to the car.

CHAPTER 13

I was nursing a terrible feeling. A feeling that gnawed inside me like one of those bot flies. You've seen the YouTube videos, right? They burrow into your skin and, when you squeeze, some big larva comes out, all plump and juicy from its comfy hibernation in your warm flesh. I wanted to throw up just thinking about it, and cursed myself for all those YouTube rabbit holes I so often went down. I start watching videos of cute cats and somehow land up on a weird Russian woman pouring slime over a microphone while whispering the alphabet at you in a mysterious way.

After leaving the cemetery, I went back to the hotel and sat in my room trying to type up a response to that letter. But it wasn't working. *How the hell was I meant to respond to that, when I'd never experienced anything close to that kind of love and devotion before?* I'd certainly never been loved like that—a love that seemed unselfish and kind. Who was this woman who was so utterly adored? Everything I tried to write seemed so lackluster and pale in comparison. Well, of course it was. I had no great love story to pull from. All my "love stories" had been utter disasters. I'd dated a much-older man in college, and I didn't need a psychologist to tell me I'd been looking for a father figure. It had ended abruptly when we realized we had absolutely nothing in common and there was no passion. Then there was the son of the lady I'd worked for, but I'd liked her more than him. She had been so nice to me and taken me under her wing. Again, probably just an attempt to create the family I'd never had.

I'd been looking more for a mother than a partner. And then, finally, the man I'd considered to be the great love of my life, only he'd had another love and it wasn't me. My psychologist had pointed out how I'd probably unconsciously chosen him because he was unavailable, like my dad. My dad was dead, not unavailable. Sometimes psychologists just took it too far.

After going round and round for two hours unsuccessfully, I stopped trying to write. The beanbag I was sitting on was uncomfortable and I was starting to get a strange pain in my shoulder blade. I also found myself suffering from cabin fever in this room, which seemed smaller than it had when I'd first walked in. The walls were making me anxious, and I kept looking to the door, hoping it was unlocked. Getting trapped in the elevator had definitely made me feel unsettled in confined spaces. I left my room in the hope of finding something else to do, and I very quickly found myself sitting at the hotel bar, *not* drinking, simply staring down at my Coca-Cola, watching as the bubbles fizzed away, making the edges of the ice cubes smaller and smaller. I started to imagine that those ice cubes were the story I was trying to tell, and the bubbles were a carbonated combination of all my fears, anxieties, insecurities and growing guilt, making my ability to tell the story less and less. I downed the Coke so I couldn't watch it anymore. I needed to get to that willow tree; maybe if I saw the engraving that she'd made, I would have more of a sense of her and would be able to write. But how? I needed to have at least 80,000 words written in less than twenty-one days, and that thought was driving me crazy.

I heard a huge cheer and looked to my left. A group of guys was watching the rugby on the TV in the corner of this fine establishment. The nineties rave-esque decor of the hotel had also spilled into this small bar. This was evident from the lime green, vinyl bar stool I was sitting on and the ultraviolet light that was making my pale pink nail polish look luminous white. The cheers from the corner were getting louder and it seemed that the big game was reaching its conclusion as manly high-fives mounted. Clearly, their team had won. I didn't really pay much attention to things like rugby—or any sport, for that matter. It reminded me a little too much of an uncomfortable part of my childhood. I looked down at my phone; I needed a distraction. You know the kind of thing I'm talking about—the kind where you're blowing up bits of candy, or decorating your virtual fish tank, or imaginary living room. So gratifyingly mind numbing. Meditation for the modern mind. Ten minutes later, while I was happily adding some bright pink sun loungers to my gorgeous patio in Belize, I felt a tap on my shoulder. I jumped in my seat and swung around, and then looked straight at *him*.

"Uh, *you*! I . . . didn't see you, sorry, I got a fright," I said, as my heart pounded in my chest. I didn't know why it was beating so fast—because I'd gotten a sudden fright, or because he was standing there, so close to me?

"Sorry, I didn't mean to frighten you," Captain Magic Mike said, and then he smiled at me. He was wearing civilian clothes, as they might say in his profession, and looking . . . looking . . . so, so . . . *wow*!

Breathless.

Stupidly breathless.

And did I mention he was smiling at me?

CHAPTER 14

"*F*ancy seeing you today . . . again," he said with a strange smile.

"I guess we did make it a hat-trick," I heard myself say in a flirty voice that I seemed to have barely any control over.

"I guess we did," he said. His cheeks were slightly flushed, his hair ruffled and the casual T-shirt he was wearing was clinging to his broad chest and shoulders like a second skin. I don't think the shirt was meant to be tight—it was loose everywhere else—I just think this man was so genetically blessed in his upper region that he would make any shirt look slightly dirty, and I don't mean the kind of dirty that warrants a go in the washing machine. Oh no, Mike was a completely new kind of dirty. One I'd never set eyes on before.

"So, what are you doing here?" I asked, looking around to see if there was a someone—a female someone—with him.

He gestured behind him, to the corner. "Watching the game," he said, with a smile. "With my friends," he quickly added.

"Aaaah, the game," I replied flatly.

"I take it you're not into watching the game?" he asked, looking a little amused now.

I shook my head. "Not really my thing; although, at one stage in my life, I had to pretend it was. That's probably why I really don't like it now."

He started to pull one of the bar stools out, and then stopped and looked at me. "Can I sit? Do you mind?"

"Sure! Yes!" *Shit—I think I said that a little too enthusiastically.*

He sat down and suddenly I was acutely aware of his presence. It was overwhelming. As if I'd turned around and then looked back to find that a wall had magically appeared right next to me.

"Why did you have to pretend you liked the game?" he asked, resting an elbow on the bar.

"Long story. Boring story. You probably don't want to hear about it," I said, looking away from him.

"I like your stories," he said. I could hear an amused tone in his voice and I turned and looked at him.

"What stories?" I asked.

He shrugged playfully. "You know, detective novels and cousins who don't exist."

I blushed. "Oh, so you know I'm not related to any Sharon Letty, then?"

"There is no Sharon Letty." He gave a small chuckle at this and my eyes widened.

"So you let me say all that, let me think I had gotten that right, let me make all that stuff up . . . ?" I shook my head at him and smiled.

"So, what were you *really* doing there?" he asked.

"Again, a long and probably boring story," I said, looking down at my empty glass.

There was a silence between us for a while. It felt strangely comfortable, as if we knew each other. "What say you tell me your boring stories over another drink? What are you drinking?"

"Coke," I replied. "And you?" I asked.

"I'll have one of those too," he said, waving the bartender down. The bartender was none other than Techno Tannie herself.

"Hi, Mike," she said, when she'd reached us.

"Hi, Crystal." His voice had an air of reticence. An air of expectancy. "Soooo?" he asked, looking at her and raising one of his brows, as if this conversation had happened a million times before.

"Well, it's just the usual, really," she said, leaning over the counter.

"Nothing too hectic to report, other than those cat fanatics parking me in at the grocery store the other day. But, other than that, just a normal week in Willow Bay."

He cocked his head to the side. "You wouldn't be the one responsible for the red lipstick 'graffiti'—" he gestured air quotes at her—"that was drawn on the hood of one of the cat people's cars, would you?"

"What? Me?" She put her hand over her heart. "I would never! You know me!" She said it with the faintest smile dancing at the corner of her lips.

"Mmmm, that's the problem: I do know you, Crystal. I know you too well."

"To know me is to love me." She smiled at him.

"Ain't that the truth," Mike said, with a smile in his voice. "Still, if you know the person who was responsible for the lipstick vandalism, I would be very appreciative if you told them to stop. The last thing Willow Bay needs now, especially slap bang in the middle of tourist season, is a lipstick vandal on the loose. Especially considering what the lipstick vandal was drawing."

She gave him a huge smile. "I'll be sure to pass the message on. If I ever happen to find out who this lipstick vandal is." She winked at him and he shook his head.

"That's a nice lipstick color you're wearing, by the way," Mike teased.

"Thanks. It's called Russian Red. Suits every skin tone. Would even suit a redhead like you," she said to me, and then smacked her lips together.

Mike sighed and she smiled even more.

"Would you like some?" she asked me, taking it out from a small make-up bag she kept behind the counter.

"I'm okay," I replied.

"Come on," she urged. "You'll look great. Every girl should wear red."

"I really don't think fire-engine red would suit me." I glanced down at the lipstick now; she'd rolled the whole thing out.

She shook her head. "Every skin tone," she reiterated. "Even a pale person, like you."

"Pale!" I exclaimed, and then stopped. "Yeah, I'm pale."

"Although," Mike leaned in, "looks like you got a little bit of sun today. Were you outside much?" He flashed me another smile. Killer smile.

"Ha ha." I felt a little giddy from his obvious flirtation.

"Come on, try it." Techno Tannie started leaning over the counter and the lipstick was coming closer to me. I pursed my lips together tightly in defiance and gave my head a tiny shake.

"Come on," Mike echoed.

"What is this? Peer pressure?" I asked.

"Come. Bring me those lips," she said, not really giving me a choice because the lipstick was now centimeters away.

I sighed. "Fiiinnne," I conceded. "But, I'm telling you, I'll look like a clown."

"You're wrong," she said, as she started painting my lips with great focus and care.

I looked over at Mike; he was watching intently, his eyes glued to my lips, and I wished I could see what was happening.

When she'd finished, she stood back and looked at me.

"Stunning!" she declared loudly.

I highly doubted that, and turned to face Mike. He was smiling at first, and then suddenly he wasn't. His eyes zoned in on my lips and a look flashed across his face. *What was that?*

"Looks like someone is speechless," Techno Tannie teased, rolling the lipstick back up and putting the lid on with a click. "My work here is done," she said, and then she slipped the lipstick back into the bag and zipped it up with a dramatic flick of the wrist, as if she were performing.

"You look . . ." Mike finally spoke. "Good," he said softly. "She's right—it suits you."

"Uh, thanks," I said, hoping my cheeks weren't also now Russian Red. Mike continued to look at me and I held his penetrating gaze. And then he opened his mouth and said some words that rendered me rather speechless. "That black and white author photo was a mistake. So were the glasses. They should have just taken the photo like this," he said, not taking his eyes off me.

I swallowed, despite the fact that my tongue felt big and swollen in my mouth now.

"Soooo, what are you two lovebirds drinking?" Crystal asked, breaking the strange moment between us. We both turned and looked at her.

"Love . . . huh?" I asked quickly and awkwardly. "We're not . . . um . . ."

"No!" Mike added.

"We just met." I pointed at him and then to myself. "Today. So, no."

"Sorry," she said quickly. "It just looked like you were on a date."

"What gave you that impression?" I asked.

"Just the vibe you're giving off to each other," she qualified.

"Vibe?" I asked.

"Yeah. Awkward looks, blushed cheeks, coy bar-stool sitting." She pointed down at Mike, and I looked.

"Coy sitting?" Mike piped up, adjusting himself on his seat.

Techno Tannie rolled her eyes at us. "Hey! I run a bar. I see first dates all the time and this is what they look like."

"Psssht. Oh, pleeeaase!" I tsked.

"We'll have two Cokes, please," Mike mumbled. "And it's not a date."

She smiled at us. "Fine. Whatever you say, mister." She glanced back at me. "You look good in red lipstick." She turned around and took a couple of Cokes out the fridge. I could see she didn't believe us.

"Anyway, if you were on a date, you'd both be seriously *cheap* dates." She pushed the Cokes towards us. "Shall I put this extravagant beverage on your tab, sir?"

Mike nodded, then turned to me, raising his glass. "Cheers!" he said, then he smiled slyly at me. "You must be thirsty."

"What?" I asked.

"It's just that climbing fences is really hard work; I would be parched, if I were you." He looked at me over the rim of his glass as he took a sip.

"If you recall, I didn't actually climb the whole fence. I barely made it up a meter."

"Still, it looked like you were really exerting yourself," he teased.

"Playful teasing; small, shy smiles . . ." Techno Tannie cooed.

I shot her a pointed look.

"Fine, I'm going." She finally moved off and Mike and I were alone again. He put his glass down and moved an ice cube around with the tip of his finger. I stared at it, mesmerized by his finger.

He finally stopped playing with the ice and looked at me again. "So, tell me your boring stories," he said.

I shook my head. "Nah, you really don't want to hear them."

"I do, trust me. I really want to know why you were lurking in a cemetery, pretending to visit your dead uncle."

"You'll think I'm strange, if I tell you," I replied.

"I already think you're strange," he said, with a smile.

I looked down at my glass and tapped it with my fingernails. It made a nice noise, melodic, almost calming. Like wind chimes or something. "I just like cemeteries," I said slowly.

"You do?" He sounded genuinely interested, and, for some reason, I continued.

"My father died, before I was born, and I like to go and sit and talk to him. I know that probably sounds strange and—"

"It doesn't," he cut me off. "I get it. My grandmother died, and sometimes I find myself just standing by her grave, saying random things."

I looked up at him and our eyes met. We smiled together, slowly at first, and then both looked away. We sat there in silence for a few moments, both sipping on our drinks. I could sense something in the silence. Something under it that was noisy and trying to break free of it.

"Okay, I have a confession to make," Mike suddenly said, turning to face me on the bar stool.

I leaned towards him slightly. "That sounds scandalous. Do tell."

"Okay." He took a deep breath, as if he was getting himself ready. "It was me that read your book, not my friend. I bought the book for myself and I . . . well, I'm not afraid to say it—even if it might emasculate me terribly, when I am trying to be very masculine around you—I cried at the end."

I burst out laughing. "Cried?"

He nodded. "Yes. Well, maybe twice, if I'm totally honest with you . . . Maybe even more than twice . . . Okay, okay, I cried several times throughout the book, not just at the end." He looked at me through those long lashes. The long lashes that framed those deadly green eyes of his. His pupils were big and black and took up most of the green now. I felt compelled to look into them, as if there was a law written somewhere: *Must look into Mike's eyes!* "So, do you think less of me now, as a man?" he asked, with a smile that was clearly a teasing one.

I laughed. "Maybe just a little bit."

"I thought women liked men with emotions." He took another sip of his drink. The black liquid slipped through his lips. He swallowed, and then licked the corner of his mouth.

"What women like is a very complicated thing, Mike," I said, pulling my eyes away from his mouth.

"Really?" He raised that sexy, scarred, Drogo-esque brow at me again.

"Well, I mean, in general, since I have no idea what I want, specifically," I said.

"Please, enlighten me. What do women want?"

I looked at him and shook my head. "I can't. I'd be betraying my sex if I told you, and then I'd have to kill you."

"Really?" He leaned in closer to me.

"Yup; we all take a secret oath when we're born, you see."

He laughed at this. "I knew it! It's what I've always suspected."

"We're like the illuminati, actually."

"That is so true!" he said. "You even have your own secret handshakes and secret looks and codes and mysterious languages that you speak that we're clearly all incapable of understanding, because our brains are just not wired to extrapolate that 'Yes, I'm fine' actually means that you're not 'fine', or that 'Nothing's wrong' actually means that *everything* is wrong."

"Oooh, sounds like someone has been on the receiving end of a very angry woman."

He shrugged. "I may have, in the past, misinterpreted some female signs and made a few guy mistakes along the way."

"Aaaah, and what guy mistakes have you made?" I asked, my cheeks feeling flushed with the giddiness of our obvious flirtation.

"Well, I possibly didn't notice a new haircut once," he said, looking up at me with those malachite eyes.

I gasped. "And how long were you guilty of that?"

"It was hard to say, but, in my defense, she did wear a cap during the day, so it was hard to see she'd cut bangs."

"She cut bangs and you didn't notice?! You're clearly not very observant!" I laughed.

"Funny, that's what she said, too." He said it in a joking tone, but I sensed an air of sadness in his voice, and suddenly my stomach tightened.

"I take it this was a serious relationship?" I asked, looking back at my drink so he couldn't see the expression on my face.

"Well, I thought so, until she dumped me for someone else. Clearly, I'm very bad at reading girl signals." He turned and gave me a small, tentative smile.

"Well, if it makes you feel any better, I'm notoriously bad at reading man signals."

He laughed. "Impossible! We are very simple creatures."

"No, you're not," I said.

"Trust me, we are," he said again.

"Nope." I shook my head. "You are so complicated. Not to mention very, *very* confusing."

"How so?" he asked.

"Well, the problem with most of you is that, when you get into a relationship with someone, you somehow manage to sneakily take the reins, without us even knowing you're doing it! Until a year later you wake up and can't believe where you've landed up. And for a moment, you think you were the one who landed you there, until you realize that it wasn't you. You never actually had any power, you had just been steered along, taken for a ride you didn't even know you were on, or signed up for. Because if you had known, you would *never* have signed the indemnity form!" I concluded.

Mike looked at me for the longest time and then started to shake his head. "Nah, sounds like your ex was just an asshole," he said, bringing his eyes up to me. He looked at me intently, as if he were searching me for something. Looking into me.

I sipped my Coke again and gave a big nod. "That he was. That he bloody was. And what about yours? She sounds like a real piece of work, too."

Mike shrugged. "Well, she just fell in love with someone else. What can I do? And now they're married with their first baby on the way, so . . ." He shrugged. "I don't know, Becca. Matters of the heart are confusing, aren't they? You know what I mean. You wrote a book about it."

I looked at him for a while, taking him all in, and then a slow, small smile spread across my lips. "Okay, fine. I'll break the girl code and tell you what women want, because it seems like you really need some help in this department."

He turned in his seat and looked straight at me. "Okay. Tell me."

"Right, we want someone sensitive, but not too sensitive. We still like manly. We want someone who is funny and can make us laugh, but not so funny that they can't ever be serious. We want someone gentle, but not so gentle that they can't be a little bit rough sometimes, when required. We want someone who can listen, and we mean *we really want you to listen*. And there will be tests; we will ask you random questions from time to time to make sure you heard us. And we definitely want someone who thinks we're the most beautiful woman in the world, and tells us this. Tells us often, but not so often that it sounds insincere. And we might say things like, 'I don't like flowers,' or 'Please, don't make a big deal out of our anniversary,' but, really, we want that. We really do, even if we don't think we do . . ." I paused and looked at him, my face flushing a slight shade of red—I could feel my cheeks tingle.

"Really?" His smile changed now, from amused to a little bit naughty—and a lot flirty. "For someone who doesn't know what she wants, that sounded very specific," he said slowly.

"I was speaking generally," I quickly said.

"I see." Mike moved in his seat, a little closer to me. "So, you don't think crying is *too* sensitive?"

I shook my head. "No. In fact, it's kind of sexy when men cry," I heard myself say.

"Sexy?" He leaned a bit closer.

"Definitely," I said, my voice getting a little whispery.

"Are you talking generally again?" He leaned in a little more. "Or are you being specific?" he asked, equally seductively.

Oh boy, how had this conversation gotten here so quickly? But I knew the answer to that. It was crystal clear. I had known the answer to that from the moment we'd laid eyes on each other, and then hadn't been able to take our eyes off each other as we'd driven away down that dirt road, him casting glances at me in the rear-view mirror, and me, waiting for them.

"I might be being specific," I said, playfully, sexily, teasing.

"And who, specifically, are you being specific about?" He matched my teasing tone and I heard a small giggle escape my lips. This was all so strange, and somewhat exhilarating; I hadn't been flirted with in ages, let alone flirted back with anyone—well, not anyone worth flirting with. And Mike was definitely worth flirting with. Suddenly, his hand left his glass and moved up to my face, and then, without warning, he was pushing a long strand of hair out of my face. I watched his finger out of the corner of my eye as he tucked the hair carefully behind my ear, my skin prickling and shivering as he did it.

He smiled at me. "It was hanging in your drink."

I quickly looked at the strand and, noticing that the tip was wet, I cringed. "Sorry, that's a bit gross. That's, uh . . . not exactly sexy." I pushed the strand back into the messy bun at the top of my head.

"Are you trying to be sexy, Becca?"

At that, I burst out laughing again. "You must not have noticed the coffee-stained sweatshirt I'm wearing, or my knotted hair piled up on my head, and I'm pretty sure my mascara is smudged."

"At least you're wearing red lipstick and your clothes aren't ripped," he said, with a very pleased-looking smile.

"Mmmm. So, you noticed that?"

"Well, you did have your hands between your legs—unless that was something else? And, if it was, I do want to point out that, under the disorderly conduct statute, lewd behavior in public is punishable by a hefty fine, and, in some cases, jail time."

I bit my lip as the conversation slid further and further south, towards the gutter. "Jail time?" I asked.

"In some cases."

"What kind of cases?" I asked.

He leaned in. "Only the very serious ones."

"I see. And, if you were to arrest me, would you use your hand-cuffs for that?" I asked.

His eyes widened for a second and then he smiled. "Depends if you're into that kind of thing or not?" It was a question.

"Only one way to find out," I said.

CHAPTER 15

*H*ot wet kisses.

Kisses on my mouth.

On my neck.

Snaking up to my ear.

We barreled into my room, wrapped up in a flurry of fast, hungry kisses.

Yeah, yeah! I know! This was practically anonymous sex. Don't judge me, okay? I'm a grown-ass woman and, *yes*, I have had a few one-night hook-ups. Nothing wrong with that!

Kisses. More. Harder. Faster. Crazier and more frantic as the energy between us became explosive. Like petrol to a fire, a match to a stick of TNT, two live wires . . . You get the picture. This was like nothing I'd ever experienced with anyone before. Never had I felt this level of hunger and desire, and never, as he ran his hands over my body for the first time, had anything felt so, so—

But suddenly he stopped kissing me.

"Wh . . . wha . . . what?" I asked, quite breathless.

"Oh. My. God! So this is what one of these rooms looks like," he said, looking around. "Wow."

"I know," I replied.

He looked back down at me and our eyes met. "Well, this is a first for me," he said, bringing his lips to mine. He kissed me again, and then pulled away quickly. "Just to clarify: it's a first for me in terms of being in this room, not . . . *you know*?"

I chuckled and pulled him towards me. I couldn't get enough.

I started peeling his T-shirt off.

Rock-hard abs. Steel-like, yet warm to the touch.

T-shirt slipping higher and higher.

Oh God—his chest! Hard and smooth, like polished marble.

T-shirt coming off.

Strapping shoulders that bulged and demanded that I dig my nails into them!

He moaned as I did, and I held on tighter as he lifted me off the ground.

I wrapped my legs around him as he pulled at my shirt, pulling it over my head in one move and cupping my ass in his big hand.

He tossed my shirt on the floor and then dropped me on to the bed and climbed on top of me.

Bra off.

His hands on my breasts, his lips, tongue, teeth pulling at them.

I arched my body towards him . . . *I needed him.*

He raised himself up on his knees, sitting over me, and started undoing his belt. I helped him out and unzipped him.

A moment.

A pause, as if we were catching our breath, and then . . .

Hands everywhere again.

Breathing becoming jagged as he slipped his hand down my pants and I pushed my hands into his.

Gripping him tightly.

Slipping his fingers under my panties.

"Oh God," I cried out.

I closed my eyes and moved my hips in circles.

Faster.

My hand still gripping him.

Faster.

Tighter.

And then, when I could no longer take it, I pulled him down on to me and opened my legs for him.

His weight on top of me, crushing me into the bed, and then . . .

"Wait!" we both said at exactly the same time, pulling away from each other.

"Condom?" I asked, looking at him.

He shook his head and raised an eyebrow. "Condom?"

I shook my head back and then crawled out from underneath him and opened the bedside drawer. This establishment was the kind of place that would keep condoms by the bed, I was sure of that.

"Shit," I cursed, when I found the drawer completely empty.

"Other one?" he asked, looking at me. His cheeks were even more flushed now, his hair was messy from me running my hands through it and a fine layer of sweat was glistening on his forehead. In a word, *hot*. Smoking, steaming, sizzling hot.

"Yes. The other one!" I climbed on to all fours and crawled across the bed to the other drawer. I opened it and—

"Shit!" I looked over at him and shook my head.

His shoulders slumped. "Don't suppose this is something we can call room service for?" he asked, with a smile on his face.

I laughed. "Not sure about that."

He flopped back down on his back.

"Don't suppose Uber has started a division where they drop condoms off?" I asked.

I heard a small chuckle next to me. "Don't think so, but there's an idea for a small start-up." He rolled over, perched himself up on his elbow and looked at me.

"Condom drop dot com?" I asked, also rolling on to my side. My breasts were squeezed together by the move and his eyes immediately drifted down there. He slowly lowered his lips to them again and ran his tongue over my nipple, pulled it between his lips and—

We were kissing again.

Harder and hungrier than before.

Hands through hair.

Hands on hips, pulling, grinding . . .

But I needed more!

"Shit!" I hissed against his lips. "We *reeeeeally* need a condom."

He sat up. "Convenience store. Two blocks away." He was on his feet, pulling his shirt back on already, almost before he'd even finished the sentence.

I jumped up, too. "Why didn't you say so?" I quickly pulled my clothes on and made a run for the door. Mike followed close behind me.

"Crap—left my car keys inside," I said, as we were heading across the parking lot, and I started to turn around again.

"Got mine!" He dug in his pocket and pulled a set out, waving them in the air as he ran.

"Good. Good!" I followed him to his car, expecting to see his police car. I paused when I saw a very ordinary-looking Honda.

"Well, I don't drive a police car all day," he said, opening the car and climbing in.

"Aha! Of course." I nodded as I got into what was clearly a man's car. A can of deodorant lay on the floor by my feet, as well as an empty tin of energy drink.

"Uh . . ." He looked over at me. I could see he was embarrassed. "I don't have many passengers," he said defensively. "Well, not ones that aren't criminals, and you'd be surprised how little they care about how your car looks."

"It's okay." I pushed the cans away with my foot as we drove off.

The store really was only two blocks away and we could have walked. As soon as we parked, we both jumped out the car with a sense of urgency and then rushed inside, a little bell announcing our arrival. We ran up to the counter. A man was behind it and I immediately opened my mouth and started talking.

"Hi! Can we please have a box of—" I stopped talking when I saw the strange look that had washed over Mike's face. He'd gone white and his eyes were as wide as saucers, as if he'd seen a ghost. *Who the hell was he looking at?*

CHAPTER 16

"*M*ichael."

I swung around when I heard the voice. It was coming from an older-looking lady. She stood next to us, clutching a shopping bag.

"Mrs. Devereux," Mike said sweetly, and then looked over at me in panic. "This is my primary-school teacher, Mrs. Devereux," he said, very pointedly. It took a few moments for my brain to click. Excuse me for being somewhat slow, but my brain had been very much occupied with something else entirely.

"Oh! Oh!" I said. "Nice to meet you."

"I was also his grandmother's best friend," she added. "I used to change his diapers when he was a baby, if you can believe it."

I looked at Mike as his face went slightly red, and I tried to bite back a smile. "You don't say."

"And who might you be, dear?" she asked me.

"Sorry, this is Becca," he jumped in quickly.

"Becca." She extended her hand for me to shake. "So nice to see Michael with a lady friend. It's been ages since he's been seen with a female companion. Well, not since April, anyway."

"Uh . . . Well, it's only just May, so that's not very long ago," I said.

She burst out laughing. "Oh, you are a funny one. I meant April the girl, not the month."

"Mrs. Devereux, please, I'm sure Becca doesn't want to hear about that now," he said, shaking his head a little.

"Took him by complete surprise, that did. Took us all by surprise.

I mean, half the town was sure they would get married, but, as it turned out, she fancied someone else altogether. If you ask me, she was always a little cold. But her father was Swiss, you know." She whispered that last part, as if it had some great significance. And then she leaned in and lowered her voice even more. "Very strict people, the Swiss, what with their watches!"

"Aaaah," I said, trying to figure out whether I agreed with this sweeping assessment of an entire nation. I looked over at Mike and he rolled his eyes.

"There are no secrets in this place," he said, half under his breath.

She looked at me and smiled. "He's been quite the most eligible bachelor in town since she broke his heart, all those years ago."

"He is, is he?" I tried to stop my smile again.

"No." Mike shook his head at me again. "Not true."

Mrs. Devereux nodded. "Turned into such a good man, despite the fact he was a terror as a child."

"Really?" I asked.

She nodded. "So misbehaved in class. And, when he was a teenager, he had the whole town talking when he and his friends drew some rather obscene graffiti . . ." She leaned in and whispered to me. "It was a big, purple phallus. Right on Anthony Hopewell's front wall. He nearly had an angina, the poor soul. He'd only just had his other hip done, you know." She shook her head and then tutted loudly. "Mind you, maybe he deserved to have it. You know, he left his poor wife Violet for his physiotherapist . . ." She leaned in even closer to me now and looked around, as if making sure no one was listening. "She was from the Channel Islands. The mistress."

I looked at her and she eyeballed me as if I was meant to know what that meant. As if I was meant to understand what being from the Channel Islands had to do with any of this. I had no idea, but I started nodding, anyway. "Well, you know what they say about people from the Channel Islands," I offered up, lamely.

And then she winked at me. "Oh, I do know, dear," she said.

"You do?" I asked. *What* do *they say about people from the Channel Islands?*

And then she put her finger over her lips and made a shushing sound. "We'll keep that to ourselves, though, won't we, dear?"

I nodded again. "We sure will." I quickly made a mental note to google people from the Channel Islands.

"Yes," she said, looking back at Mike, "he was quite the naughty one, growing up, but look at him now."

I gazed at Mike. He was hanging his head now, looking embarrassed.

"Sounds like he was quite the rebel!" I said.

"Oh, he was." She looked over at the man behind the counter. "Sorry, I disturbed you. You were busy buying a box of . . . ?" She looked at us, and Mike quickly jumped in.

"Cigarettes!" he said, still sounding somewhat panicked. He looked over at me, as if he wanted me to confirm this. I nodded.

"Michael Charles Wooldridge!" Mrs. Devereux suddenly grabbed a magazine from her basket, rolled it up and hit him on the arm.

"Does your mother know you smoke now?" she scolded him, and his demeanor changed a little, as if he was a small boy again. I put my hand over my mouth to stop the chuckle from escaping. "Your grandmother would be rolling in her grave if she knew you were sucking on those cancer sticks! Rolling in her grave!"

"They're for me," I interrupted.

She turned around and looked at me with that scolding teacher look. "Young lady!" she exclaimed loudly. "And does *your* mother know you're smoking?"

I hung my head in shame, playing along. "No, she doesn't."

"You know those things will kill you," she said, eyeing me. "Just last week, Laura Jacobs was diagnosed with lung cancer, and she smoked for forty years! She smoked through all five of her pregnancies, too, you know." She leaned over to me. "Of course, no one knew it was bad for you then, like drinking Scotch. Everyone did it!" She paused now, and it looked like she was thinking about something. "Mind you . . . her one son did come out very short. Very short indeed."

"I see," I said, trying not to smile at this strange oversharing.

"He's also quite unfortunate looking, but I'm not sure that's from the cigarettes. But you can't really tell, can you?" she added.

"Can't tell," I echoed.

"And his father was such a tall, strapping man. But, still, one never knows what causes these things. It might be the cigarettes, so best not to smoke them, right?" She glared at me.

I nodded. "Sure. Best not to smoke them," I agreed.

"You're absolutely right," Mike said. "And that's why she's going to quit." He took my hand. "Isn't that right, Becca?" he said, turning to ask me.

"So right!" I said. "I am definitely quitting! I wouldn't want short or unfortunate-looking children."

"Good for you!" Mrs. Devereux exclaimed happily.

Mike tugged on my arm. "So, we'd better get you out of here, away from all this temptation."

I nodded as he dragged me out of the shop.

"It was really nice seeing you again," Mike said to his old teacher as we made our way towards the door.

"You too. You must come over for biscuits soon, and please bring your lady friend. You are most welcome." She gave me a toothy grin.

"Thank you," I said, as Mike pulled me out of the store and into the parking lot. "What are you doing?" I asked him.

"Well, I can't buy a box of condoms in front of my primary-school teacher, now, can I!" he said.

I burst out laughing. "Who used to change your diapers," I added, teasingly.

"You see my dilemma." He looked over at the shop. "We'll have to wait for her to leave, and then you'd better go in by yourself."

"Why by myself? In case someone else who used to change your diapers is shopping there?"

"Exactly!" he said.

"Just how many people changed your diapers?" I asked, feeling so amused by all this.

He rolled his eyes at me. "It takes a village to raise a child."

"Clearly," I said, and started laughing again.

"Please, just go in by yourself. I know everyone in this town and I'd like to try to maintain some iota of privacy—for example, by not having the whole town knowing when I'm getting laid."

I laughed. "You're getting laid?"

"Well, I assumed I might." He smiled at me. "Unless I've read the woman signs wrong again?"

"No, you read them right. But, if you call it *laid*, you might just not get laid." I smiled at him, and his smile widened even more. There was something about his ability to go from sexy-filthy, to boyish-cute in a matter of seconds. And it was making my knees very weak.

"Sure, I'll go in by myself," I said to him.

"Thanks." Cue boyish-cute smile again. "When you live in a small town, nothing is sacred, not even your sex life. People in small towns survive on gossip and rumors, and like to spread them as if it was the town hobby. And I wouldn't want this spreading and being discussed by everyone. Next thing you know I'm—"

"I'm your mistress from some chain of small oceanic islands somewhere, with questionable Swiss heritage and a bad hip," I teased.

"Exactly. And we wouldn't want that," he said, playing along.

I shook my head. "No! We would not want that kind of scandal spreading here, in Willow Bay."

He smiled at me and then sighed. "Do you know how cute you are?"

"Cute!" I exclaimed . "Um . . . is that a compliment, or a . . . I mean, *cute*? Puppies and kittens are cute!"

"Compliment. Terribly cute."

Cue sexy-filthy smile.

Cue kneecaps turning to liquid and pooling on the floor.

"And fucking sexy, with red lipstick on!"

"I'll . . . um . . . just go into that shop now . . . should I?" I stumbled over my words as his eyes searched me.

He gave me another smile and walked off, throwing a sexy-sounding, "I'll be ready and waiting in the car!" at me.

CHAPTER 17

I lurked in the parking lot for a while, until finally, *finally*, after what felt like hours, Mrs. Devereux exited with a wave and I quickly slipped back inside and straight to the counter.

"Hi," I said to the man once more. "Please can I have a pack of condoms?" And then I felt my cheeks flush. He knew I was about to have sex! And he knew that I knew that he knew. It was embarrassing. Like going to the pharmacy and having to ask for a vaginal cream when there are people standing behind you in the queue and you want to turn around and scream, *I was on antibiotics!* so they don't make some strange assumption about you.

"What kind?" he asked, pointing at the MASSIVE row of them.

"Uh . . . wow!" *When had condoms bred like this?* I hadn't bought condoms in years. Call me very unfeminist, but I sort of expected the guy to handle that, since we have so many other ovary-related things to deal with—it's the least they can do, right?

I scanned the row: ribbed, studded, warming, kiss of mint, glow in the bloody dark (why? In case you were having trouble finding it?), bareback, long love, fire and ice (well, that didn't sound nice). I stared at them, feeling confused.

"And what size?" the man asked.

"Size?" I asked.

"We have XL, if you need?" He seemed so casual about this, as if he did it all the time.

"Uh . . . Uh . . ." I stuttered. I didn't really know. "Can you just hold that thought a moment, please?" I held my finger up and then ran out the store, across the lot, and knocked on Mike's window. He opened it.

"So," I said nervously, when he looked at me, "I was wondering, uh, what type you would like? I mean, there are A LOT! I mean, lots."

"What do you like?" he asked.

"Normal," I said quickly. "Totally normal."

He smiled at me. "Me too."

"Great, great." I started walking away and then stopped again. "And, uh, what size?" I asked nervously.

He sat up in his seat and his eyes widened. "I guess . . ." He suddenly looked very uncomfortable. *Damn, it was cute.* "Normal," he quickly said.

"So, average then?" I asked.

"Well, no. NO, not average-average, I would say. Maybe, uh, a—"

"So, XL then?" I cut him off.

"I wouldn't say . . . XL." He looked so uncomfortable as he squirmed in his seat. "Maybe more medium to large, but more on the, uh, uh . . ." He leaned out the car and whispered now. "Can't you tell?" he asked, looking at my hand. It tingled at the memory.

I looked down at it and then back up at him. "So, like, six inches then?" I asked, with a teasing smile.

"Well . . ." He cleared his throat. "I'm sure it's a bit more than avera- . . . but, I suppose that six to seven, maybe, should do the, uh, trick."

"The trick, eh?" I smiled at him and started backing away from the car. All this talk was making my temperature rise very rapidly again.

He smiled back at me. Slightly boyish, a little bit dirty. "Maybe *trick* wasn't the right word."

"Mmm, and what's the right word?" I continued walking backwards towards the store.

"God, you're hot." He ran his eyes up and down my body—slowly, deliberately, hungrily. *Oh God!* His smile grew and my stomach started to flutter.

"Okay, okay, hold that thought! Hold it!" I giggled and then ran straight back to the convenience store.

"Hurry!" he called after me.

"Hurrying!" I bolted into the shop at such a speed that, when I stopped at the counter, I did a little skid.

"Those ones!" I pointed. "Hurry!"

CHAPTER 18

~

"*W*hat the . . . ?"

I stood in the parking lot and looked around. There wasn't a car in sight. Nothing. *Nada*. No car and no Mike. I swung around to make sure I hadn't missed some parking lot behind me that had suddenly come out of nowhere and magically appeared with his car in it.

But, as I suspected, there wasn't one. I could feel the packet of condoms burning a hole in the palm of my hand.

"You're kidding me!" I threw my hands in the air. "You. Are. Fucking. Kidding. Me!" *Had I just been stood up?* It's one thing being stood up on a date, but to be stood up in the almost-middle of almost-sex, for heaven's sake, with a bag of prophylactics in your hands—well, this was just a whole new level of embarrassment.

Wait . . . Maybe he was parked on the street, to avoid being seen? I walked through the lot and looked up the street. Nope. I looked left and right, and left again. He'd stood me up. The bastard had gotten me all hot under the collar and then had just dumped me, with a box of condoms in my hand! He definitely wasn't XL, that's for sure. Someone who was XL would have had the balls, not to mention decency, to tell me they were leaving. That they had changed their mind.

I stood there for a few moments, trying to decide what the hell to do with myself now. I could see my hotel from where I stood, so I guessed the only thing to do was to walk back. I sighed. Turned around. Tossed the box of condoms in the trash can and then walked back to the shop, dragging my feet behind me. I opened the door and the little bell rang out again.

Great! Just announce my arrival. Announce the arrival of the girl *not* having sex right now!

I strolled to the first aisle and grabbed a few things: some chocolate to dull the humiliation, a biscuit or two to push down the feelings and, last but not least, salty crisps to rub in my gaping wound. I walked up to the counter and put my stuff on it. The man, who had, two minutes ago, sold me a box of condoms, looked up at me questioningly.

"I think I just got stood up," I said, pulling some cash from my wallet and sliding it over the counter.

"What can you do, right?" the man said, as he rung my stuff up slowly on one of those old cash registers. *Why didn't he have a fast one that scanned the stuff?* It was painful, standing there in silence as he pressed the buttons with one finger. "You know," he said, looking up at me, "my son is a doctor. He lives in Cape Town."

"Huh?" Was this man serious? Was he trying to set me up with his son, at a moment like this?

He stopped ringing my things up and pulled out his phone, and then handed it over to me. I took it and looked at the picture on the screen.

"Mmm," I mumbled. "Very . . . He looks . . . uh . . . *like a doctor*," I finally managed, after not knowing what I was meant to say to this.

And then he leaned over the counter and whispered, "And he's never painted a purple you-know-what on someone's wall. That poor man, he'd just had his knees done—"

"I thought it was his hip," I interrupted.

He shook his head. "No, it was his wife who got the new hip. If you ask me, she only got it done because she was having an affair with his chiropractor."

"I thought it was his physiotherapist? And wasn't *he* the one having the affair?" I said flatly, leaning on the counter now.

He shook his head again. "No, *she* had the affair. She was from the Canary Islands, you know."

"I thought it was the Channel Islands." I hung my head and shook it. What was wrong with the people of this town? Did none of them have anything better to do than know everyone's business?

"Definitely Canary. She was as mad as a bird."

"She was, was she?" I sighed deeply, taking it all in. How had I gone from almost having hot sex, to having a discussion about someone's decrepit hips and knees and a woman who may or may not have been from some island?

"And you know what they say about people from the Canary Islands," he said, and continued ringing my items up.

"Mmm. I sure do," I lied. The people of Willow Bay were definitely a bit strange!

Finally, after what seemed like an eternity of hell, he put all my snacks into a bag and handed it over to me.

"Thanks," I said dryly, and started heading for the door again.

"Good luck with the . . . uh . . ." he said.

I gave him a thumbs up, walked out the shop and stood in the empty parking lot again. I walked across it and jumped as a blast of bright light hit me. I turned and looked straight at all the motion-activated security lights.

Great! As if this moment needed any more highlighting—now, I was flooded in lights, as if on the stage. *Behold the woman who did not have sex*, the lights seemed to say, in a mocking tone. The walk back to my hotel was a quick one, and soon I found myself sitting on the purple velvet duvet on the bed. I had laid my junk food out in front of me in a semicircle, to give me good and equal access to all of it.

"What does one eat when one is stood up in a parking lot with condoms in one's hand?" I muttered to myself. *And what the hell was the song for a moment like this?*

"I Hate You So Much Right Now" by Kelis came to mind.

I reached for the Mars Bar and ripped it open with my teeth. I took a bite and chewed as fast as I could, not even tasting the food. My phone beeped and I looked down at it. It was a message from my author page on Facebook. I opened the app and looked at the message.

I can't wait for your next book!

Just seven little words, and yet they had the power to strike terror into me. And they were really the last thing I needed to read, right now. I started scrolling through my other messages. I hadn't responded to any of them; seeing messages from readers asking for my next book usually struck terror into my heart and I found it was always better to ignore them. Denial can be a very powerful weapon against the harsh glare of reality. Denial is like sticking your finger into the dyke. It will help momentarily, it will keep the water back, but soon it will blow. And blow it always does. It had certainly all blown up on me. I mean, look at me—in a strange town, plagiarizing some letters, in a hotel room, alone, not having sex . . .

I took another bite of the tasteless lump of chocolaty sugar and chewed.

There was another reason I ignored these messages, too. I still couldn't get used to total strangers reaching out to me, wanting to know me and hear from me. I hadn't had many friends, growing up; I'd never stayed in one place long enough to make any, I suppose. And now, as an adult, I guess I'd never really honed the skills needed to make any . . . and so I hadn't. I had acquaintances, sure. But not that one "ride or die" that everyone seems to have, that everyone rubs in your face on social media.

I continued to scroll through the messages on my page. They were making the knot in my stomach tangle even more, each one telling me why they loved my book and how much they were looking forward to my next one and . . .

HATED IT!

"What?" I sat up and read the message.

I usually never write to authors, but I had to write to you to tell you THAT I HATED YOUR BOOK!! WORST BOOK EVER WRITTEN. DON'T QUIT YOUR DAY JOB!!!

"Wow, wow, wow!" I whispered to myself. What on earth had I done to warrant so many capital letters, not to mention all those exclamation marks? I continued this self-destructive scroll. God, I had no idea there were so many messages. So many expectant readers. My insides started to crawl as I thought about my looming deadline, my agent's smug face, her total belief that I was going to fail, and I also wondered if everyone would hate my next book. What if I was just another one-hit wonder? A "Ninety-Nine Red Balloons," an "Ice Ice Baby," an "I'm Too Sexy For My Shirt" . . . You know who else was too sexy for his shirt? No. Stop, Becca. Just stop this! *Stop, calibrate and listen!*

"Shit!" I climbed off the bed. I was here to write and save my sinking career, not have almost-sex with people who clearly didn't want to have almost-sex with me and get lost down the rabbit hole of bad reviews and . . . *I just couldn't get distracted right now.*

I walked over to my computer with a renewed sense of (panicky) purpose. Screw Mike! Well, not *screw* him, screw him. That hadn't happened. Clearly! Or I wouldn't be alone, stuffing my face with calories and plagiarizing on a pink beanbag. Screw him and screw that naysayer with all his exclamation marks.

I put my fingers on my keyboard and forced myself to type.

CHAPTER 19

*H*aving a good sleep in a surprisingly comfortable bed had made me feel a lot better about the *almost-but-definitely-not-laid-last-night* thing, as well as the *I-hate-your-book-double-exclamation-mark* thing, and not forgetting the *I-can't-wait-for-your-new-book* palaver, too. So had that huge greasy breakfast I'd eaten at my hotel, followed by the two cups of strong black coffee that I'd almost inhaled. And, with all that fueling my system I was ready for a better and more productive day of criminal espionage, or whatever else you might want to call it. And so that is how I now found myself crouched in my car, parked outside the entrance to the Willow's Eco Estate, like a real spy, trying to figure out how the hell to get in. I'd also downloaded Techno Tannie's song and was listening to it. It was actually, strangely enough, the perfect soundtrack to this mad moment. The repetitive sound of cymbals and the hard hammer of the drum, along with those strange synthesizer sounds that reminded me of a UFO's door being opened, really added to the atmosphere.

I'd been sitting there for over an hour, observing how people drove in and out. The residents seemed to scan their fingers on the way in, and all visitors punched a code into the keypad. And, since there was no way of getting someone's finger without risking spending time in a maximum-security prison for grievous bodily harm, I wondered how one would go about getting a code for this place.

God, all I needed now was a bloody cloak and a dagger to complete this criminal look. I imagined I was some awesome P.I. chick. Some leopard-crawling, police-dodging, fence-climbing, plane-parachuting P.I. that was undercover on some important mission to catch the head of the Russian mafia or something—not that I am trying to stereotype, here, but . . . well, you know!

I was in full police stake-out mode. My seat was pulled back and I was reclining in it, surreptitiously peeping through my window in the manner of a cat hunting a mouse. But, after another hour like this, my back was sore, my neck had a crick in it, I needed to pee and I still had no idea how to infiltrate the enemy lair! And, honestly, did I even want to? The effects of the caffeine were diminishing, as was my sense of reckless bravado. I sighed and hung my head. This was just so ridiculous. What was I doing here, parked outside, waiting and watching like a stalker? This wasn't me. I reached for the steering wheel and squeezed it—I'm not sure why, but I felt like I needed to do something physical, to let out this building tension inside.

Maybe I should just give up. This was madness, after all.

Maybe I should turn around, head back to Jo'burg without a book and face whatever consequences were waiting for me. So what if I became another taxidermy casualty on my agent's desk? So what if I became another has-been, a *once-was-someone* no one?

My phone beeped and I almost jumped out of my skin, I was on such high alert. I looked down at the screen and immediately felt like I'd been punched in the throat. It was a picture from Daphne "the second esquire" Kingsley-Hawthorne. A picture of an article. I swallowed as I read the article.

A release date has been set for the highly anticipated second book from Becca Thorne. She burst on to the literary scene three years ago with her dazzling debut, but, according to her publishing house, Lighthouse Books, this book will be even better than her first. We're calling it the "Most Anticipated Read of the Summer."

"Fu . . . uuu . . . ck!" I lowered my forehead to my phone and tapped it against my head a few times. The pressure felt like it was crushing down on me like an anvil. I felt like I was about to drown in my car. Another message pinged on my phone and I looked down again.

> **Daphne (the second esquire):** I hope you're writing. Wordsmith Books just put an order in for 50,000 copies and I've just sold Russian and German foreign rights and have a phone call with Netflix this afternoon.

"Fuuuu . . . uuuuuu . . . ckkkkk!" I looked back at the estate. I had no choice, now. I had to go in. I had to find a way to get in there and read that engraving on the tree; it was imperative to this story.

And then I saw it. I sat up in my seat and watched the car drive in after punching some numbers into the keypad . . .

"Yes!" I scrambled for a pen and paper, writing down the name and number on the side of the car. I pulled my phone out and started dialing.

"Hello, Emerald Realty, Zintle speaking," the voice answered immediately, in that sweet tone that estate agents usually had, estate agents and second-hand car dealers and people trying to sell you death and disability insurance.

"Uh, yes. Hi, my name is . . ." Shit, what was my name? I didn't want to give a real one. I glanced around the car quickly. "Porsha," I blurted out stupidly. "And I'm really interested in the home you're selling at the Willow's Eco Estate." I held my breath. It was a guess, a good one, but still I didn't actually know if anything was for sale there.

"Hi, Porsha," she said happily. "Which house are you interested in?"

Jackpot! "Um . . ." *Crap!* "The one with the . . . uh . . . You can see the river from it?" I guessed.

"That's all of them. In fact, all my listings are riverfront properties.

Very elite. Most desirable in the estate. Which one were you most drawn to?"

"The one with the great, big, uh, the large . . ." I was stumbling, grasping at recyclable straws.

"The one with the big basement?"

"YES! Exactly. I like to store things . . . in a basement." I breathed a sigh of relief. "When do you think I could come and see it? I'm available now, but, I mean, if you're not there, or—"

"Porsha, it's your lucky day," she cut me off. "As a matter of fact, I am heading to that property now."

"Oh, WOW! Wow, what a coincidence—it must be a sign."

"Yes, maybe even a *sign on the dotted line*," the estate agent said.

I played along and fake-laughed. "You never know, Zintle. You never know!" I shook my head as I said it, though. I wasn't going to be buying a house today, or ever. I could barely afford to keep my apartment, let alone buy a luxury house in an uptight eco estate.

"Is this your mobile number?" she asked.

"It is indeed, Zintle." *Why was I saying her name so much?*

"I'll message you a code that you can use to get in. Security is excellent at the Willows. Real grade-A stuff. In fact, in all the years since it opened, there has never been a single security incident. We are very proud of that."

"Great, thanks. And when I'm inside?" I asked.

"Follow the road that takes you parallel to the river and it's the house at the end—198."

"Great, I'll see you in about fifteen minutes, would that be okay?" I asked. I needed to wait a little so it didn't seem like I was parked outside, which I was.

"Perfect. Blessings." She hung up.

I looked at my phone. "Blessings?" I repeated thoughtfully. *Blessings for what?*

* * *

"Please, please take your shoes off," Zintle said, as I stood there by the front door to the massive house.

"Uh, sure." I took my shoes off somewhat reluctantly. I didn't really like walking around barefooted.

"Is that your car?" she asked suddenly. The tone she used when asking this question was very judgemental, and from that I gauged that I was driving the wrong kind of car. "It's not very eco-friendly, is it?" She looked at me. "I'm not sure your neighbors will be happy with—"

"It's powered with biofuel," I quickly said.

"Oh, really?" She perked up. "Well, that is a good sign. Before buying a house here, you have to be approved for residency by the eco committee."

"The . . . ?" I asked.

"There are very strict rules, here, and the Willows only likes to open its gates to those who share in the same sustainable ideals. Like-minded individuals only. That's why this development chose me as their official estate agent; I share their ideals."

I nodded. I barely recycled. "Of course. I agree wholeheartedly. I mean, it is just terrible what's happening to the seahorses," I added.

Zintle gasped. "I know! Did you see that photo of the poor seahorse holding a cotton bud in its tail?"

I put my hand to my heart. "Tragic. Truly, it kept me awake at night."

Zintle lay her hand on my shoulder in commiseration. "So sad," she said. "Come, let's go inside."

I could see by the look of seriousness on her face that this was going to be a very thorough tour, and I wasn't going to be let off the hook very easily.

Before letting me inside, she stopped me once more. "Do you mind taking your cell phone out and placing it in that box, there?" She pointed to a box on the wall.

"Why?" I asked.

"They don't allow electronics in the house. To protect against microwaves and radiation," she said. "That box traps all the harmful rays inside."

I nodded. "Of course. What an . . . an . . . excellent idea. I really must start doing that." I tried not to roll my eyes as I put my phone into the small box that seemed encased in some strange black-looking rocks.

"Shungite crystals," she said. "Very powerful stones."

"Mmmm," I mumbled. Like my useless rose quartz table that was supposed to have brought calm and harmony into my home. Well, if that thing had brought me even an iota of that, I wouldn't find myself here now, would I? I'd have written a damn book, and, right now, I would be leisurely sipping on cappuccinos while editing my manuscript before sending it in. So much for rocks!

We walked into the hallway and I looked around. This house appeared perfectly normal inside—that is, until she started talking about it. Very soon, I realized that there was nothing normal about this house.

"The whole house is made from green bricks." She ran her hand over the wall.

"Green?" I asked, genuinely puzzled.

"Yes—made from hemp, lime and water."

"Mmmm, I see." I nodded, trying to look impressed. But I wasn't. In fact, I was more concerned about whether something so flimsy-sounding could really hold up a house. Some bloody marijuana seeds did not seem like a good addition to any part of a house, let alone the walls. What was next, chia-seed cement?

"And this paint—feel how smooth it is." She rubbed the wall and I placed my hand on it too. "Soap, berries and cornstarch. Makes a totally natural paint. Completely non-toxic." She smiled at me and I smiled back.

"Fabulous," I said, patting the wall.

"And the floor." She dropped her bag suddenly and got down on all fours. She looked up at me. "Come, come," she beckoned.

"Uh . . ." I kneeled next to her.

"Smell it," she said, lowering her nose to the floor. "Go on," she urged again, when she saw I hadn't jumped.

I leaned in and put my nose to the floor, taking a small sniff.

"No—a big sniff. Inhale." She squished her nose to the floor and took it all in. "Do you smell that?" she asked.

I shook my head. "I smell nothing."

"Exactly. You would never know this is made with cow dung, just like my Xhosa ancestors used."

"Sorry. WHAT?!" I sat up.

"I know. It's very exciting." She stood up and we continued our tour of the house. I was told things I had never heard about before: crystals in the geysers to neutralize chemicals in the water, moss carpets, bamboo water pipes . . .

Zintle finished showing me the house and we stood by the door again. "So, what do you think?" she asked.

"Gorgeous," I said. "I really must get my husband here to see the place."

"Well, this is my card." She handed me her business card and I looked down at it. "Hemp-seed paper," she said quickly. "As this estate's official realtor, I think it's essential that I represent its unique selling points." She smiled. She'd already said that to me. It made me wonder if she didn't really believe in all this stuff and was actually just going along with it. I smiled at her. I could relate to going along with something you didn't necessarily believe in, or like. Like me pretending I enjoyed watching sports on Sundays, because my cousins did and I was just trying to fit into the strange family I'd been thrust upon.

"Couldn't agree more," I said, meaning it. "So . . . tell me—" I was trying to act casual—"I heard there was a really large, old willow tree here. I would love to see it."

"Yes, it's over 200 years old. Unfortunately, it's on a neighbor's property, and, until you buy here, I'm not sure they would be comfortable with you going there." She smiled at me again.

"I understand." My stomach dropped. *How the hell was I going to get to that willow tree?*

"I'm sorry, I have to run; will you be okay getting out?" she asked.

I jumped. "Do you mind if I use the loo first?" I asked.

She looked reticent for a moment, but then leaned in and whispered, "I won't tell if you don't." She gave me a quick wink and I ran into the guest toilet.

I was so desperate to get my pants off and pee, it rushed out like the Niagara Falls the second I sat down. Private investigators must really train their bladders in some special way. If I was a P.I., I would completely blow my cover when I went looking for a toilet every few hours.

I reached for the toilet paper and stopped. *What the hell?* It was brown. I pulled a sheet off and it was as rough as sandpaper, and were those . . . ? I examined the fibrous-looking paper and I swear I saw a small twig in it. I wiped and it felt like I'd just run a grater over my lady parts.

"Don't you love the handmade toilet paper?" I heard Zintle say from behind the door.

"Mmmm," I muttered. "Divine!"

"It's amazing how versatile cow dung is!"

"Cow . . . ?" I dropped the paper in the bowl and tried not to gag! This place was *not* for me.

CHAPTER 20

⌒

I hadn't left the estate. Instead, I had parked my car behind a huge bush and was waiting for the cover of darkness so I could sneak out and look at the willow tree, up close. I could see it from where I was sitting. It was huge and impressive, and watching its leaves blowing back and forth in the breeze was really quite mesmerizing. But I was fucking bored, too, and so, to pass the time, I started typing up one of the letters.

23 June, 1948

Dearest Edith,

The world around us doesn't want us to be together, and I say we should find ourselves our own world, or create a new one, just for us. Because this one is wrong.

If I close my eyes, I can imagine what it would be like. In our world, we'd be able to walk hand-in-hand through the streets together. We could sit on the same bench to feed the pigeons in the park, ride the same bus and be free to love each other. In our world, the sun would always shine (because I know you hate winter), it would always be spring, so that I could pick as many daisies as you want.

In this turbulence that surrounds us, you and I need to find our own special places, little worlds within this one where we can be together, where we write our own laws and live by our own rules . . .

You, me, forever.

My fingers glided over my keyboard as I finished the first letter and then moved on to the next one.

1 July, 1948
I've found it. I've found the perfect place for us. Under the willow tree on the banks of the river. No one will find us there. It can be our own magical world. Let me know when you can meet me there. I know it's getting more difficult to sneak out, and I'm sorry things at home with your father have been so trying. I wish I could be there for you and hold you and make it all better. I'll be waiting for you under the willow tree tonight. I hope you can make it . . .

I stopped typing and looked at the tree again. When I'd first seen it, it had looked like a normal tree: green leaves and bark. Nothing more. But now I knew better. That wasn't just a tree, it had been their own private universe where they could escape and be themselves. A place where they could shut the world out, a sanctuary for their love to be whatever it wanted to be. It dawned on me . . . the sheer injustice of it all, being told who you were and were not able to love. This place was so special to them. And all this made me want to see that engraving more than ever.

CHAPTER 21

Although it was dark by half past six, I waited another whole hour before I felt ready to act. And so, with a very rumbling stomach (not a full bladder, since I had relieved myself in the bush!), I climbed out of my car at half past seven and closed the door as quietly as possible.

I'd found an old black hoodie on the back seat, and I put it on now and raised the hood over my head. I scuttled across the large, open grassland with the stealth of a black puma. I ducked behind bushes and hid behind trees with the cunning of a leopard on the hunt. I threw myself on the ground and crawled with the grace of a . . . *Fuck, no*—there was nothing graceful about this at all. In fact, my body was really not made to wiggle on the ground like this.

And soon the tree was very much in my grasp. It was only about twenty meters away and I decided to make a final sprint for it. But, as I did, I almost ran into two jogging women on the path. At the last second, I managed to evade detection by jumping out their way. Unfortunately, this jump also led to a rather uncontrollable roll. A roll down an embankment I hadn't seen. I tried to stop myself, but gravity was a bitch and the embankment was steep and I'd gained too much momentum and now I was being tossed around like a shoe in a tumble dryer. Around and around and around and then . . . *Splash!*

"Crap!" I screamed, as I fell into the muddy shallow waters of the river. I tried to get up; the mud squelched beneath my feet and dragged me deeper and deeper into it. "Oh my God!" I waved my arms around frantically to stop myself from falling backwards. I tottered and teetered and grabbed on to the low-hanging branch of a tree to stop myself from losing my balance. But then . . .

Chaos!

A hundred ear-shattering squeaks and squawks!

The gale-force wind of hundreds of birds taking off in panic whipped at my face.

The rain of bird splatter, thick and warm and gooey.

I screamed as the beating of wings grew so loud that I felt like I was standing behind a Boeing 747 that was taking off. I was terrified as the noise surrounded me like a raging hurricane. And then, just as quickly as it had started, it was gone. I looked up. The moon was completely obscured by what seemed to be hundreds of birds flying into the night. My God, I had never seen so many birds together in my entire life. But then, suddenly, the night wasn't so dark anymore.

It was bright and I couldn't work out where the light was coming from. It seemed to be coming from everywhere all at once. I was disorientated and stumbled forward again, trying to rub the combination of bird crap and mud from my eyes. I threw myself forward and gripped on to the long grass of the embankment, pulling myself out of the river. And then I heard it. Another noise filled the air. Dogs and shouting and running and . . . *what the hell was going on?* I finally managed to open my eyes, and, when I did, I froze.

There, surrounding me on all sides, like an army, angry-looking residents were holding torches, and all of them were pointing at me.

"Mommy, it's a swamp monster!" I heard a child shriek.

"No! No!" I stepped forward and waved my hands at them. "I'm friendly. Not a monster," I said. Which only seemed to cause more screaming.

"She's coming for us!" another child yelled, and then another one burst into tears, and suddenly concerned-looking mothers were dragging their children away. *Did I really look that bad?*

"Who are you and what are you doing here?" Someone with a massive torch stepped forward. He was probably the leader of this mob! "Are you aware that this tree is off limits?" he said.

Then someone else spoke. "Are you aware that you have just disturbed the sacred nesting spot of the black-crested night budgie that has migrated all the way from São Tomé and Príncipe."

"Huh?" That sounded made up, if you ask me.

"It hasn't nested here in over 200 years, and now it will probably never return, thanks to you!" another angry person shouted.

"And it only lays one egg a year, before plunging to its death in the Strait of Gibraltar."

"It plunges?" I asked. "Like a lemming?"

"Oh God," one moaned loudly. "We might never hear their sweet song again."

"What?!" I stared at these people. They all seemed more concerned that I'd disturbed some nesting birds than the fact I was breaking and entering. This thing sounded totally made up and I decided to challenge them.

"And how do you know they only nested here 200 years ago?" I asked indignantly.

A gasp rose up from the crowd. "Who the hell are you?" the man asked again.

"She must be an eco-terrorist!" shouted one person.

"Wait, wait!" I put my hands in the air again. "I didn't even know those birds were nesting here. And, let's be honest, they looked like pigeons, if you ask me."

At that, more gasps. As if *pigeon* was a dirty word.

"And, trust me, I am not an eco-terrorist. I don't know the first thing about the eco-bloody-system."

"Have you not seen those pictures of the sea—"

"Horses?" I cut her off and sighed. "What's with all this seahorse talk?" I threw my hands in the air and people began to back away from me as if I was mad.

"I suppose you don't care about the orangutans either?" someone asked. They sounded as if they were on the verge of tears. *Who were these people?* Of course I cared about the orangutans, of course I worried about forests and global warming, but I still liked Nutella! Although, I didn't think I should say that.

I sighed in total resignation. This night was not turning out the way it was supposed to. I looked to my left; the willow tree was right there. Within my grasp, but so far out of reach, what with this mob surrounding me with torches. And then a familiar voice cut through the chatter. I turned and looked, and . . . *I was not pleased!*

CHAPTER 22

ↄↄ

*A*ll I saw at first was a large silhouette. The light of tens of torches created a halo around him. He loomed there, like a dark shadow, for a few moments, and then he took a step forward and I shielded my eyes from the light that rushed towards me as he moved.

"God!" I squinted into the light. Why was he always backlit? Why? Was this some kind of movie? Seriously? No one walked around in real life being backlit. No one but him.

"Becca?" Mike said, and I let out a long, loud sigh, because now I could see all of him. And he was standing there in his uniform, looking hot and sexy, and very much like the man that had left me standing in a parking lot with a pack of condoms in my hand. *Non XL!*

"What are you doing here?" he asked. He looked as surprised as I felt. As if he'd hoped he would never see me again. I bet I was the last person in this ridiculous town that he wanted to see.

"This woman broke into the estate and she disturbed the nesting birds," the ringleader yelled.

"I didn't break in," I objected loudly.

"Then how did you get in?" the man asked.

"I came to look at a house. An estate agent let me in," I said defensively.

"You're looking to buy here?" someone else asked, with an incredulous and somewhat patronizing tone to their voice.

"Yes."

"Well, as head of the eco committee, I can tell you now that, as someone who has just ruined the natural nesting place of the black-crested night budgie, we would not welcome you here."

"Oh my God, do you know how made up that sounds?" I asked. "And they were pigeons!"

More gasps, and now I was just feeling very indignant.

"Well, for your information," I started, "I would not want to live in this shitty, birdy, stuck-up, cow-dung-floored place, anyway. And you know what else? My Porsche uses petrol and the fuel consumption is BAD! I mean, really, really bad. Like, shocking. My fuel consumption is probably responsible for melting at least one ice cap a year." Okay, maybe that was taking it too far, but the desire to throw it back in their faces was just too great.

Even more gasps. What was with these people and their shocked gasps? They sounded like a recorded sound-effect that was played on sitcoms, like laughter or clapping.

"Okay, okay, everyone, let's just all calm down." Mike stepped forward in an authoritative way.

"It's illegal to trespass! Arrest her!" one of the residents shouted.

"Oh, please," I said, and chuckled. But then I looked at Mike and stopped chuckling. He raised a rather serious-looking eyebrow at me. *Come on.* There was no way he was arresting me. For what? Disturbing some birds' sexy time?

"I'm afraid I am going to have to take you in," Mike said.

"Take me *in*!? HA! And now you want to 'take me in.'" I gestured air quotes. "Now you want to commit to something like that. Are you going to use handcuffs?" I teased.

Mike approached me quickly and lowered his voice. "Let's not do this here; we can talk about that later."

"*Do* it here? Oh, if I know anything about you, I don't think we'll be 'doing it'—here or anywhere, actually." I was really throwing around the old air quotes now.

"That is seriously uncalled for," he whispered under his breath.

"Is it?" I asked sarcastically. "I could name a few other things that might be considered uncalled for, like—oh, I don't know—standing someone up in a parking lot with—"

"SHHH! Okay, okay . . ." He turned and looked at everyone. "Nothing to see here, folks. I will deal with this and you can all go back home." Nobody moved. And then he turned to me and looked very, very serious. "You're going to have to come with me now, Becca."

"What? Are you being serious?" It hadn't really occurred to me that I actually might get arrested over something as silly as trespassing and disturbing a . . . *What was it* . . . ? Blacky-crested budgie-majiggy!? I put my hands on my hips defiantly.

"Look, we can do this the easy way, or we can do this the hard way," he said.

"The hard way?" I mocked. "Interesting that you should mention *hard* ways."

"*Becccaaa* . . ." he hissed. "Please. You're being very inappropriate."

He took a step closer and I knew it was now or never. The willow tree was right there and I knew this would be my last, *last chance*, to see what was engraved on it. And I had to see it! I'd come this far and I was covered in bird shit—I deserved this. I looked at the tree and then looked at him. His eyes widened suspiciously, as if he knew I was up to something. I had to do this very quickly, and then . . .

I bolted. Ran! As fast as I could.

"Becca! Don't do this!"

But I did do it. In fact, I made it all the way up to the tree. I ducked under its hanging branches and entered into the most magical world. The long leaves hung like soft green curtains, surrounding the largest tree trunk I had ever seen. The light from the torches lit the green curtains up and made them shimmer like emeralds. The breeze blew and every now and then the curtains opened just enough to allow a shaft of light to break through. But there was no time to admire this. I ran up to the trunk and there it was. I could see the engraving. I could almost read it, almost . . .

A symbol.

Two words.

What the hell?

But then I fell to the soft mossy ground as something heavy pulled my feet out from under me. I turned around to see Mike, holding on to my ankles.

"Are you kidding me? Now you want me horizontal? I don't think so." I wiggled out of his grasp and threw myself at the tree, but I felt the tackle once more and I was down on the ground again. Flat on my back. From here, I could see a slight opening in the green curtain, and one star peered down at me through the gap in the branches.

"Becca, why are you making me do this?" He sounded so frustrated, I wiggled from his grasp. I must have knocked him over, because suddenly he fell, on top of me. His face was right in front of mine, and his eyes seemed to be pleading with me.

"Please, Becca," he whispered softly. "This is the last thing I want to be doing, right now. Please, just come quietly."

I burst out laughing. "Come quietly?" I asked. "Really? Well, you didn't give me that option last night."

"Becca," he said, his eyes coming to rest on mine now.

Suddenly, something happened. His face softened and he leaned in, until our noses were almost touching.

Enclosed in that shimmery green curtain, the world outside seems to disappear . . .

Here, with you, under the willow tree, the world around us vanishes. It melts away into obscurity and it is only you and I, my dearest Edith.

I looked up into his eyes, they seemed to draw me in. I felt sucked in by them somehow, as if I was falling into them, unable to stop. Some magnetic force pulled me deep into him. We leaned towards each other, our noses touching now. I could feel his breath on my lips as he looked deep into my eyes . . .

And then, when I look into your eyes, my love, I know that every-thing is right again. Just the way it should be. As if looking into your eyes is what can save me. As if looking into them is essential to living, just like breathing.

"Have you got her?" A loud voice snapped us out of the green spell we'd fallen under.

Mike and I looked at each other and suddenly everything felt awkward.

"Sorry . . . I . . ." Mike quickly climbed off me, stood up and dusted himself off.

I climbed to my feet, unable to look him in the eye now, as if something had just happened between us.

"I've got her," he called, and then held out his hand for me to take.

I stared down at it. It was a really nice hand. Big and broad. Long fingers—the kind you wanted intertwined in yours. The kind you wanted to hold on to. Protective hands. I sighed. It was a defeatist sigh; I knew I'd lost this battle. "Fine. Let's go," I conceded. My fingers slid between his and, as soon as they did, he gripped my hand tightly, as if he wasn't going to let it go.

CHAPTER 23

⟋

"*T*his isn't a jail cell," I said, looking into the room. I'd just arrived at the police station after being put in Mike's car and driven there. Granted, he'd let me sit in the front seat and had decided against handcuffs and flashing lights, but still. I'd never been in a police car before. I'd never been in this kind of trouble before. But trouble seemed to be my new middle name.

"We turned our holding cell into a storeroom a few years ago; we needed a place to store town records and, believe it or not, we hardly have any criminals here." He looked at me meaningfully.

I tutted. "You're not really going to put me in there, are you? I'm not even a real criminal! This has just been a really huge misunderstanding that—"

"Becca." He cut me off. He looked serious now and, for a moment, my heart jumped into my throat.

Oh God, maybe I was actually in trouble. Maybe I could go to jail. But then I thought about my agent's face, and my publisher's face, and *his* face, and all my readers' expectant faces, and I realized that jail was way less scary than facing them.

"You trespassed, Becca. You broke into a secure estate, and this wasn't the first time, either. Yesterday, I caught you trying to climb over the fence, and you lied to me about it. So why don't you tell me what you're *really* doing here in Willow Bay?" He leaned against the wall, waiting for me to speak. He'd crossed his arms and they bulged and strained against the material of his police uniform. I tried not to stare at those ridiculously muscular arms. It was both sexy and amusing, all at the same time; this man was a total cliché—an uber-hot policeman in uniform. Up until this moment, I'd mainly thought such creatures were a myth, an invention created by the minds of romance writers the world over, but he was very much real. Real and hard and big and—God, he smelled nice. Just as he had the night before, when he'd walked me backward, towards my bed, and pushed me down on it.

"You didn't really seem to care what I was doing here, last night, when you came back to my room," I said snappily.

"I was off duty," he replied.

"And now you're on duty?" I looked him up and down.

"Yes," he said, matching my snappy tone. "Well?" he asked again. "What are you really doing here?"

"I told you—I'm a writer. I am doing research for my new book."

"Yeah, to see whether you can climb over a fence or not." He didn't sound convinced.

"Mmmhmm." I nodded.

He shook his head at me. "Becca, you're putting me in a seriously difficult position, here. I'm law enforcement in this town, and *you* broke the law."

"Where did you go when I was inside the shop?" I asked. "You know I was standing in the parking lot with a box of condoms in my hand? Did you just decide you didn't want to . . . *you know*?" I felt embarrassed and vulnerable asking the question, but I had to.

"What? NO! I wanted to. Trust me, I really, really wanted to, but . . ." He paused and looked at me as if he was going to carry on speaking, but he didn't.

"But what?" I asked, my throat drying up and tightening.

"You probably won't believe me, but an emergency came up," he said.

"Really?"

He was right. I didn't believe him.

"I got a call and had to rush to help someone. I tried to let you know, but there was no time to spare. It was urgent."

"I thought you weren't on duty last night?" I looked at him smugly.

"Well, yes, technically . . . but if there's an emergency, then I can't just say, 'Sorry, I'm off duty.' It's my responsibility to help."

"Help who?" I asked, folding my arms.

"Mrs. Van der Merwe. She stays in the old-age home, and every now and then she escapes and runs away. I get called to find her."

"Really? And at the exact moment that I was in the shop, buying condoms, you got an emergency call to find her? Seems rather convenient to me."

"I did," he said, pushing himself off the wall. He walked into the jail-cell-cum-storeroom and I followed him in.

"I see. And you didn't think to pop in and tell me this, like a decent human being?" I asked.

"There wasn't time. I was worried about her. She has Alzheimer's. Someone saw her standing on the highway; I was concerned she would be run over."

"Interesting," I said slowly, still not sure whether I fully believed him. I looked around the room. Rows of shelves containing files lined the walls. A desk and a few chairs were in the middle of the floor, and the rest of it was covered in overflowing boxes. "You really want me to stay in this room?" I turned and looked at him after my visual inspection.

"Well, you are officially under arrest," he said. "And I have nowhere else to put you."

"And what am I being charged with?"

"Trespassing. Breaking and entering. Possible eco-terrorism. Take your pick."

"Don't I get a phone call? Don't I get to call my lawyer?" I asked.

"Do you have a lawyer?"

"No. But I could call one."

"Sure. Go ahead," he said. "But, I must warn you, we only have one lawyer in town, and he's busy." Mike walked over to the desk and opened the drawers.

"What are you doing?" I asked, as he took all the paper clips out and slipped them into his pockets.

"You could pick the lock with these."

I burst out laughing. "You think I can pick a lock? Newsflash: I'm not some career criminal who goes around picking locks. I've never been in jail before."

"I found you trespassing on private property today, and yesterday you were climbing a fence, not to mention lurking suspiciously in a graveyard."

"I told you, I like graveyards," I said. "Besides, if you *really* thought I was a dangerous criminal, you wouldn't have almost had sex with me last night, seeing as you are the law around here." That was a good argument. Didn't need a lawyer for that one! And I seemed to have got him, because he was looking at me blankly now, as if he didn't have a rebuttal.

"There's a chair there, and there are even some magazines you can read."

"Wait—what if I need the toilet?" I asked. I was feeling a little panicked now. This was starting to feel a bit real. *Maybe too real.*

"Do you?" he asked.

"Not now. But I might need it soon."

He looked at me and shook his head again. This man was a head shaker, for sure. He looked torn, as if something in him didn't want to lock me in this room. And I wanted to believe that. I *needed* to believe that the man I'd shared an intimate moment with last night was having some trouble locking me away like this, like an animal in the zoo.

"You can call me when you need to go, and I'll take you to the office toilet." He started moving towards the door.

"You'll take me to the toilet?" I asked.

"Well, I won't go inside with you, if that's what you're thinking." He looked somewhat uncomfortable, now, as he edged his way towards the door.

Suddenly, I panicked. "Wait!" I jumped forward. "You can't seriously be locking me up?"

"What do you want me to do with you?"

"I don't know—release me, turn a blind eye to it. It's not like I killed anyone, for God's sake."

"Honestly, I wish I could, but you just pissed off the eco crowd, and those guys don't let up. You couldn't have messed with a more uptight crowd if you'd tried."

"What if I'm bored and get scared in here by myself, or there's an emergency?" My voice was high-pitched and shaky.

"What kind of emergency?" he asked.

"I don't know." I looked around the room. "What if I'm allergic to old files and dust, and go into anaphylactic shock and need a stab with an EpiPen?" I asked.

"Are you? Allergic to dust?"

I shook my head. "But I could be. I'm slightly allergic to cats."

For the first time since seeing me tonight, he smiled. It was small. It barely tickled the corners of his lips. He shook his head again, as if caught somewhere between amusement and irritation. "You really are a writer," he said.

"I am," I replied softly. Although I wasn't so sure if this statement was entirely accurate, these days.

He looked at me for the longest time, and then, slowly, he took his walkie-talkie out of his pocket and passed it over to me. "Only use this if there's an emergency."

I took the walkie-talkie and he showed me how to use it. And then he turned and started walking away. This time, he didn't stop. He walked straight out the door and closed it behind him, and I . . . Oh shit, I was officially under arrest.

CHAPTER 24

"Hello, hello? Come in, Mike. Over and out, over and out," I said into the walkie-talkie.

"Becca." I heard his voice come through all crackly and distant sounding. "What is it? Is there an emergency?"

"I just wanted to make sure this thing was working. Over and out," I said.

"Well, great, now you know." He hung up. *Wait*—do you call it "hanging up" when it's a walkie-talkie?

I sat and waited for a while, but he didn't say anything else. Then I walked around the room a few times, completely alone and bored. I read the names on the spines of the files—nothing exciting. Nothing like you see in the movies: a room full of unsolved serial-killer files, laden with evidence and jars of body parts for DNA testing. I walked over to the desk and opened the bottom drawer. A folded piece of paper caught my attention and I pulled it out. I placed it on the desk and flattened it with my hands.

"Oooh," I said out loud, when I saw what it was. It was a slightly younger-looking Mike, without a shirt on, cradling a small, white, fluffy kitten to his big chest. I smiled to myself and picked up the walkie-talkie again.

"Come in, Mike. Come in, Mike. Over and out," I said into the thing.

"Yeees?" he returned, sounding irritated at my interruption.

"Why is there a picture of you without a shirt on, holding a kitten, in the bottom drawer of the desk? Over and out."

"Why are you going through the desk?" he asked.

"I'm bored and you're still not answering the question," I said.

"It was for a charity calendar," he said, very quickly and matter-of-factly.

"Charity? For what?" I asked, staring at the picture of him. He looked good, holding a kitten. Mind you, he'd probably look good holding a sewer rat, too.

"SPCA."

"So, all the cops took their shirts off and posed with kittens?" I was amused now.

"There are no other cops in this town," he returned.

"So it was just you? Twelve shots of Mike without a shirt on, cradling various animals?" I didn't bother to stifle my laughter.

"It was for charity," he reiterated.

"And can one still buy this intriguing calendar?" I asked.

"No. Limited print run."

At that, I laughed. "Limited print run," I repeated. "So, when I get out of here, will you autograph this picture for me?"

"Just stop it!" he said.

"Stop what?" I asked innocently.

"I really have to work," he said, after a small pause.

"Fine. Fine. Over and out, Mr. January, February, March, April—"

He cut me off mid-calendar, and, once again, I was all alone. With a shirtless picture of Mike. I lasted about five minutes before I called again.

"Come in, Mike. Over and out," I said into the mouthpiece.

He replied quickly this time. "You don't have to say 'over and out' every time. What's wrong?"

"What other animals were you holding, in the shoot?"

"Alright, that's it, I'm goi—"

"NO!" I yelled into the mouthpiece. "Please don't go. I . . . I don't like it here. I'm claustrophobic." That was sort of the truth—ever since that elevator incident, anyway.

"You should have thought about that before you broke into private property."

"I know, I know," I said. "I should have thought about a lot of things before I did them, but I don't. That's my problem. I hardly ever think before I do things. It's a disease or something. Maybe there's a pill for it, or . . . I don't know." There was a long, silent pause and I couldn't bear it. "So, what are you doing?" I asked.

"I'm busy trying to write up an incident report. You won't believe how much paperwork there is to fill out when someone trespasses."

"I could help you with that. I'm a writer, after all," I said hopefully.

"I couldn't let you write up your own report, Becca. That would be seriously illegal and, believe it or not, I'm not into breaking the law."

"Except when you were a teenager and drew purple penises around town," I offered up.

He huffed. "You know way too much about me."

"Hey, it's not my fault you live in a small, strange town that likes gossip."

"I have to go." At that, he hung up on me and I was all alone again. Shit, maybe I was in real trouble here—and for what? I'd seen the engraving on the tree, but I didn't understand it.

I grabbed a piece of paper and a pen from one of the drawers and drew it as I remembered it. A symbol, like an eight . . . *Wait!* That was the infinity symbol.

I rolled my eyes when I realized that. I had been expecting something a little more—not an infinity symbol, which every person who falls in love gets tattooed on them.

Then I wrote the word *fool* in one side of the infinity symbol and drew a heart in the other side, just like I'd seen.

I sat back and looked at it. *What the hell did that mean?* Fools and hearts? Fools and love? I hated not knowing the answer and I folded the piece of paper up and slipped it into my bra, since my wallet had been taken away from me and my pants didn't have pockets.

CHAPTER 25

~

"*H*elloooo, Mike. Hello, Mike. Are you there? Over and— Uh, no, I don't say that. Mike?"

"What is it now, Becca?"

"I need the loo."

"You're just saying that," he said.

"No, I'm not," I insisted. But I was lying. I didn't need the toilet. I just wanted to get out of here.

"I don't believe you," he returned.

I dialed up my acting skills. "Pleeeease. I'm *soooo* desperate. I'm going to burst! Eeeeee." I made a noise that was meant to mimic the sounds of a person with a full bladder. It was ridiculous and he probably wasn't going to buy it. I didn't buy it myself. I paused and waited. Held my breath. My heart thumped in my chest when I heard footsteps, long and loud and wide, coming down the passage towards me. I looked at the door when I heard the key slipping into the lock, and I jumped to my feet in anticipation. Key turning, door handle turning, and . . .

There he was.

He stood in the middle of the doorway—it framed him, as if he were some great painting. And, lo and behold, the bright florescent light from the passage was behind him again, creating the perfect silhouette. A thin strip of white light outlined him perfectly.

"Do you know that, whenever you enter anywhere, you're always backlit? Do you have a lighting crew following you around, back-lighting you for added drama?"

He looked at me blankly. "I don't know what you mean."

I stared at him and blinked. "Never mind," I said. "It's just ridiculous, that's all! It adds to the whole mystique thing you have going on."

"Mystique?" he asked, stepping to the side and into the light again.

"Yeah. You, appearing suddenly from thin air, and disappearing, too. All large and intimidating and . . . and . . . *hot*." I said it before I could stop it.

His face scrunched up and he looked at me curiously, or was that suspiciously, or was that . . . *Was he confused?* It was cleared up pretty quickly when he opened his mouth and started talking.

"You know, Becca, you confuse me," he said, his tone a little softer this time.

I folded my arms. "Ditto," I said curtly, feeling somewhat defensive.

"So we both confuse each other," he stated.

"Something we have in common, it would seem," I replied. He looked at me for a while before speaking again.

"Here," he said, producing a towel from behind his back.

"What's that?" I asked.

"Thought you could use it to clean up. You're covered in—" he looked me up and down—"budgie shit and mud."

"Pigeon!" I insisted.

"Pigeon, budgie. Budgie, pigeon."

"Thanks." I reached out and took the towel.

"I also put a change of clothes in the bathroom for you," he said. "An old tracksuit. It will be too big, but I thought it would be better than what you're wearing now."

"Oh!" I was surprised by this kind gesture and didn't really know what to say. "Thanks," I mumbled, feeling guilty now.

"Shall we go to the toilet, then?" He moved out of the doorway and gestured for me to follow him.

"Sure." I walked out defiantly.

* * *

"I don't hear anything," he said through the toilet door.

"Don't you?" I tried to sound surprised, but I wasn't. No matter how much I pushed, nothing was coming out.

"I knew you were screwing with me."

"I'm not a robot! I can't just go on command, and certainly not with you standing right outside the door. Haven't you ever heard of stage fright? I bet you can't just pee in front of strangers."

"I have to stand here, or you might escape out the window," he replied.

I looked up at the window and then laughed. "God, you clearly haven't seen my ass properly yet, because, if you had, you would know I am not squeezing through that window in a hurry." I said it in jest, but, the second the words were out of my mouth, I suddenly remembered his hands all over it and sweat prickled on my forehead. I heard an awkward throat clearing and a shuffle of feet.

I looked at the sink and saw a small glass on it. I rolled my eyes and reached for it, filling it up with water. I then, very carefully and gently, poured it into the toilet bowl. But I clearly underestimated the amount that would come out, and there was a short, too-loud *splash*.

"Really? Really?" I heard him say sarcastically.

"Okay, whatever!" I pulled my pants up—the large tracksuit pants that I had changed into—and flung the door open. "You got me. I didn't need the toilet. You happy now?"

"Happy?" he asked, looking somewhat angrily at me. "Do you think arresting someone that I quite like makes me happy?"

"You quite like me?" I asked, stunned.

He looked down at his feet now, as if feeling coy. "Well, yeah!

Wasn't it obvious? Despite what you probably thought, I don't just do that with women all the time. In fact . . ." He paused. "I just don't."

"Oh!" I was stunned by this sudden confession. For a moment, I felt my mouth opening, and I felt the words *I quite like you too* bubbling to the surface. But I didn't let the words come out. Instead, I shrugged. "Could have fooled me," I said, and strode back down the corridor, towards my jail cell.

CHAPTER 26

I sat on a chair in the middle of my "cell" and waited for him to close the door on me. I was trying to be slightly offish and non-chalant about this whole thing, but that was really just to hide how much I was starting to freak out inside. But he didn't close the door. Instead, he simply looked at me. I could see his mind was racing. I could see thoughts swirling around in his brain. I imagined some hectic piano concerto was playing in his head right now, fingers slapping down on piano keys frantically, off-key and hard and strange, making his skin crawl and making him feel slightly mad. Well, that's how I felt as he stood there and glared at me.

What the hell was he thinking? What the hell did he think of me? And, when the glare was finally over, he hung his head.

"I can't," he said softly.

"Can't what?" I asked, standing up slowly. That statement had such an ominous, final kind of quality to it, I didn't know what to make of it.

He stepped away from the door and gestured for me to walk out of it. "You hungry?" he asked.

I smiled at him. "Are you kidding? I'm starving." I exited the room as quickly as I could and followed him down the passage and into a small room at the end of it. It was a dark office, by the look of it. There was a large desk and an old brown couch that looked like it had come from a student's dormitory, bits of sponge sticking out of the corners that had been worn down with time. Mike pulled a seat out for me and I sat down. The tracksuit top I was wearing was huge, I was drowning in it, and I had to pull up the sleeves again.

"Is this your office?" I asked.

He nodded and opened one of his drawers. He pulled out a Tupperware box and slid it across his desk. "We don't have Uber Eats here, let alone any restaurants that are open at this time." He looked up at the clock on the wall behind him and I couldn't believe it. It was already midnight. He opened the Tupperware and I gazed inside. Neat little sandwiches with no crusts, wrapped in wax paper, sat inside like soldiers. He reached in and passed me one. I took it and looked at it.

"Pastrami and gherkin." He took a bite of his and then leaned back in the chair, putting his feet up on the open drawer of the desk.

I bit into the sandwich and my stomach immediately growled at me. I was starving. I hadn't eaten since breakfast. We sat chewing in silence for a while.

"So where is everyone else?" I asked, looking around the office.

"It's just me tonight. There is someone else that works two days a week and then every second weekend. But he's not here."

"I thought you said there were no other people for the calendar?"

"Well, no other people who could have taken their shirts off." He seemed slightly coy, having made this statement.

"Ooooh," I said. "So you think you can take your shirt off, do you?"

He stopped chewing, swallowed and raised his eyebrows at me. "Do you?" he asked, and his voice had a slightly husky tone that was making it hard for me to swallow.

I felt my head nodding before I could stop it. He smiled at me and our eyes locked. A wave of something moved through me and suddenly I was feeling very awkward.

"Delicious," I mumbled, with food in my mouth, trying to steer the conversation away from semi-nakedness.

"The secret is the Dijon mustard," he said, his smile growing as he looked at me.

"Well, it's not a secret anymore," I said quickly, feeling like I needed to fill the silent moments with words, because something strange seemed to be buzzing in the spaces between the words and I wasn't entirely sure what it was, and nor was I that comfortable with it.

We finished our sandwiches in silence and, when we were done, sat there looking at each other for a moment.

"You've seriously put me in a very difficult position, Becca." His tone was serious, now. Quiet and thoughtful and reserved.

"I know. I'm sorry."

He reached into his drawer again and pulled out a bag of crisps.

I looked down at the bag. "Oh my God—my favorite," I said, lighting up at the sight of them.

"What? No one likes this flavor." He looked at me.

"I do!" I opened my hand and he poured some wasabi-flavored crisps into it. "I can never find this flavor in stores, though."

"Amazon," he said, shoving a few in his mouth. "I order them in bulk."

"Really?" I said, mouth full of crunchy, burning crisps. "I never thought of that."

We chewed and smiled at each other. I'd never met anyone else that actually liked this flavor before. I'd always felt alone in my strange taste in crisps and my need to slather my sushi with the green stuff.

"It's an acquired taste," he said, swallowing and putting some more into his mouth.

"Our taste buds are clearly just more sophisticated than other people's," I teased.

He nodded at me, and then something in the drawer caught my attention. I pointed over at it and then his cheeks went slightly pink.

"You really did read my book," I said. The copy in his drawer looked old and worn, like he'd read it more than once.

"It was a good book." He said it so matter-of-factly that it felt like one of the best compliments I'd received in a while, maybe even ever. I looked down at the desk and something else caught my attention. I pulled the piece of paper towards me.

"What's this?" I asked. I could see my name at the top of it: Pebecca Thorne, without the sloping line.

"Incident report. I've been sitting here, deciding whether I should fill it in or not." He tapped his fingers on the desk.

"So, are you? Going to fill it in?" I asked.

He pulled some more crisps from the bag and popped them in his mouth. He chomped them while looking at me thoughtfully. He swallowed and then wiped the side of his mouth.

"I don't want to, Becca." He said my name in a whispery tone and I felt myself crumple into the seat as I stared into those green eyes of his.

"Then don't," I whispered back, feeling like I was slipping and sliding across the desk towards him.

"I've been seriously thinking about that. I've been thinking of letting you go and telling all those people that you have some kind of an emotional problem and that you weren't really in charge of your faculties when you broke in and decimated the nesting place of the— what was it? Black budgie thing?"

"Pigeon," I said quickly. I smiled at him. "You know they totally made that bird up, right?"

"Made up or not, the fact is that you were there and you broke in and you caused a scene."

"I know." I leaned over and stuck my hand into the bag of crisps again. "God, I could eat these all day."

He sighed and put his head in his hands. "The perfect woman in so many ways, other than the fact she's a criminal." He chuckled under his breath and I didn't really know what to say to this, to be honest. One minute he was telling me that he liked me and I was the perfect woman, and now he was telling me I was a criminal. He stopped chuckling and looked up at me.

"You know, I read your book four times. At least."

"Really?"

He nodded. "It was *that* good."

"Thanks," I replied.

"And you know what I thought when I read it?" he asked.

I shook my head. "No."

"Maybe this is going to sound stupid, but I really felt like I knew you. Not the character in the book, but you. And I kept wondering if you'd had your heart broken like the character, because it was so real and I could relate so much."

"I guess I did," I said softly.

"And you poured your broken heart into the book?"

"Something like that." I looked down at the desk and started picking at a small wooden splinter sticking out of it. "I guess writing the book was cheaper than going to therapy." I looked up at him and forced a small smile.

"Reading your book was cheaper than going to therapy for me, too." He smiled back at me, but it seemed slightly forced. The kind of smile you give people when you're trying to put on a brave face. "Your book made me feel less alone," he said. "I knew that, somewhere out there, a writer called Becca Thorne was going through what I was."

"With April the girl, not the month?" I smiled at him.

"I blame her Swiss father," he said, in jest.

"Me too, what with his watches!"

Mike laughed a little and then started swinging back and forth in his chair. "Thank God he wasn't from the Channel Islands," he joked.

I laughed. "You live in a strange town, Michael Charles Wooldridge."

I reached over and grabbed another handful of crisps from the bag. "The people here are all nuts!"

He smiled. "You'd fit in well, then."

I rolled my eyes at him playfully. "Do you know, that guy in the shop tried to set me up with his son after I bought the condoms?"

"He what?" He leaned forward now. "Seriously? Mr. Reddy, of the Right and Reddy Store, tried to set you up with his son?"

I nodded. "He is a doctor, so it was very tempting."

"Tempting?" He leaned over the desk even more. "I thought you were more into rugged policemen with backlighting?"

I burst out laughing. "No, actually, I prefer my policemen holding kittens."

"Are you flirting with me to try to get out of jail?" he asked.

"Is it working?" I enquired, and then our eyes locked on to each other's and stayed there for the longest time.

"Pebecca Thorne." He finally broke eye contact with me, and something in his voice had changed. The flirty air was gone now.

"Yes?" I asked.

"I'm going to let you go, but you're going to have to make me a promise." Suddenly, he looked somewhat sad and serious.

"What promise?" I asked, feeling something change in the air between us.

But he didn't say. Instead he stood up and walked over to the couch. He pulled a pillow and blanket out from behind it and put it down. "Try get some sleep," he said, looking at me. "It's been a long night."

I nodded. I was tired. Exhausted actually now that I thought about it.

"What are you going to do?" I asked.

"I've got to patrol," he said.

"Are you leaving a criminal alone in the police station?" I asked. "Isn't that against policy?"

He shrugged. "Probably."

"Couldn't you get into trouble for that?" I asked.

He shrugged again. Bigger than before. "You've already got me into trouble, Becca," he said and then exited.

I watched him walk away and then moved over to the couch and lay down. The pillow smelled like him and I inhaled deeply. I closed my eyes and soon the pull of sleep came.

CHAPTER 27

⮂

"*So* this is it?" I asked, looking at him. A sense of loss and emptiness had crept up on me, although I hadn't lost anything, other than maybe my sanity. *Then why did it feel like I was losing something I didn't even know I had?*

"This is it!" He leaned into my car window and looked at me with those green eyes that seemed almost luminous in the early morning light. We had collected my bags from the motel and my car from the eco estate, and then Mike had escorted me out of the town. Now, we were both parked on the long and empty road that headed back in the direction of Johannesburg.

"Well, I guess . . . Goodbye, then." I could hear the reluctance in my voice as I said those words, gripping my steering wheel tightly as I did.

He exhaled, long and loud and slow. "Goodbye, Becca. It was really nice meeting you. I just wish things had happened a little differently, or it had been under different circumstances." He sounded sad. I felt sad. This was sad! More sad than I think it should have been, given that we barely knew each other. But this was also mad! Sad and mad. And now my inner monologue was a Dr. Seuss book.

"Uh . . . me too," I blurted out.

"I really did love your book, though." He smiled a little. "And I'll definitely buy the next one."

"Even though I caused havoc in your town trying to write it?" I asked with a small smile.

"Yes." He smiled back at me and a little ball of panic formed inside me. "Good luck writing it. I really, *really* . . ." He paused, and suddenly the air felt like it was being sucked out of my lungs. He looked emotional, and I wanted to cry. "I wish you well, Becca, I really do."

My eyes were starting to sting and I could feel the tight ball of tears starting to form in my throat. "I wish you well, too," I whispered back quickly, as if I couldn't get those words out fast enough.

"Okay, Becca, it's time," he said, and I nodded. "It's time to drive off and promise me that you won't ever come back here again." He looked at me questioningly.

I started nodding, slowly, tentatively. "I won't. I'll stay far away from this place. I promise."

"Good," he said. "Because, if you come back, I really will have to arrest you next time." And then he did something unexpected. He leaned all the way into the car and slowly, softly, so tenderly, he placed his lips on my cheek and kissed me. I quickly turned my face, letting my lips come into contact with his. I pressed them into his. God, they felt nice. We stayed like that for a while—lips touching, but not really kissing—until he finally pulled away from me and stood up.

He tilted his head down to look at me through the window. "You drive safely, now," he said.

"I will. You too."

"I will. And good luck writing your book."

"Thank you." The goodbye was awkward and stilted and drawn out. But, finally, after standing there a little while longer, he turned around and walked away. I panicked again.

"What are you going to tell the eco people?" I blurted out loudly, mainly because the thought of him walking away right now was so unexpectedly painful.

He turned around again and put his hands in his pockets. "Well, I'll either say you escaped from our storeroom, or I'll tell them you are a little crazy and I released you into the custody of the mental institution you came from."

"Which one are you leaning towards?" I asked.

He looked up, as if he was thinking. "I haven't decided yet."

"I doubt they'll believe I escaped. I didn't do a very good job of breaking in, so . . ."

He gave me another smile. Dazzling, heart-stopping. *Shit!* Suddenly, the thought that I was never going to see that smile again made me feel cold inside.

"Crazy it is, then." He took his hands out of his pockets and then slowly raised one of them in the air and gave me a wave. I held my hand up and waved back.

"Goodbye," he said, and then turned away from me, not waiting for a goodbye back.

I sat in my car and watched him walk away from me. My heart felt like it had slumped into the tips of my toes. I didn't want him to walk away and I didn't know why. I didn't know him, not really, and yet I felt some strange familiarity with him that had me wanting to climb out of the car and run up to him and stop him from walking away from me.

"Shit!" I hissed under my breath. I was so torn. I needed to be back in that town to continue my investigation. But I'd promised him that I wouldn't go back. Not just promised—if I went back to town, I would be breaking the law. Arrested on the spot. And so I sat in the car and watched as he drove off, unsure of what I was meant to do next. *What the hell?* This was a dilemma I didn't know how to solve, like one of those algebraic equations that never seem to end and get more and more confusing as you go.

"Crappitty crap!" I started drumming my fingers on my dashboard, creating a little soundtrack for this moment of indecisiveness. My tune landed up sounding more like the *Jaws* theme, which left me feeling deeply unsettled. A small sense of doom and danger started nibbling at the back of my mind. As if someone bad was coming . . . As if—

I flinched as the phone rang. I looked down at it. *Was this a moment of divine intervention*? No, not divine—there was nothing divine about this at all. It was the opposite of divine. It was from the devil. My agent's name flashed across my screen and, in that moment, I knew what I needed to do. Come hell or high water, rain or shine or snow or eco-freaks or hot sheriffs or promises made . . . I needed to be back in that town, because I needed my bloody story!

I didn't answer the call—obviously. The woman drove a metaphorical icy dagger into my heart. But I did start my ignition and pull off, and then commit a very illegal U-turn. And then, even though I knew I really shouldn't be doing it, I started driving back to the small town that I had just been kicked out of.

CHAPTER 28

~

$\mathcal{I}$ pulled into the small gas station on the outskirts of town to grab myself a drink, and I also needed a moment to think. I couldn't just drive back into town—that would be a bad idea. I needed to be more sneaky about this; I needed a moment to figure out my game plan. How was I going to get around without being noticed by Mike? And, also, where was I going to stay? I couldn't check back into the hotel he'd checked me out of this morning. And, last time I'd looked, the entire town was booked up. *I really didn't like cats!*

I was also driving a Porsche, which stuck out like a sore thumb. At least it wasn't red! I looked at my tiny back seat; there was no way I would be able to sleep in there, if push came to shove. I sat in the parking lot and looked around. I was hungry; I needed food and I thought better on a full stomach, anyway. I went into the shop and raided the junk shelf, and then walked back to my car, thoughtfully. How was I going to pull this off? Was it even possible to go back to town and somehow fly under Mike's radar . . . ?

And then I saw it. And it dawned on me. *This* might be my best, my only chance to get back in unseen and blend in. I looked around to make sure no one was watching me, and then I tiptoed towards the car with the photo of a large cat on the side, and the words *Lady Catterly of Kitashia* written in gold underneath. The car was like a shrine to Persian cats. It was completely overboard, right down to the fluffy tail stuck on to the rear window. I crept closer. A bumper sticker or ten had caught my attention—*Persians are my life* and *May the fluff be with you*, which depicted a Persian cat wielding a light-saber. Under normal circumstances, a girl like me might have laughed, but my circumstances were not normal. Come to think of it, my circumstances had been very abnormal since I'd walked out of that damn elevator. I blamed the elevator for this! Was it possible to blame the elevator for the fact that my whole life seemed to have gone off on a strange tangent? Since I'd found those letters, things seemed to have spiraled out of control, as if someone else was in charge of my life and I was just going along for the mad, crazy ride.

I reached down quickly and picked at the corner of one of the stickers with my nail. It peeled back and I pulled it off. And then I pulled another one off for good measure. I walked back to my car as casually as possible, whistling a made-up tune as I went. I walked around to the back of my car and looked down at my license plate. A smudge of mud on it caught my attention . . . *Dare I do it?*

But I did. I reached down with my finger and, using the smudge of mud, I turned the *P* on my license plate into an *R*. I burst out laughing. The *P* was finally getting its little sloping line! I was pretty sure fiddling with your license plate really *was* breaking the law, and I realized it probably wasn't enough to fool Detective Mike. *Mike* . . . the irritatingly attractive policeman who'd tackled me and then shackled me. Who'd cuffed me and kissed me, but not in the way women fantasize about. Who'd locked me up and then released me. Who'd made me want him more than I cared to admit to myself . . .

"Whateves," I hissed under my breath, as I stuck the Persian-cat stickers on to my bumper and climbed back into the car.

Now to (hopefully) find some kind of accommodation. I opened the booking app and typed in the parameters of my search. I clicked and waited with bated breath, and there, lo and bloody behold, two places miraculously came up. One was right in the center of town, a typical-looking budget hotel, and the other one was slightly out of town, five kilometers away. The one in the center of town was probably a bad idea—more chances of bumping into Mike. I looked at the pictures of the out-of-town one, and a strange feeling welled up inside me. The house seemed familiar in some way, and yet I'd never seen it before. But there was something about it that seemed to make it impossible for me to look away from the photos. And they were gorgeous. It was an old colonial-looking mansion, set in a magnificent green garden. The available room was huge. Wooden floors, pressed ceilings, a fireplace, and a desk that looked out over the river. It was perfect—much better than that beanbaggy Ibiza desk I'd had in the other place. I could imagine myself writing there. I quickly pressed the *Book Now* button and breathed a sigh of relief when the transaction was approved on my credit card.

I sat there and thought about what I was about to do, and I quickly realized that the illusion I was trying to create was not yet complete. I needed one more thing before I could head back to town. And I knew where I would get it.

CHAPTER 29

I drove up the long driveway to the house. I parked my car and looked up at the cat key ring that was now swinging from my rear-view mirror. I'd found it in the back of the second-hand shop, along with some soft cat toys which I'd bought and placed on my dashboard. The house seemed even bigger in real life and looked like it had been here for hundreds of years; the way the creepers had grown over it, encasing it in their green fingers, and the way the trees that lined the driveway reached all the way up to the sky, told me that this house had been part of this land forever.

Looking at the place, I had the feeling of stepping back in time. Round archways led up on to a gorgeous wrap-around veranda, with intricate patterned tiles. Upstairs was a balcony, and I could see chandeliers hanging from the ceiling of the room beyond. Bay windows, terracotta-colored chimneys and white shutters completed the look. I half-expected a butler to come running out to meet me with a cup of tea and a warm towel for my face. But no one of the sort came out; instead, I was greeted by a young, happy-looking woman, who came bounding down the stairs, her long, purple skirt billowing behind her. She looked like an artist, and this was confirmed when I saw a long, red paintbrush pushed through the messy bun on top of her head. She stopped in front of me and smiled.

"Hi! Are you Sam?" she asked.

I cringed at the sound of that name coming from her lips. My name was Pebecca Samantha Thorne, but I'd lied about my name in case Mike had some way of scanning all the bookings in the town. Or was that just something they could do on TV?

"Yes," I said, extending my hand. We shook.

"I'm Ashley. But call me Ash—everyone does. I see you're here for the Persian parade." She pointed at the cat hanging from my rear-view mirror.

"Yes. Yes, I am," I said, lying through my lying teeth. If teeth grew every time you told a lie, like Pinocchio's nose, I would have fangs by the end of this and would be left with an inability to close my mouth ever again. Front teeth so long that they dragged on the ground as I walked.

She looked around. "Where's your cat?"

"Oh! Oh, yes." I giggled. I went to the car and grabbed the cat cage I'd bought from the charity store. I'd draped a towel over it, hoping no one would ask to see her. I really had thought of everything. Maybe I *would* make a good criminal, after all. Well, if my career as an author didn't pan out, I'd be sure to check out all jobs requiring criminal maneuverings, although I seriously doubted those were advertised on Craigslist.

"Oh, let's see!" she said, stepping towards my invisible cat.

"NO!" I said quickly. "She's resting. Big, big day tomorrow."

Ash nodded, as if she understood; I was pretty sure she didn't, but I gave her a big smile anyway. I grabbed my suitcase and started walking towards the house.

"Don't you need a cat box?" she called after me.

"Uhhhh." *Shit.* "I've trained her to use the toilet," I blurted out.

"Really?" She looked surprised. I was surprised.

"She even flushes it herself with her little paws. She's very clever."

"That's amazing. I didn't know they could do that," she said.

I should have effing left it there! But I didn't. "Yeah, it's actually incredible what cats can do with their paws, when given the right training." Why?! Why had I just said that? *Whhhyyy?*

Ash stopped walking. She looked at me, genuinely interested. "What else can they do?"

Yes, Becca . . . What else can cats do with their paws when trained correctly? "They can paint!" I blurted out.

Her face lit up at that; she looked genuinely excited by this prospect and maybe that's why I stupidly decided to weave my story even more.

"Mine is quite the artist, actually," I said. "A real little Pi-*cat*-so!"

Ash laughed at my stupid joke and I laughed back. It was a nervous laugh, an *I-can't-believe-you-found-that-funny* laugh.

"Well, I would be honored if Picatso would come and paint with me sometime," she added.

I nodded. What was I doing? "I'm sure she'd love to," I said, and started walking again. I needed to keep my feet moving so they didn't keep landing up in my mouth. We climbed the steps that led up to the magnificent veranda.

"This is the guest section of the house," Ash started saying. "You have your own entrance and driveway, and, back there—" she pointed to the other side of the house—"that is where I live. But, don't worry, we have our own entrance and parking, too, so you won't be disturbed."

"Oh, great—that's good to know." This was exactly what I needed to get my book done.

"And you're the only person staying inside the house; the three guest cottages are full, but they also have their own entrance and are situated on the other side of the garden, so you shouldn't bump into them, either."

"Great!" I said happily. This place was perfect.

We walked inside, and I gaped. The entrance hall was massive; the ceiling was the highest I'd ever seen, painted a deep blue that gave it the feel of a sweeping night sky. Huge, elaborate crystal chandeliers hung overhead and, when you looked down, the floor was a vast chess board of black and white tiles, that if you looked at for too long, played tricks on your eyes.

"It's beautiful," I said, taking it all in.

"It's been in the family for over 200 years, but it's too big for us. We turned it into an Airbnb so other people can also enjoy it. It's called Sugar Manor because this used to be a sugar plantation."

I ran my eyes over the majestic place and felt something prickle at the back of my neck, as if something had suddenly walked behind me. I swung around and looked; there was nothing there. I shivered to myself, hoping this place wasn't haunted. Not that I believed in such things, but still, the feeling I was getting from Sugar Manor was completely strange, as if my subconscious knew something about it that my conscious mind didn't. As if it had sensed a secret that I wasn't privy to yet.

We walked down the hallway and passed a few closed doors as we went. "We've only turned one room on this side of the house into a guest room. When there's more time, we'll do the rest. We're doing everything by hand, ourselves. But you're staying in the best bedroom," Ash said, slipping a key into an old wooden door. The door opened with a creak and I stepped inside. The room was exactly like the photos, and the big bay window immediately beckoned to me.

"There's firewood for the fire; it gets a little chilly here at night, by the river. Breakfast is served between six and nine, and that's in the room at the end of the passage. If you need anything, I'm on the other side of the house. You can go outside and walk round it, or there's a door at the end of the hall that leads through. We don't use it that much, so it could be full of spider webs. Or you can just call me anytime, if you need anything!" she said happily, and I found myself smiling at her. She seemed to be one of those genuinely happy people; you don't meet them very often, but when you do, you know. The kind that breezes through life, not because their lives are easier than yours, but because they approach everything with a certain upbeat, roll-with-the-punches kind of attitude. I definitely wasn't that kind of person. I didn't take things in my stride, my glass was usually half-empty and I found navigating the corridors of life hard at the best of times, let alone the times when stuff was hitting the fan, like now. I'd always envied people like this. I usually didn't like them, for that reason, but Ash seemed different. There was something about her that I instantly liked, and I didn't instantly like many people.

I gazed around the room again; everything looked perfect, especially that free-standing bathtub that was just calling my name.

"I love it," I said, with a smile.

"Great. Call if you need anything." She started to leave.

"Do you do dinner here, or is it just a bed and breakfast?" I didn't really want to venture into town, for fear of bumping into a certain man in uniform.

"Sorry, only breakfast."

"No worries; I'll just run into town, then," I assured her.

Ash exited and I was on my own again. I put my invisible cat down on the floor and started unpacking my suitcase. I needed to get some work done. Now that I knew what the engraving on the tree said, I could use that in one of the letters—not that I fully understood what it meant, at all. I took a handful of the letters out and started reading them. I'd transcribe them later and creatively color in some of the blanks.

CHAPTER 30

 ~

*B*y the time I'd read almost all of the letters, I was getting a good sense of the man behind the words, and a good sense of their relationship. But, as I settled down to write, I found I was still having trouble finding my female voice. Obviously, it had a lot to do with the fact that I didn't have any letters from her, except the one. But maybe it was more than that. Maybe it was the strange feeling I got every time I tried to think about her or picture her in my head—a feeling I couldn't quite name or pinpoint. Not to mention the fact that making up her words felt fundamentally wrong. It was one thing copying his words, but making hers up . . .

How could I do this? And, if I did, surely there was no way I could do their story justice?

These two had been so deeply in love and they had been so cruelly separated by the world. It was an injustice so great and profound, I couldn't even wrap my head around it properly. A strange feeling churned in the pit of my stomach, and little voices started whispering in the back of my consciousness.

One of these voices, I'm guessing the sensible one, was telling me not to do this. This was *not* my story to tell. I had no permission to tell it, and, if I did, I would be nothing more than a common thief— and a common thief of the worst kind: the stealer of other people's stories.

And then there was the other voice, the one telling me that, if I didn't do this, my life as I knew it would be over. No doubt a public humiliation of some sort would follow, some article or other out there in the publishing world about Becca Thorne's fall from grace. I didn't think I could live through something like that, *again*. I grabbed my stomach as anxiety made it bubble and growl at me. I felt physically uncomfortable in the chair, and in my skin. I stood up and tried to take a deep breath, count to five, calm myself, inhale into my third eye or chakra or spiritual vortex, or whatever. I looked out the window; the river at the bottom of the garden was flowing calmly and smoothly, and I focused all my energy on looking at it. I could feel myself starting to spin out a bit, starting to feel that terrible sweaty-sticky-itchy feeling that comes just before . . .

Shit! I gripped the desk and held on, trying to steady myself as the waves of panic made my heart beat faster and my fingers tingle. I'd suffered from anxiety for as long as I could remember. Waking up in a new bed, in a new town, with a new family, and experiencing more first days of school than any other child I knew, had certainly helped cultivate that anxiety, and now it was a fully developed dark monster that always seemed to lurk somewhere in the back of my mind, waiting eagerly to sneak up and pounce on me, usually in the moments when I least expected it.

I told you I was flawed. There was something intrinsically wrong with me. I'd even rushed myself to the hospital a few times, so sure was I that I was having a heart attack, only to be sent home with some tranquilizers and told to go to therapy. And this situation had really opened the door for the dark monster to sink his claws in.

I couldn't do this! I couldn't write this book. If I did, I would probably spend the rest of my life looking over my shoulder, waiting for someone to bust me as a fake, a cheap stealer of words and stories.

But this was the only idea I'd had in over a year. Do you know how many days, weeks and months I'd sat and stared at the empty white Word document, while that little cursor flashed at me, taunting me? But the longer I'd sat, the more it felt like I couldn't move. Paralyzed.

As if my muscles had atrophied. The cycle was vicious. The more I did nothing, the more I couldn't do anything at all.

I closed my eyes and took some deep breaths, like I'd been taught. In—*five, four, three, two, one*—hold—*five, four, three, two, one*—out—*five, four, three, two, one*. My heart started to beat a little slower; the dizzy, nauseous sensation started to lift a little. I opened my eyes again and looked out over the river at the bottom of the garden. I focused all my attention on the rushing water until, finally, I felt better. I let go of the table and stood up straight.

I had to do this. I had no choice. Because, if I didn't, I would be right back where I started. A nobody. A failure, even. And there would be those who would relish my failure. *He* would relish it, my ex-boss. *He* would absolutely love to watch me publicly humiliated *again*, to watch me crash and burn, just like the last time. It had been almost three years since my previous life had fallen apart, and I was still so desperate to prove him wrong, especially after that review he'd given me in the papers. I'll never forget it: *A vacuous attempt at literary fiction that has no poetry, no passion and no substance to it. Nothing more than the immature ramblings of an "author" out of her depth in the genre.*

I took another breath. I imagined the look on *his* face that day that he'd fired me from the job of my dreams, and, as if that wasn't enough for him, he'd then humiliated and shamed me publicly, after also breaking my heart.

But then I started to smile to myself when I remembered the look on his face when he'd discovered that, despite his scathing review, my book had become a bestseller, that it had sold hundreds of thousands of copies and I was now driving around in the car of *his* dreams.

I pulled the chair out and sat back down at the desk and flipped my laptop open. But, before starting, I looked down at the surface of the desk. I ran my fingertips over an old carving in the wood. A small heart, the letter *A* and what was clearly meant to be a small flower.

The sun was setting, and I watched it paint the sky pink as it started disappearing over the hills on the other side of the river. The sun cast colorful reflections on the usually brown waters. It was really beautiful and for some reason, spurred me on to start writing again. But a knock on the door soon disturbed me.

"Sam?" Ash called out from the other side of the door.

I got up, walked over to the door and opened it.

"Would you like to join us for dinner?" she asked immediately, with a bright, breezy voice. It was such a kind offer. "It's nothing fancy. But you would be more than welcome." She smiled at me. Her smile was big and wide, and something about it set me at ease immediately.

"Sounds good," I heard my usually antisocial self say, before I could stop myself.

"Come by at seven? In an hour?"

"Sure."

"I just used that passage I was telling you about, at the end of the hallway. I managed to clean some of the cobwebs out, so it's safe, if you want to use it. It's a bit cold outside."

"Great. I'll do that," I replied.

"See you soon." She turned and walked away.

CHAPTER 31

⌒

At seven, I walked to the end of the passage and, sure enough, there it was: an old, wooden door that looked like it hadn't been used in years. I opened it and peered inside. It was dark and not very inviting. In fact, it was reminiscent of *any* scene from a horror movie—take your pick.

Girl walks into strange, dark passage, only to be eaten by a man wearing a clown suit and holding a red balloon . . . The *It* soundtrack started playing in my head. My head has always been filled with soundtracks for as long as I can remember. Listening to music when I was younger was a kind of escape for me.

I still remember the first CD I ever got, as if it were yesterday. I'd saved all my pocket money for it. Roxette, *Crash! Boom! Bang!* (three exclamation marks!!!)—God, I thought they were so cool; her, with her short, white hair, and him . . . my first official celebrity crush. Although, looking back now, I'm not sure what it was that appealed to my ten-year-old self. Mind you, he's probably one of the least embarrassing celebrity crushes I've had in my life. Let's just say there was a point in time when I thought the guy from Nickelback was quite the catch. I shuddered, just thinking about it. Now, when a Nickelback song came on the radio, I couldn't wait to turn it off.

I walked into the dark corridor, put my phone torch on and waved it about. This corridor looked old and unused, and I wondered why it had been built in the first place. I wondered what clandestine things had happened in here—I could almost see them, if I closed my eyes. Secret illuminati meetings, mysterious men in long, purple, velvet coats, or women with caldrons and the skulls of small creatures. My imagination started running wild, as it usually did. I finally reached the end of the passage and was just about to knock on the door when I heard a car coming up the driveway. I looked out the small, dusty window, and my blood flash froze.

What the hell was he doing here? Wait, was it even him? Or were my eyes deceiving me? I blinked a few times to make sure I wasn't seeing things. But I wasn't.

I watched, my jaw dropping in horror, as the police car drove up the driveway and came to a stop. I held my breath, waiting to see who was going to climb out, waiting to see if it was . . .

Yup! Fuck! It was him. Mike. Magic, mystical Mike really knew how to appear out of thin air when you least expected it. I watched as he strode up the driveway towards the house. I moved to get a better look. And—boy, oh boy—did I get a *look* alright. Ash came out the house, she walked up to him and then . . . they hugged.

Hug. *(Verb)* Squeeze (someone) tightly in one's arms, typically to express affection.

"Bastard," I hissed, under my breath. No wonder he rushed off. No wonder he left me holding the condoms. Clearly, he'd had some kind of last-minute guilt crisis, or needed to rush back to his wife, or girlfriend. My heart thumped and I felt more wounded than I think I should have felt. I took a step backwards, away from the window, and my back crashed into something—a wooden wall. The sound was loud and suddenly I heard Ash's voice.

"Sam, hang on! I'm coming!"

Shit! I couldn't let Mike see me here, and so I ran. I bolted up the dark passage. But then it seemed to split. Wait—I hadn't noticed this before. *Which way was I meant to go?* I heard the door open behind me and I went right. I went right and I didn't look back. I raced down the passage and pushed the door open and . . . *Cold air?*

It took me a second to realize that I was now outside, in the back

garden. I looked around, disorientated. A stone fountain, a rose garden and, far behind that, horses' stables. I'd clearly taken the wrong
turn. *Typical.*

"Sam?" I heard Ash call again.

"Who are you looking for?" It was Mike talking this time.

"I invited one of our guests for dinner. I thought I'd heard her at
the door."

I ran through the garden to the front of the house, grabbing my
car keys out of my handbag as quickly as I could. I jumped into my
car and pulled off, doing a little wheelspin as I raced out of there.

How was this possible? Out of all the accommodation in the town,
what were the chances that I would land up staying at the place where
Mike lived, or was visiting? This was too much of a coincidence—or
was it more than that? My stomach plummeted, like it had in the
elevator. *What was going on?*

I drove. I didn't know where I was going, but I just knew I needed
to be as far away from that house as possible, as far away from Mike.
There were two reasons, really. One: he was going to arrest me if he
saw me again. And two: I'm not going to lie, my heart was feeling
just as bruised as my ego was to learn that he had a partner. Suddenly,
his line about wishing we had met "under different circumstances"
took on a whole new meaning.

I felt an all-too-familiar tug on my ribcage. I recognized that feeling. The same one that comes from hearing those words from your
work colleague: *But everyone knows he has a girlfriend.* He was the
editor at the paper where I worked as a junior journalist. Her words
came too late, though; I'd already given him my heart on a silver
platter after our romantic weekend away in the winelands, where
we'd drunk fine wine and made love until noon. He'd happily taken
my heart and then deceived me—the young, naïve junior writer
with stars in her eyes at the famous, award-winning editor, who'd
hired her and taken her under his wing. And then I'd done something I deeply regretted: I'd continued my affair with him, even after

I knew about his girlfriend. I can justify this by telling you how many times he told me it was over between them, how many times he told me she meant nothing to him and I meant everything and he was ending it today. But, honestly, there isn't really a good enough justification for becoming the other woman.

I drove all the way to the outskirts of town and found myself right back at the same gas station I'd been at that morning. I pulled into the parking lot and looked at the time. There was only one thing to do, now. I was officially out of options. I was going to wait here until it was late enough that he and Ash would be asleep, then I would creep back to Sugar Manor, pack my bags and leave. Leave without a book, and just face whatever consequences would come of that.

But, strangely enough, for the first time, the thought actually made me feel relieved. I could finally let go, now. Let go of writing this book that seemed so hard and insurmountable.

I breathed a sigh of relief and suddenly I wanted to cry. All this lying and breaking-and-entering, and plagiarizing wasn't me, and I could finally let go of it. I looked at the convenience store. The words *hot dog* flashed at me in neon lights, so I climbed out and grabbed a few. I would sit in my car and stuff my face until it was safe to return, and then I'd get the hell out of this strange little town. And get as far away from Mike as possible.

CHAPTER 32

*I*t was three a.m. when I finally returned to Sugar Manor. All was dark and quiet when I arrived. His car was still in the driveway, so it was official: he was sleeping over. I could imagine them cuddled up together in bed. I felt sorry for Ash—she was so lovely and didn't deserve a canoodling wandering husband/boyfriend! But that wasn't my problem, was it? My problem was getting all my things packed and then hightailing it back to Johannesburg. I packed my bag as silently as I could. I was almost done, when one of my shoes fell into the gap between the bed and the wall.

"Damn it." I tried to grab it, but the space was too tight. I attempted to pull the bed away from the wall, but it was heavy and made a squeaking sound as it went.

"Shit!" I paused and held my breath, hoping that the sound had not traveled to the other side of the house. And when I was sure no one had heard me, I stuck my hand into the gap and felt around for my shoe. I couldn't find it, so I turned my phone torch on for a better look, and that's when *everything* changed.

"What the . . . ?" My breath and the words got stuck in my throat. *Impossible!* I pulled the bed away more, not caring about the noise this time, and shone my torch on the wall in utter disbelief. I ran my fingers over the lines and white powdery cement came away on my fingertips. My heart started racing in my chest, thumping like the hooves of wild horses. This wasn't possible. But there it was . . .

I raced over to the letters and started going through them frantically, until I found what I was looking for.

It's been thirteen days since I saw you. I've been making markings in the wall behind my bed, like someone in prison might do. Because that's what it feels like without you—that I'm trapped in prison.

I rushed back and counted the markings on the wall; thirteen days and more. My mind whizzed around and it started to fill with other images and pictures and words and . . . I ran and grabbed more letters, and frantically paged through them, looking for specific paragraphs.

I'll meet you in the passage tonight. I'll be there at midnight. Don't worry, I won't be seen. I'll hide in the stables and wait until it's dark. I can't wait to see you.

This was totally, utterly impossible! I dropped on to my hands and knees, so hard that the wooden floorboards shook. I lowered my head to the floor and rested it there, my brain racing and swirling so much that I gave it a little bash against the wood in the hope that it would stop. But, as I did, I heard a noise. I felt something move. I pulled my head up and looked down at the floor. A floorboard seemed loose. I stared at the thing. Instinctively, on some strange subconscious level that I had no understanding of, I knew what was under it. I knew what I was going to find, before I'd even looked. I took a deep breath, then I reached out with trembling fingers and slowly pulled on the panel of wood. It popped out with a click. My heart thumped as I scrambled to find my phone torch. I grabbed it with a very shaky hand and looked inside the hole in the floor. And, as I did . . .

I gasped and dropped the phone as the hairs on the back of my neck prickled again, just as they had when I'd first walked into the house. *This house.* This house that, on some level, I'd felt I recognized. This house, this room, this bed, these floorboards . . .

"Oh my God, oh my God." I scrambled to my feet and looked down at the hole in the floor, almost too afraid to reach in and take it, to acknowledge what was there. But I had to. I slowly crouched back down and lowered my hand into the hole . . .

CHAPTER 33

I reached in and my fingers immediately touched it. I paused—another deep breath—gripped it and then pulled it out. The smell hit me first: dusty, musty and burnt. I sat back against the wall and flipped the bedside light on. I looked down at my hands; I was cradling what was clearly a diary, but one that had been burned. It looked like it had been pulled out of the flames at the very last moment, just before it disintegrated. I opened the first page and recognized the writing immediately. It was her—Edith.

I opened it gently. It was so damaged and fragile that bits of burnt paper fluttered out of it like dead butterfly wings. I tried to pick them up, but they disintegrated in my fingers—disappearing along with their words and secrets. An entire page fell out and I picked it up and looked at it. A tear came to my eye the moment I started reading it.

Dear Diary,
I sat at my desk today for hours, just staring at the river
and thinking about A. I kept looking at the river and
wondering where it came from. I know it runs into the
sea, but where does it start? I bet it starts somewhere
exotic. Somewhere better than here—mind you, anywhere
is better than here. Maybe it starts all the way up at the
top of Africa, by the pyramids of Giza. Maybe it travels
through tangled jungles, large, open savannas, hot,

*sandy deserts and over great mountain ranges, just to
get here.*

   *If only A and I could build a boat and sail away together,
right back up that river. Sail as far away from this place as
possible. We could find a little spot together, somewhere
on its banks, away from the world, and we could live there
like castaways. It would certainly be an adventure.*

I stood up slowly, clutching the diary to my chest, and walked over to
the window. *How could this be?* The coincidence seemed too great
and I wondered if I wasn't grasping at straws, here, making associa-
tions where there were none to be made. Maybe I was so desperate
that I was seeing what I wanted to see? Or maybe this was a dream,
a hallucination?

I opened the diary again to a random page, but it was too badly
burnt to read, so I carefully flipped to the next page, and the next,
until I was able to see handwriting.

Dear Diary,
*I couldn't sleep again last night. I lay in bed, staring up at the
crack in my ceiling—the crack that runs the entire length of
it, dividing it into two separate halves. When I looked at it,
I couldn't stop thinking about A and me. How we are so
separated. How a crack runs a line through the middle of our
lives and pushes us apart, forces us into two separate parts.
Him on his side, me on my side, and never the twain shall
meet. Well, we did meet. I can't ever unmeet him, and nor do
I want to. But we can't be together, either, and it is tearing me
apart. Ripping me in two . . .*

Slowly, I looked up, and the same crack that she'd looked up at
stared down at me. My fingers loosened. The diary fell from my hand
and cascaded to the floor, burnt pages falling out like brown autumn

leaves dropping from the trees. My heart raced, adrenalin making me nauseous and dizzy as it ripped through my veins like a speed-boat cutting through the surf. I shook my head in utter disbelief. This could *not* be happening. But it was. How was this even pos-sible? And who the hell was Ashley? If this house had been in her family for 200 years … I stifled a gasp as it started to dawn on me, like wiping the condensation off a window and being able to look outside again and see the bigger picture. Was she Edith's granddaughter?

I sat down on the bed. There was no way I could leave now. This was a sign, if ever I'd seen one. I had to stay here and find out more. It was as if someone was handing me a gift on a shiny, silver plat-ter. But something also gnawed at me, something in the back of my mind, reminding me that silver also tarnishes. It goes black and its sheen disappears; it doesn't last forever. And, before you know it, you're scrubbing the damage away until your hands bleed.

I lay down on the bed and looked up at the ceiling again. I won-dered if she'd ever thought of giving up on her love for him, whether she'd considered just walking away from the man she loved. It would have been so much easier, after all; it would have been legal, too. But she hadn't. From what I'd read so far, she had stayed strong, right up to the very end. This idea both humbled and crippled me. How could someone so young have been so brave in the face of so much? She'd clung on, despite what the whole world around her had thought about her and the relationship! I wasn't like that at all. She was ten times the woman I was, or would probably ever be.

Some barely-there voice in my head seemed to call out to me. I tried to listen to it, but couldn't quite hear it clearly. I climbed off the bed and walked back over to the diary. I started picking the pages up gently and slotting them back into the book as carefully as I could, not to cause any more damage. One of the pages caught my atten-tion; it had been decorated with intricate patterns and hearts, and, in the middle of the page, four words …

This is my story . . .

And then I heard what the voice in my head was trying to say. "Tell it," it said to me.

I stood up and looked at the ceiling, and something inside told me what I needed to do.

CHAPTER 34

꩜

 awoke that next morning with a renewed sense of purpose. *Awoke* isn't really the right word, since I'd barely slept. I'd spent what was left of the night combing through the letters—and now the diary, too—looking to fill in the gaps in the story, looking for more clues that would lead me to more places. There were a few references to a small room under the stage at the town hall where the two of them had met. And, today, I was going there.

But there was something else on my agenda first. I had to think of some excuse about last night and apologize to Ash, because I wanted to find out as much as I could about this house and Edith, who I now suspected was her relative.

I made sure that Mike had left before I walked round to the front of the house. I didn't go through the passage this time; I didn't want to surprise her. I walked up to the front door and stopped. It was grand: an old stained-glass door with a big brass bell hanging from it. I rang the bell and waited. I still hadn't quite worked out my excuse yet. I was toying with three in my head and I was sure the right one would pop out of my mouth when I saw her, now that I was such a bloody seasoned liar.

The door swung open and Ash was standing there, paint-stained as ever.

"Hey," I said, and then launched right into it. "I'm so sorry about last night. I was just—"

"No worries!" she cut me off quickly.

"No worries?"

"Yeah, it was a very casual thing. No worries if you couldn't make it; you can come round another time," she said, with a smile.

Well, that was easy.

"Thanks," I said, feeling relieved that she had spared me my bullshit explanation, but I decided to add one anyway, just in case she thought something bad about me. "Stomach thing. I had to go to the chemist."

She nodded. "Nasty. You okay now?"

"Much better."

"You want to come in?" She opened the door even wider.

"Do you mind?" I said innocently. But of course I wanted to come in.

"Sure." She walked back inside and I followed her into another grand entrance hall with big, golden chandeliers and black and white tiles. Dark grey, velvety-looking walls made the pristine, white, pressed ceiling pop. Antique chairs, covered in dark green damask, lined one of the walls; they looked like they'd been put there because they had nowhere else to go.

"I was just busy painting," she said, walking through the huge hall. I followed close behind her. The walls here were covered in old oil paintings, all set in ornate gold frames. I stopped and looked at one.

"Oh, those are my great-great-grandparents and their family." She came up behind me and said, "This was in the 1940s."

"Wow—that's amazing." I scanned the picture, looking at the faces of the children. One of these could be Edith. But which one?

"He had four daughters," she said, behind me. "In those days, it was a tragedy not to have sons. My grandmother said that her father was very strict. Dictated who they married, dictated their lives." She shook her head. "Women really had it hard then."

I nodded. "They did." I wondered if she knew just how hard one of these four daughters had it. "Are any of them alive today?" I asked, still scanning their faces. I was trying to see inside them, to look past their painted eyes to the person within, who may have written that diary.

"No, they're all gone now. My one grandma only passed away last year, though," she said softly.

I turned and looked at her. "Sorry for your loss."

She shrugged. "She had a really good innings, you know. She was over ninety when she died. That's when my brother and I inherited this place."

At that, I swung around. "Your . . . uh . . . brother?" My heart started drumming a big rock solo in my chest.

"Yes—Mike. He lives here, too," she said casually, not knowing that the information she'd just given me was like music to my ears.

"Brother?" I asked again, in case I hadn't heard correctly.

"He's two years younger than me. We fought like cats and dogs when we were little, but get on like a house on fire now. Weird," she said.

Weird. That was an understatement. If Mike was her brother, that meant he was also related to Edith. He was her grandson. How was this all happening and unfolding like this? Like there was some preconceived plan out there that was playing out, and we were all just pawns in it, falling into place, falling into predestined roles. Did I even believe in all that? But what was the other explanation? That this was all some huge coincidence, right from the moment the lift had fallen?

"My brother is actually the sheriff of this town." She smiled proudly.

"Really? I'd better not get in any trouble," I quickly joked.

"Funny you should say that. God—he was a naughty little shit, growing up. I never imagined him as 'the law,' but I guess that just happened by accident." She carried on walking up the hallway and I followed behind her. "So what do you do?" she asked me.

And, before I could make something up, I said it: "I'm a writer."

"Really? Wow!" Ash spun around and looked at me with a smile.

I quickly played it down. "I should say *aspiring* writer. I've written a few articles, some blog stuff . . . not much else." I shrugged.

"Still, that's amazing. Well done!"

"Huh?" I looked at her, confused, taken aback. She just smiled and kept on walking. No one had ever just said *well done* to me. *What the hell was going on?* I had known this woman less than a day and she was being nicer and more supportive to me than anyone in my life. And I was trying to use her for information . . . God, I was a bad person. Truly, I was horrendous. And there is no need for you to dislike me right now, because, trust me, I disliked myself enough.

We continued walking and I looked around. This house was configured in exactly the same way as the other one. "This place feels like two houses that were joined together by a passage," I said.

"They were," she said, over her shoulder. "The one you're staying in was the original family home where my grandmother lived as a child, and this one was built a little later. I'm not really sure why, to be honest."

"Are all of these paintings of the family?" I asked.

"Yes." She stopped and pointed at one.

It was definitely the man from the letter, right down to the scar on his cheek. I shivered as I looked into his icy blue eyes. "Scary," I said, without even realizing it.

"Apparently he was. A very, very hard and difficult man. We don't really talk about him much, and some of his pictures were taken down because we didn't want them up."

"Why?" I asked.

She shrugged and suddenly looked embarrassed. "He was very . . ." She paused and swallowed hard—I could hear it. "He was, uh . . . very . . . racist," she said quietly.

"Oh. OH!" I said, although this wasn't news to me.

"His daughters were all scared of him; I think that's why they all moved away. Except for my grandmother, Edith—she was the only one who stayed here. But I don't think she stayed of her own free will."

"Really?" The pennies began dropping. I could almost hear them in my head, the sound of them falling into a tin can. "Can I see a painting of her?" I said quickly.

"I can do better than that." Ash walked further down the hall and I followed her. "There's a beautiful photo of her from her wedding day."

My heart thumped in my chest as Ash stopped at yet another gold-framed picture. I was so eager to see her, but, when I finally did, I felt like crying. She looked so beautiful in her vintage wedding dress, holding her bouquet of white flowers that hung all the way down to the floor. She stood next to a handsome man. There was no doubt about it, he was very good looking—clean cut and smiling from ear to ear. Edith was smiling too, but her smile was different from his. She had a Mona Lisa smile, the kind that concealed something. And her smile certainly didn't extend to her eyes, which seemed distant and far away, as if they were looking at something else.

"She looks sad, right?" Ash said, leaning closer to the picture.

"Yes, she does," I immediately returned. "Why?" I asked.

"It was basically an arranged marriage. Her father organized it. I think she was terrified."

I leaned in and looked closer. She wasn't terrified. She was heartbroken. She didn't know how she was going to live without the man she loved, let alone breathe without him.

"But I guess they grew to love each other. They had three kids," she said. "My mom was one of them. Apparently, I got my artistic abilities from my grandmother; she was an artist."

"Oh? Do you have any of her paintings?" I asked.

"There was a fire and they were all destroyed."

"Really?" I perked up.

Ash looked over at me. "She never painted again, after that. Who knows, maybe she had an artistic temper and burned them all herself because she hated them. I can relate to that," Ash said, dismissively.

But that wasn't what had happened at all. I knew that. I looked back at the photo of her.

"What date did they get married?" I scanned the picture for a date.

Ash reached up and pulled it off the wall. She turned it around in her hands and read out the date: "The first of December, 1949."

My heart thumped. The letters had ended just before this date. This was where my love story technically ended, but I just couldn't see it *really* ending there. My mind was ticking away, forming connections, joining the dots and creating images and pictures and filling in the gaps.

We continued walking until we got to a massive room that was completely unfurnished, apart from some canvasses standing in the middle of it. I looked around in wonder. I'd never seen such a big room in a private home before.

"This used to be the dining hall," she said.

"It's enormous!" I exclaimed.

"I know. It's pretty impressive. It's actually where my grandmother got married."

"Really?" I swung around and looked at her in surprise.

"The aisle she walked down was right there, where you're standing."

I looked down at my feet and was overcome by such devastation. She'd walked over the very spot where I was standing as she made her way down the aisle to marry a man she didn't love. Leaving behind, forever, a man she'd loved with her entire heart and soul. I could almost hear her footsteps as she walked over the wooden floor towards a destiny that was not hers. Sad, tentative footsteps.

"Wait!" Ash said. "Why aren't you over at the cat show? It's starting soon."

"Huh?" I looked up at her, almost forgetting, and then quickly remembered. "I, uh . . . just wanted to come here quickly and apologize for last night, and then I was going to go."

Ash looked down at her watch. "It starts in half an hour; you should get going."

"I will," I said. "Thanks for showing me around."

She smiled at me and I hurried out. I wished I could have stayed longer, but I had to keep my cat story going, even if I wasn't really going to go to the show. I was going to go to the town hall to see if I could find the secret room under the stage.

CHAPTER 35

I drove to where Google told me to go, but, when I arrived, I got quite the fright and couldn't believe what I was seeing. The place was packed with cars and cats and people carrying cats.

I looked up at the massive banner that hung from the roof of the hall, flapping in the cool autumn breeze: *Annual Persian Parade 2019*. Just my luck. There was only one place I needed to see, and it was inundated with cats. I slung my bag on to my shoulder and climbed out the car. A huge queue had formed outside and I stepped into it and waited. But when I got to the front . . .

"I'm sorry, but I can't let you in unless you have a ticket," the man at the door said, when I failed to produce such a thing. He looked like a real "cat person." He was such a stereotype, right down to the T-shirt he was wearing that said, *Cats, because people suck*.

"Are you sure?" I asked.

"Yes," he replied flatly. The real reason he thought people sucked was probably due more to his bedside manner as a human, and less to do with humans at large. Because this man had the social graces of an aardvark. He had beady eyes, his shirt was covered in cat hair, he wore thick glasses and, quite frankly, there was a strange smell that seemed to linger on him.

"I lost my ticket." I tried to put some flirt in my voice; it didn't work. I fluttered my eyelashes a little, too, hoping that perhaps my feminine wiles would get me in . . . *Wait—what was I thinking?* This was 2019! Women didn't do that anymore. How truly un-feminist of me! It didn't work, anyway; the man was unswayed.

He shook his head. "No ticket, no entry. We have been sold out for months, now."

"Pleeeease, is there noooooo way I can get in? Pleeeeease?" I tried a new approach. Begging. It was undignified and revolting and I hated myself for doing it, but I was desperate.

A few people behind me sounded like they were getting irritated. They looked like they were dying to go in, as if this was the highlight of their entire year. The man looked at me blankly. Still unmoved. Concrete features on his face. Unblinking.

"I guess that's a hard no, then?" I asked, raising an eyebrow. He didn't respond. "Okey-dokey, a hard no it is. I get it." I left the queue, much to the relief of the others.

I turned and looked at the hall. *Crap!* I needed to get into this place. A potential clue was waiting inside, but the man was still staring at me, as if he knew I was up to something. I started whistling a tune and made my way around to the back of the building, where I found a steel door labeled *Exit*.

I grabbed the handle, but it was locked. There was no way in. I was just about to turn around and leave when a woman burst through the door, looking agitated. She reminded me of the woman in the lift—the one with the brows. She held the door open with her foot and lit a cigarette as if her life depended on how quickly she managed to inhale it. She released the smoke with a huge sigh.

"Hey," I said, acting casual.

"Hey!" She sounded pissed off.

"Bad day?" I asked.

"Our cat groomer couldn't make it. The show is in less than an hour."

"Oh, that's a pity," I said, playing along.

"I don't know what I'm going to do." She looked like she was on the verge of tears, and that's when I jumped without thinking. Without even pausing to think about thinking, without even—

"I'm a cat groomer."

"Oh yeah?" she asked, looking at me suspiciously. "What are you doing out here?"

I rolled my eyes and gestured at her cigarette. "Trying to quit."

The woman looked down at her cigarette. "Tell me about it."

"Have you tried vaping?" I asked, adding some more details to my story for authenticity, even though I thought vaping was literally one of the worst things ever to have happened to the world.

"Didn't work," she said.

"Me neither. I even did hypnotherapy once," I said. "I did manage to stop biting my nails, though." I held my hands up and she smiled at me.

"So, who have you groomed?" she asked.

"Uh . . . Well, last year, I groomed Lady Catterly of Kitashia," I said, thinking about the car I'd stolen the sticker from.

"Lady Catterly won last year!" She dropped her cigarette and put it out with a stomp of her foot.

Shit. I hadn't really meant to choose such a high-profile cat. But it was the only cat's name that I knew.

"Are you grooming her this year?" she asked.

I shook my head. "No."

"How much do you charge?" she asked.

"Oh . . . uh, you know. Industry norm."

"So, about 500 rand?" she asked.

"Exactly." I smiled. "Would you like me to . . . ?"

"Yes! But where are your tools?" she asked, looking at me.

"Oh, they're inside," I said quickly.

"Great! Thanks. This is such a lifesaver. I really feel like Countess Claw-dette has a real chance, this year."

I smiled at her. "It's my pleasure."

"Sorry, I didn't catch your name?" she asked.

"Sam." I smiled as I said it, walking straight inside.

"I'm Greta." She closed the door behind us and I couldn't believe my luck.

I was in!

CHAPTER 36

Oh My God!

I looked around as I followed Greta through the room. I'd never seen anything like it in my entire life. It was literally full of people and cats, and I felt my nose itch.

"Here we are," she said, as we arrived at a table with a cage on it.

I looked inside the cage; the bloody cat was huge! An enormous grey thing with bright green eyes, its squished face gave it a distinctly grumpy look.

"This is Countess Claw-dette." She opened the cage and placed the massive ball of fluff on the table in front of me. The fluff immediately collapsed, stretching out regally. It looked like a particularly lazy thing. Not the kind of cat that was out hunting small creatures and climbing trees.

"She's gorgeous." I didn't know the first thing about cats. This could be a cross-breed runt with a gammy paw and I wouldn't know.

"You think?" Greta asked quickly.

I nodded. "Definitely. Very regal."

Greta smiled, and I suddenly felt *very* bad. Oh God, why did I keep getting myself into these terrible situations? Was I just a terrible person? Greta looked at me expectantly and I jumped.

"Right. Yes!" I took a step closer to the cat. "Better get started, then. Time to turn lovely Claw-dette, here, into a paw-fect winner."

Greta laughed at my lame joke, and now I felt really bad! I looked down at the cat. There was so much of it, where did one start?

I didn't know what to do, I'd never groomed a cat before, so I reached out and placed my hands on its head. Greta looked at me, clearly confused.

"I like to gauge the cat's vibe first," I said, answering her silent question of, *What the hell are you doing to my cat?*

"And?" she asked, looking interested.

"Great vibe. A real winner, here. She seems very psyched for the competition," I added quickly, as I stroked the cat and smiled up at her.

"You communicate with them?" she asked, with wide eyes.

Oh, damn—what had I just done? "It's more of a feeling I get, you know. A sense of the animal."

"That's incredible." She smiled at her cat as if it were her most prized possession. "What else are you picking up on?"

"Uh . . . well—" I put my hands by the cat's head again—"she loves you very much."

Greta raised a hand to her chest. "Aaaah . . ." She seemed genuinely touched by this. "Can you tell her I love her, too?" she asked.

For fuck's sake, Becca! How had I gone from groomer to pet psychic in thirty seconds? This was all ridiculous and I really needed to put an end to it. "She knows, Greta. She knows." God, I needed to get out of here. "Oh damn," I said. "I need to fetch my tools from the other table. I'll just go and get them." I started backing away from her, but she reached out and stopped me with a hand on the shoulder.

"No worries; I have everything you need." She pulled a brush out of her bag and handed it to me. "We've lost enough time, already. We need to get started."

Double damn!

I took the brush and moved towards the cat again. *Just brush her. Just brush her.* How hard could this be?

"Hey, kitty," I said to the cat, who looked very unimpressed with me. Or maybe it was just her face. This cat had a real resting bitch face.

"Her face needs a trim, too, as you can see," Greta said, passing me some nail scissors.

The cat's whole body looked like it needed a bloody trim.

"Her eyes also need cleaning, and her nose."

"Of course," I said, feeling this massive wave of performance anxiety push down on me as I started to lower the brush towards the cat. It was as if it went in slow motion, as if the whole world was watching me, waiting for the brush to come down on the cat—and, as it did, the cat purred. I smiled, thrilled that I'd done the right thing.

"She likes you," Greta said. "She doesn't like many people."

"I have a way with cats," I said, as I brushed her thick fur.

Greta gave an even bigger smile and her shoulders relaxed. "Well, I don't know about you, but I could do with a cup of coffee." She took a step away from me. It looked like she was leaving. Perfect!

"No, thanks, not for me." I smiled at her as she turned and started to walk away. Lying to this poor woman was one thing, but then also taking coffee from her? I couldn't do that.

"Trim the face. Don't forget," she said, over her shoulder.

I nodded. "Doing it right now." I lowered the scissors towards the cat's face as Greta left.

I was just about to put the scissors down and walk away when someone came up behind me. I turned and saw an elderly woman with a badge that read *Judge*, and she was looking closely at Countess Claw-dette.

"Hi," I said.

"Are you the groomer?" she asked.

I nodded.

"Beautiful cat. I think she stands a real chance, this year—but you didn't hear that from me."

I smiled and raised my finger to my lips in silence.

She winked at me and then leaned in and whispered, "Trim above the eye." And, with that, she quickly walked away.

God! The pressure! The pressure! The fucking trimming. For some reason, I now felt compelled to do it, since everyone seemed to be telling me to do it. I lowered the scissors on to the cat's face and focused my attention on the hair above her eye. I was about to cut, when . . .

AAATISHHHOOOOO!

I sneezed. And froze. I realized instantly that something very, *very* bad had happened. I opened one eye slowly, terrified to see what I'd done. Then I opened the other eye, and there wasn't even time for me to respond, because I heard a gasp next to me. Then I heard a smack, followed by a splash, and then I felt a hot, wet burst of liquid at my ankle. I looked down. A cup of coffee lay on the floor. I followed the familiar legs up to Greta's face. She was standing there, eyes wide and hands over her mouth, staring at her cat.

I turned slowly, and finally looked at the cat. I didn't need to be a professional to know I'd made a terrible mistake.

"Oh no, oh no," I said, staring at the cat.

"WHAT HAVE YOU DONE?!" Greta screamed, and people turned around. "You have mutilated my cat!" she yelled, pointing at the stripe of hair that was now missing from above one of the cat's eyes.

"I . . . I . . . Sorry. It was a mistake. I . . ." I rambled loudly as a crowd started to gather.

Greta was fuming; she was turning a bright shade of tomato. "I can't believe you let this woman groom your cat last year," she said, and I swung around to see who she was talking to. As I did, I came face to face with a man and woman wearing very familiar-looking T-shirts. *May the fluff be with you.* This was so bad. The couple stared at me.

"I've never seen this woman in my life," the man said, after looking at me for a while.

Another gasp. Even bigger than before. And then a finger was pointed in my direction. A big, shaking finger. God, this felt so familiar. Why did I inevitably cause a scene everywhere I went? "You're not a groomer. Who are you?" Greta asked, with a trembling voice.

"I . . . I . . . I can explain," I stuttered. Why do people who are caught red-handed always claim they can "explain," when clearly they can't? And then I did it, once again—I turned and ran.

CHAPTER 37

⌒

"*I*MPOSTER!" I heard a yell as I ducked behind a wall and hid.

"Where is she?" Greta sounded frantic, and then I heard a familiar voice.

"What's going on here?" the voice asked.

I peered around the pillar and looked.

Oh my God! It was him. Why was he everywhere I went? Why couldn't I escape this man, no matter how much I ducked and dived? I dropped to my hands and knees and crawled behind a mountain of cat cages.

I couldn't hear what was being said, now, as the general sound level in the room shot up. I peered around the corner again and saw, with horror, that Mike was walking in my direction. I needed to hide. I needed to get out of here or I was going to be in such trouble. I looked around, trying to find a way out. The stage wasn't that far in front of me and, if the details in the letters were correct, all I had to do was crawl under it and there should be a small door there that led to a secret room. It was only a few meters away; I decided to make a run for it, but Mike was coming closer and closer—too close. I needed a disguise, I needed something to hide behind, something big, something that would cover me, something like a . . .

I turned. A massive black face stared at me from behind the bars of its cage. Our eyes locked for a moment, and I knew what I needed to do. I opened the cage and pulled the massive black thing out.

I held it up to my face and stood up slowly. My timing was perfect, because, at that precise moment, Mike walked right in front of me. He was so close that I could smell him as he went. That soapy, clean smell; that musky, spicy . . . And then, instead of walking off, he stood there—stopped and looked around the room, right in front of me.

He was no more than a few feet away from me, standing so close that, if I reached out an arm, I would be touching him. *Touching him*. Suddenly, the desire to do that overwhelmed me. I held my breath and kept the cat in front of my face (please, don't sneeze) and waited, still as a statue. I really needed to get out of here; if Mike turned around and looked behind him, he was sure to recognize me. So, I did the only thing I could think of: I started walking straight to the stage, with the cat to my face. But, as I reached the stage . . .

"Countess Catatonia!" A piercing shriek brought the entire place to a standstill; even I looked around to see what was wrong.

"Countess Catatonia is gone! SOMEONE TOOK HER!"

Oh my God, who would have taken a ca—? *I stopped*. I turned my head slowly and looked back at the cat in my hands. It glared at me with a look of total and utter disdain. "Oh!" I said flatly, as I looked at the name tag hanging from her pink collar. The cat slowly licked her lips, as if she was contemplating taking a chunk out of my finger.

"What does Countess Catatonia look like?" I heard Mike's voice again. God, he was such a busybody. Always coming to the rescue of something—a mythical mating bird, a fat black cat.

"She's a black Persian!" The scream was so frantic, so panicked, that you would have thought the woman had lost her child in an aisle at the shopping center.

The black cat blinked at me, as if she knew exactly what was going on, as if she knew that everyone was now talking about her. And then chaos and pandemonium broke out once more. I heard another voice, and I wanted to cry.

"I know who took her! It's that Sam woman who's pretending to be a groomer."

"Oh shit," I mumbled, and looked at the cat.

"What does she look like?" It was Mike again.

I couldn't stand there any longer. I ran to the edge of the stage, put the cat down on it, and then, as quickly as I could, I threw myself under the stage and crawled to the back of it. Once I was there, I collapsed with my back against the wall and closed my eyes. I could hear the madness in the hall. People rushing around. People calling out to each other. Loud whispers and gossip spreading like wildfire through the room, and I had caused it all.

"I found her. I found her!" I heard the frantic woman scream when she'd clearly found her cat on the stage. I opened my eyes and looked around. It was dark everywhere, except for a small shaft of light rushing through a hole in the wood. I crawled towards it and stuck my eye to it to see what was going on outside. I could see legs—a lot of them. One pair of legs belonged to Greta—I recognized that pattern on her pants—and another pair definitely belonged to Mike. I held my breath as I looked through the hole at what was happening. So many voices were talking at once and I couldn't make anything out clearly, until a phrase jumped out at me and my heart thumped in my chest.

"Press charges?" I heard Mike say. "What would the charges be?" he asked.

Exactly!

"Animal cruelty. Impersonating a professional groomer. Emotional distress for both me and especially my cat." It was Greta, and she was so beside herself.

Oh, please! This was such an act.

"Do you remember what she looked like? The woman who pretended to be a groomer?" Mike asked, and my blood stopped pumping. I held my hands over my mouth for fear that a squeal might slip out.

"YES! Absolutely." She said it so emphatically that my whole body stiffened up. "She had these wicked eyes. You know, eyes you can't trust. I should have known."

At that, I rolled them.

"Can you give me some more details, please?" he asked.

There was a pause, and then she spoke again. "And there was something about her mouth, too."

"Her mouth?" he asked.

"Yes, she had a very puckered, witchy mouth. You know the kind. Like she was sucking on a sour lemon."

"Oh," Mike said flatly.

"Very evil-looking indeed."

"Uh, well, maybe I could get my sister to come down here. She does our police sketches, when need be. And then we could get a sketch into circulation around town."

"Yes, that would be great," she said.

This was all so ludicrous. If I wasn't legitimately in trouble, here, I might have popped out from under the stage and pointed that out. Cat hair grows back, and it's not like I fucking stole that other cat and was halfway to Mexico with the thing and about to make it into guacamole. And now they were actually talking about a police sketch! I sighed, moved away from the hole and lay down on my back under the stage. I wanted to laugh. I wanted to cry. I wanted to . . .

Shit. I didn't know what I wanted to do.

CHAPTER 38

⌒

It had been fifteen minutes since I'd "stolen" the cat, and in that time Ash had arrived. I was still lying there, listening to it all—listening to Greta describe me as Ash drew, listening to Mike talking to the organizer of the event, who also happened to be staying in the damn eco estate and now had concerns about the security in this town generally. At least I didn't have to worry about the identikit drawing of me; I mean, no offence, but I'd seen Ash's art lying against the walls in the dining room—it was more abstract. I was about to pull my phone out and play Candy Crush while I waited for all the chaos to subside, when . . .

"Mmm, there's something familiar about this face."

I sat up straight when I heard Ash utter those dreadful words. Surely it wasn't possible that, between Greta's mad ramblings and Ash's avant-garde flair for art, they would have gotten anything that could be identified as human, let alone me.

"She seems so familiar," I heard Ash say to herself.

Shit! I crawled over to the hole and pressed my eye to it again. Adrenalin swooshed in my veins as I waited for the grand reveal. The minute it was shown to Mike, he would recognize me. I didn't have to wait long.

"Mike," Ash said. "I'm done. You can get this photocopied."

The moment of truth.

"Let's see," Mike said.

I could see his legs moving again. He took a few steps, stopped, and then I heard some rustling of paper. There was a long pause and then I heard it. His tone was such a giveaway that I knew my time was very much over.

"Are you sure this is her?" he asked.

Oh, dear Lord!

"One hundred percent," Greta said. "I will remember that face for as long as I live." Her voice cracked when she spoke, as if she was about to cry.

Great! So now I was a face that she would remember forever. Just what I needed.

"Okay," Mike said, sounding strange and tentative. "I'll go over to the station and get some photocopies of it and start distributing it around town."

"Thank you," said the man that I'd identified earlier as the organizer of the event.

And then the crowd started moving off. I waited to see what Mike would do next, peering through the hole like a creepy stalker.

Ash was also still there, and she whispered, "Jesus. I recognize that face."

"Me too," Mike said. "Me too." And with that cliffhanger (cue dramatic cliffhanger music in my head), both of them decided to walk away, leaving me crouching there, feeling sweaty and sick with nerves.

Well, this was it. As soon as I stepped out from under the stage, I would be recognized, apprehended and this time probably "booked" or whatever they called it. In a few hours' time, I would have a criminal record, so I might as well look around and get what I came for, and then I would leave and march myself straight into the police station. Maybe Mike would take pity on me. But probably not.

I crawled deeper into the space under the stage. According to the diary entry, there was a small door that led into a room. It was unlikely that whatever I was looking for was still there. I mean, what were the chances that this room had not been disturbed in seventy years? I crawled my way past some old costumes and props. A pile of old velvet curtains that had obviously been taken down and replaced with new ones. I crawled past an empty Coke can, a discarded condom wrapper . . . *Eeeew*. I crawled a little faster and finally I got to the back and found what I was looking for. There it was, the—

"Shit!" I hissed to myself when I saw it. "No." I reached for the pieces of wood that had been hammered over the small door and pulled on them. They were not going anywhere, unless I had a crowbar in my bag, which I did not.

All of that drama for absolutely nothing! All that cat maiming and stealing and running and hiding and getting my face plastered all over town . . . for nothing. I hung my head and slumped against the wall, feeling totally dejected. Maybe I had been wrong about this whole thing. *Maybe I wasn't meant to tell this story, after all.* Not that I was basing that on anything scientific, other than some half-imagined voice that I thought I might have heard in the early hours of the morning.

Seriously, what was wrong with me?

CHAPTER 39

I waited until the stream of people started filtering out of the hall before I decided to step out myself. I was bracing myself for that moment when I got recognized by one of the cat crowd, because God knows what they would do to me. Would I be tarred and furred?

I walked out of the hall and into the throng of people in the parking lot, who were all getting ready to parade their Persian cats down the street. God, this was a bizarre ritual. I needed to get to my car, but there were at least a hundred people between me and my vehicle.

I could see someone handing out bits of paper and could hear them saying, "Have you seen this woman?" I shrugged to myself. Clearly, my days of being a criminal mastermind were over. I pushed past a few people and came face to face with the man handing out flyers. He stopped and looked at me for a moment or two.

This was it! The moment that the alarm bell was sounded and I was dragged off. Only it wasn't. The paper was thrust into my hands and the man didn't even say a word to me. I turned and watched him walk away, no recognition on his face whatsoever.

Slowly, shakily, nervously, I raised the poster to my face. I gasped when I saw the image, and then burst out laughing—so loudly that people around me stopped and stared.

I waved the poster at them. "Just terrible! Terrible what someone can do to a cat!" I said, and then walked off to my car, a sense of amusement and utter relief washing over me.

I knew why this poster looked familiar—because apparently I looked like the love child of Liza Minnelli and Frank-N-Furter.

* * *

It was already late afternoon by the time I left the cat parade and headed back to the house. I did a few drive-bys first to make sure there was no sign of Mike. There wasn't. I walked into my room and the first thing I noticed was a small folded note on the floor. I opened it and peered inside.

> Since you're a writer, I thought you might be interested in our library! No one goes there anymore, but I unlocked it for you. It's on our side of the house, first door in the passage in front of you. You can come by and use it anytime you like. It has some really old books in it—many belonged to my grandmother, too! Ash.

I dropped the note on the bed. A stab of guilt and shame and other bad feelings wacked me in the belly. She was so nice, and I was . . . was . . . a . . . I was, uh—

"Library?" I uttered to myself. Why did that sound so fam—?

"Oh my God!"

I raced over to the letter and opened it.

> *I've found a better hiding spot for my letters to you. You will be able to get them there. I'm putting them inside my "favorite book." Please go and look for them as soon as you can, in case there is a change in plans.*

My mind started to race again, and I ran over to her diary. I opened it carefully, so as not to cause any more damage, and started scanning the pages as I went, looking for any reference to a book. A passage caught my eye and I stopped to read it.

Dear Diary,
Miriam tried to deliver the letter to A today, but he was gone.
His house was empty, all his things had been packed up and no
one knows where he went. And now I don't know where he is—
I even packed my bag, ready to run away with him, but he's gone.
Miriam thinks it's for the best that he's left town. She says she
doesn't want to see me arrested—but, if I can't have A in my
life, they might as well put me in jail, anyway.

I brought my hand up to my mouth when I read that. Edith had wanted them to run away together and he'd just disappeared. Where had he gone? I continued leafing through the diary, looking for a clue as to what this "favorite book" might be. But there was nothing, only more heartbreaking entries about how she was being forced to marry a man she didn't love.

I closed the diary, stood up and started pacing the room. *What was her favorite book?* I felt like I knew the answer to the question, I felt like it was right in front of my eyes somewhere and I just wasn't seeing it. I stopped walking and looked at the bath—I probably needed one. I'd barely slept, had been wearing the same clothes for two days, and my pants were covered in dust and spider webs from crawling under the stage. And clearly I wasn't going to figure this mystery out. I peeled my clothes off as I ran a bath, and then I slipped into the warm water. I was just about to fully submerge myself when I looked down; there was something stuck to my boob. I pulled it off and looked. It was the folded piece of paper I'd stuck inside my bra, two days ago. I was about to toss it on to the floor when something stirred inside me. I sat up in the bath and slowly opened it. I looked at the drawing through the veil of steam that was curling up from the hot water.

"Shit!" I sat straight up when it dawned on me, when it clicked into place. I knew what her favorite book was!

CHAPTER 40

⌒

J waited until the clock struck midnight before I went to the library. I'd managed to catch a little bit of sleep after my bath, and was feeling slightly more human. I crept out of my bedroom and down the long hallway, pushing the door at the end open and walking inside. The passage felt completely different this time, now that I knew of all the things that had happened in here. All the kisses at midnight, the secret liaisons, the writing of letters. This passage held so much more meaning for me. I stopped walking for a moment and closed my eyes—listening, wondering if I could hear the echo of what had happened here, a soft whisper from the past. I touched the wall; it was cold, but I could imagine that, at some point, warm bodies would have been pressed up against it in passion.

I smiled to myself. This story was becoming so much more to me than *just* a book. The more I read his letters and her diary, the more they crept into my heart. I could picture their faces so clearly. I could picture their clothes, their voices as they whispered sweet nothings to each other. I opened my eyes again and looked around, feeling a sudden sense of loss. Would I ever have a place like this? A person like him? Someone that loved me, for me? When I was younger, I had longed to be a part of a family. And, as I became a little older and more aware that you could create your own family, I had longed to find someone and get married, to have babies and a wonderful life of my own, with a family I could call mine. Little did I know that, as I got older, I would also develop this uncanny ability to choose the wrong men. I would find it hard to mingle with people, or make meaningful connections with them . . . *although* . . .

It hadn't felt that way with Mike. It had felt so surprisingly easy and effortless. There had been this strange connection, from the moment we'd met, that I couldn't quite explain. Mind you, most of the things that had happened over these last few days defied explanation—well, defied any explanation that made sense, that wasn't rooted in some esoteric, *the-universe-is-doing-this* kind of thinking.

I continued down the dark, dingy passage and pushed the door at the end open as slowly and silently as possible. I walked to where Ash had said the library would be and slowly opened the door. I knew that Mike was close to me, now, sleeping. It felt strange being this close to him, and yet so far away. Being so near him, without him knowing I was there. I hoped it would stay that way.

I stepped inside the library and closed the door behind me as quietly as possible. I flicked on the lights and looked around. It was incredible. Exactly as I'd imagined an old library to be: dark wood paneling, the dusty, musty smell of old books hanging in the air. Old, frayed Persian rugs covered the floor; large, brown leather couches surrounded an old stone fireplace; there was a huge mahogany desk with old papers on it that looked as if they'd never been touched, and, in the center of the desk, a large bust of a man I didn't recognize. But the most striking thing about the library was the wall of books, with one of those cool ladders that slides from left to right. I could imagine Edith in this library, slipping her favorite book back on to the shelf after reading her favorite quote from it . . .

We are all fools in love.

It was one of the most famous lines from *Pride and Prejudice*, and I don't know why I hadn't seen it immediately. The word *fool* and the heart inside the infinity symbol that had been carved on to the tree were a clear reference to it. I scanned the wall for the book, and when I couldn't see it anywhere, I started climbing the ladder.

I'd recently proved to myself that I wasn't good at climbing fences; I just hoped I was a little better at ladders.

I climbed the ladder carefully. It was so dusty, it was slippery. Also, my nose was starting to tickle and I could feel a sneeze coming on. This was the last thing I needed to happen, now, especially considering the last time I'd sneezed had basically caused an international incident. And then, suddenly, one of the rungs shook. I wobbled a little, but managed to hold on. With my current streak of strange luck, though, I'd probably fall and break a bone. At least I was touching wood!

"Please, please, please!" I whispered at the ladder, begging it to stay intact for a little longer. "If you don't break, I promise I will dust you when I'm done," I said, feeling slightly mad that I was trying to communicate with this inanimate object. I climbed higher and higher and finally reached the top shelf.

I started scanning for the book, where (hopefully) I would find a gold mine of letters. My eyes drifted from one spine to the next, and then . . .

I stopped. My eyes scanned the words; I read them twice, just to make completely sure I was right. There it was. *Pride and Prejudice.* It was staring at me, beckoning me to just reach out and take it. My fingers tingled as I reached for it. They were practically on fire as I wrapped them around the book and pulled. I was so excited, so eager to peer inside that I didn't wait to get down. Instead, I opened it right there and then, and, when I did, disappointment wracked my body. Nothing! Without thinking, I stamped my foot and—*shit*— that's when disaster struck.

I looked down just in time to see my foot crash through the rung, splinters shattering and wood snapping. I started to fall. I yelled as I plummeted and then, in one hard, loud thump, I hit the floor. I winced in pain as I climbed to my hands and knees, grateful that I wasn't too hurt. And then I heard a noise. Footsteps descending the staircase. The door handle starting to turn. I stared in horror as

Mike burst through the door. Then I heard another noise and looked up as books began to fall from the shelf, pummeling me like falling baby elephants. I felt an explosion of pain on my head. I closed my eyes momentarily as the pain kicked inside my skull like a drum. But my eyes flicked open again when I heard him.

"You! What the hell are you . . . ? Becca, I mean . . . what?! How . . . ? Why . . . ? Becca, WHAT?"

I looked up at him as he stuttered away, clearly trying to make sense of this moment. Why was I, the girl he'd personally driven out of town, now on her hands and knees in his library? He pointed at me, his face going ashen white.

"What?" I asked, raising my hand to my head in alarm. I felt wetness and pulled my fingers away. They were coated in blood. "Blood," I said, suddenly thinking about the woman in the elevator . . . *I hoped she was okay.*

"Sam!" I heard a shout from behind Mike; it was Ash, and she was looking at me with horror.

"Sam?" Mike asked.

I tried to shrug, but my head hurt like hell.

Ash slapped her brother on the arm. "What the hell are you just standing here for? We need to get her to the hospital. Come, come." She rushed to my side and started pulling me up. She shouted over her shoulder, "For God's sake, Mike, what are you doing? Help Sam." She was already pulling me to my feet.

"Sam?" he asked again, like a stuck record.

"Yes, Sam. The guest I was telling you about."

I was on my feet now, feeling dizzy and somewhat peculiar around the edges.

"What are you doing here?" Mike looked at me.

"For God's sake, bro. Come *on*. I told her she could use the library. MIKE!" she shouted, and that was it. Suddenly, he was also at my side, clutching my arm, both of them pulling me out of the room.

"Get her to the car," Ash said quickly.

"I'm okay. I'm okay." I protested, backing away from them both and trying to wiggle free of their grip.

"You are not okay. You have blood running down your face!" She looked at me firmly and then turned to Mike, as if she wanted him to confirm this.

He nodded. "I think we should get you to the hospital," he said. *Did I detect a slight hint of panic in his voice?*

"Bloody right we're getting you to a hospital," Ash said forcefully.

We exited the house and I was quickly put in the car again—the police car. Ash had insisted on it and had also insisted that Mike put on the lights and sirens, since the hospital was all the way in the next town.

"Jesus—drive a little faster." Ash hit the back of Mike's seat as we drove out of Willow Bay. Clearly, this town was too small for things like hospitals and real jail cells.

I looked to the front and caught Mike's eyes in the rear-view mirror. They seemed to be filled with something—questions, I was guessing. He probably had a lot of questions for me, right now—questions I wasn't sure I would even be able to answer. Our eyes locked again and something surged inside me. This time, it wasn't the feelings I'd had before; now, it was guilt, and it was the worst feeling in the world. I'd promised him I wouldn't come back to town, and yet here I was, in his car again. He gave his head a tiny shake and looked away, as if disappointed in me. After that, I sat quietly in the back and looked out the window until we finally arrived.

CHAPTER 41

$\mathcal{M}$ ike sat there, staring at me. The stitches in my forehead were stinging and so was I. The intense look he was busy shooting at me from the chair in the corner of the room was as sharp as throwing spears, making everything sting.

"So?" Mike finally spoke. His voice was cold and steely-sounding.

"Mmmm?" I looked up at him innocently from my hospital bed, although I knew there was no amount of wide-eyed innocent looking that was going to get me out of this situation.

"I'm waiting," he said, folding his arms. He sat back in his chair and his shirt tugged against his broad chest; for a moment, I remembered how good he looked, almost naked.

"Still waiting," he said, sounding even more irritated than he had a second ago.

"Waiting?" I asked.

"For an explanation!" He crossed his legs now too—very sexy, and yet surprisingly intimidating.

I nodded. I'm not sure why, but I did. I looked around the room, hoping someone would appear at any moment and save me from this situation. But Ash had gone to get snacks from the vending machine and, for the first time since Mike burst in on me in his library, we were alone. Honestly, at this stage, I would have taken a nurse with an enema to avoid this conversation.

He jiggled his foot in the air and I knew I needed to say something soon. Wait . . . A thought hit me. Maybe I could pretend that the wound on my head had caused temporary amnesia, and that I had no memory of who I was or what I was doing. *Was that even possible?* Or were things like that only possible in soap operas and romance novels?

"Becca, Sam, Pebecca—whatever your name is—what is going on, here?" He uncrossed his legs and leaned forward in his chair. "Last time I saw you, I thought I'd made it very clear that you were *not* to come back."

"You did," I said, my voice trembling a little.

"Well, an explanation for why you're suddenly here again—and in my house, no less—would be great!" he replied sarcastically.

"I didn't know you lived there when I checked in," I snapped, in my defense.

He shook his head again; clearly, he didn't believe me. "And, not only do I find you in my house, when you're not even meant to be in this town, I find you—*yet again*—sneaking around in the middle of the night, and I have to ask myself, and you, the same question again: what the hell are you *really* up to?"

"I told you—"

"Yeah, yeah, I know. You're researching a book." He looked dubious; I didn't blame him, but it was the truth. In fact, that was the only bit of truth I'd probably spoken in several days.

"It's the truth," I said, as sincerely as I could.

"And what are you researching, exactly? I mean, what kind of book requires all this sneaking around?"

"I told you, it's a book on a P.I." That didn't sound as sincere, and I could see he'd picked up on that immediately.

"Okay, now that part was a lie," he said.

I shrugged. "I . . . I can't tell you what the book is about. I'm contractually bound not to say what it's about yet. If I did, I could get into trouble with my agent and publisher." This was a half-truth, but it flew out of me so easily, it might as well have been the gospel truth.

He eyed me, but it felt more like he was dissecting me. His gaze moved over me like some kind of scanner—one of those powerful radars that they used to look inside the Giza pyramids, searching for all the secret hidden tunnels that lurked deep inside them. I tried to keep my facial features in check as he scanned my innermost corners, looking for my hidden secrets, but my lips kept twitching for some unknown reason as he dragged his eyes slowly over my face.

"The thing is, Pebecca." *Dear God, he was calling me by my full name—this was bad!* "Thing is, since you've arrived in this town, there has been nothing but chaos. We never have any incidents; in fact, Willow Bay is one of the most peaceful places in South Africa. But, since you've been here, we have had a break-in, damage to property—and by that I mean a cat is missing its eyebrow—and then we had a cat stolen by a mysterious women called Sam, who was impersonating a groomer . . . Coincidence?" These were obviously rhetorical questions.

I hung my head. Everything he'd said was right. But I wasn't usually like this, and I wanted him to understand that. "I *am* researching a book," I reiterated. "I wanted to see the town hall today, and, yes, I might have—without thinking—impersonated a cat groomer. But I put that black cat down, and she was found!" I said quickly.

"So it *was* you?" he asked.

I nodded and then cringed a little. "Would it help if I told you that I regret doing it and wish I could take it back?"

"But why?" he asked. "Why not just buy a bloody ticket and go inside, like a normal person?"

"It was sold out."

"And you were that desperate to go to a cat show?"

"Well, I was researching . . . *something.*"

"For the book?"

"For the book," I confirmed.

"The book?"

"Yup, the book." I nodded.

"Becca, just how much trouble are you prepared to get into for this book?" he asked. "Is it worth it?"

I laughed. Small at first, but then it picked up momentum. "Now that, *that* is the question of the year, Mike," I said, and then looked down at my hands and picked at one of my cuticles. "That's a really good question, actually, and I'm not sure how to answer it."

"Maybe you should, before you land yourself in some real trouble," he responded.

I looked up at him and he stared straight back at me. Silence—strange and stretchy and making me feel a little insane. I was filled with so many contradictory feelings. I was so happy to see him, to be in the same room as him; I'd missed him, but . . . I hadn't wanted to see him under these circumstances. I could see he was angry with me—disappointed, even—and it hurt.

"So—" Ash burst into the room—"I have some chocolate, which should be good for blood sugar—I'm sure yours is low at the moment—or, if you need something more substantial, then I have crisps—not that that is substantial, but it was all I could find in the vending machine. What do you want?" She was like the Energizer bunny as she put all the snacks down on my bed. Then she did something that truly took me by surprise. She sat, took my hands in hers with care, and looked me straight in the eyes. "How are you feeling?"

I could tell she genuinely cared and it almost brought tears to my eyes. "Much better," I said. "It stings a bit and my head's a little sore, but I'm all good."

"Oh, thank God!" She placed her hand on her chest. "I feel terrible. I told you to use the library, but I didn't know the ladder was that bad. If I'd known, I would never—"

I put my hand up to stop her. "Seriously, it's not your fault. I should have known better than to climb an old, wooden ladder."

"And probably not at that late hour?" Mike said pointedly.

My head snapped up and I looked at him. "Probably not," I admitted.

"And how is the patient feeling?" The friendly doctor who'd stitched my head came in. This was such a typical small-town area—the kind where everyone knew everyone else's business, even in the next town over—to the point that, while stitching me up, the doctor had told me that he'd delivered both Mike and Ashley, and, when Mike had been born, he was so chubby that the doctor had mistaken him for a girl because his "boy parts" were hidden!

"Much better," I said to him, as he sat at my bed.

"Good." He examined my head wound again. "Well, I'm happy with that. You can go home now."

"Home?" Ash jumped. "Surely you should keep her here to monitor her, in case she has a concussion."

"Did you lose consciousness when the book hit you on the head?" the doctor asked.

"No, I don't think so." I looked up at Mike.

"No, she didn't lose consciousness. Well, she did close her eyes for a little while, now that I think about it," he said.

"She did?" The doctor looked at me again. He took a small torch out and shone it in my eyes.

"See!" Ash said. "Don't you have to be extra careful with head injuries? She shouldn't sleep tonight, right? Just in case."

"Uh . . ." The doctor looked like he was considering this. "I don't think it's necessary, but if it would make you all feel better, then it won't do any harm, keeping her awake tonight."

"Great!" Ash clapped her hands together. "My brother and I are going to look after you so well tonight, we won't leave your side for a second, and we'll entertain you all night long. You won't want to sleep!" She smiled so broadly, but I could see that Mike wasn't too thrilled with the idea. In fact, he looked like this was the last thing he wanted to do.

"So, what do you guys say . . . ? Movie night!" She clapped her hands together excitedly.

"Yay," I said, trying to sound upbeat. I looked over at Mike.

"Mmm, yay," he whispered, half under his breath.

CHAPTER 42

I sat on the couch next to Mike; to say it was awkward would be an understatement. *Is there another word, other than* awkward, *that one can use?* I scanned my brain, going straight to the place where my inbuilt thesaurus lay. But no other words seemed to describe adequately the strange feeling of sitting next to this man. My head was still stinging and I could feel a tender bruise developing around the wound, but that wasn't what was worrying me the most . . .

His proximity. The warmth I could feel radiating off his body. The smell of him, too—familiar and exhilarating, but unnerving. I felt both comfortable and uncomfortable, all at the same time. Excited and terrified. Warm and cold. A contradictory mix of every feeling and emotion thrown in and stirred about. I was grateful when Ash finally came back to the room.

"Move up—popcorn coming through." She sat on the couch and pushed me further into Mike, until our shoulders were pressed into each other.

I tried to lean away, so as to relieve the pressure, but there was no space. His shoulders tensed against mine and I tried not to move too much.

"This is fun," Ash said. "When did we last do movie night?" She leaned forward and looked at Mike.

"Not in a while." He sounded rather flat.

"Okay, what should we watch?" Ash picked the remote up and flicked on the TV.

"Uh . . . whatever," I answered.

"Not 'whatever.' You are the guest of honor—you choose." She passed the remote over to me and I started flicking through the channels, and then Ash jumped up excitedly. "Let's watch that!" She pointed at the screen.

"No—please, no," Mike mumbled, next to me.

"I luurve *The Bachelor*!" she gushed.

I turned and smiled at her. "I love *The Bachelor*, too!" Because I effing did. Give me any cheesy, over-the-top reality TV show—whether it was a bunch of hot estate agents in tight dresses and super-high heels, or pregnant housewives in tight dresses and super-high heels—and I was game. To me, reality TV was like watching a slow-motion train crash; you just knew something bad was about to happen, but you couldn't look away.

"Done," Ash said, taking the remote away from me and turning the program on.

"*Tonight on* The Bachelor—" that familiar voice filled the room—"*will Jay finally see Eliza for the back-stabber she really is? And will Jessica find the courage to tell him the secret she has been keeping? Stay tuned for unbelievable scenes like you've never seen before in* Bachelor *history!*"

"I don't know how you can watch this stuff." Mike shuffled next to me. "It's not real!"

"Of course it's real." Ash sat forward and looked at him. "You can see it in their eyes, when they like each other. I mean, it's obvious that Jay is totally into Jess."

"Oh, please. The whole thing is so manufactured. There's no way you can fall in love, *real love*, under such ridiculously strange and staged circumstances. And so quickly—no one falls in love that quickly!"

"What?!" Ash sat forward even more, and so did Mike. These two looked like they did this often—sibling arguments. I sat back and watched them; it was almost more amusing than the TV show.

"Love blossoms instantly," Ash shot back, "and in the least likely places, when you meet the right person. Trust me!"

"Really?" He sounded unmoved. "Okay, name one person we know who found love like that." He turned on the couch and faced her, his knee bumping into mine, and a strange feeling zipped up my leg.

"What about Brendan and Sue? She hated him at school, and then they met by accident, five years later, in a restaurant, because they'd both been stood up by their blind dates, and then they got engaged a month later, and now they're married with children." She folded her arms and looked pleased with herself, as if she knew she'd won the argument. I had to give it to her, it was a good argument.

"Okay, that is the exception, though," Mike said.

She shook her head. "Nope! I'm telling you, bro, love comes when you least expect it *and* in the strangest of ways, and it can be totally instant, too. Sometimes, you can fall in love with someone without even knowing you love them."

"Impossible," Mike said.

"Possible," Ash fired back. "People who are soulmates always seem to meet in strange, fateful ways. Like being stood up by blind dates, or being stuck in an elevator together, or finding the other person's dog when it ran away, or accidentally sending an email to the wrong address but realizing that that person is your soulmate when you start communicating."

Mike laughed. "That stuff only happens in romcoms. For the most part, people meet normally—or abnormally, like on Tinder and all that crap."

"Nope. People meet in strange, mysterious, fortuitous ways all the time. What about you and that girl on the fence?"

"Huh?" I choked on the popcorn I was busy shoving into my mouth. *Did she mean me?*

"ASH! Stop!" Mike sounded very firm.

"No, no, it's a good example of what I mean." She tried to continue talking, but Mike became very agitated and cut her off.

"No, it's not. It's NOT!" he said loudly.

"Yes, it is. You said it yourself: you met her totally by chance, and then you had this strange moment with her when you felt something you couldn't explain. As if you knew her on some level, or you'd met, but you didn't know where. And then you met her again, in a grave-yard, of all things strange and peculiar, and then AGAIN at the bar, same day, and then—well, the other stuff is not for now." She looked over at me and winked. "Not in front of guests."

"Ash, stop!" Mike sounded downright panicked now.

"And then, the next night, again! There is something to that, little brother," she said.

"It's a small town," Mike quickly added.

"Not that small. Besides, what did you say?" Ash started.

"Stop it!" Mike held his hand up.

"The saddest goodbye to a person you didn't even know," Ash said thoughtfully. "I thought that was really beautiful! You can be so sen-timental, you know."

"WHAT?" I heard myself screech.

Ash did a double take and looked at me strangely. Suddenly, the air around us was thick with uncomfortableness (is that a word?). I could almost feel it buzzing around me. I tried not to look at Mike, but something compelled me to glance over into his eyes . . . *green eyes*. Emerald pools. Lush, tropical jungles. There was no way to describe how green they really were. I looked and then I slipped and then I fell into them. I could hear a sound in my head that accompanied the fall. It sounded like two great things colliding together. Thumping. My eyes locked with his and I couldn't pull them away.

"Waaaaiiiiit." Ash jumped up and looked down at the two of us. "Why are you looking at each other like that? Why are you giving each other *that* look?"

"What look?" I asked innocently.

"There's no look," Mike mumbled, next to me.

"Oh, yes, there is. I saw a look!" Ash folded her arms and looked from me to Mike and back again.

I shook my head at her quickly and then looked away as I felt my cheeks get warm.

"Hang on . . . Have you guys met? Do you know each other?" she asked.

I shook my head even more. "No."

"Never met her in my life," Mike grumbled.

"*NO!*" Ash exclaimed, so loudly that I flinched in fright. "NOOO!" she said again.

I looked up at her. "No, what?"

She pointed her finger at me and started wagging it up and down. "I see. I see." She sounded terribly excited.

"Ash, please." Mike jumped out of his seat.

"*You're her!* I don't believe it." Her eyes were as wide as saucers, and then she burst out laughing. "Is this her?" she asked, looking straight at her brother.

"Me? What? Who?" I stood up now, too, totally confused. I was at least three sentences behind in this conversation. I'd zoned out somewhere around Ash saying something about Mike feeling something for me, or something . . . "What?" I asked again.

"You're the girl that Mike caught climbing over the fence," she said to me. It was a statement, not a question. "Did you know Mike stayed here?" Ash asked. "Is that why you booked in?"

I shook my head. "No. I had no idea he lived here."

"Oh, wow!" She threw her arms in the air now. "I need a minute to process this all." Ash paced the room a few times, looking highly amused. "You're the 'hot out-of-towner' that he found climbing over the fence and then met at the bar the other night when he came home late. The one that . . ." She burst out laughing again and raised her hands to her mouth. "You're kidding! No wonder he looked so shocked when he saw you in the library! This is perfect."

"The one that what?" I asked.

"Ash, please. No!" Mike was begging now, and Ash was shaking her head from side to side.

"This is priceless. This is like the best thing that has ever happened. I mean, the girl you dubbed 'best kisser in the world' checked into *our* B and B, by accident. The poor woman who you ran out on, mid make-out sesh, to help Mrs. Van der Merwe!" Then she turned to me. "This is all making so much sense now. You didn't have a stomach bug last night, did you? I was *soo* sure I'd heard you in the passage, and then, when I opened the door, I was sure I saw you running away. You saw Mike! That's why you didn't come to dinner, right?" She looked at me and was nodding happily to herself.

My eyes drifted back to Mike. "Best kisser in the world?"

Ash burst out laughing. "Oh my God! This is brilliant. This is truly amazing."

"You told her I was the best kisser in the world?" I looked at Mike. I was harping, I knew that, but it was really all I'd heard.

He looked flushed in the face now. A little embarrassed. He nodded.

"Oh, he tells me everything," Ash said.

"What?" My eyes widened in shock.

She shrugged. "No, not *that* much!" she said sarcastically. "But just enough . . . and you are quite the jailbird, aren't you?" She looked at me with a massive smile. "Wait—your real name isn't Sam, is it? Don't you have a strange name, like Pebble or—"

"Pebecca," I cut her off.

"That's right!" She snapped her fingers. "So, let me get this straight . . . you broke into that weird eco place, Mike arrested you and ran you out of town, and then you . . . what? Snuck back, chose a fake name and checked into this place . . . *by accident*?"

I started nodding my head.

"Wow. You really aren't a very good criminal, are you?" Ash sat down and crossed her legs. She leaned back on the couch and watched us for a while. "My God, this story is insane. I love it. I can't wait to tell Emelia." She burst out laughing again and then stood up and started walking towards the door. She was almost in hysterics now.

"Wait! Where are you going?" I asked, as she started to exit.

"Uh . . . I'm leaving. I think you guys can manage to keep each other awake all night . . . Besides, a little black-crested night budgie told me you might have some unfinished business." She laughed even harder and then disappeared out the room and closed the door behind her. I heard her laughing all the way to the other end of the house. Suddenly, Mike and I felt very, very alone.

CHAPTER 43

I stared at the closed door in a kind of stuck-in-the-mud horror. The kind where your body feels like it's sinking into the ground . . . *slowly*. My body felt like it was getting heavier, and heavier. As if it were being pushed down by something. Well, I'll tell you what it was being pushed down by: the thick, heavy air of *Awkwardness!* (capital *A*, exclamation mark) that was filling the room. I could feel his presence behind me, I could hear his soft breathing, smell his cologne, but I dared not turn around. We froze there together for a few moments, as if we were both trying to disappear, until it became unbearable to no longer talk. I turned around slowly and looked at him.

"Well . . ." I stuttered. Dry, scratchy throat.

"Well," he echoed.

"This is not awkward. At all," I said.

"Not at all." I heard Mike swallow.

"What else did you tell your sister? I mean . . . did you tell her—?"

"No! Not any details!" he jumped in. "Just the bare necessities."

"Bare? I hope you didn't tell her about anything that was bare?" I replied. "Not that we were very bare, actually. Just partly bare. Not all the way . . . *bare*." How many times could I say the word *bare* in a sentence? Clearly too many, judging by the small smile that was beginning to play on his face.

"No *bare* details were shared. I'm a man who doesn't kiss and tell." He stepped closer to me and smiled. I smiled back, stupidly. His big, green, smiling eyes were a little like a drug. One hit, and you were addicted. One hit, and you needed more. One hit, and you were always searching for the next one. But then he took a step backward and started walking away from me.

"What?" I said, with a clear hint of desperation in my voice.

He continued to back up, until he reached the wall. He leaned against it and folded his arms.

"We should probably finish that conversation we were having at the hospital," he said, so abruptly that the mood in the room changed once more.

I nodded. "Sure."

He ran his hand through his hair. "I just . . . I . . . You were . . ." he stuttered. He sounded frustrated with me and like he was searching for the right words to use. "You aren't supposed to be here—you know that, right?" He said, sounding frustrated.

"I know! I know!" I said. "But aren't you just a tiny bit glad I am here?" I looked up at him and smiled.

I could see he was fighting it. I could see it in the way his forehead was crinkling and that sexy scar above his eyebrow was quivering. But then, slowly, surely, tentatively . . . *a smile*.

I felt myself go weak inside. Like something bendable and malleable. "You felt something for me?" I heard myself ask in a very breathy voice.

His smile grew. "Don't push it," he said. "Technically, I should be arresting you, right here and now."

"So why don't you?" I asked.

"Well, you're injured." He pointed at my head. I'd almost forgotten about that. "Maybe when you've recovered in the morning, I'll arrest you." I wasn't sure if he was being serious or not.

"And lock me in what jail cell?" I asked, with a smile.

"You know, if those cat people see you again, I might not be able to stop them from pressing charges," he said, in a very serious tone.

"It's a good thing the cat parade is over, then, and that Greta thinks she saw Liza Minnelli instead."

At that, Mike laughed. "It really didn't look anything like you."

I shook my head. "No." I smiled at him and he smiled back.

"You know, I'm really trying to be angry with you, right now, but you're making it very hard. Because I should be angry with you!" He pointed at me, now. "I really, really should be furious with you."

"But you're not?" I asked.

"Unfortunately." He pushed himself off the wall and walked into the middle of the room and looked around.

"So, what do you want to do?" he asked.

I shrugged. "Watch *The Bachelor*?"

"I'll watch anything else but that." He moved back towards the couch and sat down. I sat down, too.

"Mike?" I asked.

"Becca?"

"What's going to happen in the morning? Are you going to run me out of town again?"

I felt his shoulders shrug next to me. "I don't know. I really don't know what to do with you. You're like a boomerang that keeps coming back. If I ran you out of town again, I'd probably find you up another ladder or fence somewhere tomorrow."

"I think my climbing-up-things days are over."

"Well, they should be. You suck at climbing," he replied.

I laughed a little. "I do."

There was a little lull in the conversation. A pause. I waited for him to speak again.

"Did you really, really not know I lived here?" he asked, looking over at me.

I locked eyes with him. "Honestly, honestly, I had no idea you lived here. Not until I saw you when I was coming for dinner."

He smiled at this and then shook his head. "That's crazy," he said, half under his breath, "that, out of all the places in town, you landed up here."

"There weren't many free rooms to choose from," I said.

He nodded. "We've only just finished that room, Ash put it up on the booking site a couple of days ago."

"I must have seen it moments after it was listed, then." I smiled at him.

Another silence fell over us and this time I could see something, an emotion, playing in his eyes.

I cleared my throat. "I broke a promise to you when I came back to town. And I feel really bad for that. I'm sorry," I said.

He nodded. "What are you really researching in this town?" he asked.

A bolt of guilt-tinged anxiety shot through me. I didn't want to lie to him. But this story had just taken on a whole other meaning, because he was now involved in it personally. *Shit!* It suddenly hit me how terrible this was. Secretly researching his family. Staying in their home. Enjoying their hospitality when I was really just . . . *using them?* I was such a bad person.

"The book is set in a small town . . . I was just trying to get a feel for one, that's all," I stuttered.

"Why this town, specifically?" he asked.

"I googled 'Best small towns in South Africa' and this came up. It looked quaint and perfect."

He looked at me for a while, his eyes peeling back my layers, trying to look inside. "I've asked this before, but, seriously, is researching your book really worth all this trouble? You got injured today, for heaven's sake!"

"That was an accident. I just wanted to see the library. I couldn't sleep and I needed a distraction."

"And yesterday you were the most wanted person in town."

I got up and walked around in a small circle. And then I stopped. "I've had two years to write this book. TWO! And do you know how many words I've written? Zero—that's how many." I shook my head. "I've had this writer's block . . . No, it's more than that. I've been plagued by this fear, this terror that maybe I only ever had one book in me. And how the hell am I supposed to write another one that can compete with the last one's success? How is that even possible? What if it fails? What if it's not as good? What if no one buys it? What if it gets bad reviews? What if . . . ? What if . . . ?" My anxiety was rising by the second.

Mike walked up to me and put two big hands on my shoulders. Comforting, warm hands.

"It's okay," he said. "It's okay. It's going to be okay."

He smiled at me and my anxiety immediately started to disappear. I forced myself to smile back at him.

"I'll help you," he said. "I know this town. I know how small towns work. What do you need to know?"

I started to shake my head. "No," I said emphatically. I couldn't let him help me when I was secretly researching his family. That would be wrong. On so many levels. "I can't let you do that. I've already caused too much trouble and put you in a bad situation," I said. "But thanks for your offer. I probably don't really deserve it, after all I've done." I moved away from him, and felt the emptiness immediately. The steady weight on my shoulders had been reassuring.

"I disagree. If I help you, I'll make sure you stay out of trouble." He walked over to the couch and sat down. "At least I can keep an eye on you." He said the last part with an amused tone of voice.

I turned around and looked at him.

"How's your head feeling?" he asked.

I reached up and touched it. The pain was ever so slight. "It's okay," I said.

"That's good." He turned the TV back on and I sat down next to him again. But, before we were able to settle on anything, his phone rang. He pulled it out of his pocket and answered quickly.

"Shit," he said, with a sense of urgency in his voice.

I immediately turned and looked at him; his face took on a frown.

"Where?" he asked, into the phone. There was a pause. I couldn't make out the words being said, but I could hear that it was a woman's voice and she was speaking frantically.

"What time?" He looked down at his watch as he spoke, and then he nodded. "I'll go there now." He hung up and stood up immediately.

"What's wrong?" I asked.

"Well, you know the reason I left you in a parking lot, holding condoms?"

"Yes."

"It's that again. Petra Van der Merwe. She's escaped from her home and someone said they saw her by the beach." He started walking towards the door. "I have to go now."

"Okay. I guess I'll see you sometime, then." I followed him into the entrance hall and watched as he grabbed his car keys.

"You're coming with me. You're not meant to sleep tonight, remember? Doctor's orders." He pulled a jacket off a coat hanger and held it out for me. "Come. It's cold outside."

I walked up to him and he slipped the huge jacket on to me. "Thanks," I said, running my hands over the coat.

"Pleasure," he mumbled, and then held the door open for me.

I walked through it and into the chilly night air.

"You warm enough?" he asked, as we ambled towards his car— not his police car. This was confusing, having two cars. How did he decide which one to drive?

"Yes, thanks. But what about you?" I looked at the T-shirt he was wearing. "Isn't this yours?" I indicated the jacket I had on. "Shouldn't you also be wearing something warm?"

He shrugged. "Don't worry about me." And then he smiled at me again—that big, bright smile that made his green eyes sparkle—and I felt myself go warm and fuzzy inside. Suddenly, I no longer needed anything to keep me warm.

CHAPTER 44

❧

"Mrs. Van der Merwe, please come with me." Mike started walking slowly towards the old woman on the dark beach in front of us. She was barefoot and alone, silhouetted against the white clouds that were lit up by the bright, full moon. I climbed out of the car into the cold sea air. The wind was strong and it was whipping cold droplets of water off the crashing waves. The wind howled in a way that was eerie and loud.

She turned around briefly and looked at Mike, and then looked back out at the waves in front of her. The waves were black and the breeze coming off the sea was so icy that I shivered. She didn't respond, and Mike took another step towards her.

"Petra," he said, in a voice that was so soft and caring, it made my heart flutter. "Petra, can you hear me?" he asked.

She turned around, looked at him and then smiled. "Pierre, is that you?" she asked, happily.

"Yes," he said. "*Dis my, Ma*. It's me," Mike said softly, speaking half Afrikaans and half English. I could tell from the way he spoke to her that he'd done this many times before.

"Pierre, where have you been? *Waar?*" she asked, and then rushed up and hugged him with all her might. My heart broke a little bit, just watching her.

"I've been right here," he said, as the old woman took his face in her hands and looked at him happily.

"You need to shave." She ran her hands over his chin and I smiled. "You know what Dad always said."

He nodded. "Cleanliness and godliness," Mike said.

And then Petra turned to me and smiled. "Bianca?" She rushed over to me and pulled me into a hug. "You look so well." And then her hand reached down to my stomach and she laid it across it. I flinched and almost pulled away, but her words stopped me. "You're hardly showing."

"Uh . . . Sorry, what?" I looked up at Mike.

"The baby," Mike said to me. "*Our* baby," he reiterated, with a firm and pointed nod.

"Our . . . What? The what—?"

"Baby," he said again, raising his eyebrows at me. "The one that you're carrying." He pointed at my stomach and I didn't know whether to be offended or not.

"Baby. Yes! The baby—our baby." I played along when I understood what was going on. I'd been cast in a strange movie that I had no idea I'd even auditioned for. I looked back at Petra. "Yes, I'm still small," I said to her. "My mom was small, too—it's a family trait, I think."

"But you're taking good care of her?" she asked, with great concern.

I nodded. "Of course, the best." I looked up at Mike and gave him a shrug. He gave me a small, relieved smile. Our eyes locked and my mind decided to run down a very strange path, one where I was actually imagining what our child would look like, what with all those good, green-eyed genes that he was sure to pass on. I quickly looked away and turned my attention back to the woman in front of me.

"Have you thought of names?" She looked at me and then over to Mike. Her face was old, time had etched deep lines in it, but she was smiling.

I shook my head as Mike walked over to me. "Not yet; we're still trying to decide." I slipped my arm over Mike's shoulders. It wasn't totally necessary for the scene, but it felt like something I wanted to do.

Petra looked at us both. "You'd better hurry," she said. "It will happen in the blink of an eye." And then her smile faltered and she looked out over the sea again, as if she'd zoned out of this reality and into another one—one where she was remembering something. "Trust me, blink your eyes too many times and it *all* happens. It happens so quickly that, soon, it's all over."

A knot formed in my stomach at her words. Mike slipped his arm around me, too. "We like Emily," he said, and nudged me.

"Yes!" I said, playing along with this strange charade again. "And Abigail," I added. "We like Katy, too."

"Yes! And Jennifer," he said.

"Jessica, even," I added.

"Yes, Jessica," he confirmed. "We like the *J* names."

I nodded. "Joanne."

"And Jolene," he said quickly.

"What?" I looked up at him. "Jolene?"

"Yeah, what's wrong with Jolene?" he asked.

"Well, it just reminds me of that song."

Mike smiled at me. "You can't say you don't like a name just because of a song."

"Of course I can dislike a name for that reason."

"No, you can't. Jolene is a really pretty name."

"So is Eileen, but you can't name someone that, or, every time anyone met them, they would go, 'Come on, Eileen,' in their heads. Or, worse, out loud."

Mike's smile grew, and suddenly the cold air felt a little warmer.

"So, you're saying we can't name our daughter Billie Jean, either?" he asked, a teasing quality in his voice.

"No," I said. "Definitely not. You have to think carefully about a name, you know? A name is for life. Just look at what happened to me."

And now he was beaming at me.

"What?" I asked.

"You're really taking this seriously, the naming of our daughter," he said, and, at that, I smiled back. Our eyes locked; the stars seemed dull and muted in comparison to his eyes—they were the brightest things in the night.

"Well, she *should* take that seriously," Petra said, and I snapped out of it. I'd almost forgotten she was even there!

I leaned over to the old woman. "Who knows—" I winked at her—"maybe her middle name should be Petra."

At that, her face lit up. "You would do that?" she asked, sweetly.

"Of course," I said.

"Come, Ma." Mike let go of me and slipped his arm around her small, fragile-looking shoulders. "Let's get you home; it's cold outside."

She nodded and Mike started guiding her back to the car. She stopped and turned around again. "You're a good boy. Always looking out for me. You were always such a good boy," she said, and then turned to me. "You got a good one." She patted Mike on the arm and he looked over at me awkwardly.

I smiled at him. "I guess I did."

"You must always take care of each other," she said, that sad tone in her voice again. "It goes so quickly."

Mike and I looked up at each other, and something unseen and barely there passed between us, like a thin wisp of something. A whisper, an echo of a thought. A fragment of a half-formed feeling.

"We will," he said, as he helped her into the car.

CHAPTER 45

⌒

"Come, let's get you into bed." The nurse at the old-age home took Petra by the hand and led her over to her small bed. I looked at her bedside table; she only had one photo on it. It was of her and a young boy—I assumed this was her son, Pierre. My throat tightened as I looked at that smiling picture of her and then looked back at her profound sadness as she climbed into that bed, all alone. She turned to Mike and me again.

"You will come back soon, Pierre?" she asked, urgency in her voice.

"Of course." Mike walked up to the bed and took her hand in his. "I'm not going anywhere," he said, patting the back of her hand. And then he did something that brought a salty sting to my eye—he leaned in and gave her a small kiss on the forehead as she closed her eyes.

We all started backing out of the room slowly, when she opened her eyes and looked at me again. "Bianca, you must take all your vitamins, and do what the doctor tells you," she urged, "so my grandchild grows strong and healthy."

"Of course," I said. We all exited and closed the door behind us.

The nurse, whose name tag said *Sister Cynthia*, looked over at Mike and gave him a smile. "Thanks for doing that again."

"How did she get out, this time?" he asked.

"We have no idea; she's a real escape artist," Cynthia said, with a hint of affection in her voice.

"We found her on the beach. Something serious could have happened to her."

"Oh, God." Cynthia shook her head. "We'll have to assign someone to watch her all the time. We're short staffed and we're doing our best, but, with the recent cutbacks and—"

Mike put a hand on Cynthia's shoulder. "I know. You're doing a good job, here. You're doing your best."

Cynthia nodded. "We'll figure something out," she said softly and thoughtfully. "I have to go do my rounds, now, but thank you." She looked over at me, as well.

"Oh. Pleasure. No problem. I hope she's okay," I said.

Cynthia gave me a sad smile. "She won't remember any of this in the morning."

"She won't?" I asked.

Cynthia shook her head, looking solemn. "I don't think she has that long to go, either. We'll miss her when she's gone. She's been with us for a long time." And, with that, with those few words that held such gravitas and importance, she turned and walked away from us. I stood there and watched her go, then cast my eyes back to Petra's door. She was so alone, right now. Physically and emotionally. My heart was breaking for her; she seemed like the saddest person I'd ever met in my entire life.

"Come," Mike said softly. "It's been quite a night for all of us. Let's go home . . . *wife*." He gave me a small smile; I guess he was trying to lighten the mood somewhat. It worked, and I found myself smiling slightly back.

"Wife?" I started walking down the corridor with him. "Funny, I don't remember you ever proposing to me." I gave his shoulder a small nudge with mine and he nudged me right back. "Come to think of it, if my memory serves, I don't think we ever consummated our relationship, either, so it must be the immaculate conception."

"I'm not going to live that down, am I?"

"Probably not. But I do forgive you, though. Now that I see your excuse was real." I looked up at him and we shared a small, sad smile together. We walked out into the cold night again and climbed into the car.

"What happened to her?" I asked.

"She has Alzheimer's. She's stuck in a moment in time. It's like a daily loop," he said.

"What moment? Where are her son and husband?"

"Her husband died some years back. And, about forty years ago, their son got married and moved to the UK with his pregnant wife. She's never met her grandchildren."

"What?" I swung around in my seat and looked at him.

"I don't even think she speaks to her son anymore," Mike said thoughtfully.

"Why?"

"I don't know the full story, but I know he married someone that the family—mainly the father—disapproved of. He was disowned and moved away."

"And Petra also disapproved?" I asked. "Why?"

He shrugged. "I don't know all the details, only bits and pieces that the nurses from the home have told me. All I know is that there were cultural, religious differences. Bianca is Jewish, and Pierre's family are very observant Christians. Pierre chose to convert and he and Bianca wanted to raise their children as Jewish. This didn't go down well. His father disowned him."

"I can't believe Petra would have felt the same way. You saw her with me tonight, when she thought I was Bianca."

"Apparently her husband forbade her to speak to Pierre ever again."

"Why? I mean, that's just . . . crazy. It's her son. How could he do that?"

Mike turned and looked at me. "Families have beliefs and biases. They have fights and falling outs. I don't know all the circumstances, and maybe there were more factors. All I know is that it's heart-breaking, that's for sure." His voice became weak and small.

"Has anyone tried to do something to fix this?" I asked.

Mike shook his head. "I'm not sure."

"Someone has to do something about it," I said, getting worked up.

"What?" he asked.

"Can't we phone her son and tell him that she wants to see him? I mean, she clearly does. That's all she wants in the whole world."

Mike shook his head. "We can't do that. You can't get involved in family matters, as much as you want to."

"You've thought about doing it?" I asked.

He nodded. "About a hundred times, but . . ." He paused and looked at me earnestly. "Family matters are complicated, they're just . . . *complicated*. Take my family, for example. I thought we were normal, but, a year ago, I discovered things were a lot more complicated than they appeared to be."

"What do you mean?"

"My grandmother was also in love with someone she shouldn't have been in love with. Someone the family disapproved of."

"Really?" At that, I perked up. "Who was she in love with?"

"Again, I don't know the full story. I don't think anyone does, actually. All I know is that the relationship was very much frowned upon and she was forced to marry my grandfather, Ian. She wasn't free to love who she wanted to love." He sighed and looked out of the windshield. The streetlights illuminated the contours of his face and he looked . . . *beautiful*. "I think some of us take for granted that we can fall in love with and marry who we want. It certainly isn't like that for many of us."

I felt a tear come to my eye as I thought about it all. As I thought about the lonely woman who longed for her son. The son who lost his mother and the grandchildren that had never known their grandmother. I thought about Edith, longing for a man she couldn't have, and about him, thinking that she no longer loved him. I was overcome with this feeling of utter loss and my heart physically ached. And then guilt. Mike was opening up to me, and these were the things I wanted to hear, but this felt so one-sided. Like I was using him for information, like I was . . .

"My family is complicated, too," I blurted out, without really thinking.

He turned in his seat and looked at me.

"My father died before I was born. My mother was a wreck for a long time—she still is, in many ways. We're not close, at all," I continued.

Mike scanned my face again; he always seemed to look at me in a strange, specific way. As if he was trying to see me for who I was. He wasn't just looking at me, he was . . . well, it felt like he was . . . *seeing me*.

"Must have been hard growing up with a grieving mother?"

"I didn't grow up with her," I said sadly, sharing the most intimate part of my life. I never shared this with people. Mike was an exception. "I was looked after by relatives, mainly. A lot of them. But I never really felt welcome anywhere, you know? I was always an imposition—that's how it felt, anyway." A small tear escaped my eye and rolled down my cheek. I couldn't help it.

"Hey, hey . . ." Mike reached out and touched my cheek. He caught the tear on his fingertips and wiped it away. It felt so incredibly intimate that another tear immediately ran down my cheek. "Are you okay?" he asked, wiping the other tear away.

I shook my head, unable to speak. Everything was sort of crashing around me. Thoughts and emotions slammed into me like stormy waves against the rocks. It had also suddenly dawned on me, in that moment, just how huge and important this story was that I was trying to tell. This wasn't a story about two people who weren't allowed to be together and love freely. This was a story about everyone who's ever had that privilege taken away. A basic human right to love whomever you want to love—romantic, platonic or otherwise. Edith hadn't been allowed to love the person she wanted to love. Petra hadn't been able to love her son or her grandchildren in the way she should have, and then there was me. I hadn't been able to love my father, and, as for my mother, well, she and circumstances had made it impossible to love her the way a daughter wants to love her mother.

"Don't cry, Becca." Mike leaned in closer to me and placed his hands on the sides of my face.

"Sorry, I . . . just feel emotional." I pulled away quickly and wiped my face, embarrassed by this sudden show of emotion.

He smiled at me. Killer smile. Smile to end all smiles. Smile that held the power to melt Neptune, melt hearts, melt me . . .

"Becca, you are a strange one," he said.

"Strange?" I enquired.

He shook his head and continued to smile. "Fence jumping, bestseller writing, nesting-bird scaring, library breaking, graveyard stomping, head banging, wife acting, chaos causing, cat stealing, fake naming, cat maiming, wasabi eating—"

"Hang on, hang on!" I held my hand up and cut him off. "You can't label me with all those. There are some serious extenuating circumstances that led me to do all of those things," I said, in my defense.

His smile grew even more. "With-everything arguing—"

"That doesn't make sense," I cut him off again. "What you just said is all very grammatically incorrect, thus meaningless."

He laughed. It sounded amazing. Like my favorite song. The soundtrack I had been waiting to hear. He leaned closer to me and his sudden closeness was so palpable, so tangible, that all the muscles in my body contracted and suddenly I felt like I was sitting more upright than I had in a while. As if every part of my body was standing to attention, like those soldiers with the fluffy hats outside Buckingham Palace. And then his smile faltered, he hung his head and shook it.

"What just happened?" I asked.

"I've got a real problem on my hands, here." He kept shaking his head.

"What problem?"

He looked up, reached out and tucked a strand of hair behind my ear, like he had that night in the bar.

A long, loud breath escaped my lips. *Shit*, I hadn't meant for it to be that loud. "Wh . . . what problem?" I repeated, as his hand grazed the side of cheek, slowly, deliberately.

"It seems I'm really attracted to the criminal elements." He came closer to me, his lips almost touching mine.

"You . . . you said, if I came back to town, you would arrest me. Are you going to? Arrest me?" I asked, his lips brushing against mine.

"You've put me in a very tricky position, here, Becca." He ran his thumb over my bottom lip and I felt my whole body melting into the seat. "I should arrest you, but . . ." He trailed off.

"You can't?" I asked.

He shook his head and his eyes moved down to my lips. "What is it about you, Becca?"

I shrugged. "I don't know."

"Ever since you came to town, I haven't been able to stop thinking about you." He placed his other hand on my cheek, cradling my face between his big hands. I closed my eyes and drifted away a little, allowing myself to indulge in the warm feeling of his hands on my skin, the coolness of his breath as it danced across my face like a soft, gentle breeze of breeziness. So airy and breezy and wispy and . . . did I say *breeziness* . . . ?

CHAPTER 46

⌒

I was climbing on to his lap.

The breeze was gone now, and it was a hurricane of heat, and every single part of my body was burning as he ran his hands over it.

And we were kissing . . .

Or we weren't. I don't know. I couldn't tell. Because everything we were doing felt so natural and automatic, like breathing or the beating of your heart. It's something you cannot control, it just happens, even when you're asleep. And I was asleep. Awake, but enjoying the best dream of my life. Lost in a kind of waking dream where everything felt more alive and intense than it had ever felt.

Hands and mouths and bodies did their own thing, as if we had no control over them. They were moving to some soundtrack that I couldn't hear over the buzzing in my ears. I think I started unzipping his pants. I think he had his hands up my top, pulling at my bra, trying to get it off just as frantically as I was trying to get into his pants.

And then, as quickly as it had all started, it stopped. Our eyes connected and . . .

"No!" I looked at him and gasped.

"Shit!" he said, reading my mind.

"Condoms! Please tell me you have some this time?" I asked breathily.

"No, I don't, because I didn't think I would ever see you again. I wasn't really planning on sleeping with anyone else so soon."

I smiled at him. "I'm flattered." I slumped forward and rested my head on his shoulder.

"What's the time?" He pushed me a little and looked at the clock on the dashboard. "It's four a.m.!" he said, shocked. "Reddy's won't be open now."

"No." I slumped even more.

"What about the condoms you bought the other night?" he asked, perking up.

"Oh, so *now* you want those," I teased him. "I threw them in the dustbin."

"Which dustbin?" he asked.

"The one in the parking lot . . . *Wait!* You're not being serious?" I asked, appalled.

"Garbage collection happens on Monday, and wasn't it a sealed box?" he asked.

"What?" I gasped even more now. "I might really, really want to do this, but I don't think I am soooo desperate that I'm prepared to fish a box of condoms out of the garbage can, despite how good your hands feel on my, um . . . on my . . ." I exhaled sharply as his hands crept under my shirt again.

"On your?" he asked, teasing me with his thumb.

"Uh, my, uh . . ." His hands slipped under my bra and I winced as his hard, hot palms grazed against my nipples. I moaned loudly as he took them between his fingers and squeezed. I threw my head back, arching my body towards him. I started moving in his lap, grinding my hips in small circles. He was hard; I could feel it beneath me, so close, yet so far away. I gripped his shoulders as he brought his mouth down on one of my nipples and sucked, hard. His hands moved down and gripped my ass; he held me in place as he started a slow, steady thrust underneath me. The feeling was electric and every single one of my nerves was alive and awake and begging for more, more, mo—

"OKAY! Fuck it!" I climbed off him in one swift movement and jumped into the passenger seat, pulling my shirt back down. "Let's go get them. But, if there is a hole in the box, or a rat, or a dirty diaper, or anything like that even close to them, then that's it!" I laid down the law.

He turned the key in the ignition as quickly as possible and pulled off at speed. "Deal," he said, driving off in the direction of the parking lot.

* * *

"No, you can't stick your arm in," I said, looking down at the sealed box in the bin. To my surprise, it had landed perfectly on an old sheet of newspaper, totally separated from the crap below it, whatever that might be.

"It's almost on the top, though, and it's on paper."

"Still, I'm not letting you touch me after your arm has been in the dustbin," I said firmly.

At that, he laughed. "God, this is ridiculous, you know that." He looked at me and I smiled.

"I know. I know." I looked into the bin and my mind started racing for a solution. "If only we had a fishing rod with a hook on it, we could get the hook through the loop at the top and pull them out."

"Uh . . . I kind of do have a fishing rod," he responded, looking over at me.

"You do?"

"This is a coastal town. I fish."

I looked around; the streets were completely empty and we were in the shadows. But surely we couldn't get a fishing rod out of a car to fish a box of condoms out of the dustbin? Were we that desperate for sex? Mike was standing there with folded arms, muscles all bulging and busting, chest all broad and hard, eyes all dazzling green and lips all red from kissing, hair all ruffled from me running my hands through it and . . . and . . .

"Oh God." I threw myself at him and kissed him again. He grabbed me around the waist and pulled me closer, held my ass in place and moved me over him. I pulled away, trying to catch my breath and my senses. But both were gone. I stuck my hand into the dustbin and grabbed the box!

CHAPTER 47

*B*ack in the car.

Decided couldn't drive home.

Have to have each other, now!

Right now!

Right here!

In car! (Thanks, tinted windows!)

Parked in secretive make-out spot.

Hands again.

Lips, tongues, clothes coming off.

Box of condoms ripped open. (Hands quickly disinfected!)

Pulling at the wrapper with my teeth . . . Pulling at the wrapper with my teeth . . . Pulling at the wrapper with my teeeetthhh . . .

"Shit, I can't open this thing." I passed the condom to him and he tried to rip it with his teeth, too, unsuccessfully.

"It's not opening!" He pulled it as hard as he could; the plastic inlay only stretched and nothing ripped off. "Bloody hell." He reached into his cubby hole and . . .

"Whoa!" I held my hands up as he produced a pocket knife.

He shrugged and stabbed the condom packet. "I feel like Mac-Gyver," he said, laughing.

"Don't put a hole in it; we wouldn't want a real Jolene." I smiled at him and, just then, as the condom was being taken out the packet, as it was being lowered and was just about to be slipped on . . . *his phone rang!*

"Don't answer it, don't answer it," I whimpered.

He looked at his vibrating phone on the passenger seat. "I have to. Could be work."

"The only criminal in town is in this car and she wants to have sex with you . . . She really, *really* . . ." I took the condom from him and slipped it between us, seeking him out. I found him and started rolling it down over him . . .

"Oh God," he moaned, looking at me. He looked at the phone, then at me, then at the phone again (repeat a few times). "Shit! Hold that thought." He put his hand over mine, stopping me mid-roll, and reached for the phone. He took a deep breath before answering it.

"Hello, it's Mike—"

He hadn't even finished speaking when I heard the voice on the other end. It sounded loud and angry. I tried to listen, but couldn't hear the actual words, just the muffled screech of them.

"Uh-huh." He nodded as he listened. "Okay. I see." He looked at me and widened his eyes. "I agree. Sounds totally suspicious." He listened some more. "Of course, I'll take a look." He nodded and gave me an apologetic look. "That definitely sounds like something that should be checked out."

I climbed off his lap and shimmied over to the passenger seat again. This was starting to feel very familiar, our habit of *almost-sex*.

"Right. Okay. Well, don't approach the car, then. Keep your distance," he said into the phone. "Can you tell me where it is and I'll go there as soon as I can?" He listened for a second and suddenly the atmosphere in the car changed. Mike ducked behind the dashboard and pulled me down with him.

"What's happening?" I mouthed.

He quickly put his finger to his lips to silence me. He looked a little panicked and I could see he was trying to zip up his pants and put *himself* away. "I think the best thing for you to do is to drive away. No need to watch them anymore; I'll be there and I'll handle it. Go home; it's late." He peeped over the dashboard and then his head shot back down.

"What. Is. Going. On?" I mouthed, silently this time.

He put his hand over the receiver, pushed it into his chest and whispered across to me. "A resident just phoned in about some suspicious behavior. A white car parked secretively! Movement inside it!"

I tried to stifle a giggle.

"It's not funny!" he mouthed. He raised the phone back to his ear and spoke into it again. "Give me five minutes and I'll be—" The voice on the other end interrupted him again and this time the color drained from his face. "NO! No, I do not think it's a good idea that you approach the car, AT ALL!"

My eyes widened as I watched him.

"Get back into your car; there could be people inside . . . uh . . . They could be, uh, criminals, you never know . . ." He was flapping now. Words tumbled out of his mouth frantically. He listened again. "WHAT? You're already approaching the car?!" He looked at me in panic, and also as if he was asking me what to do. *Why? Because he thought I was a criminal mastermind?*

"Drive away!" I mouthed, and pointed frantically at the car keys hanging from the ignition.

Mike nodded at me and peeped over the dashboard. I did, too, and there he was—the little, inquisitive man, coming towards us with a torch. I reached out and turned the key in the ignition. The car sprung to life.

I heard the man shout down the phone, "Someone has started the car!" He yelled so loudly, I heard him both through the phone and from outside the car.

"Okay, now, listen to me," Mike said in a calm voice. "Get back into your car. I'm on my way." It seemed like the man agreed, because Mike's shoulders slumped in relief. "Okay, great. I'll be there soon," he said, and then popped his head back over the dashboard. He looked across at me and mouthed the words, "Seat belt."

I put it on quickly, as Mike pulled off, wheels skidding slightly.

"That's great news," he said into the phone. "I'm glad they've gone. Uh . . . you didn't get their license plate, did you?" he asked, another hint of panic in his voice. "Oh, darn. Well, that's too bad. Goodnight, Bruce," he said, and finally hung up.

He looked over at me and shook his head as we drove off down the road.

CHAPTER 48

$\mathcal{W}$e'd arrived at the house and pulled into my side of the driveway. Mike turned the car off and we sat in silence again for a while.

"I'm not a superstitious man, and don't believe in the power of crystals and vibrations and karma, but, if I was, I would say that someone out there is really trying to stop us from having sex," he joked.

I laughed. "You know, I once bought a coffee table made of rose quartz because I read that it would bring peaceful vibes into my home."

"Did it?" He turned in his seat and looked at me.

I smiled at him. "Do I look like the kind of person who's imbued with spiritual peace?"

He laughed. "No."

We smiled at each other, stupidly—the kind of smile you can't help.

"You know what you are, Becca?"

"No."

"A whirlwind of chaos. Everywhere you go, you bring chaos. And anyone who gets too close gets swept up in it." He smiled, and I could tell he meant it in an endearing way, otherwise I might have been seriously offended, even if there was a great deal of truth in it.

We continued our smiles. The sexual mood was long gone, and I was starting to feel exhausted from my night of no sleep. I looked over at the clock on his dashboard—it was five a.m. already. "Do you think it's safe for me to go to sleep yet?"

"I'm not a doctor, but I think this constitutes a night of no sleep."

"I have exactly four hours to sleep, then," I said.

"Why? What chaos do you have planned for nine o'clock?" he asked.

"Nothing. I just can't sleep in later than nine. If I do, I always wake up feeling strange and groggy."

"Well, I guess this is goodnight, then?" he asked, looking torn.

"I guess it is."

"Thanks for helping me with Petra," he added.

"Pleasure. I wish I could do more; she seems so sad." I would never forget that look she had given me as she climbed into her small, single bed.

"I'm not sure much will help, other than seeing her son," he mumbled. "And her grandchildren."

I looked out the car window towards the house. "It really is a beautiful home."

"We're really lucky to have it. It's steeped in so much history and so many memories, both good and bad."

At that, my stomach contorted into a knot. A cloud of guilt, peppered with a good deal of shame, descended. *If he knew what I was doing . . . what story I was* really *researching . . . what would he do?* I suddenly felt like I needed to be away from him, before I burst into tears and blurted it all out.

"I better go." I reached for the door handle and, before he could say anything, I'd climbed out of the car.

"Sure." I could hear the surprise in his voice. "Thanks again," he called after me, as I speed-walked towards the house and didn't look back.

CHAPTER 49

I couldn't sleep. Ten minutes of lying in my bed, staring at the ceiling, was proof of that. I felt unsettled, for so many reasons. At least I knew what they were, though:

1. I was so attracted to Mike. More than attracted. There was something about him. Since the moment I'd laid eyes on him, it had been as if my body knew something about him that my heart and mind wasn't quite aware of yet.
2. I felt guilty about lying to him.
3. I felt desperate to write this book.

The last two were in direct conflict with each other, and, together, were in even greater conflict with the first.

I was just about to get out of bed when a knock on the door disturbed me.

"Who is it?" I called out. There was a small pause.

"Me," the voice returned.

I reached for the door handle, but stopped myself before opening it. I took a deep breath, hoping that all the unsettledness wouldn't show on my face. I twisted the door handle and swung open the door. There he was.

We looked at each other for a moment, zoning in on each other's eyes, and suddenly my heart was beating in my throat again, a now familiar feeling that I'd only ever experienced around him. His eyes drifted down to my mouth, and then to my neck, as if he could see my heart beating in it, but, when they kept on drifting, it dawned on me where they were going. I wasn't wearing a bra, and the thin, white T-shirt I *was* wearing was probably accentuating that fact.

He took a step forward, straight into my room. He kicked the door shut with his foot and I knew exactly what was going to happen. *The inevitable.* Since the moment we'd first seen each other, this destiny seemed to have been etched in some stone somewhere. A cosmic rock where our future was worked out and written down for us. He took my face between his hands and kissed me.

He pressed his body into mine and I could feel he was hard; I wanted to touch him, *again.* I slipped my hand down his pants and wrapped my fingers around him. His whole body tensed and he reached out and gripped my shoulders. I watched his face as his eyes closed and he threw his head back, with a bang, against the wooden paneling on the wall. I kept going, his breathing becoming faster and faster. He bit down on his bottom lip and then, suddenly, his eyes flipped open. He shook his head violently as he reached down and pulled my hand away.

"Stop," he whispered. "You need to stop."

I smiled at him and nodded.

"Fuck, Becca, do you know how crazy you make me feel?" Without any warning, he reached between my legs and pushed them open. He pulled me in for another kiss, walking me backwards across the room while his hands slid over me. It was hard to walk like that, hard to feel my legs as his kiss deepened and his fingers slipped into my panties.

"Crazy good, or crazy bad?" I whimpered, stupidly.

"Now, that is the question, isn't it?" He planted hot, wet kisses down my neck and then all the way up to my ear.

"So what's the answer?" I threw my head back, feeling dizzy as his hand moved under my T-shirt and his palm covered my breast. It was slightly cold against my warm skin and I moaned loudly.

"I'm still trying to work that out," he said, still walking me across the room.

"Where are you taking me?" I moaned again as his fingers traced circles around my breast.

He stopped what he was doing and then looked at me seriously. "Where do you want me to take you?" he asked, a wicked, naughty, dirty smile on his face.

I smiled back at him and then looked around the room. "I guess the bed is usually the preferred choice."

His smile grew. "Bed it is." He continued to push me towards it.

"But that doesn't mean it should be *our* preferred choice." I stopped him.

"Really?" His pupils were dilated, eating up the green part, but, in the middle of the black, there seemed to be a spark. A flame. A small, bright diamond shining back at me.

In that moment, I took charge. I put my hands on his chest and started walking *him* backwards. I knew exactly where I wanted him. The back of his knees hit the chair and he stopped.

"Sit," I whispered, firmly.

"You are trouble, Becca. You know that, right?"

I nodded and climbed on to his lap, straddling him. I sat straight up and looked down at him as I pulled my shirt off and tossed it to the floor. I was completely exposed and his eyes drifted down to where I wanted them to go. He pulled me closer and buried his head between my breasts, trailing his tongue over them and then up my neck. I arched my back as he gripped my hips and slid me across his lap.

Things became frenzied, after that. Nothing followed in any logical, rational order, as we pulled at each other's clothes, hair, dug our fingers into flesh and kissed each other, completely missing mouths as it all built to the moment where, finally, we were both completely naked.

"Condom," I managed to whisper in a tiny, lucid moment.

He gave a small chuckle and looked into my eyes. "This time, I've got them."

CHAPTER 50

⌒

I had the strangest dream in the half an hour of sleep I'd gotten. Well, I wasn't sure if it had been a dream or not. It must have
been, though, because these kinds of things don't really happen in
real life, do they?

That moment when someone is kissing you softly and slowly,
when their fingers are gently tracing the length of your spine, when
they're inside you and your bodies are moving as one. Slow and purposeful. Each movement in perfect unison. Your breathing in perfect
harmony, the small whimpers and moans escape your mouth at the
same time, both moving slowly and steadily towards no finishing line
at all, because it's all about the journey. It's all about what is happening now, about the way he's staring into your eyes, looking deep
inside you, and, suddenly, without any kind of explanation that
makes any sense whatsoever, you feel completely and utterly in love
with the person who's telling you how beautiful you are.

Love at first sight?

Does it even exist? And, if it does, can it possibly be real? How
can you feel something so strong for someone who you just don't
know? I knew next to nothing about the man I was making love to,
in the true sense of the word. Not sex. Not fucking. Making love in
that slow, intense way, when stars and fate and everything align. As
if your bodies had been designed to do this from the start and had
been going through life looking for each other, the last puzzle piece
that slots in perfectly and completes the picture.

It went on for ages, like that. Me on his lap, him exploring every inch of my body with his eyes and lips and hands, making me feel things that I'd never felt before for any human being. Making my body feel things that it had never felt before. With words being communicated silently. And, when it was over, I collapsed on to his chest and he wrapped his arms around me and held me there, our sweaty bodies pressed together. I closed my eyes and breathed him in; the smell of him was intoxicating. And then, later, when he picked me up in his arms, walked me over to the bed and tucked me in, I was even more intoxicated by him. He climbed in next to me, wrapped his arms around me and pulled me close, as if this was something we did all the time. As if it was natural, as if this was the way it was meant to be and was how we'd done it a million times before. I fell asleep like that, but only for a short while, because something woke me up from my dream and sent me straight into a nightmare.

I opened my eyes. He was standing at the window with his back to me, completely naked. I appreciated the dimples at the bottom of his back for a few seconds before I felt the atmosphere in the room. Before I tasted it. It came at me like cool steel. It was like biting down on a piece of tinfoil, the smell of burnt hair and the iciness of a winter's morning, all at once.

"Mike?" I whispered softly, my mouth dry. My heart was pounding.

But he didn't turn around.

I climbed out of bed and stood on the floor, feet planted firmly, because my legs felt as if they were swaying.

"Mike?" I said again.

This time, he turned around. Slowly. He was holding something in his hands and I immediately looked down. In one hand, the burnt diary; in the other, the letters.

"I . . . I can explain," I said.

"Really?" he asked, looking like he'd already made his mind up about me.

"It's not what it looks like . . . Uh, well, it is, but it's not . . . uh,"

I stumbled and stuttered. I had no idea what to say. There was not really anything that could explain or justify this.

"I would recognize this writing anywhere." He held the diary up and my heart sank. "Question is, what are you doing with it and where did you—?" And then he stopped talking, mid-sentence. He nodded his head and smiled to himself. "I see. I get it now. I should have seen this, but I guess I didn't, or didn't want to, or . . ."

"Get what?" I asked.

"Your research. Your new book. This has something to do with it, doesn't it?" He waved the letters and the diary in the air now. "You're not writing a private investigator book, set in some random small town, are you?"

I shook my head. "No, but—"

"Oh my God!" He cut me off with a loud gasp. "You're research-ing my family! What about me? Is that why you booked into this place? Because you knew I was here?"

"I . . . I—" I tried to speak, but he cut me off again.

"And the library, this makes sense now, of course you were snoop-ing around. You looked guilty when I found you." He spoke rapidly, as if he was following a trail of bread crumbs, clues that his brain was throwing at him in logical succession. "What were you looking for in the library? Why do you have these letters and this diary? Where did you get them? Did you steal them? Did you steal them from some-one in the eco estate? Is that why you broke in?"

"Uh . . ." My head was spinning. So, so many questions. No easy answers for any of them. So, I said the first thing that popped into my head: "I almost died in an elevator, a few days ago."

He blinked at me several times. "Sorry, what? What does that have to do with anything?"

"It has everything to do with this. As crazy as it sounds, that ele-vator has led me here—to this town, to the diary. To you. If I had gotten into a different elevator, a minute later, I wouldn't be here."

He shook his head rapidly and blinked at me.

"I know, it's not making sense. It barely makes sense to me."

"Try to make it make sense, please. I really want to understand," he said.

"A few days ago, I got into this elevator in my building. I had my favorite bag with me—this beautiful old vintage bag I found in a charity store in Johannesburg. The lift plummeted and I grabbed on to it, but it ripped, and I found those letters inside this secret compartment in the bag. It looked like they had been sewn into it."

"Who wrote them?" he asked, looking down at his hands.

I shook my head. "I don't know yet, but they were written to your grandmother."

He looked down at the diary. "And this is her diary."

I nodded. Guilty. Red handed. "I found it here, under the floorboards, behind this bed."

He shook his head as if none of it was making any sense. And, to be honest, the more I heard it out loud, the more it seemed so jumbled. So improbable. "How did you know it was here?" he asked.

"I didn't. I found it by accident."

"Bullshit!" he spat. He looked angry with me now, and my pulse raced. "Stop lying. You've been caught. For once, tell the fucking truth."

"What?" I was so shocked by his tone and the language he was using with me now. How had we gone from last night, on the chair, to *this*?

"Come on, Becca, you've been lying to me since you got here, since the moment I found you climbing over the fence. Do you deny that?" he asked.

I looked at him. Emotion welled up inside me—mouth dry, tongue sticking to the top of my palate. I bit my lip to stop the tears. "No," I said quietly. "I don't deny it. I've been lying to you."

"Thank you for finally admitting to that." He paused for a while before talking again. "So you've been investigating my family since you arrived here, behind my back?"

I nodded. "I didn't know it was your family until I saw you here."

He turned around and looked out the window for a moment. "You know what's worse than sneaking around behind my back? What's worse is that you let me offer to help you with your research. I was offering to help you secretly investigate my family. Do you know how twisted that is?" he asked, and my heart plummeted. He was right. Of course, he was right about everything. And there was no excuse in the world that would make this okay.

He turned around and looked at me with sad, disappointed eyes. "Were you only getting close to me because you were researching me, or—"

"NO!" I cut him off quickly. "No. I'm getting close to you because I . . . I like you. I . . ."

"That's a bit hard to believe." His voice was soft and sad.

Deep remorse and regret washed over me. "I'm telling the truth. I didn't know who you were when I met you. I didn't know you lived here when I checked in. I didn't know the diary was here."

He sighed loudly and then shrugged. He clearly didn't believe a word I was saying. And, suddenly, I became uncertain too. Suddenly, I wasn't so sure if I was telling the truth either. I mean, what are the chances of finding the diary of someone you're researching, in their house, because you accidentally booked into it? The chances are impossible. They are needles in infinite galaxies. And yet, here I was, finding them.

I started to feel panicky. I started to feel like I wasn't there anymore, like I was stepping backwards into myself and the world in front of me was disappearing and dissolving. *Was I lying?* Had I known the dairy was here? Had I known he lived here? I felt like I couldn't trust my mind anymore. It all seemed so strange and illogical. I took a step back and sat down on the edge of the bed again. My thoughts were spinning so fast, the facts and events twisting and turning in my mind, and, before I lost them forever to this strange confusion, I opened my mouth to speak . . .

"I found those letters in my handbag. The one that was ripped in the lift. I was on the way to a meeting with my agent—who, by the way, was furious with me and has been threatening to fire me. My new book is due in three weeks and I haven't written a word and people are waiting for it. *Do you know what kind of pressure that is?* And they've paid me a lot of money for the book and I've bloody spent it all because I'm bad with money. I buy things stupidly that I don't need, I buy things to make me feel better about myself, or to show people I'm doing well, or . . . I don't know. So, when my agent asked me if I had written anything, I don't know what came over me, but I said yes, and I read her one of these letters. And it was so beautiful and moving that everyone cried. And then I told her I was writing a book about two young people in love, telling the story through a series of their love letters. But I didn't have the other letters and I couldn't just make them up. I needed some context, some setting to get a sense of the characters. So I googled, and I realized that Willow Bay was where the letters had been written. And I came here, and—by chance, by accident, by fate, by I don't know—I booked into this place and I found that diary under that floorboard. And that is the truth! That is the truth!" I finished and there was a deafening silence that I waited for him to fill. But, when he finally did, I hated myself a little more.

"Character?" he asked. "You called my grandmother a *character*," he repeated slowly. "But she's not. She's a real person, who I loved, and who loved me, and who died."

A tear slipped down my cheek. "I know. I'm sorry," I whimpered, softly.

He shook his head. "I still don't get this. Did you write your first book yourself?"

"Yes." I nodded.

"But you're stealing someone else's story for your second book?"

More tears. "Yes." The weight of the shame and guilt were almost too much for my shoulders to hold up, and it was crushing down on my skeleton.

"But your first book was so good—why would you do this?"

"Because I'm stuck. I feel paralyzed with fear. How am I supposed to write something as good again? What if I can't? What if my first book was an accident? What if I'm not good at this? What if I fail? What if I really am who they say I am? A nobody."

"Who says you're a nobody?" he asked.

"Everyone. Me. My mom must have thought that or she wouldn't have palmed me off to everyone else. My ex. My ex's partner. I'm an unremarkable someone with the wrong name. Writing a book is the only thing I've ever done that has meant anything. And I am going to lose it all, and then who am I? Who am I?" I felt like I was struggling to breathe as I said it. I hadn't actually said anything so personal out loud before. I'd thought it a million times, but I'd never uttered the words, and I was even more terrified hearing them out loud than thinking them in my head, late at night. I gripped my sides, because my ribcage felt like it was closing in on me.

"Becca, breathe," I heard him say. His tone had changed a little, now.

I nodded and tried to inhale.

"Breathe," he said again, as I managed to get some air into my lungs.

I focused on my breathing for a while and, finally, it started to feel possible again. I didn't look up at Mike—I couldn't—but, out of the corner of my eye, I saw him pull his clothes on. The act seemed so final. A full stop to something. I heard him sigh and then sit in the chair—the one that we'd made love in last night.

"Your self-worth shouldn't be wrapped up in something like that. It's not healthy," he mumbled.

"Easy for you to say," I said back quickly. "Your thoughts about me changed when you realized who I was and what I'd done. We probably wouldn't be here if you hadn't been a fan of my book and a fan of Becca Thorne—"

"That's insulting!" He cut me off angrily. "I actually quite like

Pebecca-with-the-wrong-name, who likes hanging out in cemeteries. The person who doesn't wear intelligent-looking glasses and pretends to be something she clearly isn't. I quite like the person who I met at the bar, who opened up to me, the person tonight, who was kind and gentle and shared personal stories with me, and shared . . . *everything*."

"Oh," I said, quite taken aback by his statement.

Silence engulfed the room. This time, I could almost imagine a melancholic tune playing. A sad solo violin, the bow dragging slowly against the strings, causing that agonizing, heart-piercing sound that reverberated through my entire being. The sound had such a finality to it, as if it were the very last note played by the orchestra before the curtain came crashing down.

"Where are the letters from my grandmother to whoever this is?" Mike said, after the silence. His tone was much calmer than before. I almost wished he was still angry with me, because this tone made me feel like he had decided on something and he'd resigned himself to it.

"I don't have them," I murmured.

"But you have her diary?"

"Yes."

He stood up again and walked over to me. I felt the bed dip next to me as he lowered himself on to it. Another silence stretched on between us. It was the silence that two strangers would share. This broke my heart, because we weren't strangers, not after what had happened between us last night. We'd been so close, connected, but I guess we weren't like that anymore. And it was my fault. I'd messed everything up. I was a mess. I waited for him to speak, trying to imagine what he was going to say, or what he was going to ask me, but I wasn't expecting what came next, even though I probably should have been.

"I'm going to have to ask you to leave, now," he said.

I started to nod my head. I was trying to hold back my tears, but it wasn't working. "I'll start packing." I stood up and rushed over to my suitcase.

"I don't just mean leave *here*," he qualified. "I mean, I'm going to have to ask you to leave this town and to never come back again."

"And . . . what about us?" I stuttered, heart shattering into small shards, piercing my lungs, making it hard to breathe.

"What about us?" he asked. "There doesn't get to be an *us* when it's based on lies and deceit, like this."

"But last night was—"

"It was." He cut me off again. "But, let's face it, it wasn't really real, now, was it?"

"It was real for me," I said.

"Yeah, I sort of thought that, too, until I woke up this morning and realized that everything about you is a lie."

I inhaled sharply. Yes, that was the sound of my heart breaking.

CHAPTER 51

One hour gone, four and a half to go. I was in my car again, driving back to Johannesburg. Mike had escorted me to the town limits once more, and, this time, there had been no kiss goodbye, no lingering look, no *I wish we'd met under different circumstances*. I was sure he wished he'd never actually met me. Truthfully, I wish I'd never met me. The new me. This me that lied and manipulated and was devious and deceitful. But that still didn't change the fact that my heart was breaking, right now. It had broken before, but not like this. This felt nothing like what Blade Sanders had done to me.

Blade was my famous and charismatic editor and ex-boss—even his name was charismatic—the man I'd admired more than I can say. He was a journalist supreme, going undercover in crime rings and cracking open some of the country's biggest stories. It all added to the legend and mystique of the man who had given me my dream job, plastered me with praise and compliments and poems, and then stolen my young, naïve heart.

Let's keep it a secret at work, he'd said. *Wouldn't want anyone here to think I favor you*, he'd said. The secretiveness had made it that much more thrilling. Those late-night moments in printing rooms. Stolen kisses in the elevator, the basement, on his desk, under it, in the locked boardroom. Late-night calls, sexting at our desks . . . It was all so thrilling for my younger self. I had been so naïve.

But all the secrecy had had nothing to do with our work situation, and everything to do with the fact that he had a live-in girlfriend.

How had I not known, when apparently it was common knowledge? She was the editor of one of South Africa's bestselling women's magazines.

It's over between us.

We don't even sleep in the same bed.

We haven't had sex in years.

The lines that he'd kept feeding me had kept me hanging on for so long. Looking back now, I can't believe I bought it all and allowed myself to become the mistress in a bad movie for another year. In my defense, I was a star-struck twenty-five-year-old. At that age, you're still just teetering on the precipice of true adulthood, and any shove in any direction can either set you back or propel you forward. Well, I was pushed back—especially on the Monday morning he'd come to work engaged to be married. He'd announced it nonchalantly in our regular Monday-morning meeting . . .

Got engaged.

How? someone asked.

Took her to her favorite restaurant. Put the ring in the bottom of the champagne glass.

What does the ring look like?

Very simple and elegant. Princess cut. One and a half carats.

Did she cry?

She did. She did.

It was as if the whole world stood still in that moment. The board-room table that I'd been resting my elbows on vanished and I fell through it, like a ghost moving through a wall. I felt like all the blood had drained out of me, leaving me cold and empty, and the coffee cup fell from my hand. The hot, black liquid spread fast over the polished table and dripped off the edge, on to the carpet. I still remember that sound, that frantic *drip, drip, drip, drip*. At the time, it was the loudest sound I'd ever heard.

I'd lost it—broken down in front of everyone in the room. Tears and snot and trying to gulp in air between sobs. Thinking back on that moment now, I cringe at the sheer embarrassment of it all. He'd pulled me out of the room, dragged me into his office, slammed the door and we'd gotten into a screaming match. Everyone heard, and when I walked out of his office, five minutes later, broken, bruised and rejected (*didn't I know I was only a bit of fun?*), I had to do this walk of shame across the newsroom floor. Later that day, I'd gotten it into my head that I needed to call *her*. She needed to know. One woman to another, I needed to tell her, to save her from the biggest mistake she would ever make: marrying him. I wish I'd had some-one to sense-check that thought, though. If I'd had a good friend or a close family member to turn to, maybe they would have saved me from that moment. Because it turned out to be a big mistake.

Of course I know. Just like I known about all the others, she'd said.

What others? God, I had been so stupid.

She'd laughed. *Did you think you were the only one he was fucking? Do you think you mean anything to him? Look at you. You're just a jun-ior writer who is fucking her boss. How pathetic can you be? You'll never get anywhere, after this. Your career is doomed. No one likes the girl that fucks her boss.*

It was true, what she said. No one likes that girl, especially the boss she'd been fucking. He tried to get me to leave. Said it was awk-ward, now, in the office. He even offered me a retrenchment package, but I refused to go. I had something to prove, now. To her, to him, to all my colleagues who now looked at me like I was just sleeping my way to the top—as if I was a talentless writer and this was the only way I would make it. My refusal to leave was what ultimately led to my downfall. The big, public downfall. The one where I wrote that big, political story and "misquoted" our finance minister.

Mr. Mcube said that budget cunts were coming.

It had been printed like that and you can imagine what happened next. Think funny Facebook memes, think a lawsuit, think the whole country laughing at that unintentional joke. Thing is, my copy hadn't said that when I handed *him* the article to go to print. I had written "cuts"—let's be clear about that, there was no "n" in the version I submitted. See what a problem just one wrong letter can cause?

He'd deliberately changed it so he had a reason to fire me and then publicly humiliate me and kill all my future prospects as a journalist. He'd take some slack, too, as the editor, but he'd managed to emerge on the other side with his reputation fairly intact—his biggest mistake was trusting a *too young, too overzealous journalist*.

My stomach twisted at the memory, but I continued to go down the dark rabbit hole of my thoughts. In fact, I was so far down the rabbit hole, I was about to drink the potion to make me fit through the door, when . . .

I heard the siren. It must have been going for ages, because I'd been vaguely aware of some red and blue lights.

"Fuck! What now?" I pulled over at the side of the road. I was sure I hadn't been speeding, but, then again, I had been so deep in thought that I might have been, and this car was naturally fast—you had to really concentrate to keep it moving slowly . . . God, why did I buy it?

The police car stopped behind me and I started scrambling for my license. I swung around as I felt the shadow of the man beside my car. I opened my window and launched into it.

"Hi, officer. I hope I wasn't speeding." The sun was behind him and I shielded my eyes so I could see his face, but, when I did, my jaw fell open.

CHAPTER 52

"Mike, why are you . . . ? What have I . . . ?" I asked.

He took his sunglasses off and ran his hand through his hair. He looked pained. He leaned one arm on my car and suddenly I heard him tap his fingers against the roof, like some frantic beat.

I waited for him to speak, but the silence and the tapping continued.

"I read some of the letters and the diary," he finally said. "And, the thing is . . ." His voice trailed off and he didn't speak again.

"Thing is?" I asked, after what felt like a torturous wait.

"I was with my grandmother when she died." He stopped tapping his fingers; the sudden silence acted like an exclamation mark to those words. "I was holding her hand when she passed."

"I . . . I'm so sorry. I didn't know that," I replied. I could see the pain etched into his face as he stared off past me and the car, as if he was looking down a dark tunnel, trying to see what was at the end of it.

"I'm not saying it because I want you to feel sorry for me; in fact, it was probably one of the most special moments of my life. To be with someone, like that, when they are at their most vulnerable and . . ." He paused and swallowed, as if the words were sticking in his throat. "It was a privilege to be there at the end with someone I loved."

"Of course it was," I whispered, trying to hold back my tears.

"She told me something, though." He finally tilted his head down

and looked at me. Our eyes met with the intensity of a thousand galloping horses. Hooves hitting the ground hard, kicking up dust.
Thunderous. Painful.

"What did she tell you?" I asked, unable to look away from him.

He tapped the roof again. "There had always been these whispered
stories when I was growing up. I mean, I knew snippets. I knew she
hadn't loved my grandfather when she'd married him, that it had
almost been this arranged marriage. I'd always gotten the feeling that
there was more to the story, but no one spoke about it. It was as if no
one was allowed to speak of it. Our family had a secret, I just didn't
know what it was . . . until I read those letters and her diary." There
was a long pause again, and I waited for him to say what he needed to
say. "She loved someone once, someone she wasn't allowed to love."

"She did." I nodded.

Then he looked away again. "You know what she said to me, as
she was holding my hand and taking her last breath?"

"No." I shook my head, tears starting to form in my eyes as I pic-
tured the scene he was describing.

"She told me that she was going to die with only one regret. And
that regret was that she had never spoken her truth and told her
story. She'd kept it locked up inside and held on to it, a secret, for so
many years. At the time, I didn't really know what she was referring
to, but, now, I guess I do." His voice was overflowing with emotion.
He was struggling to get the words out and I was struggling to keep
the tears in. "She told me . . ." He paused. I actually heard the breath
and the words sticking in the back of his throat. "She told me to
always follow my heart. To love who I love without fear of judgement, and to never keep it a secret. To scream my love from the
rooftops and let the world know, because she hadn't let anyone know."

The tears could not be held back anymore and they trickled down
my cheeks. He started walking away from the car, and I watched as
he stood in the middle of the empty road and looked up at the sky.
He put his hands on his hips and stared, as if he was trying to find

some answer that would come down to him from the clouds. And then he started walking back towards the car.

"What do you need to tell this story?" he asked.

"What do you mean?"

"You obviously need something, or you wouldn't have been running around stealing Persian cats and breaking into secure estates. Just what is it that you are actually looking for? No more lies. Tell me the truth."

"I'm looking for clues," I said. "Things to give me more insight into what they were both like. I wanted to see the places in the letters. I wanted to see the engraving under the willow tree, the room under the stage. I wanted to see all of that so I could get a better sense of them. I was also trying to figure out how their story ends, because it seems to end so abruptly in the letters, but there's got to be more to it. It can't just end like that."

"She gets married to someone else," he said. "That's how it ends."

I shook my head. "You've read those letters—their story could not have ended there. It just couldn't have."

"So you think there's more?"

"I do. And I also think there's another stash of letters somewhere."

"Inside her favorite book?" He raised his eyebrow at me.

"Yes." I reached up and instinctively touched the scar on my forehead.

"So, basically, Becca, you came here with the express purpose of taking someone else's story and making it your own," he said.

I nodded. So ashamed. "Yes," I admitted.

He tapped on the roof of the car again. "Are you calling this a work of fiction?" he asked.

"Yes." More shame.

"Could you say it was based on a true story? Could you say that, in your book?"

"Yes. I could. I don't see why not."

"So, you could put her story out there in the world, like she wanted it to be?" he asked.

"Well, it would be a creative interpretation of it, since I don't have her letters."

"So you would be filling in the blanks?"

"Yes. But as accurately as I can. Which is why I have been traipsing around your town."

He looked down at me and nodded. There was another long pause. It looked like he was holding his breath. I held mine, too.

"I think she would want this story out in the world," he said.

I straightened up in my seat. "What . . . ? What are you saying?"

"She couldn't tell it when she was alive, but you can tell it now."

"You want me to keep writing it?" This was the last thing I'd expected to hear.

"But if we do this—*if* we do this—there are going to be some rules," he said.

"Sure. Whatever. Yes, I agree," I gushed.

"If you come back to Willow Bay with me, consider yourself in my legal custody."

"Huh?" I looked at him and blinked a few times.

"If you come back with me, if I let you back into my town, into my house, consider yourself under arrest. You're not to go anywhere or do anything without me. You're not to leave my side. And, when this is over, when you have it all, I still want you to go."

I started to nod. "Yes. Sure. Whatever you say," I agreed.

"And I want to be very clear, here: I'm not doing this for you; I'm doing this for her. She never got to tell her story and it was her one regret. This is for her. That's it! Nothing more."

I nodded again, even though my heart felt like it was being ripped out by claws. "I understand," I whispered.

"Are you sure? Because I don't know if you do understand. Last time I thought you understood, you turned your car around and came straight back into town, like a hurricane."

"This time, I understand. I get it. I won't do anything without your permission. I won't do anything else to cause trouble."

He huffed loudly and then put his head in his hand. "This is probably a monumentally bad idea. I've never met someone who causes so much trouble and chaos wherever she goes. And now I'm bringing you back. I must be mad."

"I'm sorry," I mumbled.

"Sorry for what?" he asked.

"Everything," I said quickly, meaning it completely.

He tapped the roof of my car again—harder, this time. "And this thing between us . . ." He cleared his throat. "This thing . . . is not a thing anymore. You understand that too, right?"

Jesus. Final dagger through once-beating heart. "I understand."

"Good." And, with that, he walked back to his car and climbed in.

I started my engine and waited for him to pull off. He did, and indicated that I follow. I made a U-turn on the long country road and headed straight back to town for the second time. This time, though, I had a police escort, and I was to consider myself in his custody.

CHAPTER 53

"*W*ow," Ash said, looking down at the letters and wiping the tears away that were running down her face.

"Wow," Emelia, who had just been introduced to me as Ash's girlfriend, also said. We were all sitting around the table in the kitchen, drinking cups of warm tea and eating biscuits.

Ash looked up at me, wide-eyed, and I wondered if she was going to be as angry with me as her brother was. "Wow," she simply said again.

"They're amazing letters," Mike added.

"It's not just the letters, though," Ash said, and Emelia nodded.

"It's not?" I asked.

"This whole story!" She threw her arms in the air. "What . . . *WHAT* are the chances? That you, living over five hours away, in the city, find a bag at a shop, get stuck in a lift, find these letters, find this town, come here and accidentally check into the very hotel that used to be the home of the person in the letters, and then you find her diary. It's as if this was meant to happen. There is no other explanation for it. It's as if Gran is reaching out from beyond the grave and making this all happen."

"You don't really believe that, do you?" Mike asked.

"How else do you explain it all?" Ash looked at her brother. "The alternative is that this is all some massive coincidence. No." She shook her head. "I don't believe that." She turned and pointed her finger at me. "You were meant to find these. You were meant to come here, find us and tell this story." She sat back in the chair and exhaled, and then tears came to her eyes. Emelia put her hand on her shoulder and squeezed.

"How did her bag get to Jo'burg?" Mike asked.

"I took some of her things to the charity shop in town, including the bag," Ash said.

"Someone must have bought it and then decided they didn't like it," I added. "They must have taken it to the shop I went to."

"I can't believe this whole thing." Ash put her elbows on the table and rested her head on her arms for a while. "I knew it, though."

"Knew what?" I asked.

"I knew there was something about you." She looked up at me. "Besides, I knew a cat couldn't crap in a toilet and flush it!"

"What?" Mike asked.

I hung my head a little as Mike looked over at me.

"Didn't you know? She pretended to have a cat, when she checked in. Told me she had trained it to use the toilet, that's why she didn't have a litter box with her."

Emelia burst out laughing. "I can see why you're a writer," she said.

Ash smiled at me. "I should have seen it. You didn't seem like a cat person." She looked at me for the longest time, as if deciding whether or not to like me again. I guess she decided that she did, because she gave me another smile.

"Do you know how sad this is?" She held a letter up. "Do you know how awful this is, that they were not allowed to love each other because of the color of their skin? Gran went through her whole life loving someone that she could never be with . . . right up until the day she died. She loved him until her last breath, in this house." Her words spilled into the room and the profound weight of them made us all silent. "Do you think she ever loved Grandpa?" Ash looked up at Mike.

"I'm sure she loved him in some way. They had children together and shared a whole life together."

"I guess there are different kinds of love," Ash offered. "But I don't think she loved him like she loved this guy from the letters."

I shook my head. "I don't think many people get to love like that." I pulled one of the letters towards me and felt compelled to read it out loud.

3 January, 1949

Dear Edith,

I still remember the first time I met you. It was just after three o'clock—I remember this because the church clock had just struck. The sky was overcast, it looked like it was going to storm and I remember thinking that there was a strange energy in the sky. You know, the kind of energy the sky gets just before a lightning storm, as if everything in it feels alive, as if everything is standing to attention, waiting for something great to happen. There is an anticipation in the air, a kind of invisible fire that you can feel, but you can't see. And I remember thinking that I was waiting for something to happen, waiting for something special, but I didn't know what it was.

I looked around, and at first I didn't see anything, but then you appeared. You were running, as if you were late for something. I didn't know what you were running towards, but I remember thinking that it had to be important. I watched you closely when you came to the fork in the road. You looked down the left fork and then you looked up the hill. I knew what you were thinking: short cut up and over the hill, or take the long way. I smiled; I knew which way you were going to choose before you did, because I could see what kind of person you were. You were going to take the short cut up the hill. It's harder, there is a fence to climb over and a steep slope, but I could see you were an adventure seeker. Most people take the easy way, but not you. And I was right, because suddenly you were running up the hill. I watched you carefully. I could see you weren't a runner. You were out of breath and covered in sweat, and this made me smile. Because someone as unfit as you should probably take the easy way, but you didn't! I liked that a lot. I admired it and it made me think that you were different from any of the other girls around town. But then you tried to climb over that fence! To be honest, I didn't think you were going to make it. But you were so determined. I watched you struggle up it and slip a few times, but you never gave up. I remember thinking to myself that this was what I'd been waiting for. For some strange reason, I had been there at that exact moment because I was waiting for you. I didn't really understand that thought at first, but, looking back on it now, looking back on that moment a year later, I know what it all means.

You slipped and fell—remember that? You fell on your back and, for a moment, you couldn't breathe. You'd winded yourself and you looked so panicked, and that's when I ran up to you. Do you remember what I said to you then, when I took your hands in mine? I told you to be calm, be patient and the air would come. You would be able to breathe soon, you just had to hold on for a second longer and the air would come.

Well, that was a total lie. I know that, now. Because, when you're not with me, I cannot breathe. I wait patiently and I try to be calm, just like I told you to be, but it doesn't work. When you're not here with me, I feel like I'm drowning. I go through my day trying to gasp for air that never comes. It's only when I'm finally with you, when we can sneak away together, that I can breathe again. It's only in those quiet moments with you—in the willow, under the stage, in the cove—that I get to breathe again. So, like swimming under water, I take as many deep breaths as I can with you, because I never know when I'm going to be able to come back up to the surface again . . .

You, me, forever.

I slowly lowered the letter to the table again.

"That's . . . that's the most beautiful thing I've ever heard." Ash was wiping away a flood of tears now. "I had no idea Gran was so in love with someone else."

"It's terrible they couldn't be together," Emelia said, and then she looked down at Ash. "In a way, that could be us. If we had been born in another time, or in another country, or to another family. Can you imagine that? Not being able to be together?" She laid her hand on Ash's shoulder. "I mean, how dare someone tell you who you're allowed to love? Especially the government," she continued.

"This story has to be told." Ash stood up suddenly. "Gran would have wanted that. It was basically her final wish."

I looked up at Mike; he seemed like he was somewhere else, that he wasn't present in this room. His body was here, but his mind was elsewhere. And then, without a word, he reached down and started gathering up all the letters and the diary from the table.

"What are you doing?" I asked, as he walked towards the door.

"Some investigating," he said, exiting the room.

"Shame, this seems to really have affected him," Emelia said, when he was out of earshot.

"They were really close," Ash said.

"Becca!" Mike called out loudly, sticking his head back around the door.

"Yes?" I jumped.

"You better not go anywhere."

"I won't," I said.

"Don't worry. She can hang with us. We'll keep an eye on her," Ash said.

He nodded, and his head disappeared again.

"Hey!" Ash said. Her whole tone and demeanor had changed, now. "Didn't you guys meet for the first time on a fence, too?"

"What?" My jaw dropped open and I looked at her.

She smiled at me—a strange smile, as if it held a secret—and then she looked over at her partner Emelia and the two exchanged some kind of a *look*.

My heart started thumping a soundtrack in my chest, and the blood rushing past my ears created an orchestra of accompanying sounds, until I had a full-blown concerto playing in my head, making me feel rather dizzy.

CHAPTER 54

I was woken up by the frantic knock on the door. I'd been so exhausted after my sleepless night with Mike that I'd fallen into bed at seven and had slept deeper than I had in years. But I'd dreamed the same dream over and over again, playing in a loop, like a stuck record.

In the dream, I was the girl in a hurry, trying to climb the fence—not unlike real life. And Mike was the man who came to my rescue. Each time the dream reached a certain point, it stopped, and started again. It stopped at the moment that he held my hands, looked into my eyes and told me to breathe. And then, when I did finally breathe, I inhaled deeply and the smell of night jasmine filled my lungs and Mike leaned towards me and lowered his lips to mine and we were just about to kiss and then . . .

I am the girl climbing the fence again.

"Becca. Becca!" The knock on the door continued and I thought I heard Mike's voice. And, when I didn't answer immediately, he burst through the door.

"WHAT?!" I sat up in my bed.

"Oh," he said flatly, looking at me in the bed. "I thought you might have disappeared."

"No. I'm here," I said. "I promised I wouldn't go anywhere." I tried to smile at him, but he didn't smile back.

"You've made some promises in the past that you broke."

Oh God, he was still so mad at me. I'd hurt him so much, and, in the process, I'd hurt myself, too, more than I can describe.

"I'm sorry," I whispered, looking down at the duvet on the bed.

"Doesn't matter. Come to the library. I have something to show you. Ash and Emelia are already there."

"Okay." I climbed out of the bed and Mike immediately averted his gaze. I looked down and realized that I'd gone to sleep in an oversized T-shirt and panties, nothing else. And, during the night, the T-shirt had clearly become bunched in my panties and now I was fully on view.

I turned around quickly and immediately realized that I'd just made the situation worse, since my ass was now fully on display. And, by the feel of it, one of the sides of my panties had magically disappeared into the crack (as they do, sometimes) and now I was half-mooning him. I quickly reached around and pulled the panties back out. God, this was truly undignified. I heard him clear his throat awkwardly; I knew he'd seen.

"Library," he said loudly, and then I heard him scuttle out of the room. "There's coffee there," he muttered. I turned around just in time to see his hand pull the door closed. Only the night before last, that hand had been all over my body, and now it was very clear that that hand, and the man attached to it, wanted nothing to do with me.

* * *

I walked into the room and gaped. I couldn't believe what I saw. Mike had made photocopies of all the letters and diary entries, and had stuck them up on the walls in what looked like a timeline of events. In between them all, he'd stuck up other things, too: hand-written notes, photocopies of what looked like architectural plans, actual photos of people, newspaper articles. Some of these had bits of colored wool pinned to them, linking them to diary entries or letters. It was a spider's web of information.

"You . . . you've created a serial-killer wall!" I exclaimed, looking at Mike.

Ash laughed. "You're right. This is a serial-killer wall. They all have these."

"They do." I nodded.

"Hey, if you were a serial killer, what would your MO be?" she suddenly asked me.

"What do you mean?" I replied.

"Like . . . would you stick your dead victims' bodies to the ceiling with chewing gum, or would you cut off all their toenails and use them to make sandpaper, or would you pluck their eyelashes out and stuff a pillow with them?"

"Ash!" Mike exclaimed.

"I'm just asking, cos she's a writer and I bet she would come up with a good one."

"My *not* morbid girlfriend," Emelia said, handing me a cup of coffee with a smile. "I don't know how you like it; there's milk and sugar there."

I liked Emelia. She was uber-cool—one of those androgynous-looking women who have the guts to cut their hair short and dye it blue, who have the guts to get a nose ring and a tattoo on their neck.

"So?" Ash asked again. "Your MO?"

"I'd probably kill them with millions of tiny paper cuts," I said.

"Oooh, that's good." Ash raised her coffee mug at me in a toast and we both took a sip.

"Right, now that we've finished murdering people, can we get on with this?" Mike interrupted.

"Nothing like the smell of coffee and murder in the morning." Emelia sat down on one of the brown leather couches and I joined her. It was cold and I cradled the warm cup between my hands.

"So," Mike said, walking up to the wall. "I've put all the letters into a timeline, and slotted the diary entries in between. Becca, you were looking for another bunch of letters that were put into her favorite book, *Pride and Prejudice*?" He looked at me and I nodded. "Well, look at the plans of the house and the date of the letter."

I stood up and walked over to his wall, reading the dates on the letters and plans.

"The library in the house hadn't been built yet?" I asked, looking up at him.

He nodded. "Exactly. So she wouldn't have hidden the letters here."

"But where, then?" I asked.

He pointed to a newspaper article and I read the headline aloud. "*Willow Bay's library is renovated.*" I stopped and thought for a while. "You think she put all the letters in a public library?"

"That makes sense. She wanted him to find them, right? She wouldn't have stashed them here, inside the house, if she was expecting him to come and get them," Emelia added.

"Sure, I guess. But there's no way that they would still be there now. How many people have taken *Pride and Prejudice* out since then?" I asked.

"But maybe they're not in a book. Maybe it's not that obvious. Maybe there is a panel in the shelf. She wouldn't have just put them inside the book," Mike offered up.

"Maybe it's not in the library at all. Maybe she had a secret hiding spot for the book," Ash added.

"Where?" Mike asked.

"Under the stage at the town hall," I blurted out.

"Did you see anything there, under the stage?" Mike asked.

"You've been under the stage at the town hall?" Ash asked, looking confused. "But your cat was fake; why would you go there if you . . . WAIT!" Her eyes widened. "Were you the one who stole the cat and cut—?" She burst out laughing before she could finish her sentence. "Oh my God, it *was* you, wasn't it? I drew you!" Her laughter grew and I gripped the sides of my coffee mug even tighter. "Wow. You really get around!" Ash exclaimed.

"Yeah, she does." Mike cut her off in a gruff, stern voice. "And it's not funny; they might not have the Persian parade here again because of what Becca did, and that would be bad for tourism. Well, they won't have it here unless the infamous catnapper is apprehended, which puts me in a very difficult situation, being as I'm actually harboring the catnapper here, in my house." His tone was harsh.

God, he really was angry with me. This wasn't something that was going to blow over very easily. Maybe it would never blow over. Maybe I had really ruined this thing between us, permanently. Maybe the most I could hope for after this was for him to be able to look me in the eye again. Maybe, maybe, maybe . . . *Too many maybes.* I felt sick. My stomach knotted as the strong black coffee hit it.

"You okay?" Emelia asked. I hadn't realized I wasn't hiding my feelings.

"Just coffee on an empty stomach, making me feel a bit—"

"OH! Hang on!" She jumped up. "That reminds me." She raced out of the room and I looked after her.

"She's got something in the oven. She's a baker," Ash said.

"Really?" My stomach immediately growed at the idea of baked goods.

"She's very good. I always say I fell in love with her the second I tasted her muffin," Ash said, and then burst out laughing again.

"Ash! God!" Mike shook his head and smiled.

I also laughed, but Mike quickly ended it.

"So, did you find anything under the stage?" he asked, in a loud, very formal manner.

"No. I couldn't get into the room; it's been boarded up," I said.

"You couldn't? You couldn't—?" He cut himself off and then shook his head. "Seriously? You didn't get in, after all the trouble you caused? After all that, you didn't get what you came for?"

I shook my head. "No."

Ash laughed again. "Did you see that drawing of you? The one I did?"

"Yes." I smiled.

"Don't you think it looked a little like that guy from *The Rocky Horror Picture Show*?" she asked.

"YES!" I said immediately. "That's exactly what I thought when I saw it." We laughed together for a moment before Mike cut us off again.

"I'm glad you guys find this so amusing. Half the town is demanding that I arrest the cat-maiming person, and those people at the eco estate—who I managed to talk *out* of pressing charges against you by telling them you weren't sane—would also love to see you charged with something!"

"Oh, chill!" Ash stood up, walked over to her brother and looked at the wall behind him, giving his shoulder a hard squeeze. "At least she isn't a serial killer."

"Ha ha—" he started, and then stopped when Emelia came bursting into the room.

The smell was instant. The warm, sweet, sticky smell of freshly baked goods. It made my mouth water.

"Oooh, what did you bake, babe?" Ash asked.

"Chocolate croissants," she said, putting the tray down on one of the tables.

"God—did I mention how much I love you?" Ash reached out and took one.

"I swear, if I wasn't a baker, you wouldn't have asked me to marry you," Emelia replied playfully.

"Sorry, what?" Mike looked flabbergasted.

"Well, we were going to tell you this morning, but you woke us up so early and forced us down into this room and have been talking non-stop since we got here," Ash said to her brother.

"You guys got engaged last night?" I asked.

They both smiled at me. Beamed. And then Ash slipped her arm around Emelia. "After reading that letter . . . It really made us think about what was important in life and what we wanted. And we want to be together, forever. Those letters inspired us." She leaned over and kissed her fiancée, and I immediately looked at Mike.

"Really?" Mike asked, with a smile that lit up his green eyes.

Ash nodded as Mike walked up to them and pulled them both into a massive hug.

I felt tears in my eyes again. Not sad ones, this time.

"I guess we have you to thank for this, then—bringing the letters into our life, like that." Ash pulled me into a hug.

I wrapped one arm around her, tentatively. "I didn't do anything," I whispered, full of emotion, and then I wrapped my other arm around her and gave myself over to the hug. Something I don't do very often.

"You did," she said, pulling away and smiling at me. "Trust me. You've done more than you think." She said this in a strange tone, and I was just about to ask her what she meant, when she took me by the hand and pulled me towards the food. "Come, you need sustenance," she said. "I'm sure my brother has big plans for all of us today!"

CHAPTER 55

~

$\mathcal{W}$e parked the car outside a very different-looking town hall. Gone were all the cat cars and cat enthusiasts; instead, it was empty. We'd agreed to divide and conquer today. Ash and Emelia would go upstairs into the attic and search through old photo albums and anything else that was up there, while Mike and I checked out the room under the stage. And, if we found nothing there, we'd check out the library. The tension between us on the short drive had been tangible, like a heavy fog hanging in the air between us. Cold and clammy. We hadn't said a word to each other, other than me congratulating him on his sister's engagement, to which I'd really only gotten a half-hearted grunt in response.

"Let's go." He jumped out the car and I followed behind him.

We walked into the empty hall. The sound of our feet on the wooden floorboards bounced off the high ceiling and seemed to ricochet off the walls, creating a kind of ominous movie soundtrack. I could almost imagine us as characters from an Indiana Jones film, creeping towards some hidden treasure or other. We reached the stage and stopped. Mike turned to me and made brief eye contact, then looked away.

"Lead the way," he said, pointing with the crowbar that he'd brought with us.

"Okay." I got down on my hands and knees and shuffled under the stage, making my way past all the discarded props again. I crawled all the way to the back, to where the sealed door was, and stopped.

I turned and looked over my shoulder. Mike was following me on his hands and knees, crouched low, trying to fit under the stage without bashing his head.

"Here." I pointed at the door and Mike crawled up next to me. As he did, his body brushed mine, and I became hyperaware of his presence.

"Someone really didn't want anyone to go in, now, did they?" He took the crowbar and slid it under one of the wooden beams that was keeping the thing shut. He gave a large tug and the first beam popped off with a crunching sound as the wood split and splintered. He made quick work of the next one, and the next. He was strong, after all; anyone who could pick me up the way he had the other night was . . .

I shook my head. I really couldn't afford to be thinking like that again—thinking about that night together.

"You know," he started. I could hear he was slightly out of breath from the physical exertion. "I don't think I've ever broken into anything before."

"I don't think it's breaking in, if you phone ahead and ask for permission to do it," I said, referring to the call he'd made to the caretaker of the hall. "What did you say we were doing here, anyway?" I asked.

He looked over his shoulder at me briefly and then went back to cracking the fourth piece of wood. "I didn't need to say anything; he owed me a favor."

"Really?" I asked.

"I caught his sixteen-year-old son and some of his friends drinking beer on the beach, a month or so ago."

"Ooooh! I see," I said.

"I could have made a bigger deal of it, but I let it slide—with a very firm warning." He stopped what he was doing for a second, as if thinking about something. "I remember what it was like to be that age."

"I bet you do," I said, with a smile. "According to Mrs. Devereux, you were a terror."

He looked over his shoulder at me again and then stopped what he was doing. "And you?" he asked. "I bet you were an absolute horror as a teenager. I bet you were always in trouble, if your current behavior is anything to go by."

I thought about the answer to that question for a while. It was a complicated one for me. "I was what I needed to be at the time," I said thoughtfully.

"What does that mean?" he asked.

"I was never in one place enough to become who I was meant to be, I guess. If the people I was staying with were into sport, then I was into sport. If they were into church, then I was, too. When I was with one set of cousins, I dressed in black and listened to metal, because they did. When I was staying with my other cousins, I was into cycling. Even though I hated it. I was what the situation called for me to be." I sat there, thinking about it for a while. Thinking about being this little lost person, moving from place to place and never really fitting in.

"Why couldn't you just be yourself?" he asked.

The question caught me off guard. "Um . . . I . . . I don't know," I stuttered. "That's a good question. I guess I don't know." Only, I think I did know the answer. I couldn't "be myself" because "myself" clearly hadn't been quite good enough.

He nodded at me. He looked like he was going to say something to me, but then stopped himself and pulled the last piece of wood off.

CHAPTER 56

⌒

The small room under the stage was exactly as I'd imagined it. It was physically empty, but, at the same time, it was full. It was so full of history and secrets and sweet nothings whispered that you could almost feel it. There was something strangely magical about this little room under the stage and the secrets it held—the hopes, the dreams.

"There's nothing here," Mike said, once he'd walked around the small space.

"There is," I replied, looking up at the dusty beams of the ceiling that were covered in so many spider webs that they looked like a Halloween prop.

Mike looked up. "Where?" he asked, his eyes seeking out the place that mine were seeing.

"There's nothing here physically, but can't you feel it?" I knew how I must have sounded, a little woo-woo and esoteric, but I really could feel it. It was as if an energy had been caught in this room, years ago.

"Uh, I think you might have inhaled some hallucinogenic spores from the dust, because there's nothing in this room," he grumbled.

I smiled at him. "You could be right, actually. Did you know that the pages of really old books can be covered in fungi that have hallucinogenic properties? You can literally get high from sniffing the pages of an old book."

He chuckled. It was small, but it was like music to my ears.

I hadn't heard him laugh in what felt like forever. And it was everything.

"They also think hallucinogenic fungi are responsible for most reports of ghost sightings in old houses," I added.

"I thought I saw a ghost once," he said. "I was about eight. I was staying over in Sugar Manor when it happened, actually."

"What did you see?" I asked, intrigued.

"Well, I was walking up the stairs and I heard a creak behind me, as if someone was following me, and when I swung around, I thought I saw a flash of something white, as if something flew away quickly."

"What did you do?" I asked.

"Screamed. Cried. Slept with Mom and Dad," he said.

"And you think it was a ghost?" I pressed.

He shook his head. "Nah. Probably just an eight-year-old's imagination. Also, my friend had stolen his parents' VHS copy of *It* and we had all watched it, and it was fucking terrifying."

"Yup, that will do it. God, I was terrified of clowns, after that film." I cringed. "I can't even think of a clown without feeling freaked out." I looked around the room again. "Crap, and this place is rather reminiscent of a sewer, and now I'm just expecting to see a red balloon come creeping out of the dark corners and—"

I screamed when I felt it and saw it. The furious flurry of something black passed my face, the wind on my cheek and the loud screech in my ear.

"Oh my God, oh my God! What the hell is that?" I flapped my arms around and almost fell to the ground. And then it came again, and again, and . . . "What are they?" I yelled, running in circles as the things whizzed past me. "Are they bats? Are they bats?" I was quite frantic now.

"It's okay. They're not going to fly into your hair," I heard Mike say. But the air around us was full of them, the small room was alive with frantic flapping.

"Oh my God. Oh my God," I squealed, running around in small circles, covering my face with my hands so nothing would fly into it. I screamed when I felt the swish of a wing by my arm, so close I could feel the rush of air against my skin. And then another wing grazed one of my hands. By this stage, I was quite hysterical. All I could think of were hundreds of bats flapping about in my hair, twisting it into knots, and me having to cut the flapping creatures out in chunks.

Suddenly, I felt two arms around my waist. And then I felt myself being pulled down. The sound in the small room was ear-shattering, filled with the screeching of what felt like a million bats.

I fell to the floor. Not hard, though; something cushioned my blow, something soft and warm and . . . I opened my eyes and looked. My head was on Mike's chest, his big hands were cradling me towards him.

"Ssshhhh," he whispered. "Let's just stay down until they settle."

His hand across my cheek . . . *warm*. His hand around my back . . . *protective*. His smell . . . *intoxicating*. His soft voice . . . *calming*. I wrapped my arm around him, across his big chest, and I closed my eyes tightly and waited for the last of the bats to disappear. It took a while until the room was completely silent once more, until they'd flown out of some unseen hole, or flown back to their little devil perches. And, when it was all over, I opened my eyes, tilted my head and looked at him. I could see his eyes were open, scanning the ceiling. And then, slowly, his head began to tilt down. His lips arrived in my field of vision first, followed by his nose and then his eyes and then . . .

Down here with you in this room, Edith, I can pretend I know what it would be like to live together. Sometimes, I imagine this is our house. I can almost see it . . . Me, coming home from work. You're waiting for me, because you've been painting all day, because you're a great artist and we bought a small house that has a cottage out back that you turned into your studio. The windows are big, so you can watch our children playing in the garden after school while you paint your masterpieces. And, when I come home, you're all there to open the door for me. My wife, and my beautiful children. That's what this room is like for me—it's our imaginary home, the one we'll probably never get to have. But when I lie here with you on my chest, looking up at me, for a few blissful seconds it's real. And when I look into your eyes and you into mine, I know I have come home. To you. You are my home, even if we do not have four walls of our own.

You, me, forever.

CHAPTER 57

I quickly sat up, turned my back to him and straightened my hair anxiously. The moment was officially over—he'd made that very clear when he suddenly looked away and started sitting up, pushing me off him. I tucked my messy hair behind my ears, and *gathered myself towards myself*, as my grandmother used to say. I'd never fully understood that expression as a child, but, as I'd gotten older, it made more sense to me. On many occasions, I'd had to gather together the scattered Becca debris, the little chunks of myself that had become loose and dispersed themselves in a usually very disorderly fashion. I'd had to pick all those pieces up and then click them back into place, where they belonged.

"So—" Mike stood up—"what are we looking for?"

I climbed to my feet and dusted myself off. My legs and back were covered in spider webs and dust—and, I suspected, some bat droppings, too. *Wait—don't bats carry rabies?*

"We thought that maybe she'd stashed her favorite book here," I replied.

I felt a little lost, stranded between this moment and the one that we'd just shared, staring deep into each other's eyes while my head had been on his chest and my mind was remembering moments from the letters. But Mike didn't look lost in any moment, he was busy walking the perimeter of this small room. He walked it in a very police-ish manner, running his hand over the stone walls.

"Looking for a hidden compartment?" I asked.

"I don't know what I'm looking for. This place seems totally empty." He stopped walking the perimeter and turned around, surveying the room from a different angle.

"I'm sure whoever closed it up cleared everything out," I said. "The chance of finding something in this room, after all these years, does seem incredibly small."

"Don't be so sure about that," Mike said, looking up at one of the beams on the ceiling.

I looked up, too, but couldn't see anything. "What?" I asked.

"This." He reached up and pulled something down.

I moved closer. "What is it?" I looked at the rectangular object wrapped in cloth and my heart started to beat a little faster. I had this strange, uncanny feeling that I knew what it was. And I couldn't wait to see it. I pulled it from Mike's hands and, without a second's hesitation, unwrapped it, and, when I did, I gasped.

After all this time, I was finally looking at *him*. His voice had lived in my head for days, now, and I felt as if I'd gotten to know him. But seeing him for the first time brought tears to my eyes. I ran my hand over the edges of the burnt canvas. This must have been the only painting left of him. And, like the diary, it had been fished out of the fire. I gently wiped the dust off the picture with my palm.

"It's him," I said quietly, in absolute awe. "The man who wrote the letters."

I looked into his eyes first, and I was overcome with this feeling that I knew him. I had seen these very eyes in my dreams at night, and imagined them reflected in his letters. They were big and brown, and she'd painted them perfectly, capturing what can only be described as a bright spark, right in the center of them. His eyes were smiling, as was his mouth. It was open, mid-laugh, as if the artist and her subject had just shared a joke. His cheeks were indented with big dimples and his face was dotted with just a tiny amount of stubble. And then there was the color of his skin, the thing that had become absolutely everything. I traced my finger over his cheek; the light caramel color of his skin was almost golden because of the warm light the picture had been painted in.

So much attention to detail had been frozen on to this canvas: the tiny freckles that dotted his skin, the laugh lines in the corners of his eyes, the deep lines etched into his forehead, the individual hairs of his eyebrows. The painting was so realistic that, from far away, one might have thought it a photo. But, on closer inspection, one could see the small, individual brush strokes that made up the face. Each one vital and important in its own way, capturing something of the subject. His light, his laughter, his spirit, a little piece of his soul. Captured, mixed into the colors, painted in a million strokes and saved for posterity.

I looked at the old cloth that the painting had come out of and wanted to weep. This painting should not have been hidden behind a dusty ceiling beam. This painting was created with more love than I'd ever seen, and, as such, should have been hanging proudly on a wall for all to see, as a celebration. People should stand in lines to see this painting, to look into the eyes of someone who was truly loved, deeply, with every breath and every beat . . . *Now, how many people can truly say that they know what that's like?* To love against all odds. To love with courage and strength when the world is trying to pull you apart.

"We should take this home and hang it on the wall," Mike said, next to me, as if he'd been inside my head, thinking the same thoughts that I had been. "This deserves to be seen."

I nodded. I couldn't open my mouth to speak, because so many emotions were suffocating me right now. Besides, what words could I use, in a moment like this? It seemed too big and too momentous for words. Words didn't do it justice, as I looked at him on the canvas.

We hadn't found what we thought we were looking for, *but we'd found everything.*

CHAPTER 58

After not finding anything relating to her favorite book, *Pride and Prejudice*, in the room, we headed to the library. Not that I had any idea what we were looking for there. We both agreed there was no way her letters would be stashed inside a copy of the book, just sitting on a shelf, waiting to be found. I held the painting in my hands as we drove; I hadn't been able to look away from it since finding it.

"Does he look how you imagined?" It was the first thing Mike had said to me since climbing into the car.

"No, not at all. I imagined him differently."

"Different how?" he asked.

"Less smiley, more smoldery, I guess."

"Smoldery?" He turned and half-looked at me.

"He has laughing eyes, in this picture. I don't know. I was imagining someone with more piercing, bedroomy, look-into-your-soul eyes."

"Seriously, who has eyes like that?" he asked, a faint hint of amusement in his tone. Ever so faint, though.

"You do," I said impulsively, without thinking.

Suddenly, with just those words, the atmosphere between us changed; it became prickly and awkward. I regretted saying it, since he'd made his feelings for me so clear. What had he said, exactly? Maybe I needed to remind myself. *Nothing had been real, because I had been lying to him.*

"Sorry," I muttered. "I didn't mean to say that. I know we're trying not to say things like that to each other—well, at least, you're trying not to say things like that to me . . . Not that you are, I guess. But . . ." I stopped rambling. "I don't know what I'm saying," I blurted, and then shrugged.

There was a pause, a lull in the conversation, as if there was a giant gaping hole in front of us and we were both standing on the edge, looking into it, trying to figure out how to fill it. I kept my mouth closed. I wasn't going to fill it with another mindless stream of words.

"You're making this so hard, Becca," he finally said, tossing at least one thing into the hole. But it was still completely empty; those words hadn't even made a dent in the abyss.

"What am I making hard?" I asked.

"This. Us."

"I thought there wasn't an *us*," I said snappily, before I could stop myself.

"There isn't," he said softly, "but, down in the room, when we lay there, I don't know, I felt . . ." He trailed off.

"Me too," I said.

Another pause. I could hear my heart beating and I wondered if he could, too, it was so loud. That's how loud it felt, anyway.

"Let's just drop this, shall we?" His voice also had a snap in it.

"Fine." I gently put the painting on the back seat and crossed my arms over my body. "Let's drop it," I agreed, as we pulled into a parking place in front of the library. It was painfully clear to me that, whatever we had once shared, no matter how fleeting, it was so over. I should just pack away any feelings and any hope I was holding on to at this point.

* * *

The library was just as you would imagine a little town library to be. It was a small room, crammed with shelves full of well-used books.

The shelves were overflowing, in parts, and little towers of books had sprung up all over the floor. The smell was distinct, too—musky and old. To be honest, I hadn't set foot in a library in years—a fact I should probably have been ashamed of, as a writer. In the middle of the floor stood an old, rickety-looking table and chairs, and, in the far corner, the counter, where an older woman was sitting. She looked up and I recognized her immediately.

"Mrs. Devereux," I said, smiling at the old woman.

She looked over at us and immediately stood up. "My, my! And what brings you here?" She walked over to the two of us and put her hands on her hips.

"Mrs. Devereux," Mike said, sounding formal.

"I didn't know you worked . . . here?" I said, without thinking.

"Why, just because I'm over ninety, I shouldn't be useful?" she asked.

"Sorry, I didn't mean that," I said quickly.

"I brought Becca here; she was looking for a book. Maybe you can help?" Mike jumped right into it, no small talk, and he said it defensively, as if he was making sure that she knew he had brought me here for business, nothing else.

"What are you looking for?" she asked.

"*Pride and Prejudice*," he blurted out.

"Last shelf, there, under *Classics*." She pointed to the other side of the room.

Suddenly, the door opened with a loud ring and three older ladies walked in. Mrs. Devereux's demeanor quickly changed and she became very stiff.

"You'll have to excuse me," she said, and then hurried off to the group of women, who were now lurking suspiciously around the counter. I watched for a while as some hushed whispers were exchanged. They all looked up at us and then looked back down again. *Odd.* I glanced at Mike to see if he'd noticed it, too, this strange exchange that was happening right in front of us.

"What do you think is going on there?" I whispered to him.

"I have no idea." Mike turned his back to them and walked to the last shelf. We found four copies of *Pride and Prejudice* and immediately started flipping through them. But, as suspected, there were no letters inside any of them.

I looked at Mike and he shrugged. He seemed thoughtful for a few moments and then spoke: "Well, it's exactly as we thought."

"It was worth a try, though, I guess."

Mike pulled a few more books off the shelf and then ran his hand over the wooden shelf panel.

I folded my arms. I wasn't expecting him to find some secret, hidden compartment or—

"I don't believe it," Mike said, his eyes going wide.

"What?" I asked.

"Look." Mike pulled, and a piece of wood moved.

"Oh my God! A secret compartment. What are the chan—? Oh," I said, when I rushed over and looked at it. It wasn't a secret compartment at all; the shelf was just so old that parts of it were falling off. I looked through the hole that had been created and I could see all the way to the other side of the library, to where Mrs. Devereux was. "What the . . . ?" I leaned in and looked closer. She was surrounded by a new group of women, now, and they were definitely up to something.

"What the hell?" Mike whispered, as he also watched.

"What are they doing?" I asked. "It looks completely clandestine and—look, another group of women are coming through the door. Since when is a library this busy?"

We watched in fascination as more woman came; they handed their books to Mrs. Devereux, who quickly took them out of the covers, and then, as fast as lightning, she slipped other books into the same covers and passed them back to the women.

I looked at Mike in utter confusion. What the hell could be going on there?

"Let's investigate," Mike said. He walked around the shelf and started striding across the library, back towards the counter. Everyone at the counter suddenly turned, and then, as quickly and quietly as they had all appeared, they dispersed. Some headed for the door, others ducked between nearby shelves, and another one scuttled out the back door, marked *Exit*.

The closer Mike got to the desk, the stiffer Mrs. Devereux became. She met Mike's eyes and smiled, pushing a book across the counter, as if hoping Mike wouldn't see it. He had. He reached out and placed his hand over hers, stopping her. Her smile faltered as Mike picked the book up. He looked at her and raised his eyebrow, as if asking her a question. At that, her demeanor changed again. Her shoulders slumped and she raised her hands in the air in resignation.

"Oh, well. What can I say? You've caught us," she said, and sat back down on the chair behind the counter.

"Caught you?" I asked, peering at the book in Mike's hands. On the surface, it was *Black Beauty*, but when Mike slipped the cover off . . .

"*Claimed Under the Full Moon: A Werewolf Erotica Collection*," Mike read, slowly.

"A what?" I gasped and reached for the book. Turning it over in my hands, I read the back out loud. "*When Sasha goes for a jog in the park, late at night, the last thing she expects is to have all her wildest fantasies fulfilled by a sexy, shape-shifting werewolf . . . A what?!*" I burst out laughing and turned the book back over in my hands, looking at the male torso on the front cover. I glanced up at Mrs. Devereux and she shrugged again.

I picked up another book from the counter and slipped its fake cover off. I immediately laughed when I saw it: *Merman Ménage: Get Slippery*. On the cover was a sexy merman, draped over a rock, holding what looked like a nubile virgin in his arms.

Mike shook his head and then turned back to Mrs. Devereux.

"You know, just because we're old, doesn't mean we stop liking sex!" she said, and it looked like Mike's jaw was about to fall open.

I laughed even louder. "I get that," I said, "but can't you be into normal things? Not . . ." I turned the book over in my hands and read again. "*Six steamy paranormal romances, featuring a merman ménage and a sexy, underwater, reverse harem!*" I shook my head. "What the hell is a reverse harem?"

Mrs. Devereux blushed. "I guess, after that *Fifty Shades*, we were all looking for something a little . . . *wilder.*"

"So *Fifty Shades* was the gateway drug to *this*!" I looked at Mike and he face-palmed.

"I've discovered an underground porn ring being run by my ex elementary-school teacher." He sounded amused. "And to think I was embarrassed to buy a box of condoms in front of you!"

Mrs. Devereux smiled. "Do you really think I didn't know what you two were doing, red lipstick smeared all over your necks like scarlet letters?" she said.

"Oh," I mumbled.

She gave us both a knowing look and then casually took the other books out from behind the counter and started putting them into their fake covers, ready for collection.

Mike turned and looked at the women who were starting to emerge from behind the shelves. He waved at one of them. "Mrs. Christianson . . ." He waved at another one. "Mrs. Edwards. Hope you're having a nice day."

They smiled back at him and then both of them darted for the door.

"So, does everyone in town read these books?" Mike asked.

"Well, none of us know how to use the bloody Google, so we can't do those Kindle things. Besides, those are terrible for your eyes, especially if you wear bifocals."

And now I was in stitches. This was possibly the greatest thing I'd heard in ages, and Willow Bay was probably the strangest town I'd ever set foot in.

"So, if none of you know how to use 'the bloody Google,' how are you getting all these?" he asked.

She averted her gaze, looking sheepish. "You'll have to ask Emelia about that."

"Emelia? My Emelia? As in, Ash's Emelia?" Mike asked.

"My lips are sealed." Mrs. Devereux put her finger over her lips.

Suddenly, the door tinkled again. We all turned and an older woman walked in. She looked at Mike and then quickly closed the door and hurried off again.

"That's Violet Masters. She likes Mafia," Mrs. Devereux commented.

"Mafia?" Mike asked.

At that, she pushed over what had once been a Jodi Picoult, in its past life. Mike removed the cover and we both looked down at the book.

"*Captured and Bound by the Bad Mafia Boss*," Mike read out, and then paused. "Wow. Just . . . wow. I'm not sure I have words for this."

"It's an acquired taste," Mrs. Devereux said.

"And who around here is into law enforcement? Like, *Cuffed by the Cute Cop*?" I teased, playfully.

Mrs. Devereux leaned across the table and smiled conspiratorially. "I think you'll find that, around here, they're all into that, dear."

"Okay! Enough! Enough!" Mike threw his hands in the air. "Here, take your . . . your . . . uh . . ." He struggled to find the words.

"Erotic literature?" she offered up.

"I was going to say 'porn,' but, sure, erotic literature it is, then." He handed her the book and she took it from him.

"And you?" Mrs. Devereux turned her attention to me. "What are you into, dear?"

"Oh God," Mike mumbled, under his breath.

"Uh . . . Well, I don't know, actually," I said. "What would you recommend?"

She looked me up and down for a few moments and then clicked her fingers together. "I think I have an idea." She bent down and disappeared behind the counter, only to emerge with a book. "What about this, dear?"

She passed it to me and I took its fake cover off. I suspected that Donna Tartt would be utterly appalled if she could see what secret *this Secret History* was hiding.

"*Bedded by my Handsome Brontosaurus*," I read, and, had I had coffee in my mouth, I would have spat it out. I turned the book over in my hands and gaped at the copy on the back: *Tiffany is a time-traveling paleontologist, but, when she goes back to the Cretaceous period, she gets more than just a crush when she falls for a handsome Brontosaurus.*

"Dinosaur erotica is very popular here. It must be the sea air," Mrs. Devereux said.

"Okay, I've heard enough for one day." Mike took me by the arm and pulled me towards the exit. "In fact, I think I've heard enough for an entire lifetime; I'm just going to pretend that none of this happened. Thanks, Mrs. Devereux. Bye!"

"Wait!" she called after us, and we stopped. "Did you find *Pride and Prejudice*?" she asked.

We both turned and then shook our heads.

"I was sure there was a copy, here; it was your grandmother's favorite book, you know."

At that, Mike and I clocked each other, as if both coming up with the same idea at the exact same time. We headed back to the counter.

CHAPTER 59

~

"How long were you and my grandmother friends for?" Mike asked Mrs. Devereux.

"About as long as I can remember," she replied. "We used to play together as children and teenagers—our parents were long-time friends—and then we got very close again a little later in life, just after she got married."

I could see Mike's mind ticking away, as if he'd heard something in that statement that I hadn't.

"So, you were friends when you were kids and teenagers, and then only after she got married. What about just before she got married? Say, around age twenty, twenty-one? Were you not friends then?"

Damn! He'd asked the right question, because Mrs. Devereux looked like she was squirming.

"Well, I guess you change in your early twenties, and then . . . I guess, after marriage, our interests sort of aligned again, you could say." Her voice sounded shaky.

"So, what interests of hers didn't align with yours when you were both in your early twenties?" he asked.

God, he was good. If I were a *real* criminal, I'd be scared of him.

She looked at us for the longest time, from me to Mike and then back again, as if she was trying to decide whether to tell us something or not. She exhaled slowly and then spoke again. "How much do you know about your grandmother's life?" she asked quietly, not making eye contact this time, but looking away, as if ashamed of something.

"We know enough to know she was in love with someone that 'she shouldn't have been in love with.'" He used air quotes—usually, not my favorite things—but, with his tone, his stance, the way he was using them all firmly and sarcastically . . . God, he was hot.

Mrs. Devereux cleared her throat and looked around the library, as if this was a great secret. "She was," she said softly.

"And you didn't approve?" Mike asked. God, that was a loaded question, and I doubted the answer to it was going to be good.

I leaned in a little and waited for her response; it took her a long time to talk again.

"I'm ashamed to admit it, now, but, at the time . . ." She paused, rubbed her finger and thumb together nervously, her eyes flicking from side to side. "I . . . I didn't approve of her relationship. But, back then, you must understand, it was a totally different world, a totally different country—and it was the law. There is no good excuse, I guess, but we were taught to believe certain things, back then— terrible things, which today I *don't* believe in. But I suppose I was influenced by other people's feelings and ideas. I was young. But, when I was older and made up my own mind . . . Well, it was too late then, I guess." She sighed loudly and looked somewhat defeated as she tapped her fingers on the counter, as if she didn't know what to do with her nervous hands. "It's something I still deeply regret." Her shoulders slumped, as if a lifetime of guilt and shame and remorse were pushing down on them. "I wasn't very supportive of her when she needed me the most, and I regret that."

I reached out and grabbed the old lady's hand; I could see the tears welling up in her eyes now.

She shook her head. "Thinking back, now, on how things used to be in this country, thinking back to how we all let it happen, when we should have known better, I feel quite sick about it."

"We all do," I said. "It was unforgivable. It left such deep scars and

I don't think those wounds have healed yet. I don't know that they ever really will. Perhaps some injuries are too severe to recover from fully."

"Did she ever talk to you about her relationship?" Mike asked.

She shook her head. "No. I never even saw him," she said.

At that, a thought entered my head. "Come," I said to her.

"Where?" she asked.

"Can you come outside for one minute? I'm sure the amorous ladies can take care of themselves for a moment. I'd like you to meet him," I said to her, moving towards the door.

* * *

"He's . . . he's . . ." she stuttered, holding the picture in her hands. We were all standing in the parking lot, looking at it. The moment was so hard to describe, emotionally. "He's very handsome," Mrs. Devereux finally managed.

"He is," I said.

"He looks happy." She stroked the canvas.

"I think they were very happy together," Mike said, towering behind us, looking over our shoulders. "For a short while, anyway."

She turned and looked at us. "That's more than most people can say."

"Is there anything you can tell us about the relationship? We're trying to learn as much as possible about it."

Mrs. Devereux became very quiet and thoughtful for a moment. She looked like she was reliving a bad memory.

"What is it?" Mike pressed.

"You know how they were caught, don't you?" she asked.

We both shook our heads.

"I don't know all the details, but her father followed her out one evening, down to the cove, by the beach. You know the one?"

Mike nodded. "Yes."

"I think they went there sometimes to be alone. Anyway, your great-grandfather saw them together and he was furious—he lost it. I only learned about this a few years later. Edith never talked about it to me, but she did once tell me that she'd lost something very precious once, down by the cove—*someone* very precious. I put two and two together."

I shook my head a little in disbelief. "Did you and Edith never talk about this, later in life?" I asked. "Even after you changed your opinion on it?"

"No," she said, looking back down at the picture.

"But why?" I asked.

"Perhaps she never fully trusted me enough to share it with me."

"So you don't know if she ever saw him again, after that night?" I asked.

"I don't know." She hung her head. "I wish I could have been a different kind of friend to her, back then."

"Do you know his name?" Mike asked.

She shook her head. "She never said." She looked down at the picture. "This is the first time I'm meeting him, and I'm glad I am."

She passed me the picture and I took it.

"I should have been a better person. I should have been stronger and I should have had my own mind, but I didn't." The sadness in Mrs. Devereux's voice was unmistakable, laced with a lifetime of guilt and regret.

I pulled her into a hug; I felt compelled to hold her. She hugged me back and the moment meant so much to me. And then she turned and walked slowly back to the library. Mike and I stood in silence for a while. I was trying to imagine what that terrifying moment must have been like for them, when they were caught together.

"I'd love to see the cove," I said.

Mike turned and looked at me. "Me too . . . but, uh . . ." He stopped talking and looked at me strangely.

"What?" I asked.

"It's just that the cove is interesting, these days, and it might be a bit of an issue, getting to it," he replied.

"What do you mean, 'an issue'?" I asked, as he walked back around the car and climbed in.

He looked over at me briefly. "You'll see."

CHAPTER 60

"*R*ight?" I said, as I read the sign sticking out of the sand.

"I told you," Mike said.

"Well, not really. You told me this place was interesting, so I was expecting red pebbles or black volcanic sand, I wasn't expecting . . . *this!*" I said, pointing at the sign.

"This is one of our most popular tourist attractions," he said.

I looked around at the full parking lot. "I can see," I said flatly.

"This is our busiest season, too—the Easter holidays, when the weather isn't too hot—I guess so sunburn isn't such a big . . . *problem*." He said that very pointedly, and I knew why.

"Mmmhmm." I nodded. "You know you live in a strange town, right?"

Mike cracked a small smile and my heart skipped a beat. "It does attract a rather eccentric crowd."

"You don't say." I put my hands on my hips and shook my head.

"Well, it did attract you," he said, raising his sexy, scarred eyebrow at me.

"Me? Eccentric? Whatever do you mean?" I teased.

"Mmmm," he muttered under his breath, and then looked around the parking lot. "So?" he asked.

"So?"

"Are we doing this?"

"No!" I replied.

"Why?"

"Um . . . Well, call me a square, or whatever, but I'm not sure I feel like getting naked at eleven o'clock in the morning and walking on to a beach full of nudists."

He smiled at me. "Would twelve o'clock suit you better?"

"Ha ha!" I quipped, happy that some of the tension between us had been lifted.

"Don't you want to see the place?"

"I do, but I'm not sure I want to see it as much as . . . *that*?" I pointed as a couple emerged from behind a rock. They were completely naked. And they were not models, let me tell you that. Not that I was expecting them to be. "Oh God," I moaned loudly. A flaccid penis in full sunlight is not the most attractive thing in the world, especially when it's coming out of what looks like a grey Santa beard. I tried not to stare, but it was all I could see. Bobbing up and down like that, swinging free in the sea breeze, shimmying from side to side—and I wasn't referring to his penis, now; I was referring to the other things that were clanking about like castanets behind it.

"I don't think there's anything wrong with it," Mike said. "Nothing wrong with being naked."

"Says the man with the body of a god, the abs of steel and the ass so round and perky that you could probably use it as a soccer ball, not to mention the—" I stopped myself mid-sentence. "Well, you know," I said quietly.

"No, I don't know." He folded his arms and looked at me.

"You know—your . . . *you know*," I said.

"My *you know*?" he asked. A smile was parting his lips and he wasn't even trying to hide it from me.

"Yes!"

"What about it?" he asked.

"Well, it is freakishly perfect, isn't it?" I said.

"Perfect?" Mike chuckled a little.

"Well, yes. Not too big, not too small, not too—"

"Whoa!" Mike cut me off with a hand in the air. "You make it sound like that bowl of porridge from Goldilocks and the Three Bears. Next thing, I'll be not too hot, not too cold, not too hard, not too soft."

I laughed.

"It's not funny," he said. "No one wants to hear those parts of themselves described using lines from a fairy tale." He turned to me and placed his hands on his hips, and, again, the movement caused him to perfectly block the sun out. He was silhouetted once more.

I sighed. "What is it with you and blocking the sun out?" I asked.

"Huh?" He looked down at me.

"You! You're always in perfect silhouette. You move through life being backlit by the bloody sun, like you're in a movie."

He laughed again, and my heart started banging in my chest. *We were laughing together again.*

"You too, by the way," he mumbled, under his breath, when our laughter had tapered off somewhat.

"What?" I asked, and turned to face him.

He stepped closer to me and, as he moved, the sun hit me in my face. He held his hand up to shield it from my eyes.

"Not too hot, not too cold . . . just right." He almost whispered that last part, and I had to lean in to hear him.

"What is?" I asked.

"Your body," he said, looking at me.

"Wh . . . ? Uh . . ." I stumbled stupidly now, caught in the green spell.

He was looking at me with the same intensity with which he'd looked at me the other night, on that chair. I told you, things can never return to normal after something like that.

"Uh . . . What's going on here?" I asked.

He looked away; I think I'd bloody broken the spell. "I don't know," he murmured, half under his breath.

"I thought you said we weren't a thing anymore?"

"We aren't," he said. "But I can't just turn my feelings off, and I guess they're running away a little now."

"You have a feeling switch?" I asked.

He looked at me again. "Don't you? Aren't you also trying to turn it off?"

I looked away. "It's not really working," I whispered.

"Tell me about it." He stepped away from me.

A silence descended again. There were so many words and feelings in it, but who was going to speak them?

"So, are we going to do this?" Mike finally asked.

I looked back at the beach. "We don't have towels," I said, trying to think of a reason not to.

"I have gym towels in the trunk of my car, in my gym bag."

"Gym towels are too small," I replied quickly, thinking of another excuse.

"Well, like you said, I'm not XL." He gave me a small smile, now—a forced one. The kind you give when you're trying to claw your way out of a situation with a brave face.

I acknowledged his effort with a smile back. "I kind of meant that it was too small to cover me."

"The point is *not* to cover yourself, I think . . . if I'm understanding this whole nudity thing correctly," he said.

"There's nowhere to change." Another excuse.

Mike pointed and I followed his finger.

"Oh. I see," I grumbled. There, on the other side of the parking lot, was a building labeled *Change Room. Lockers available.* "They've thought of everything, haven't they, the little nudists."

"And, look, you can also rent chairs and towels there." He pointed to another sign.

"Fancy that." I was officially out of excuses.

"Do you really think those people on that beach are going to even look at you? Think about it. The safest, most non-judgmental place you can be naked would be on a nudist beach."

"Um . . ." I was torn.

"How about this: I'll go, and take pictures for you," Mike started walking towards the change room.

"Are you seriously going?" I asked, walking after him.

"Yes," he called over his shoulder.

I looked at the beach, then looked back at Mike striding towards the change room.

"FINE!" I shouted after him. "I'm coming."

He laughed. Oh God—wrong word for the moment, Becca. *Wrong word!*

CHAPTER 61

⁓

I'd rented the biggest towel I could find and wrapped myself in it. I walked out of the change room and Mike was already there, waiting for me. He had *not* rented the biggest towel he could find. Instead, he'd gone back to the car and now had a very small gym towel wrapped around his waist. It was so small that a portion of his upper thigh was sticking out; it looked like a bloody miniskirt with a huge slit in it. I tried to look away, but it was hard. And I could see it was hard for the woman who walked past, too; she did such a double take that I was sure she had given herself whiplash.

"Shall we?" he asked, standing there casually, as if he didn't know he was the hottest man on the planet, a god, dropped down from above for us mere mortals to look at.

I clutched my towel tighter as a whole swirly array of feelings started surging through me. "Okay. Let's go."

I walked past him, towards the beach. This was the last thing I had been expecting to do today. Of all things, this seemed like the most ridiculous—especially in light of how solemn and serious everything was that we were busy uncovering. As I rounded the corner, I was faced with the full glory of this nudist delight.

"Oh my God," I whispered under my breath. I had known nudists existed, but I'd never seen this kind of gathering before in my life. What was this? A nudist convention? And they were so relaxed about it all; some were even playing a game of volleyball on the beach. And, when I say *some*, I don't mean a bunch of hot models were playing volleyball; I'm talking about people who looked just like my grandparents. But none of them seemed to care. This seemed so natural to them.

"So?" Mike said behind me. "Are you ready?"

"As ready as I will ever be, I guess." I was staring at the sign in front of me. The one that said, *No clothes or towels beyond this point.* Why? *Why?* Wasn't it enough for them that I was naked under the thing. And then, in one swift, dramatic, backlit moment, Mike pulled his towel off. I swear I heard a soundtrack playing—that one that happens when there is a giant reveal . . . *Taaa-daaaah!*

And, with that note playing in my head, he started walking on to the beach. I looked around to see if people were staring at him. They weren't. They seemed like they were just going on with their naked day.

"Okay, Becca, oookay," I coaxed myself. "Just pull it off. *Whoosh.* Pull. Take it off. In three, two—"

I did. I took it off. I flung the towel over my shoulder, so it draped over me and covered at least one of my breasts. And now for the hard part: walking. Walking and not obsessing that things were jiggling—which they were. Let's just be clear: there was definite jiggling. And wobbling. I'm sure it was not pretty, but Mike was striding in front of me and I needed to catch up . . .

Okay, note to self: do not speed-walk when naked. Just don't. I swear, one of my boobs nearly gave me a black eye! I walked across the beach, in front of people, and not one of them looked at me strangely. Not one gave me a peculiar look or even paid me any attention. And the more I walked, the more I began to relax. No— *relax* is not the right word. I was as relaxed as someone who was lying on a bed of nails might be. That kind of relaxed. Mike looked at me over his shoulder and smiled. *What was he thinking?*

This beach was rather spectacular, surrounded by a cliff face, and carved out of the cliff was a large cove. Most people had placed their chairs in the shade of the rocky overhang, and that was where Mike and I headed first. We walked further into the cove, to the place where no one was sitting, where it became darker and more cave-like. I shivered a little as the light of the sun faded and we walked into the dark shadow.

"Shall we go in further?" I asked, feeling unsure. I wasn't exactly a fan of small, enclosed spaces, especially of late.

"Yes!" Mike continued walking.

"Uh . . ." The space inside seemed to get smaller quickly, as if this massive cove was turning into a small cave.

Mike turned around and looked at me. "You okay?" he asked.

"I've recently become not such a fan of smaller spaces," I said. "You know, since almost dying in an elevator and what not."

At that, unexpectedly, he offered me his hand. I took it and he immediately wrapped his fingers around mine, protectively. He continued to walk. The cave was becoming darker and smaller, and the floor was no longer sandy, but rocky. Mike stopped at a sign that was attached to a small fence.

"*No Entry*," I read.

Mike didn't waste any time, though; he pushed the small fence out the way.

"Wait—it says *no entry*; it could be dangerous or something." I let go of his hand and wrapped the towel around myself properly.

"Since when has a no-entry sign stopped you before?" he asked.

I looked at the cave and sighed. "Fine." I held on to my towel with both hands now, and followed Mike inside.

I could see why there was a no-entry sign. A shaft of light was rushing through the roof, and a pile of stones lay on the floor below it. Clearly, a part of the ceiling had given way. But at least the hole provided some much-needed light. The small cave was about the same size as the room under the stage. *How had they found all these places?*

I looked around at the walls and instantly spotted the etchings in the rock. There were so many clues like this around town, etched into trees and rocks and rooms. This town bore the markings of a great love story that no one knew about, except us. This town held a secret that was always just out of sight, but, if you knew where to look, you could see it clearly. I traced my fingers over the carving. It was exactly the same as the one from the tree.

"It's them," I said.

"Has to be." He echoed my sentiment, and then he took a step closer to me. I knew this, because I could feel the warmth radiating off him. His body was so close, and yet so far away. So far away, because it had been mine to touch only the night before last, and now it wasn't. I felt his head come closer to my shoulder, until I could see it there in my periphery. I could hear his breathing; I could feel it on my exposed shoulder and neck. It was warm against my cool skin. I closed my eyes; I could feel the tension in the air. I could feel him wanting to touch me, but holding himself back. He took another step closer and his chest came into contact with my back. I leaned back, allowing my body to fully connect with his. Neither of us said a word; it wasn't as if we needed words. I put my head back on his shoulder, rested it there. He felt warm and safe.

We stayed like that for ages, until—slowly, tentatively—he wrapped an arm around me. I sunk into him and put my hands on his forearms, clutching him closely. I looked at the engraving in front of me—he looked, too—and suddenly I didn't know if I was Becca anymore.

We could have been them, holding each other in this small, stolen moment, while the world outside disappeared. In here, it was just us. Just this feeling of togetherness and . . . *love*. Strange, sudden, all-consuming.

But then, just as quickly as it had started, it stopped, and Mike just walked away.

CHAPTER 62

*"S*o, how was your day?" Ash asked, as we walked into the house library, which seemed to have become our unofficial headquarters.

"Interesting." Mike flopped down on to a couch and I walked to the other end of the room and sat down, too.

Interesting was an understatement, though. We'd held each other, naked, in a cave, and then, after that, everything had felt stranger than it had ever felt between us. Because Mike had suddenly just left me there, standing naked, all by myself, without an explanation. We'd driven off in silence together and hadn't spoken about what had happened.

"Oh? What was interesting about it?" Ash asked. "Find anything useful?"

Mike leaned forward on the couch. "Well, we did go to the cove."

Ash smiled. "The *cove* cove? No-clothes cove?"

Mike nodded. "And we also discovered an underground erotic book ring that is being run out of our town library, and it seems the mastermind behind the whole thing is none other than my future sister-in-law," he said.

Ash looked over at Emelia. "Told you he would find out, sooner or later."

"You knew about this?" he asked Ash.

"Those ladies were desperate for some excitement," Emelia said, "especially when the Viagra ran out in town."

"The WHAT?" Mike sat up straight.

"Remember just before Joe retired from the pharmacy, before Hector took over?" she said.

"Yes?" Mike sounded like he was bracing himself for something he didn't want to hear.

"Towards the end, when he went a bit . . . you know, forgetful, he didn't place any orders for Viagra for months. But, since Hector took over, that's all fine. Blue pills all round!" She shot Mike the thumbs up and he face-palmed.

"How do you know all this stuff?" he asked.

"I supply the ladies' weekly book club with eats. It's amazing what you overhear."

"And that's when you decided to start buying them those books?" She laughed. "It's not like it's illegal."

"Really?" Mike pointed at me. "Take your book out, Becca. Because I'm pretty sure that *that* is totally illegal."

I scrounged in my bag and pulled out my book and held it up.

"Oh, yes, I remember that one," Emelia said.

"Wait, give that to me." Ash laughed and snatched the book out of my hands and opened a random page.

"*His scales were both hard and soft to the touch. I ran my hands over the wondrous things, glistening and glimmering in the prehistoric sunlight. I had never known this kind of desire before—so primitive, so carnal and so unexpected. My brontosaurus tilted his head and looked at me with those sexy, reptilian eyes. He was so handsome, and I wanted him more than I had . . . WHOA!*" Ash put the book down and looked at us. "Tell me I'm not reading what I think I'm reading."

Mike nodded. "Apparently, dinosaur erotica is a thing."

Emelia burst out laughing. "I was just ordering what was requested." She quickly looked over at Ash. "I'm not into that—promise."

"Eeewww." Ash cringed. "I should hope not." She turned to Mike and me and held the book up. "And they are all reading this stuff?"

I shook my head. "No, some are reading about merman threesomes," I quickly added.

"What?" Ash looked at me, appalled. "Is bondage and S & M not kinky enough for them anymore?"

"I think it's cool," Emelia announced. "I hope I'm still having sex at that age. Just because you get older, doesn't mean that part of you dies."

"No dinosaur erotica allowed in our house." Ash wagged a finger at her.

"I promise," Emelia said.

"We did find something else, though," I said, pulling the other thing out of my bag.

"What's that?" Ash asked.

I stood up and walked over to her and placed the painting in her hands. I didn't need to say anything to her; she inhaled sharply when she saw it. Emelia moved over to get a closer look and, when she did, her hand flew up and covered her mouth in shock.

"This is him," Ash declared.

"Yes," I stated.

We all sat in silence and I could see that Ash and Emelia were looking at the picture in exactly the same way as I had—with a sense of absolute wonder.

"What's this?" Ash pointed at the corner.

"What?" We all moved closer.

"It looks like writing. Look—can you see it?"

"Vaguely," I said, not sure if I was seeing letters or not.

"Wait. I'm coming back." Ash put the picture down and raced out of the room. Moments later, she came back with some bottles of liquid and a few cotton buds and brushes.

"I need more light." She looked up at the ceiling—the light in this room was naturally dim—and, at the same time, we all took out our cell phones and flicked our torches on. We shone the light down on to the canvas that Ash was now carefully working on. As we watched, I could feel the collective holding of breath as something started to emerge from the ash and dirt and dust. She continued to work and soon it became clear what we were looking at.

"It's a letter," she said. "It's an . . . an . . ."

We all leaned and squinted.

"A!" Ash yelled triumphantly. "It's a bloody A!"

"Oh my God," I gasped. "It *is* an A. She calls him 'A' in her diary."

"What else can you see?" Mike asked.

"Okay, give me some time and space." Ash swatted us back with her hand and we moved. "This might take a while; you'll have to give me at least half an hour."

"Shall I make dinner, then?" Emelia asked.

"Pleeeassse." Ash looked over her shoulder and smiled at her fiancée. "And I could seriously do with a little glass of vino."

"Me too," Emelia said, walking towards the door. "All this detective work makes me thirsty."

"Me too." Mike started following Emelia out the door.

"Are you coming?" Emelia asked me. "You heard the lady—she wants some peace and quiet."

"Uh . . ." I looked at Mike; he was looking at the floor. "It's okay. I'll just go and chill in my room for a bit. I wouldn't want to disturb family dinner—"

"Oh, don't be an idiot!" Ash swung around and looked at me. "What are you talking about? Go, drink wine and relax, and we'll all have dinner together soon."

"It's fine. Don't worry about me. I'll go grab something somewhere." It was less about disturbing a family dinner, and more about getting away from Mike. The uncomfortableness between us since the cave was making my skin burn.

"God, you are a martyr, aren't you?" Ash said. She looked over at Emelia. "Sort her out," she said to her.

"Yes, ma'am." Emelia walked up to me and looped her arm through mine. "Come," she said. "You can peel potatoes." And, before I knew what was happening, I was being dragged off by her.

CHAPTER 63

"*I* don't really drink," I said, after the glass of wine had been poured and passed to me.

Emelia looked at me and did a fake double take. "And why ever not?" she asked.

"Well, it's kind of embarrassing, really," I said.

Both Mike and Emelia looked at me expectantly now.

I sighed. "I go red," I said.

"Red?" Mike asked.

"Yes—very."

They both looked at me blankly, as if they didn't understand, so I elaborated.

"It's like a mini allergic reaction. So I try and avoid it, especially when in public and especially on first dates; it can get quite embarrassing."

Mike and Emelia looked at each other and then looked back at me. "What do you mean, *red*?" Emelia asked, with a smile.

"Bright red. Tomato red," I qualified. "But not an even red—that would be okay. I go blotchy."

"Where?" she asked.

"Just my face," I said. I was embarrassed just talking about it.

Mike and Emelia then shared a smile.

"This, I've got to see." Emelia walked over to me and gently pushed the glass to my lips.

"No. Really. It's totally embarrassing and I look ridiculous and you'll all just laugh at me—"

"You're among friends. We won't judge you, as long as you don't judge my bad singing after I've had two glasses." We shared a small smile and I lowered my lips to the glass. I took a sniff. God, I missed wine. The smell, the taste, the whole experience.

"Your friends must love watching you go red when you go out for drinks. It's like a party trick," Emelia said casually, but the statement struck me hard.

"I don't really go out drinking much . . . with friends," I said quietly.

"True. Neither do we, really. We're more home drinkers. Dinner parties at home, you know. I think we're all getting older."

"Mmm . . ." I mumbled. "I meant more the 'with friends' part." I said this so quietly that I wasn't even sure they heard it.

"What do you mean?" she asked, turning to look at me properly now.

I shrugged. "I don't really, well, have many friends."

"I suppose you're so busy writing that you don't get to see them that much," Emelia said.

"No, not really. I mean . . . I just don't have many, you know, *friends*."

Emelia blinked at me. "What do you mean, you don't have many friends?"

I took another sip of wine—a rather large one, and immediately started feeling the effects. When you don't drink, two sips is enough to send you on your merry way. "I'm not so good at making them, I guess," I said.

Emelia looked at me expectantly, as if she needed more information.

I took another quick sip and started rambling a little. "I kind of moved around a lot when I was young. I was never in one place for long enough to make any friends, I suppose. Besides, wherever I went, I didn't really fit in—well, not until I *made* myself fit in. And then, I suppose, when you're pretending to fit in, you don't really make friends, because you don't actually have anything in common with anyone. Or something like that." I took another sip. My tongue was loosening. I never spoke to anyone about these kinds of things, and now it was all just flowing out of me. "I'm probably just bad at making any kind of meaningful connections with anyone. It's like if you've never learned to cook and then suddenly someone asks you to cook something, you'll probably be bad at it, even if you have a recipe!" I concluded, after another gulp of wine. "Mind you, I don't even think I was ever given a recipe. Or I was given the wrong one. It's like I'm trying to cook coq au vin, but someone gave me a pizza recipe."

Mike and Emelia looked at me blankly for a while, and I realized that I had lost them with my cooking analogy.

"Bottom line," I stated, "I'm just not good at making and keeping friends. I'm probably just not friend material."

Emelia looked at me for a while and then started shaking her head vigorously. "That's such crap! What are you talking about? I've known you for five minutes and I like you a lot. I was thinking how much I'd like to be friends with you."

"Really?" I asked softly.

"You're so wrong about that," she stated, matter-of-factly.

"You sure?" I asked.

She nodded again. "You probably just haven't met your tribe yet."

"My tribe?" I said thoughtfully.

"Everyone has a tribe!" Emelia said. "And, I'll have you know, most tribes prefer to eat pizza, not coq au whatever. So, maybe you do have the right recipe, you just don't know it."

"Huh?" I looked at her, confused for a moment or two, trying to work out how my analogy had come full circle, to this, and if it even made sense anymore.

"You're so easy to get along with," Emelia continued. "Don't you think, Mike? It's sort of impossible *not* to like Becca." She turned and looked at Mike, who'd been standing silently during this conversation. "Don't you think?" she asked again. This time, her voice had taken on a strange, knowing tone.

Mike didn't answer and, on that rather awkward note, Emelia walked out and left us alone together.

I quickly took another sip of my wine and tried not to look at Mike. I could see that Emelia's rather pointed statement was having the same effect on him as it was on me. That was obvious from the way he was shuffling his feet from side to side. The silence dragged on until it was broken by Emelia bursting back into the room. She stopped when she came inside.

"God, I could cut the tension in here with the back of a spoon." She put her hands on her hips and gave us both a suspicious look.

I shrugged. "What? It's nothing. It's . . . you know . . . nothing." I drank more wine and deliberately avoided looking at Mike.

"Nothing," I heard Mike say.

"Well, obviously, it is *something*, or you wouldn't both be saying 'nothing' so emphatically." She looked from me to him and back again.

"Well, I guess it was *something*, and then, I guess, it wasn't," I said.

I heard Mike clear his throat. "There was a very clear reason for it being *something* and then suddenly *not* being something," he said pointedly. "And that hasn't really gone away fully."

"Um . . . sure," I said, "I know that, but it seems that, in light of what's happening now, maybe that *something* shouldn't be such a something, after all?"

"Trust me, that *something* is still something. Just because everyone else is over it, doesn't mean I am."

"You seemed over it an hour ago, when you had your arm around my—*Shit!*" I cut myself off and put my hand over my mouth. I hadn't meant to say that out loud.

"Arm around your what?" Emelia asked, as if she was enjoying this far too much.

"Nothing," I quickly said.

"Something!" Emelia reiterated.

"Nothing," Mike exclaimed, a little too loudly.

"It *was* something!" I said, as loudly as Mike had spoken. Oh dear, the wine seemed to be acting like a truth serum now, and all my true feelings were tumbling from my lips. "And it meant something," I whispered into my glass.

"Interesting," Emelia said, after a moment's silence. "So, what I'm getting from you two," she said, smiling ear to ear, as if she was finding this highly amusing, "is that *something* happened between you . . . Actually, shall we just be adults and call it what it is? You had sex. And, now, I'm guessing that you're not having sex anymore—except for that moment where Mike had his arm around you—because something else happened. And now nothing is happening, but you're both struggling with that because it may or may not have meant *something* to both of you. Have I summed it up?" she asked.

I looked over at Mike. We held each other's gaze for a few seconds and then both looked away.

"I'll take that awkward semi-eye-contact interchange between you two as a *Yes, I've summed it up*," she said.

"Mmm," I mumbled, under my breath, sipping the wine and feeling the rush of it through my veins.

Emelia looked at Mike for confirmation, raising one of her pierced brows at him.

"Mmm," he mumbled back.

"Good! Good to get things out in the open!" she exclaimed happily. "We can work with this. Perhaps, Becca, you could share with Mike your first childhood memory?"

"Huh?" I said, looking at her.

She burst out laughing. "I'm just fucking with you. I'd make a terrible therapist! I'd be too damn direct."

"So, be direct," I said to her.

"I don't know. Not sure you two could handle the truth."

Mike suddenly pulled a chair out and sat down at the dining-room table. "We can handle the truth. Although, I'm pretty sure it will be way off." He looked at me and patted the chair next to him. I sat down quickly.

"Fine." Emelia sat down, too, and we all looked at each other for a while. "Should we hold hands and sing 'Kum Ba Yah' first?" she joked, and then laughed again.

Mike shot her a disapproving look and she stopped laughing.

"God—so serious. Be cool," she said to him. "Mind you, I guess going to a nudist beach and stripping down to your birthday suit is probably the definition of cool."

Mike's cheeks went a little red, and I'm sure mine did, too, as memories of what had *almost* happened in the cove came flooding back to me.

"Aaaaah," Emelia said. "I see . . ."

"See what?" I asked.

"Did *something* that means *something*, that could have been *something*, happen on the beach, perhaps?"

We looked at each other briefly.

"Oooh, I'm getting good at this stuff. Screw the bakery—I'm becoming a psychologist." Then she sat back in her chair and put her hands together in that thoughtful, psychologist way. "You know what I think?" she asked.

We both shook our heads.

"I mean, the sexual attraction between the two of you is undeniable. You can see it a mile away."

"Pssshhht, please," I said defensively.

Emelia raised a brow at me. "No amount of *pssshhht*ing will convince me you're not attracted to that man. I mean, I'm a lesbian, for heaven's sake, and even I am attracted to him!" She turned to Mike. "And you—I've seen the way you look at her when she's not looking."

"What?" I asked.

"I don't think so." Mike looked uncomfortable now.

"He's always staring at you when you're not looking," she said.

"Staring?" I asked.

"You make it sound creepy," Mike piped up. "I might steal the odd glance, from time to time. I certainly don't stare."

"No, you basically stare," Emelia confirmed. "And, as for you—" she returned her attention to me now—"I've noticed all the little coy looks and the prolonged sighs you make when he's around."

"I don't make prolonged sighs!" I objected.

"Yeah, you actually do," Mike said. "You sigh a lot."

"I do not. Perhaps I exhale a little loudly sometimes, but I certainly don't sigh."

"You sigh," she said. "You are a sigher and—" she looked at Mike again—"you stare. So, you're a starer. And I can only assume that all that staring and sighing indicates that the two of you want to, you know, do *something* that meant more than nothing that could have been s*omething*, again."

A moment's silence.

"And, from where I am literally sitting, I see no reason why you shouldn't do that something. It's clear you like each other, or you wouldn't be acting like an old, angry married couple and moping about like this."

"We're not acting like a married couple!" we both said, at exactly the same time.

Emelia laughed. "Sure, and that's why you're finishing each other's sentences now, too. Besides, you met on a fence."

"What's that got to do with it?" I asked.

Then she leaned in, she looked at us closely and mysteriously, and, in a voice that one would expect to hear from some kind of dramatic, pretend psychic, she whispered, "Oh, I think it has everything to do with it . . . *everything*."

At that, Ash burst through the door. "I have it! I have his name."

CHAPTER 64

"*Abe E*," Mike read.

"Yup," Ash said proudly.

"What does the *E* stand for?" Mike asked.

"Well, I don't know that," Ash said. "I'm an artist, not a psychic."

"Funny you should say that; seems your fiancée is a baker and a psychologist."

"Huh?" she asked, looking at her brother.

"Long story," I said, and then sighed.

"SEE? HA!" Emelia said. "You sighed."

"I . . . I . . . Okay, so I did," I conceded.

"You do sigh a lot, now that I think about it," Ash said.

Mike gave a small, self-satisfied smile. "Well, at least I don't stare."

I looked at him pointedly.

"Oh, yeah." Ash started nodding. "He does stare a lot."

"Okay, change of subject, thanks," Mike said quickly. "What do we think the Abe is short for? Abraham?"

"Could just be Abe?" I suggested.

Ash stood up straight and stretched out her shoulders. "All this detective work has made me hungry. What's for dinner?"

"Haven't started it yet," Emelia said. "Been too busy trying to solve the world's problems." She smiled at us.

"Did I miss something?" Ash asked.

"Oh, yes—*something* being the operative word, there," Emelia replied. "Something that could be nothing, or something, or whatever."

And then, suddenly, Ash looked over at me and gasped. "What's wrong with your face? You're red!"

I raised my hands to my cheeks and everyone looked at me.

"You weren't kidding," Emelia said. "You do go bright red, if you drink."

I looked over at Mike and, this time, I got a smile out of him.

"Oh, God—this is why I don't drink. Soooo embarrassing." I tried to hide my face.

Ash burst out laughing. "You go red when you drink?"

I nodded.

"That would make your job easy, Mike," she said. "No need for a breathalyzer." Ash pulled my hands away from my face. "Don't be embarrassed. It's just making you redder," she said.

"Am I splotchy, or is it at least even?" I asked.

The three of them looked at me and then looked at each other, slowly.

"It's . . . Let's just say it's not even." Mike tried to conceal a smile.

"What? How bad is it?" I asked.

"Mmmm, you know how a leopard has spots?" Ash teased.

"Nooo!" I yelped. "It can't be that bad!"

They all looked at me again, all trying to hold back smiles. I ran for the closest bathroom and looked at myself in the mirror in horror. I looked ridiculous. My face was spotty, as if I had contracted some kind of exotic rash.

"I can see why you don't drink on first dates," Emelia said, with a chuckle, when I returned. "Wouldn't want them to start thinking you're contagious."

Ash smacked her on the arm. "Hey. That's rude. She doesn't look *that* bad . . ."

I gave them all a deadpan look. "Really?" I asked. I ran my hand in big circles around my face. "This doesn't look *that* bad, does it?"

At that, all three of them laughed, and, before I knew what was happening, I laughed too.

* * *

The rest of the evening was strange. But nice. Me and my red, splotchy face enjoyed a massive bowel of pasta and more red wine—despite the fact that, every time I had a sip, a new red splotch appeared and everyone pointed it out—and then we all "retired" to the sitting room, put some logs on the fire and sat and watched the flames, like primitive man might have done. We laughed, we told each other stories from our lives. Ash and Emelia shared the story about how they'd met and fallen in love. Emelia had, on a strange whim she said she couldn't really explain (must have been fate, she concluded), decided to drop out of big-city life and move to a small town and set up a pastry shop. She'd hired Ash to paint her shop sign and, from the moment she'd seen her up that ladder, splattered in paint, she'd known! I then shared the story of my previous public shaming and humiliation at the hands of my cheating ex. They said they remembered "cunt-gate" (as they dubbed it) and all those internet memes it had sparked. And they all showed such instant hatred for this man that had wronged me! It felt good. I hadn't had a group of people rally around me like this before—a group that, on my behalf, despised the man who had done that to me. They also agreed that I should never have phoned his fiancée and, had they known me at the time, they would have all seriously recommended against it. Mike and Ash then started debating which room in the house they should renovate next, and what color they should paint the walls, and whether or not they should redo the dining room and host events in it, like weddings and parties. It was a conversation about something so seemingly banal and normal, but, to me, it was magical. To be sitting there, listening to them talk about their day-to-day things—it made me feel included in a way I don't think I had ever felt.

When the evening was over, we found ourselves all walking back to our rooms.

I said my goodbyes and walked towards the door, feeling a little skate-y on my feet. As if they weren't really walking, heel to toe, heel to toe (as they should be), but sort of moving from side to side, as if on ice or something slippery—like the squashed grapes one might use to make wine!

"Well, aren't you going to walk her to her room?" Ash piped up, and I turned around and looked at them all.

"Who?" I asked.

"Him!" Ash said, pointing at her brother. "It's the gentlemanly thing to do."

"It is," Emelia confirmed.

"I'm fine," I said. "Big girl and all. Been walking myself to places on my own for many years."

"Still, it's a long, dark corridor. It might be fraught with danger," Ash teased, as she draped her arm around Emelia's shoulders.

"Fraught with danger," Emelia echoed.

"No one uses the word *fraught* anymore," Mike said.

"We do." Ash gave her brother a small push.

Mike walked towards me. "Fine." He opened the door and held it open for me. "Shall we?" he asked.

"Aaaah, so chivalrous," Ash said.

"Clearly, it's *not* dead." Emelia pulled Ash and they started walking up the stairs together and disappeared.

I walked into the dark corridor that separated the houses, and Mike pulled his cell-phone light out and lit up the path in front of us. I tried to walk in a manner where my feet skated less and did what they were supposed to. I seemed to manage okay and soon we were standing outside my door.

"Thanks," I turned around and said to him.

"Pleasure." He looked at me and turned the torch off, plunging us into the soft, warm glow from the crystal chandeliers above us.

"Right . . ." I reached behind me and opened my door.

"Right," he repeated.

"This was a really nice night," I said softly, as I began pushing the door open. "I really enjoyed it. Thanks for having me."

He nodded. "Sure. It was nice."

"I don't do stuff like this much. I'm usually a bit of a recluse," I blurted out.

"I wouldn't guess that about you." He was leaning with his back against the wall on the other side of the passage now.

"I am. Usually just stick to myself."

"So what keeps you company?" he asked.

"I don't know. Maybe the songs and stories in my head."

"Sounds lonely," he said quietly. "You can't go anywhere, here, without bumping into someone you know. You're never lonely, here. Even if you wanted to be, you couldn't be."

"I'm not lonely . . ." I started saying, and then stopped myself, because suddenly I did feel lonely. Suddenly, after having this evening of laughter and food and drink, I felt like I was already missing it. I imagined myself alone on a Saturday night, watching Netflix and wondering what Mike and Ash and Emelia were doing. "Maybe I was a little lonely, but I didn't know it," I said, again without thinking.

Why was I saying all these things to him—these intimate things that made me feel vulnerable and exposed? I didn't like to feel like this. He looked at me, and that same familiar feeling rose inside, the one that had been rising non-stop since we'd first met.

"Anyway . . ." I said, trying to diffuse the situation, as one does when one feels uncomfortable and throws words like *anyway* and *so* about, with no real intention of actually turning them into a sentence at all . . . *Shut up!*

"Anyway, what?" he asked.

Damn!

"Nothing," I said.

"Okay." He nodded and pushed himself off the wall. "Goodnight, then."

"Goodnight, Mike . . ." And then I said it. I probably shouldn't have, and maybe it was the red wine . . . "Hey," I called after him. "Aren't I still under arrest, or something?"

He turned slowly. I could see he was trying to conceal another smile. "Technically."

"So . . . shouldn't you be watching me? Who knows what I might get up to . . . alone?" Whoa! Had I really just said that? I had. I had.

He smiled. "What might you get up to?"

I shrugged playfully. "Well . . . I was thinking of kidnapping a dog, next. Perhaps I might impersonate a human-hair stylist and start giving the good people of Willow Bay perms."

He laughed. Oh, God—it sounded good. "So, are you saying that, if I don't watch you tonight, you might get up to something illegal again?"

"Perhaps. I mean, who knows? I am a bit of a criminal mastermind, these days."

He laughed. "I disagree. You're perhaps one of the worst criminals I've ever met."

"What?! I am so offended. I'll have you know that my criminal skills are . . . are . . . are . . ."

"Really shit!" he added, with a massive smile.

I smiled back at him. "Still . . . who knows what will happen tonight, if I'm left alone?" I was flirting. I had no idea whether it was any good, but I was doing it!

He took a step closer. "So, what are you suggesting?"

"That's up to you, officer," I said.

He put his hand on the wall behind my head and leaned in. Our eyes met, and I held on to his gaze as tightly as I could, because I didn't want him to take it away again.

"You know what?" he said slowly.

I shook my head.

"I'm going to trust you tonight."

"You are?" I gasped and then almost cried. "Seriously? You trust me again?"

He looked at me for the longest time. "Please—" his voice became soft and desperate sounding—"please don't let me down and do anything to break that, this time. Not like last time."

"Are you giving me a second chance?" I asked.

"Maybe." He didn't look one hundred percent sold, but I was taking it.

"Does that mean you've forgiven me?" I asked.

"Getting there, slowly." He looked at me seriously.

I started nodding. "I won't do anything bad, I promise. I won't let you down, I won't lie again, I won't . . . I promise!" My heart felt like it wanted to leap into his hands. He was giving me another chance! Was this him accepting my apology for everything that had happened between us?

"Goodnight, Becca." He leaned in and planted the smallest kiss on my lips.

"Goodnight, Mike," I whispered against his mouth.

"By the way," he said, pulling away slightly, "I like you in red." He ran a finger over my cheek and then traced the curve of my mouth with it.

I smiled at him and then he turned and walked off.

CHAPTER 65

I was fast asleep when I felt the bed moving up and down.

"Becca!" I heard his voice and then I felt the warm hand on my shoulder. "Becca, wake up," he said.

"What?" I mumbled, caught somewhere between awake and asleep—that strange no man's land where your body feels suspended between what is real and what isn't.

"Come, get up. I think I know where the letters are," he said to me, a gentle tapping on my shoulder.

At that, I sat straight up. I blinked several times, until my eyes adjusted to the light a little better. The moon was full; it was casting a soft white light into my room and this white light made Mike look like some kind of a statue, sculpted out of a white slab of marble.

"Where?" I rubbed the sticky sleep from my eyes and shook my head awake.

"The stables." Mike flicked the light on next to my bed and I blinked rapidly as the harsh light almost blinded me. I shielded my eyes with my hands.

"What do you mean, stables?" I asked.

"I was looking through the old photo albums again, and there's a picture of her and her horse," he said.

I nodded and yawned at the same time. "I read about that in her diary."

"Well, its name was Darcy. The horse."

At that, a little shot of adrenalin woke me up. "And you think, what? That she hid the letters in the stables? That it was a cryptic clue—she didn't mean an actual book?"

"Wouldn't you make it cryptic? Something that only the person who knows you would work out?"

"Sure," I said. "It's just a slight leap, isn't it? My favorite book, to the horse stables?"

"And, think about it, the stables are all the way at the bottom of the property, they back on to the woods—he would have been able to get to them, unseen. And, also, if she was unable to get away to give them to him, because my great-grandfather was watching her, she could have easily put them in the stables when she went riding."

"You've thought about this a lot," I said. I was still skeptical, though.

"I'm going to check it out, whether you're coming or not."

I jumped up. "I didn't say I wasn't coming."

"Okay," he said, and waited for me as I skidded around the room, pulling on a pair of shoes and a jumper.

"It's inside out." He pointed, once I was done.

"Mmmm?" I looked down at myself. I had indeed put my jumper on the wrong way. "I'm not very functional in the morning," I said, trying to pull the thing off, but getting tangled in the process.

"Here." He moved over to me and pulled at my jumper. "Seems you need some help dressing yourself in the mornings." He smiled.

I put my arms up in the air and watched him as he pulled the jumper up and off me. He was looking at it with such concentration as he held the hole open for me to stick my head through. I did, and popped out the other end with a smile.

"Haven't had someone dress me in a while," I joked.

"That's surprising, since it seems you need some help in that department."

"Ha ha," I teased back, wiggling into the jumper as he pulled it down my body. But, as his hands grazed my rib cage, I stiffened and froze. Suddenly, everything around us felt different again. *Very.*

His hands stopped what they were doing. They weren't pulling on my top anymore; instead, his fingertips had come to rest on my rib cage. I could feel his hands through the cotton T-shirt I was wearing; they felt warm and soft. They tightened around me slightly and I shivered. My skin pebbled and the hairs on my arms and the back of my neck stood straight up. His hands slipped down my sides, tracing my body as they went, and then came to rest on my waist, making me feel dizzy.

"What are you doing?" I whispered, looking up at him. He was staring at his hands, as if deciding what to do with them. *Should I tell him what to do with them?* Should I let him know where I wanted them? That I wanted them all over my body, in my hair, gripping the back of my neck, on my cheeks, holding my face?

He didn't answer me, but his eyes did. They went from green to a stormy black, and an excited shiver ran the length of my body. And then his gaze left my waist and drifted back up to my eyes, seeking me out with such intensity, such a determined focus, that I was sure the room around me just disappeared.

"What are you doing?" I asked again, my mouth going dry as his hands slipped under my clothing and came to rest on my naked flesh—the soft part, where my hips ended and my stomach began. But he didn't say a word, and neither did I. This strange place we now found ourselves in seemed to be a wordless place—that is, words didn't really seem adequate to describe what was going on. We were neither here, nor there. We were neither lovers, nor strangers. We were neither together, nor apart. We could touch, but we couldn't. We couldn't fall, but we couldn't stop ourselves either. I could feel that, now. His hands moved round to my lower back, and he pulled me closer to him. I lifted my arms and wrapped them around his neck. I looked at him and smiled.

"Becca," he said.

"Mmm?" I continued to smile at him, and then he sighed. The second he did, he let out a small chuckle.

"Must be contagious." Then he stared at me, swaying us from side to side, as if we were dancing.

I laughed. "What are you doing?"

"Don't know," he said.

"Just so you know, I don't dance," I said quickly.

"Neither do I."

"So, why does it feel like we're dancing?" I asked, feeling amused.

He shrugged his shoulders. "Not sure. Maybe it's because I'm trying to decide what to do with you." He stopped swaying and we looked at each other, both our smiles fading.

"What do you want to do with me?" I asked, swallowing.

His eyes swept over my face. "Now, that is a good question, and it doesn't have an easy answer, does it?"

I pushed away from him a little. "No, I guess it doesn't." And then I perked up a little. "But, if it helps, I didn't commit any crimes last night."

He smiled at me. "That does help."

"Thanks. For dressing me," I said.

"Pleasure." He nodded and walked to the door. "We better go."

CHAPTER 66

"*Wow*—how long since these were used?" I asked, as we walked into what were clearly dilapidated stables. They were old and cold, and the walls were made of a cobble stone—the kind you never see anymore.

"I don't think they've been used since my grandmother rode. No one rides horses anymore."

"Where should we look?" I asked.

Mike pointed at a small copper sign on one of the stable doors. "*Darcy*," he read out. "That seems like a good place to look."

He pushed the sticky door open. It scraped across the old stone, fingernails tearing down an old blackboard, and my skin shivered.

We walked in. The air was cold and damp and smelled of dust and old straw. "God, it's a bit creepy in here," I said, wrapping my arms around my body.

Mike pulled a torch out and turned it on.

"And now?" I asked.

"And now, we look." He started moving along the wall again. I copied him, running my hands over the large cobblestones, like he was—although, I wasn't sure I would recognize anything, if I actually found it.

What were we looking for?

"Gross! Gross! Aaaahh!" I pulled my hand away and shook it wildly, trying to get the sticky spider web off it. I wiped it on my pants and cringed. "Gggrraaaggghh." I shook my body, feeling nauseous.

"Bleg! Bleg!" I scrunched my face up and flapped my arms some more.

Mike looked at me. "That was . . . *a lot*," he teased.

"Hate spiders," I said.

"Hate bats, too. And rare nesting birds?"

"Oh, by the way, on that note, I bloody googled that bird, and they totally made it up. There is no black-crested night budgie!"

He chuckled again, like smooth liquid gold. "They have applied to have it officially recognized as a separate species."

At that, I jumped up. "HA! I knew they made that shit up."

He laughed some more. "They seem to think they have a legitimate claim."

"They are soooo wrong," I said, putting my hands back on the wall and tracing over the stones.

"They're convinced. They even called in a bird expert."

"Well, I'm no bird expert, but those were bloody pigeons, if I've ever seen a flipping pi—" I stopped dead when a stone moved. "What the . . . ?" I gave it a little push and the whole thing moved.

"Wait." Mike rushed over and placed his hands over mine. I wasn't so engrossed in the moment that I missed how good that felt. "Careful," he said, wiggling our hands gently, pulling and sliding the stone out, until . . .

"Shit!" The whole thing came out and revealed, straight away, what I knew we had been looking for.

CHAPTER 67

There, behind the rock, was an opening—a large one—and it was absolutely stuffed with envelopes. I stuck my hands in and touched them, in case I was imagining it all, but, when my fingertips ran over that familiar surface, *I knew*. I grabbed a bunch and pulled them out. I looked into the hole. There were more letters. I pulled some more out, and there were more behind those.

"How many are there?" I asked.

I reached in again and pulled out another huge wad. Another one, another, another . . . Mike and I looked at each other in total disbelief. I dropped the massive pile of letters down on the floor and looked at them.

"I don't believe this," Mike said, reaching into the hole and taking out yet another pile.

"There are . . . are . . ." I couldn't believe I was about to say this—"hundreds!" I looked at Mike; he was pulling letters out so quickly, now, and just dropping them to the floor as he went. When he'd finished, we both looked at the huge pile in front of us. We must have stared at them for ages before either of us knew what to do. Slowly, I lowered myself on to the cold floor and sat down in front of the letters.

"They all have dates on the front," I said. "Why would they? Why would you only put the date on the front of the letter, nothing else?" I asked.

Mike crouched next to me and began leafing through the letters. "It's definitely my grandmother's writing," he said.

I nodded. "But why the dates?"

He raised one to his face and looked at it closely, and then looked at me over the letter. "You put the dates on when you want them read in chronological order," he said.

I looked down at the letters and started moving them around with my hands. "Where do you start?"

"Don't you always start at the beginning?" he asked.

"Depends on how you want to tell a story." I picked up one of the letters and read the date out. "The eighteenth of June, 2018."

"Oh my God." Mike looked at me. "That's a week before she died."

I stared at the letter in my hands. I had no idea what was contained inside it, but I could feel that it was important. I could sense it. I slowly passed it over to Mike and he took it between his fingers. I shivered as a cold breeze rushed in through the open door.

"Here." Mike pulled his jacket off and wrapped it around my shoulders.

"Thanks." I smiled at him and held the jacket close. "Read it," I said, indicating the letter in his hands.

He looked up at me nervously, but started nodding. He opened the letter, and then, slowly, he started to read.

Dearest Abe,

I think this might well be my last letter to you. I'm feeling very tired and, to be honest, I would welcome the rest. But, as I come to the end of this all, it's given me an opportunity to reflect on my life.

I haven't had a bad life. I had four wonderful children and more grandchildren than I could ever have hoped for, although I confess that I do have my favorite. My grandson, Michael, who sits by my bedside every night to see if I'm still breathing. He doesn't know that I know he's there. I can see he's exhausted during the day, although he tries to hide it. I feel like I've become such a

burden, but he will never admit it, and I can't wait for the moment
that he gets a full night's sleep again.

Mike couldn't hold it back. He put the letter down and covered his face as his shoulders began to shake. I could hear the muffled sounds of soft crying and I reached over to him and wrapped an arm around his shoulders. He didn't resist my comfort. Instead, his head fell on to my shoulder and he buried his face in the crook of my neck. I lifted my hand and placed it softly on the side of his face, cradling it, like I had a few nights ago. We stayed like that for a while, until he finally pulled away. He wiped his face with the back of his hands.

"It wasn't a burden," he said quietly.

"I know," I replied.

"I can't read this." He passed the letter over to me and I felt my breath catch in my solar plexus.

"Are you . . . sure?" I asked. This letter was so personal, intimate, and letting me read it out loud, well, it seemed like a gesture I wouldn't ever know how to repay. It was such an honest gesture. He simply nodded and I raised the letter up to my face and started reading.

Of course, I'll miss them. I'll miss them all. But there is one person
who I'll miss the most, when I am gone. I have prayed every morn-
ing that I will see you again, but, of course, when I look at all these
letters I've written over the years, I know that will never happen.

I knew, many, many years ago, that you would never find these
letters, but I kept writing them. Over the years, they became more
for me than for you. I write them for you, knowing that you will
never receive them, but it makes me feel better. I feel that, in some
small way, I am still communicating with you. And I need to feel
like that, like I need air to breathe.

Of course, I hope you find these one day, but I've long given
up hope you will. What sustained me through these years was

your letters to me. I read them so many times that I memorized them, and then I sewed them into that bag you gave me. I didn't need them anymore, because, when I closed my eyes every night, I imagined that you were reading them to me. I would try to imagine your voice. But, I confess, it has gotten harder and harder to hear your voice in my head. I can almost still hear it, but it's fading fast and I don't want to live for one single day on this earth without being able to hear your voice in my head anymore.

My husband was a good, kind man, and he loved me very much. But I was never able to give him what he deserved, and, for that, I will always feel guilty. I think I was able to give him a part of my heart, the part that grew to love him in some way. Waking up next to him every morning wasn't a chore; it was something I came to enjoy. He was a companion, and I respected him and cared for him, but he never got my full heart. That has always been for you.

The day you left was the day that part of my heart was locked away. I closed it up behind a door, waiting for you to return with the key that opened it, only you never did.

I don't know where you are, or where you went. I can only imagine that you left after you read the letter that my father forced me to write. I wish I'd never written it. I wish I had been stronger and had been able to stand up to him. I have tried to forgive him over the years for what he did, but it is hard, and, I confess, I now believe I never will.

I feel tired, now. Even as I write this, my hands seem like they won't be able to do this for much longer, and, if I don't get to write this regular letter to you anymore, it will become impossible to live. So, I guess that this letter is a goodbye to you . . .

Abe, I have loved you since the first moment I saw you. I have loved you with the kind of love that I know now is rare, and almost impossible to find. I consider myself lucky to have ever loved like that, even if it was too brief. To love with such abandon and passion. To love with all my heart, mind, body, soul. To love so deeply that sometimes, when I looked at you, my heart felt like it was going to explode. To love so blindly, right from the first moment I saw you. By the time you walked me home and said goodbye to me, that day we first met, I was completely in love, and, only having known you for such a short amount of time, I didn't know how I was going to live without you.

You were my everything. You still are.

You are the last person I will think of when I close my eyes for the final time. I will close them and I will imagine your face, not the way it was, but how it would be today. I bet you've gone grey, like me. I bet your face is lined with wrinkles. I bet your hair has migrated off your head to places you never thought you would have hair . . .

At that, I laughed a little, tears streaming down my cheeks. Mike gave a small chuckle, too.

I bet you walk bent over and your knees feel as bad as mine. I bet you have aches and pains all over that you never knew you would have. I bet all those things. I bet you look nothing like the boy I fell in love with . . . but I bet your eyes are still the same.

If I close my eyes, I can still see them. See them looking at me. See them as I painted them, so many times that I got to know each little corner of them. You always had a spark inside them, and I bet you still have that spark—well, I hope you do. I hope you never lost it and I hope that you had a good life, one filled with love and laughter, like I had . . . even though there was something always missing from it.

I love you. I always have. But now it's time to say goodbye. Please know that I will love you until my last breath, and, who knows, maybe we will meet again in the place beyond this.

I hope we do. But, if we don't, if those short moments I had with you in this life are all I will ever get, it's enough for me. Because my memories of you and my love for you will sustain me for eternity, and for whatever comes after this.

You, me, forever.

We sat there quietly, staring at the letters. As if someone had pressed the mute button, there seemed to be no sound around us at all. The words contained within that letter had silenced us, they had silenced the entire world. They had stopped the breeze from blowing, the crickets from chirping. They had stopped everything. We slowly looked up at each other, eyes shining with tears. We didn't need to communicate our feelings, because I knew I felt exactly like he did. There was no other way to feel. Finally, Mike broke the enduring silence.

"These are all the letters she wrote him, for seventy years." He started picking them up and placing them into one single pile. I watched in amazement as the pile got higher and higher, until it tumbled back down.

"And he never got to read any of them," I said, as my heart broke.

Mike looked at the fallen letters. I could see he was thinking, and then, as if propelled by something unseen, he jumped up. "We have to get these letters to him."

I looked at him, and something exploded inside me. Recognition. "Yes!" I jumped up, too. "We need to find out who he is, where he is, if he's still alive, and we need to get these to him. He needs to know how she felt about him, right to the very end. But how?" I asked.

Mike didn't hesitate. "The town census and all the other old town records. They're kept in our jail cell. We can go and look through them."

I nodded. "We don't have his surname."

"It started with the letter *E*. We'll just have to look through every-thing. Let's wake Ash and Emelia up—this is a four-person job." He grabbed as many letters as he could, and pushed even more into my arms, but there were still too many for us to take, so the rest we put back inside the cavity in the wall. We hurried back to the house, imbued with a sense of purpose.

A purpose . . . I wasn't sure that was the word for this. Because this felt like the single most important task of my entire life. Finding Abe and taking these letters back to him felt like the most meaningful thing I'd ever done with my life. And, in that moment, it all kind of made sense. It all clicked in my head, like a key into a lock. The strange string of events that had led me here—the elevator, the letters, coming here, meeting Mike—it all made sense now. It was as if all of that had been the journey I needed to go on to get here. To be holding these letters in my hands and to be trying to take them back to the one person in the world that they had been meant for.

CHAPTER 68

*"S*o, what are we looking for, exactly?" Ash asked, sliding into one of the old seats behind the desk—the very one I had sat in, the other night, during my short time as an incarcerated person.

"His name was Abe—either short for something, or just Abe. And his surname began with an *E*," Mike said.

Ash and Emelia nodded. "Where do we start?"

Mike walked over to one of the massive shelves and started pulling down files. "Well, this is from 1940 to 1950, so let's start looking here first."

"All of them?" I asked, looking at the massive files and boxes that were now in front of us on the desk.

Mike nodded. The gravity and enormity of our mission suddenly hit me. There was just so much to go through, this was a name in a haystack, and our chances of finding it were stacked against us.

Emelia groaned and looked at her watch. "It's eight in the morning. I can't start doing this without coffee."

"Me, neither!" I moaned back.

Ash nodded. "Pleeeaaasse. I would kill for a coffee right now."

Mike gave Emelia a small nod. "Would be great."

"Okay." Emelia jumped up. "I'll get everyone caffeine." She rushed towards the door and then stopped herself. "Wait—how do you take it, again?" She turned around and looked at me. "Black with sweetener, right?" she asked.

I smiled and nodded at her quickly. And then something strange hit me. A feeling. Small and almost invisible, at first. It was such a seemingly insignificant gesture, fetching me a cup of coffee, but suddenly I felt included. I felt like I was part of some special group, and I hadn't felt that in such a long time—maybe even ever. I looked at Ash and Mike, who were already flipping through dusty pages, and smiled at myself, wondering if this was my group. *Had I found my tribe?* I gave a tiny smile and then looked back down at the first book, opened it and started running my eyes over the names.

* * *

We must have been looking through the files for hours when Mike's phone rang. We all jumped in fright; it was the loudest noise any of us had heard all morning. He answered it straight away, and I immediately knew, from the look on his face and the tone in his voice, who he was speaking to and what the call was about.

"What do you mean, she's gone?" he asked into the phone. He listened and his eyes widened. "And you're sure everything is locked?" I could hear the nurse's frantic voice on the other end. "Then she has to be inside. I'll come over and help you search." Mike hung up and looked at me. "Petra has disappeared again." He stood up, reached for his car keys and started moving towards the door.

I jumped up. "I'll come help you," I said, following him.

"Don't you want to stay and continue looking?" he asked.

"We've got this, don't worry," Ash said from behind us.

"Great. Thanks." Mike nodded at me and we both ran out and climbed into his car.

"Do you think she's looking for her son again?" I asked, as we drove off in the direction of the old-age home.

"Probably. The whole place is locked, though, so she has to be inside somewhere." We drove for three minutes before we got there. This town was quite literally only a few streets big. We jumped out of the car and rushed inside. A group of concerned staff and some of the residents were waiting for us when we arrived.

"I swear, everything is locked." Cynthia, the nurse, looked devastated and frantic. "We've all been so careful since the last time."

"It's okay," Mike soothed her. "We'll find her. Where have you looked?" he asked.

"We've searched all of the rooms on the first floor, and the front garden. We were going to head up to the second floor, now, and then out to the back garden."

"Okay," Mike said. "We'll take the second floor and you take the back garden."

Everyone nodded and dispersed.

Mike and I headed straight up the stairs to the second floor. This floor wasn't in use anymore and was nothing more than a creepy corridor of empty rooms, used for storage. We rushed from room to room, careful not to overlook any nooks or crannies, but, after about thirty minutes of combing the entire place, there was still no sign of her. We rushed back downstairs and were just about to head outside when we heard a shout from the bottom of the garden. We rushed over as fast as we could.

"Shit!" Cynthia looked at us as we all stared at the open gate in the staff area. "How did she even get into the staff quarters without anyone seeing her?" she asked, and looked at the other nurses.

"It's been a busy morning, with the incident in gym class. No one would have been here," one of the other frantic-looking nurses said.

Cynthia nodded and looked over at us. "Mrs. Louw broke her hip. There was a huge commotion. Petra must have slipped out during that."

Mike walked out the gate and I followed him. It led straight out on to the road. "She could be anywhere. I'll go look for her," he said.

Moments later, we were back in his car, driving up and down the small streets and finding nothing. A sense of panic started welling up inside me. *What if something did happen to her, this time?* The sound of Mike's phone ringing broke my train of thought. He reached for it, but paused before answering. I watched in fascination as something washed over his face. I'd never seen it before. What was it? He answered tentatively.

"Hello, April," he said awkwardly into the phone, a strange tone in his voice. "Okay, I'll be there now." He hung up and looked over at me.

"Petra's at her old house. The Cliftons, who live there now, found her standing inside one of the rooms."

"Wow. Great. Great, I'm so . . . God." I shook my head, tears choking me up again. I was an utter emotional mess, at the moment.

Mike put a hand on my shoulder and squeezed it gently. "She'll be okay," he said.

I reached up and put my hand over his. It felt good to be touched by him again. "But will she?" I asked. "Maybe she'll be okay physically, but emotionally?"

Mike remained silent for a while. "I doubt she'll ever be okay that way," he said softly.

His words cut through me like a sword. Of course she wasn't going to be okay. She hadn't spoken to her only child in years, and for what? It seemed so unnecessary. All this pain, because we don't all share the same beliefs, or share the same color skin, or the same sexual preference . . . Underneath it all, we are just the same collection of flesh and blood and bones. Sinews and muscles connecting our vital bits together; lungs that take in oxygen, hearts that beat the same sticky stuff in the same direction, arms and legs and eyes and ears . . . *We're made of star stuff.* Carl Sagan's words echoed in my mind. It was just such a beautiful sentiment: billions of people, all made of the same stuff that had once exploded out of stars. Surely, the fact that we all came from the same exploding place was all the proof we needed that we were more similar than different?

We finally pulled up to the house and rushed to the front door.

We didn't even need to knock; it was already standing open, waiting for us.

"Hello, Mike." We walked in and were greeted by a woman. There was something strange and familiar in the way that she'd said his name.

"April," he said, not making eye contact. Mike's eyes drifted down to her stomach—the pregnant stomach that she was cradling.

I knew who this was: April the woman, not the month.

"How are you?" he asked, finally looking up at her. She was gorgeous. She definitely had a pregnancy glow about her. Long, blond hair, blue eyes, a better figure than mine, even though it looked like a small human was about to fly out of her. This was definitely the kind of woman I could see Mike with, and suddenly I felt incredibly inadequate. I always felt inadequate around these perfect-looking women, I always wondered what they thought of me—like that woman who'd been inside the elevator, the one with the matt lips, who'd looked me up and down.

"Good." April smiled and rubbed her stomach. "Due any day now. And you?" she asked.

"Good." His answer was short and stoic. "Ash and Emelia just got engaged."

"Really? Wow, that's amazing news. Please send them our congratulations."

Our. The word sort of echoed around us. Mike nodded. "Thanks; I will. Where's Petra?" he asked.

"She's upstairs, in the nursery. It's a bit creepy, to be honest. She's just standing there. I got quite a fright this morning, when I saw her," April said, looking over at me for the first time since we got there. "Sorry—I didn't introduce myself. I'm April." She stuck out her hand and I shook it. Smooth, soft hands.

"Becca," I said.

"Well, thanks for coming," she said to us.

We walked upstairs and into the nursery. It was yellow. The walls, the bedding in the crib, the carpet—it was as if a sunflower had exploded in here.

"We don't know what we're having yet," April said, behind me, as if she could read my mind.

I nodded. Whoever first thought that yellow was a neutral color for children was just so wrong. "It's lovely," I lied. It wouldn't have been my choice, but hey.

Petra was sitting in a chair at the end of the room, staring at the cot. When she saw us, she looked up and put her finger over her lips.

"Shhh," she said. "I've just put him down."

"Oh my God," April whispered, behind us. "This is so sad."

She didn't need to state the obvious, though. This was more than sad. This was devastating. Heartbreaking. This was the single most tragic thing I had ever seen.

Mike stepped towards her. "Petra," he called.

She looked up at him with the saddest eyes I've ever seen. Empty and hollow, desperate for something to fill them.

"We've come to take you back home," he said softly. "You remember me, right?"

She looked at Mike and shook her head.

"I'm a friend." Mike took her by the hand and started lifting her out of the chair.

"Where are you taking me?" she sounded panicked.

"Home," Mike answered.

"Isn't this home?" she enquired.

Mike shook his head. "It used to be your home. But now it belongs to someone else."

"WHO?" she exclaimed. "Did they swindle us out of the house?"

Mike smiled. "No. They bought it from you."

"Good. Because I hate swindlers."

"Me too," Mike said. "Nothing worse than swindlers."

"And charlatans," she said, as Mike began leading her out the door.

"I hate charlatans," Mike agreed. "I arrest them whenever I can."

He started edging her down the stairs, back to the front door, and she became quite wrapped up in their conversation.

"You know, someone came to my door, just the other day, and tried to sell me a Hoover, when I already have a perfectly good one. And I told him that I didn't need one, and guess what? He came back the next day, offering me a set of encyclopedias," she said angrily.

Mike nodded at her. "Well, thanks for letting me know about this. I will certainly keep an eye out for him."

She nodded. "And so you should. Dreadful man, trying to sell me things I don't need. And have you seen the tube, these days? Always selling, selling, selling. You can't turn it on without them trying to sell you something and swindle you out of your money."

Mike tutted. "I know. Terrible." And we went like this all the way back to the car and back to the old-age home.

CHAPTER 69

I stopped Mike before we walked back into the police station. We hadn't spoken since taking Petra back. This whole thing, right down to being inside April's sunflower-soup nursery, had felt so emotionally draining, and now I was just exhausted.

"Do you want to talk about it?" I asked, knowing that he probably didn't.

He shook his head.

"Must have been hard, being inside that nursery," I said, persisting a little, when I probably shouldn't have. Perhaps I was overstepping a line here.

But when he turned in his seat and started talking, I knew that I hadn't overstepped. In fact, before he'd even started, I got the sense that he wanted to get it off his chest.

"April and I broke up a long time ago," he said to me.

"Is she the one who left you for someone else? The one we spoke about at the bar? The one whose bangs you didn't notice?" I asked.

"Yes," he said. "We were high-school sweethearts. We both grew up here."

"Oh. Oh!" I said. I hadn't realized that their story had so much history.

"When we finished school here, we both went off to the big city to study. She'd always dreamed of going to the city and becoming something great, you know?" he said.

I nodded. I could relate to that. Becoming something great, something other than myself—Pebecca Thorne—was what I strived for most.

"Honestly, I don't think I actually wanted to leave, but she'd convinced me that we'd have this big, glamorous life in the city. Big dreams and ambitions and . . . *whatever*. We were these kids that grew up in a small town and we had no idea about the world out there. But we went."

"Where?"

"Cape Town. We both went to study at UCT."

"What did you study?" I asked.

He chuckled. "Well, that's a good question."

"What do you mean?"

"April always knew what she wanted to be—she wanted to be an architect—and she had this idea in her mind that I should become a great businessman."

"Why?" I asked.

"I don't know—because 'CEO' and 'architect' sound like real jobs. The kind of jobs that successful grown-ups that live in a big city have."

"So you studied business?"

"For three years, then I dropped out. I hated it. After that, I tried politics, followed by a little bit of psychology and some law. By the time I'd done the rounds a few times, she'd graduated as an architect and wanted to start creating that life she'd dreamed about—that 'we'd' dreamed about."

I listened as he spoke, the words just flying out of his mouth now.

"Only, I couldn't really give her that life. I was still trying to figure out what I wanted to do with my life. She was wanting to buy a house and take on jobs at architectural firms with those long, triple-barrel names, like Watson, Livingston, Clifton."

"Clifton?" I asked.

He nodded. "I'm sure you can figure that one out," he said.

"She left you for Clifton?"

"Anthony Clifton, partner at the architectural firm. The guy had what she wanted: money, prestige and a shiny sports car. Of course, by this stage, I was such a disappointment to her, because I was just going round and round in circles and not living up to that dream 'we'd' shared as stupid kids that knew nothing about life."

"It was *her* dream," I offered up.

"But, because it was hers, I thought it was mine too. I guess I also thought I wanted that."

"So, she and Clifton came back here, after that?"

"No. I stupidly tried to live in the big city and 'make it.'" He gestured air quotes. "I thought that, if I could be what she wanted, maybe she'd come back. I thought I was very much in love still. April and I had been together since we were fifteen—she was all I knew. And everything I'd ever thought I wanted for my life was wrapped up in her, *and us*. So, I landed up getting a law degree—"

"I'm sorry—you're a lawyer?"

He nodded.

"But you hated it?"

He nodded again.

"Wait . . . The other day, when you arrested me, you told me there was only one lawyer in town and he was busy. Did you mean you?" I asked.

"Well, I was busy. I was busy arresting you."

"So, you studied law, and now you're a policeman?"

"Funny you should mention that . . ." His tone changed and he gave a little smile.

"What?"

"Let me carry on telling you the story," he said.

"Okay." I crossed my legs on the seat and turned to face him now.

"So . . . I pretended to be a lawyer for a few years, and I pretended to have this life, complete with a fancy apartment and a shiny car and shit like that, but, after all that, she didn't really want me back, anyway. I also realized that big-city life wasn't for me, either, so I came back here."

"And became the town's policeman?" I asked.

He smiled again. "You know this job is more of a volunteer thing?"

"What do you mean?" I asked.

"I'm not really a policeman. I'm more of a police reservist. The town needed someone to man the station, and they voted me in, since I had the most law knowledge, I guess."

"Hang on . . . You're not a real policeman and you arrested me? Can you do that?" I asked.

He shrugged. "Honestly, I'm not sure."

I smacked him on the arm. "Are you kidding? You arrested me and you don't even know if you can?"

"You're the first criminal we've ever had in this town," he said. "I didn't know what to do with you."

"So, I'm technically *not* under house arrest right now?" I enquired.

"I don't know," he said thoughtfully. "Probably not."

"Why isn't there a real policeman in town?" I asked.

Mike looked at me with a deadpan expression. "You know our current population is about 550 people, right? And you know the doctor here also doubles as the vet? And the baker here also doubles as the kingpin of a porn ring?"

I smiled at him. "So, you're a lawyer doubling as a policeman."

He shook his head. "No, I'm no longer a practicing lawyer. I gave that up. I'm actually a small-business owner with my sister, and I volunteer on the side as a policeman."

"Okaaay," I said, taking this all in. "But you wear a uniform and drive a police car?"

"Loaned to our department by the real police, over in Morgan Bay. Technically, they're the real law in this area."

"Right." I crossed my arms. "Well, you take your job very seriously."

He smiled. "I'm just serving and protecting my community."

"So, this is what Ash meant when she said you became a policeman by accident."

"We were having a town meeting and I was voted in. I'd just come back to town."

"And why is April back here?" I asked.

"Oh, well, that's not really the end of the story, with her," he said.

"It's not?"

He shook his head. "No. She came back here about two years after I did. Things with Anthony didn't work out, and we got back together for a year, and then she left me again."

"What? She left you twice?"

"Told you I wasn't good at reading woman signals."

"Who did she leave you for this time?" I asked.

"She went back to Anthony, or should I say that he came here for her and won her back. By that stage, I must have been a serious disappointment to her—living with my sister, running a little B and B, volunteering as a police reservist."

"Oh my God," I said, holding my head. "She left you twice, for the same man. And she still lives here with him?"

"I thought they would go back to Cape Town, but they didn't, because they're making a fortune designing houses for the eco estate."

"Wow. Okay." I looked at him in shock.

"It's like a wise person once said," Mike started. "The heart is also just a muscle, and it takes time to heal a strain."

"You memorized it?" I smiled at him.

"I told you, your book really helped me."

"Has your strain been healed yet?" I asked him, not able to make eye contact. Feeling coy.

"Has yours?" he asked.

"What?"

"You were heartbroken when you wrote that book," he stated.

I nodded. "I am over the sprain—well, sort of. I still find myself doing a lot of things motivated by getting him back," I said. "Like my car. I don't even like Porsches; I just got it because it was his favorite car and buying it meant I could rub it in his face!"

He smiled at me. "I tried that shit once before—trust me, it doesn't work. People don't love you or want to be with you for things. They love you and want to be with you because you're you."

This time I *did* look at him. Our eyes locked.

"So, that's me. My story," he whispered.

"Thanks for telling it," I said back.

He shrugged. "It was good to talk to someone who understands. Ash just gets angry and wants to drive by and fuck April up, which puts me in a difficult position, being the official unofficial law man of this town."

I smiled at him. "Do you like what you do now?"

"Love it," he gushed, without a moment's hesitation. "I'm finally living the life I always should've been living. I run a small business with my best friend. We live together." He rolled his eyes a little. "We probably always will. A psychologist might say *codependent*; I say *close*." He gave me another shrug. "I get to wake up every day in the most beautiful place in the world, where I grew up, and I get to help people, in small ways. I make enough money to be comfortable, but not enough to stress!"

"Wow." I looked at him. "You are who I want to be," I said.

"Really?" He looked at me and raised that sexy eyebrow. "I find that hard to believe. You're a famous, bestselling novelist."

"But I'm also completely alone, living in an apartment that I can't afford, with a fucking coffee table that cost more than your car, and I'm . . . I'm . . ." A stab in my gut. A hard punch. My heart kicked in my chest and suddenly I couldn't really breathe.

"What?" he asked, leaning forward.

"I'm . . . *unhappy*." I finally said the word that I think I'd known for a very long time. The word that had hung just below the surface. That had bobbed there, just out of reach of my conscious brain. The word that had followed me around for quite some time now, like an unwelcome shadow that I didn't even know I had.

"So, be happy, then." Mike leaned even closer to me.

"How?" I asked. I couldn't help the tears in my eyes now. "I don't even think I know what would make me happy anymore."

"Writing makes you happy, doesn't it?" he asked.

"It did. But now it just feels stressful."

"So, don't do it," he said quickly.

"I can't do that," I whispered. "If I'm not Becca Thorne, bestseller, then who am I?"

He leaned closer to me. "Then you're Pebecca Thorne. The girl with the wrong name, who lost her dad and who overcame a crappy childhood and a bad break-up and then rose above that all to write a book that changed people's lives."

I looked over at him, tears escaping my eyes now.

"Why do you have to be someone else, when being *that* person seems perfect to me?"

My heart thumped in my chest and I gazed out the window. I felt like I couldn't look directly at him; if I did, I might cry. Ugly cry.

"Do you ever speak to your mom?" he asked.

I shook my head. "We lost contact many years ago. Somewhere between me living with her sister and then me living with one of her cousins. I'm not sure I can forgive her for the childhood she made me have," I said thoughtfully. I looked at the police station, and it was then that I noticed the sign that had been painted over. "Bottle store?" I pointed at the faint paint on the wall. "This used to be the bottle store?"

"I know. Nothing is really what it seems, in this place," he said, in a mysterious tone, and, before I could turn around and say something in response, he was already out the door and walking across the parking lot.

Nothing was as it seemed, here. Everything had another side to it. Everyone and everything had a story . . . *I wondered what mine was, and whether it had a happy ending?*

CHAPTER 70

⌐∿

We walked into the "jail cell," and Ash and Emelia were no longer stooped over papers; they were sitting happily at the desk, laughing together. I didn't know them that well, but, in the short time I had, I could see what a great couple they were. It was obvious how perfect they were for each other, how in love they were.

"Hey," Mike called out, when we walked inside. "Did you find anything?"

"Did you find Petra?" Ash asked.

He nodded.

"Was she looking for her son again?"

I walked up to where they were sitting. "It was so sad. She went to her old house—we found her in her son's old bedroom. Surely someone can do something about this?" I said.

"God, that's so awful," Ash said. "Imagine getting to a place like that, where you can't remember who and where you are, and missing someone so badly that you—" She stopped talking and looked at Mike. "Wait. She went to her old house, as in . . . ?"

"Yup." Mike sat down at the table and I followed suit.

"Did you see her?" Ash asked, sitting up straight.

"I did," he replied flatly. "She said I must tell you guys congrats on the engagement."

"What a bitch!" Ash said, and Emelia nodded in agreement.

"She seemed genuine," Mike mumbled.

"Oh, please! A genuine thing hasn't come out of that woman's mouth in, like . . . forever." Ash was getting really worked up now, just like Mike had mentioned. "Do you know what she did to him?" Ash looked at me and I nodded. "Broke up with him—twice!" Ash shook her head, and I couldn't help the smile that flashed over my face. She looked at me, shocked. "You think that's funny?" she asked.

"NO! No. Not at all." I waved my hand. "I didn't mean it like that. I smiled because I just think it's so nice, how upset you're getting on your brother's behalf. It's sweet to see, that's all."

Ash's face softened. "No one must fuck with my little brother," she declared, and then wrapped her arm around his shoulder.

"She put play dough down someone's pants in kindergarten because they teased me," Mike said, with a smile.

"I can't imagine you being teased," I said.

"Uh . . . You know how the doctor said that he couldn't tell whether Mike was a boy because he was so—" she inflated her cheeks—"chubby?"

"Yes?" I smiled.

"Well, he was. For a while, anyway, and then it all turned to pure, hard muscle." She poked her brother on the arm and they both laughed. If there was a prize for the best siblings in the world, these two should get it.

"He was so cute, though," Ash said.

"You should show her the photos!" Emelia piped up.

"No. Please. No photos." Mike hung his head a little.

"I'd love to see photos," I said, feeling like I was part of the group now.

"So . . . what did you guys find, while we were out?" Mike changing the subject.

"Well, do we have some good news or what," Emelia declared, pushing a piece of paper in front of us.

Mike pulled it towards himself and started reading. "Eugene Abrahams?"

"I think Abe was a nickname, and actually it's short for Abrahams, his surname."

"How do you know?" Mike asked.

"Aaah, so that's when Google came to our rescue." Emelia pulled out her phone. "Look." She held it out and both Mike and I leaned in."

"What?" I gasped when I saw the profile pic for Eugene (Abe) Abrahams. "It's him! It's HIM!" I almost yelled as I looked into the eyes I knew so well. The photo was of his younger self, and not how he would look today. "Is his profile open? Has he posted anything?"

"No," Emelia said. "And it's weird that he used that photo as a profile picture. Do you think he had it like that in case Edith ever searched Facebook?" she asked.

Mike looked up and then his face dropped. "Oh God. Towards the end, Gran asked me about Facebook, about whether you could find people on it. She'd heard about it. She asked me to help her set up a page . . . I never did."

Ash reached out and laid a hand on his shoulder.

"Shit, she was probably looking for him." Mike stood up and paced the floor a few times, as if he could no longer sit down. "I should have done it for her. I should have helped her."

"You didn't know what she was looking for," I said quickly.

"She could also have found him in others ways—like, by using a private investigator. Why didn't she look for him? She could have, couldn't she?" Ash pressed.

"Where is he? Can we drive there?" Mike asked.

Emelia and Ash shook their heads together. "He moved to England. He moved a week after she wrote her last letter to him."

"Oh, wow," I said, as the impact of those words hit home. "So, that letter that she was forced to write by her father, that really was the *last* communication between them?" I held my face in my hands, trying to imagine what I would feel like, if I was him.

"Oh my God," Emelia exclaimed.

I held my head and shook it. This couldn't be how this story ended. This story needed a happy ending; this could not be it. I jumped up off my chair.

"We have to go there, now, and give him the letters," I said. "He cannot live a minute longer thinking that last letter was what she felt about him. He needs to know the truth."

CHAPTER 71

~

"*Y*ou're squirming a lot." Mike turned his head towards me.

"There's no space." I wiggled in my seat and tried to stretch my legs out.

"Used to traveling business class?" he joked.

"Actually, yes!" I said, with a playful smile.

"Well, you're just going to have to slum it, like the rest of us."

"Did you know," I leaned in and whispered, "that men still pee on the toilet seats in business class?"

Mike laughed loudly and someone turned and looked at us.

"What's so funny?" I asked.

"Do you know how hard it is to pee standing up in a moving vehicle?"

"Do you know how hard it is to pull some toilet paper off, make it into something like a little square and give the seat a wipe, or—hey, here's a novel idea—why not lift the seat?"

"I lift the seat," Mike said to me, in a strange voice that seemed loaded with something.

"Good to know," I teased.

"In case we ever decide to co-habit." He mumbled that last part and then quickly smiled, turning it into a joke, even though it hadn't sounded like one at first. Was I imagining things? I smiled back at him and he gave me that warm, crazy, sexy smile that lit up the dull interior of the plane around us. This was better than any business class I'd ever flown.

"So, what's the plan?" Mike asked.

"The plan," I said thoughtfully. We hadn't really had a chance to formulate that much of a plan between yesterday and today. We'd only discovered the man's name yesterday, and everything had happened so quickly after that. Mike had used his fake police powers and had gotten a cop friend from Morgan Bay to track down an address for Abe, in the UK. Emelia had booked us flights there, with three clicks of a button, then we'd packed as fast as possible, then we'd all piled into my car and driven back to Jo'burg, crashing at my place for the night—everyone had fake *oooh*ed at my coffee table. Then we'd all woken up the next morning and gone to the airport, said goodbye to Ash and Emelia, and before I really knew what was happening, we were cruising 30,000 feet in the air, *in economy class*.

"The plan," I repeated, thoughtfully. "Well, the plan is that we go and take these letters to him."

"And what about your book?" Mike asked.

"What about it?" I repeated. *What about my book?* I hadn't thought about my book in days.

"How are you going to tell him you're writing it? You'll need to get his permission, now, from a copyright perspective, if I'm not mistaken," he said, suddenly sounding like a lawyer for the first time since I'd met him.

My stomach twisted a little; I hadn't thought of that. "I guess he could be married and maybe he wouldn't want this out?"

"But—as her heir and the person who inherited her estate—technically, all her letters and the diary are now mine. So I can give you permission to do whatever you want with them. You can turn those into the book; you don't need his letters anymore."

I listened to him. It was all starting to sound complicated now, and the whole idea was making me feel nervous and nauseous. Somewhere along the way, I'd almost forgotten that I was writing a book. I'd become so swept up in Edith and Abe's story, I'd forgotten I had one to write.

"It's okay." Mike slipped an arm through mine. "We'll ask his permission, but, if he says no, you can put her letters into the book. We'll photocopy them all and give him the originals. It'll be fine." He sounded so sure of himself.

I leaned my head back on the uncomfortable seat and let my mind wander. I let it wander to all the places I'd been, this last week. All the things I'd seen and done, and the people I'd met. I closed my eyes and let it wander some more; this time, it wondered what it would be like to be with Mike, permanently. What it would be like to wake up with him in the morning, in Willow Bay. I might stay at home and write at that little desk by the window, looking out over the river. He'd go out during the day and fake-police around town. I smiled to myself at the thought. Maybe, in the evenings, we could walk on the beach together, we could sit on the veranda and drink wine—and I wouldn't care how red I went. At night, we would climb into bed and sleep together, and he would hold me in the same way that he'd held me the other night. Maybe I would go out and have a cup of coffee and some cake at Emelia's coffee shop during the day. Maybe I would go and work in the library, too, in between all the hot dinosaurs and mermen threesomes. Maybe I would become friends with Techno Tannie and download her music and listen to it, and maybe I would become a regular at Reddy's, buying condoms. Maybe I would paint with Ash in the afternoons, help out around the B and B. I could rewrite their terrible web copy, I could . . .

I opened my eyes when I realized what I was doing.

"What?" Mike asked, looking over at me. "Are you okay?"

I looked at him and shook my head. Because I wasn't okay. I was in serious danger, here, of being very *not okay*, because I was totally and utterly falling—for him, for a place, for the life I wanted to have, *was meant to have*.

"I'm fine." I forced a smile, and he smiled back.

"You sure?" he asked again, as if he didn't believe me.

I nodded. "Never been better," I said, and, strangely, in some ways, that was the truth.

CHAPTER 72

"Who's going to knock?" Mike asked, as we stared at the front door. We'd only landed a few hours ago and we were already standing outside Abe's house in Chiswick.

I took a deep breath and tried to steady myself. "I'll knock." I reached out and rapped my knuckles against the wooden door. We stood there and waited as the door remained closed. We looked at each other nervously and both shrugged. I reached out and knocked again—a little harder, longer and louder, this time.

"Are we sure he lives here?" I asked Mike.

"Positive; I checked. He lives here with his granddaughter. I called her to say we were coming."

I nodded. "Okay." I knocked again and, this time, I heard movement in the house. I looked at Mike and smiled. "Hello," I called out.

"Coming," a small voice returned.

"This is it," I whispered to Mike, feeling a strange combination of excitement and nerves. I pulled the bag of letters higher on to my shoulder and clutched it tightly. I saw the door handle move and I stared at it, willing it to open. When it finally did, I gasped.

There he was.

It was him. The man I'd been searching for and had traveled halfway across the world to find. It was a strange feeling to see him, like this. He was the same, but completely transformed. It was as if he'd used the face-aging app and posted a picture of himself. His hair was grey, his face was full of deep lines that criss-crossed the planes of his cheeks and forehead and pulled at the corners of his eyes. His body was frail, his fingers and knuckles swollen and crooked with arthritis, the backs of his hands dappled with liver spots, and his skin looked thin, like a piece of rice paper.

"Hi." Mike stepped forward and held his hand out for him to take. "I'm Mike. I spoke to your granddaughter on the phone yesterday, about coming here and talking to you."

"Yes?" the man, Abe, said. His voice sounded soft and old and tired.

"Do you know why we're here?" Mike asked.

"Only that you have something for me," he said slowly, and then looked over at us. "Your accents," he said thoughtfully. "I haven't heard an accent like that in a very, very long time." He said that last part almost inaudibly.

"Yes, our accents," I said.

"Where do you come from?" he asked, looking at us.

"Can we come in?" Mike asked. "Maybe we can do this when we're all sitting down."

At that, Abe perked up. "What do you think I'm going to do, son? Drop bloody dead in the doorway?" he said, standing up straighter than before.

Mike smiled at him and shook his head. "No, I don't think that."

"Well, damn right I'm not!" Abe declared loudly.

"I think what Mike means," I said, "is that this is quite private; maybe doing it inside is better."

Abe eyeballed us, as if trying to get a handle on us. He finally stepped aside and we followed him into a small sitting room and took a seat on a floral-patterned sofa.

"I would offer you tea, but my granddaughter says I am not allowed sugar anymore, and, let's face it, tea tastes like milky water, without the sugar. That's the best part." He rolled his eyes.

"It's okay, thanks. I'm fine," I said quickly.

"Me too," Mike said.

"So, out with whatever it is you've come here for." Abe sat back in his chair; it almost dwarfed him. His frame was so small and fragile-looking, despite his fiery personality.

I reached for my bag and, without a word, I started pouring all the letters down on the table in front of us and I kept going until they were all out. There were so many that they spilled off the table and dropped to the floor, like leaves. I watched his face as he leaned forward in his chair. He reached out a crooked hand and took one of the letters. He looked at it briefly, and then, with his other hand, he grabbed his glasses off the table and put them on frantically. His hands were trembling as he raised the letter all the way up to his face.

I turned to Mike and we shared a quick, concerned look.

"Where . . . ? Where . . . ? Where did you get these?" Abe asked. I could hear his mouth had gone completely dry.

"My name is Michael Wooldridge," Mike said. "I am Edith's grandson and these are the letters that she wrote to you over the last seventy years."

At that, Abe brought the letter up to his face and touched the paper against his cheek. He closed his eyes and inhaled deeply. I gripped the side of my chair, as my chest felt tight.

"Is she . . . ? Has she . . . ?" He opened his eyes and looked over at Mike. Mike didn't say a word, just nodded. Abe lowered his head and grabbed the arm of his chair, gripping on to it so tightly that I could see the sinews in his arm tensing, like violin strings.

"I'm so sorry," I whispered to him, trying to hold back my tears. "But she loved you," I blurted out, and then started rambling. "She loved you so much. She loved you more than she loved anyone in her entire life. With her every breath, every thought. She memorized every single one of your letters and would recite them to herself every day. She loved you so much, right until the day she died. She wrote you letters for the rest of her life, even though she knew you would never get them, and she hid them in her horse's stable—"

"Darcy," he whispered, softly.

"Yes," I confirmed.

"She loved that stupid bloody horse," he said, with a small smile. "It was the dumbest mare I'd ever met!" He let out a small laugh.

I caught Mike's eye and we shared a tiny smile.

Abe stopped laughing and looked very serious again. "When did Edith pass?" he asked.

"The twenty-fifth of June, last year," Mike said.

Abe nodded. "I felt her go," he said softly, quietly, almost to himself.

I felt a breeze at the back of my neck and I turned around and looked behind me. The window was closed.

We sat in silence for a while as Abe ran his fingers over the handwriting on the envelope, over and over again.

"I think I'll have that tea, after all." He stood up and slowly walked out of the room.

"Do you think he's okay?" I whispered to Mike.

Mike shook his head. "I don't know. Would you be okay?"

"No," I replied. "Should we be worried about him?" I asked.

"I don't know."

We sat and waited for what felt like hours as the kettle boiled. Finally, he came back in holding a cup of tea in one hand and a small box in the other. He passed me the small box and sat down with his tea.

I looked at the box in my hands and slowly took the lid off. When I saw what was inside, the tears started streaming down my face. I reached in and pulled the pile of letters out. He'd kept all her letters, too, and they looked just as worn as hers did, as if they'd also endured a lifetime of reading and rereading. Something at the bottom of the box caught my eye. It was a photo. I pulled it out and found myself looking into Edith's face—her laughing, happy, joyful face.

"It's the only photo we have of ourselves together," he said softly. "My cousin took it for us, and he had to get it printed in secret, so no one would ever see it."

I clutched the photo between my fingers and bit my lip hard, to stop my tears turning into sobs.

"Oh, don't cry, young lady. There is nothing to cry about. What you're looking at, there, is the happiest day of my life," he said.

I held the picture out for Mike. He took it and I could feel his emotions from where I was sitting.

"That was taken in the summer of 1948. God, I remember that summer as if it were yesterday. I can still smell the sea air and hear the screech of the cicada beetles in my ears. They make everything so loud and alive. It was one of those sticky, humid summers, when all the ladies complained that their hair was always ruined." He smiled. "Edith used to hate what the humidity did to her hair, the way it curled up like it did. I thought she looked like a doll, though. Those big curls and green eyes, and she used to get these freckles, like a spray of stars across her nose . . ." He chuckled softly to himself. "She hated them. But, to me, she was the loveliest girl I'd ever seen in my life, and I just knew, from the moment I laid eyes on her, that I was going to love her. There was nothing not to love about her. But . . . the country didn't want us to love each other, that's the truth." He got quiet and thoughtful for a while. "I . . . I haven't spoken about any of this for a very, very long time."

"When did you last speak to Edith?" I heard myself asking.

He smiled at me—a strange, faraway smile. "Just last night. I speak to her every night, and, sometimes, if I'm lucky, she visits me in my dreams. But that hasn't happened in a while."

I smiled back at him and our eyes locked for a while; that spark that she had painted all those years ago was still there, but it was dimmer.

"Last time I saw and spoke to her was on the seventh of September, 1949. We were at the cove together. We used to go there sometimes, because no one else did. There was an old town legend about the cove being haunted by the ghost of a pirate, or something. Everyone was too afraid to go there, except us." He smiled again and looked thoughtful. "Edith used to say we were fools to go there! 'Fools in love,' she used to say. That was a quote from her favorite book."

"*Pride and Prejudice*," I added.

He nodded. " 'Fools in love forever,' she would say . . . *How wrong she was*. Her father caught us there together. I'll never forget the look on his face when he saw us. There was so much hatred in his eyes, and disgust. As if he had seen the most disgusting thing and he was going to be sick." He shook his head and closed his eyes for a moment, as if trying to remember everything. "He screamed at us. Told us he would have me arrested for this. 'You're going to rot in jail, boy,' he said. And then he started dragging Edith away. I tried to stop him, but Edith begged me not to. She begged me. She told me to run." Abe stopped talking, but kept his eyes shut, as if he was at that moment in time.

I sat and watched him, and waited for him to continue telling the story.

He took a deep breath and opened his eyes again. "So, I did. I ran."

"Did you ever see her again, after that?" I asked.

He shook his head. "No. I got a letter from her, after that, but I knew she hadn't written it. As soon as I read those words, I knew her father had forced her to write it." He stopped talking and looked down at his hands in his lap. He was wringing them now. "That photo was the happiest moment in my life, and that letter I got from her was the saddest and most terrifying. I knew how much trouble she was in. I realized just how much me loving her put her in danger. We'd always known it was dangerous to love each other, but, until I saw it, I guess a part of me didn't want to believe it. And that's when I left town. I left without saying goodbye to her, because I knew that, if I saw her again, I wouldn't be able to go. I needed to remember her as I'd seen her for the last time, if I was going to be able to go; I needed to remember her father dragging her off by her hair. I left to keep her safe—to keep myself safe, even . . . Our love was a crime. She could have gone to jail. Her entire life could have been ruined. So, I came here on a ship. I was seasick the whole time, but it still felt better than being lovesick."

"She never knew you were here," I said softly. "Why didn't you tell her where you were?"

"I wanted to keep her safe. I was worried what her father might do to her. He was a very angry, controlling man, even under normal circumstances. Edith was terrified of him."

"And you never saw her again?" I asked.

He smiled again, but this time it was completely forced. I could see he was struggling with his emotions. Struggling to keep them all contained. "I did go back to Willow Bay, years and years later. I went back to the house and . . . I saw her."

"You did?" Mike asked.

He nodded and looked distant. "She was still the most beautiful woman I'd ever seen in my life." He paused for the longest time. "Some women really do glow when they're pregnant."

"Oh God." I held my chest, as my heart ached. "She didn't love Ian like she loved you, though—she didn't. She says so in the letters," I said to him.

He looked down at the letter in his hands and smiled. "I know that now. Thank you."

I gasped for air and then couldn't fight it anymore—I started crying, proper tears. Mike took my hand and squeezed it tighter than I've ever been squeezed before.

"It could never have lasted," Abe said thoughtfully. "Our love was a crime. We loved each other in the wrong time and place. It could never have been, unless we ran away and built a house in the middle of a forest somewhere." He smiled a little. "We used to talk about that sometimes. Try and imagine what our lives would be like if we could be together. Towards the end, it was getting so hard to see each other. Sometimes, we wouldn't see each other for a whole month. Our only communication was the letters we wrote. But even getting the letters to each other was becoming harder and harder. We would write them and leave them in secret hiding spots, hoping that the other person would be able to get to it. It was the only way we could communicate with each other." Abe looked at the two of us. "Are you married?" he asked.

I was crying too much to answer.

"No." Mike spoke for us.

"If you meet someone that you truly love, don't ever let them go. No matter what," Abe said to us. "Fight for it. Fight as hard as you can. We tried to fight for it, but it wasn't a battle we were ever going to win. But at least we fought." He paused and looked forlorn for a while. "I didn't fight for my wife," he said quietly, almost under his breath. "I never loved her the way I should have; I couldn't love her like that. She divorced me and I didn't fight for her. It's for the best, though; she found someone who really loves her, like I loved Edith . . . Everyone deserves to be loved like that. Even if it's only for a short time."

Then his demeanor changed a little and he looked back at the pile of letters. "Looks like I have some reading to do. And I don't have all the time in the world to do it." He started arranging the letters on the table, with his shaking hands.

"Aren't you going to ask him?" Mike whispered to me.

I shook my head pointedly.

He looked confused. "Ask him," he urged, under his breath. "Ask him about your book."

I shook my head and jumped out of my seat. "We are going to go now, Abe. So you can read these letters in peace."

"Wait!" Mike jumped up, too. "There's something we want to ask you—"

"No, it's nothing." I grabbed Mike by the arm and squeezed it hard. "It's fine." I looked him in the eye and tried frantically to convey what I was feeling.

Mike's mouth fell open and he gaped a few times, like a fish out of water.

"We really must be going, but I am so glad we managed to get these to you," I said to Abe, who wasn't even looking at us now; he was too busy with the letters.

I pulled Mike towards the door. "It was nice meeting you," I said to Abe, as we started to leave.

"Thank you for coming all this way and bringing them to me," he called after us.

I turned and smiled at him. "They belong to you." I opened the door and pulled Mike out of the small house, and then started running towards the park in front of me.

CHAPTER 73

I ran up to a bench and sat down on it. I lowered my head and held it in my hands, trying to catch my breath.

"Why did you do that?" Mike rushed up to me and sat down. "Why didn't you ask his permission, like we spoke about? Why didn't you tell him about the book and the story and what you're writing—?"

"I can't do it!" I swung around and cut him off.

"What?" he asked.

"This. Any of this. All of this!" That familiar feeling rose inside me again. I felt breathless. I looked around for something to steady myself on and grabbed hold of the sides of the bench.

"Are you okay?" Mike asked quietly.

I shook my head. I tried to count to ten in my head. I always did this when I felt the anxiety taking hold of me. But it wasn't just the anxiety, this time; it was also the sadness. I could feel the tears, like buckets building up behind my eyeballs, climbing up my throat, just waiting for one more thing to tip me over the edge so they could all come out.

"Becca, please tell me you're okay?" Mike's arm was around me now.

That's what tipped me over the edge: his genuine care and concern for me. The sobs came and they shook my body. "No. No!" I finally managed, through the messy crying. "I'm not okay. This is not okay."

"Talk to me," Mike said gently.

"I can't write this. This is not mine to write. This is not just some story with characters and a plot twist in it. These are real people, and they are in pain. Did you see how much he loved her—*loves her*? He still loves her, after all these years. After an entire lifetime has passed without her, he still loves her." I shook my head, hard. "*I just can't do this*. This isn't my story to tell, and I know you think your grandmother told you to tell it, and Emelia and Ash feel the same way, but I don't think she meant this. I think the fact that we found those letters, and they've finally—after all these decades—found their way back to Abe, means she gets to tell it to the *one* person who is meant to hear it."

I stood up and walked over to the huge oak tree in front of me and put my hands on it and tried to take another deep breath. I heard Mike stand up behind me and walk over. I turned around before he reached me and leaned my back against the tree.

"I can't believe I even thought of doing this," I whispered to him. "How did I become so desperate that I thought I could steal someone else's story and pass it off as my own?" I looked up at Mike. "I have done some stupid things in my life, but this one . . . *this one* . . ." Down at my feet, a small beetle was scuttling over the blades of grass, and I watched him as he went about his business, totally oblivious to what I was going through.

"I'm sorry I dragged you into this." I looked up at Mike when the beetle had walked around the back of the tree and disappeared. "I'm sorry I dragged you halfway across the world and wreaked havoc in your town and . . . well, *I'm just sorry*," I said.

He smiled at me sympathetically. "I'm not sorry. Look what we just did." He looked back at Abe's house, and I did, too.

"Do you think he's reading them now?" I asked, feeling a little calmer.

"I hope so." Mike came and rested next to me, with his back against the same tree.

I thought about the willow tree and what was etched in it, and

I felt like Mike and I were etching our own story in this tree together, without even knowing it.

We stayed there in silence like that, our shoulders touching. I synced my breathing to his and my body started to relax even more.

"So, what are you going to do about your book?" he asked, gently nudging me with his shoulder.

"I don't know," I said. "I just know what I *can't* do." I took a deep breath; the air here smelled different from the air I was used to. It seemed sweeter, as if it were laced with some exotic flower. "I guess I'll call my agent and just tell her I don't have a book," I said calmly. "She'll call my publisher, who will freak. The bookstores will be told that the book is not coming, my readers will be told that there is no second book. My career as an author will be over. I'll take on a small job somewhere and sell my car and all that other crap I don't need, and I'll start trying to pay back the advance, and . . ." I shrugged. "I don't know."

"I know that the *Willow Bay Herald* would probably jump to have a writer of such caliber working for them," he said, and I laughed through my tears and then leaned my head on his shoulder.

"You think?" I asked, my cheek resting against the muscles in his arm.

I felt him nod. "Yeah, I do think."

"And where would I live?" I asked. "The people of Willow's Eco Estate will not have me."

Now it was Mike's turn to chuckle slightly. "No, they *definitely* won't."

We were silent for a while again and then Mike put his hand on my cheek. "You sure you don't want to do this? It's not too late to go and ask him. We are right here."

I pulled my head away and shook it. "This is the right thing to do." I pushed myself away from the tree and then started wiping the tears from my cheeks. I straightened my clothes and pushed the loose strands of hair that were hanging in my face behind my ears. I put on a small, brave smile when I was done.

"I'm proud of you," Mike said, out of the blue.

"You are?" I asked.

He nodded and smiled. "And, you know, I won't think anything less of you if you're not Becca Thorne, international bestseller. In fact, I think I might think more of you . . . *just like this*."

I looked down at myself. "Just like this?" I asked.

He took a step closer to me. "Exactly like this."

I looked up at the tree as a pigeon flew into it and cooed. I smiled to myself; it looked exactly like the birds from the eco estate. *Just like this*. I sighed, but it wasn't a pained, torturous sigh. It was the sigh of a person letting go. There was relief in that sigh. Acceptance. And, you know what? For the first time since starting this journey, I also kind of liked myself, just the way I was. I'd finally done the right thing. The only thing.

"What now?" Mike asked. "Do we go back home?"

I put my hands in my pockets and looked at the ground again. "No," I finally looked up and said. "There is another good thing I can still do today." I pulled the small piece of paper out of my wallet.

"What's that?" he asked.

"An address." I held it up for him to see.

"Whose address?" he asked.

I looked down at it and stroked the piece of paper in my hands. "My story might end here, but I know of another story that doesn't have to," I said, walking back towards the road.

CHAPTER 74

I rang the doorbell with shaking fingers. I had no idea what I was going to find on the inside, or whether the people on the inside would even want to see me. I stared at the mezuzah next to the front door while I waited.

"I'm not sure about this," Mike said, one last time, in my ear. He'd been saying it for the last twenty minutes, in the taxi, as we'd driven here.

"I'm not sure either," I whispered back, "but we have to do it." As I said that, the door opened and a teenage girl stood there.

"What?" she asked in a snappy tone.

"Hi. I . . . I . . . My name is Becca Thorne and this is Mike Wooldridge. We've come from South Africa and we wanted to know if your dad was in?"

"My dad?"

"Well, sorry, I'm just making an assumption that he is, but I'm looking for Pierre Van der Merwe," I said quickly.

The girl looked at me and put her hand on her hip. "Yeah. That's my dad," she said slightly venomously, and then rolled her eyes.

"Who's at the door?" I heard a man's voice.

The girl shook her head and rolled her eyes some more, in case we were not aware that she was a sulky teen with a bad attitude. "Just some people for you," she said. She walked back into the house, dragging her feet down the passage.

I looked at the staircase in front of us as I heard feet coming down it. The feet turned into ankles, knees, a torso, and finally an entire body. "Hey, where are you going?" he asked, as the teen slunk into one of the rooms.

"Watching TV," she said.

"Not until you've helped your mom with the dishes," he said.

"God, this is so unfair. It's a Sunday; it's not my fault you guys decided to have a dinner party last night."

"Now!" her dad said, in that voice that is terrifying to teenagers. The voice that lets them know they're about to get an iPhone confiscated.

I heard a sigh and then a stomp. "Fine!" She marched down the corridor and burst through the door at the end.

"Sorry." The man turned to us and my heart thumped. "What can I do for you?" he asked.

"Uh . . . I am Becca Thorne and this is Mike Wooldridge. Mike is from Willow Bay, in Sou—"

"Has something happened to her?" His eyes widened. "Is she, uh . . . ?"

"No, no. She's fine. She's totally fine," I stated, and then I stopped. "Actually, she's not fine. At all," I said. "In fact, she is anything but fine. She goes wandering around, almost every day, looking for you. Mike has to fetch her from the beach, people's houses and even from the side of the highway once."

"God." He put his hands to his face.

"All she talks about is you, and she wants to see you so badly and to meet her grandchildren for the first time and . . ."

He hung his head and looked at his feet, as if he didn't want me to see the emotion on his face.

"Your mother isn't well. The nurses at the home don't think she has much time left," I said.

At that, he stepped outside and pulled the door closed behind him. "I . . . I don't want my children to hear about this."

I nodded at him.

"Thing is," he started, "she and my dad disowned me when I got married. I didn't do anything but fall in love with the wrong person, in their eyes. I never wanted this rift between us. They did, not me. And it really hurt me, for years and years."

"I don't think your mom wanted it either, and now that your dad is gone . . ." Suddenly, I wondered if he even knew about this. Clearly, he did.

"I heard that. I didn't go to the funeral."

"The point is, she's desperate to see you."

He looked at me, his eyes welling up with tears. "There isn't a day that goes by that I don't think about her."

"Why don't you stop thinking about her and go and see her? Or start with a call, even."

He started nodding, slowly. I could see he was taking this all in, listening to every word I said.

"I had this idea of what my life would be like," he said. "I imagined hot Sundays by the river, my parents playing with their grandchildren. I imagined family holidays and birthdays, and I imagined that my children would grow up in Willow Bay, like I had. But that all changed when my father kicked me out and disowned me. He killed my dream, that day—killed the dream of the life I wanted to have. Everything I'd ever hoped and dreamed of was taken away from me, that day. All because of him, *and her*—even if she didn't want it, she was still complicit in it and never said anything to my father. I'm not sure that is totally forgivable, either," he said, and my heart plummeted. This wasn't going to be as easy as telling him his mother was dying and wanted to see him one last time. This man had a lifetime of anger and resentment inside him.

"They had no right to do that to me. To take the story I wanted for my life and to rewrite it without my permission. Do you know what it feels like to live a life you never wanted to live?" he asked me, and I nodded. Because I knew exactly what he meant.

"I . . . I actually do know what it's like. I also know what it is like to be estranged from your mother, not sure if you can forgive her for what she did to you, for the life she forced you to have, without asking your permission."

The man nodded as he looked at me. I understood him. And, suddenly, I understood everything. The truth about my entire life was laid out in front of me. And the truth was that I was living in someone else's strange version of what I thought my life should be like. *That wasn't really my story.* That wasn't what I wanted. I wasn't living the life I'd imagined for myself, and that's how I'd found myself here, plagiarizing someone else's story because I'd lost sight of my own. And, in that moment, I knew what I was meant to do. *I was meant to write my own story.*

"I'm sorry," I said to him. He looked at me, our eyes met and I mirrored back to him the emotion I was also feeling.

"Thank you," he said to me. "You've given me a lot to think about." And then he started closing the door on us. That was it.

When it was closed, I turned to Mike.

"Do you think he'll contact her?" he asked.

I shook my head. "I don't know," I replied. Because I didn't. I hoped he would contact her before it was too late, but a part of me didn't think he would. Too much pain had passed between them and maybe everyone doesn't get to have a happy ending. But, fuck it, I was going to get my happy ending, or at least something as close to a happy ending as possible. I wasn't going to become like the Van der Merwes and live with a lifetime of regret because I hadn't lived the way that I wanted to, because I hadn't lived a true and authentic life and spoken my truth out loud, like Edith hadn't. Suddenly, I smiled and I threw my arms around Mike. I pulled him into a hug and we held each other tightly.

"What's that for?" he asked.

I pulled away and looked at him. "I know what to do," I said. "I know what to write."

"Really?" he asked, looking excited.

I nodded. "I need to write my own story. Not someone else's story."

"What story is that?" he asked.

I smiled again, and then I leaned in and kissed him on the cheek. "It's the only story I need to tell. And I have two weeks to tell it, so we better get back."

CHAPTER 75

~

Two weeks later

I walked up to Mike and handed him the manuscript I'd been working on for an entire two weeks. The weeks had passed in a kind of dazed, confused, caffeinated sugar haze. There is this strange place that writers go to sometimes, where at least one liter of their blood is replaced by pure sugary caffeine fuel, and where they totally disappear and time becomes meaningless, as days blur into nights and nights blur into weeks.

I'd stayed at Sugar Manor after Mike insisted that I come back with him and work there. I stayed mainly indoors, emerging every now and again to eat something that was kindly offered to me by Emelia or Ash, or when Mike brought in a bag of wasabi-flavored crisps from his private stash.

Mike and Ash had also started renovating another room in the house for guests, and sometimes I would sit in the corner with my headphones on, listening to some soundtrack, typing away, while I watched them paint the walls and polish the wooden floors.

In the evenings, after my work, we would all have dinner together, mostly crowded around the fire, as the evenings got colder. We all talked and laughed, and I don't think I had ever talked and laughed so much in my entire life. And then Mike would walk me to my room, we'd say a slightly strange goodnight, and then he would hand me an espresso as I headed back to write into the night again. We'd all fallen into this strange and comfortable routine, and I felt like I belonged here. In a way, I felt like I had always belonged here, but I just didn't know it.

And then the day finally came when I typed those two words that I had been heading towards like a high-speed train: *The End*. But I didn't stop to bask in it; I rushed to the video-shop-come-internet-cafe-come-printing-mecca, and I printed out my entire book. I'd sat on the veranda all day, waiting for Mike to come home from work.

I heard his car pull up on the gravel driveway and my heart started beating faster. What I was about to do . . . *What I was about to do* . . . The thought terrified me and excited me, all at the same time.

"Hey," I said, as he walked up to me with a small smile.

"You're not in your room." He climbed the stairs and stopped in front of me. "Does that mean . . . ?"

I nodded. "It does!" I pulled the manuscript out from behind my back and held it out for him to take.

"Oh my God!" He pulled me into a half hug, making sure not to squish the papers between us. "Well done—I am so proud of you." He kissed me on the forehead and I closed my eyes and relished the feeling.

"You are?" I asked.

"Of course I am," he said. "Why wouldn't I be? My God, what you have done, and in two weeks! You've finished an entire book! It's insane. Not that you will tell me what the book is about yet, but I bet it's going to be amazing, like your last one."

"You're proud of me," I harped.

He nodded and then looked confused. "You look like no one has ever said that to you before."

"No one has," I said.

"What do you mean?"

"No one has told me they're proud of me for writing anything," I said.

"Why?" he asked.

I shrugged. "I guess I don't surround myself with that many people who can tell me things like that."

"Well, now you've surrounded yourself with people who are proud of you, I can't wait to tell Ash and Emelia, they'll be . . ." Then he paused. "In fact, we should all celebrate tonight! We should go out and have dinner and drinks, and celebrate this success."

"No, really, it's fine."

"No, it's not. What did you say? 'When we tell you not to make a big deal of something, we really mean you should make a big deal about it.'"

I smiled. "The girl code," I said, and nodded my head. "Okay. That sounds cool—unless, I mean, Ash and Emelia might be busy tonight."

"Are you kidding? This is important. I'm sure they're not busy. Or, if they are, they will cancel their plans for this."

He started walking towards the house. "Come. Let's get ready. I'll tell them."

"Wait!" I said, almost forgetting my reason for being here.

"Yes?"

"I need you to read this," I said, handing him the manuscript.

He took it and looked at it. "I'd love to."

I shook my head. "You don't understand. I *need* you to read this."

"Okay," he said. "I can't wait."

"And neither can I; you have to promise you'll start tonight," I urged.

"Sure, as soon as we all finish celebrating."

I nodded. I wished I didn't need to wait that long to tell him what I needed to tell him. Maybe I was being a coward, not saying the words out loud, but rather putting them down on paper for him to read. But it wasn't just *those words* that I needed him to hear; I needed him to hear all the words. The ones that aren't necessarily said out loud, that happen in the moments of silence. The words that happen in the bits in-between. But, sometimes, those are the most important parts. Because it's in those silent spaces that the magic and the unexpected happens. It's in those silent places that you realize you have fallen in love . . .

CHAPTER 76

"*W*ell, congratulations!" Ash held up her glass and I clinked mine against it.

"Thank you," I said. "I seriously couldn't have done it without you guys." I looked at them all.

"It's so cool that we know a famous writer," Emelia said.

"Ah . . . thanks," I replied coyly.

"What's everyone congratulating about?" Techno Tannie asked, as she came to our table with our second round of drinks.

"Becca is an author. She just finished her book!"

"Really?" she said, and then suddenly and unexpectedly sat down at our table. "What's your book about?" she asked.

"Yeah, what's it about?" Ash asked. "You've been very secretive about it."

I blushed, felt my cheeks go hot, and I looked down. "I can't tell you. Not now, anyway."

"Why?" Emelia asked.

I looked over at Mike and then quickly looked away. "Not until Mike's read it first."

"Apparently, I *need* to read it," he said.

"Aaaah, I see," Techno Tannie said.

"What do you see?" Mike asked.

"Well, clearly you're in it, or she wouldn't make you read it."

"Am I?" Mike turned in his chair and looked at me.

"Well, actually, you're kind of all in it—names changed, of course."

"Who?" Emelia asked. "Are we in it?" She indicated herself and Ash. I nodded.

"Wait . . . You mean you wrote about us?" Ash asked.

I looked at everyone. "No, I wrote about *me*. It's my story, but you're all a part of that, even you . . ." I turned and looked at Techno Tannie.

"Me? Really?" She perked up.

"Seriously, now you have to tell us what this book is about," Emelia said.

"It's about me and this insane journey that I made, here, into your crazy little town, with all the cats and dinosaur porn and crazy eco people."

"Hear, hear!" Techno Tannie said, holding up a glass that she'd taken from Emelia. "I'll drink to that. Those people are nuts."

"Mmmhmmm," I said. "You have no idea. Did you know that the floors of the houses there are made of cow dung?"

"WHAT?" Ash almost spat her drink out.

"I can believe that," Techno Tannie said.

"So, wait, let's just reverse here . . ." Mike said. "We are all in the story?" he asked.

"I mean . . . if that's okay. I did make up names and places, and it's not really about you guys, at all. It's about me. It's my story. You just all happen to have been such a big part of it, in a completely good way."

"What's it about, though?" he asked.

I smiled at him. "You'll have to wait and see."

"Okay, well, now we really have to rush this celebratory dinner, so I can get home and start reading."

"I want to read it, too," Ash said.

Emelia put her hand up. "Me too."

"And me," Techno Tannie said. "Did you put in there that I make music? You should. I just posted my new track on Spotify, if you want to listen," she said.

I nodded. "Your music is in there. A lot of music is in there."

"Now I'm dying to read it," she said.

"You'll all have your turn, but Mike has to read it first."

"Why?" he asked.

I smiled to myself. "You'll see," I said nervously.

* * *

I heard the knock on my door at about six thirty a.m. I was sleepy when I got up, unsure and a little disorientated. I walked over to the door and opened it. Mike was standing there, holding the manuscript. I could see that the corners were crunched and crumpled, as if he'd been reading it. He held the book up.

"Uh . . . so I read this," he said.

"And?" I asked, waking up with a yawn.

"It's . . . it's incredible," he said.

"Really?"

He nodded. "And the letters you wrote are so beautiful. I mean, they are completely made up and so different to the real ones, but they are still so accurate. You captured the feeling in them perfectly. You captured everything perfectly. The town, the people, yourself . . . everything."

"I didn't think I was going to be able to write those letters and do them any kind of justice, because I'd never experienced anything like it . . . But now . . ." I paused.

"Yes. Now . . ." he said. "That's kind of what I wanted to ask you about."

"Ask away," I said nervously.

"Well, I read something in the book that I just want to confirm, because I don't want to misinterpret anything here, and I certainly don't want to make a complete idiot of myself."

"What do you want to understand?" I asked.

"So . . ." He flipped the manuscript open and there was a high-lighted line in it. "Well, it's this part, really, that I want to just make sure I'm reading correctly." He pointed at the line and held it up in front of my face. I read it.

"What about that line?" I asked.

"Well . . ." He turned the manuscript around and cleared his throat. "It seems to imply that you—"

"Have fallen in love with you?" I asked, cutting him off.

"Well, yes." He looked up at me, malachite eyes shining in the early-morning light that was rushing through the stained-glass window.

"Yes," I repeated.

"So, I'm not reading this wrong, then?" he asked.

I shook my head. "No."

He looked back down at the manuscript and started nodding. "Okay. Okay . . ." He looked up at me and then took a step closer to me.

"You're in love with me?" he asked, with a smile.

I nodded. "Totally and utterly."

"Really?" He smiled. "And when did that happen?" he asked.

"I don't know," I replied breathily. "Halfway up a fence. Under a willow tree. In a small room under a stage. In a cove . . . Take your pick," I said softly. In fact, our love story seemed to be imprinted on to this town, in the same way Edith and Abe's was. Where their love story had unfolded, ours had, too. In all those magical nooks and crannies of this small town. The unders and overs and in-betweens.

He walked into my room and, in one movement, he took my face between his hands and kissed my lips. The manuscript fell to the floor with a bang. His smell flooded my senses—coffee and some-thing soapy, the hint of smoke from the fire. The kiss deepened quickly, obliterating the world around us. I felt dizzy, drunk on lust and love and filled with the desire to merge with him. I wrapped my arms around him and pulled him closer to me; I needed him to be a part of me, now. I'd waited for this moment for so long. And this kiss was just the beginning, the start of it, the promise of so much more and all to come.

"I'm totally and utterly in love with you, too," he said, with his lips pressed into mine. We stayed there like that for a while, lips touching, not kissing, breathing into each other's mouths as if we were giving each other life-saving air.

"Say it again," I whispered.

"I love you," he said, and kissed me again, and then started walking me back towards the bed . . .

* * *

There are a few things you need to know about me before we end this story. I think these things are important in order for you to understand why . . . *why* I landed up where I did.

I once wrote a book about having my heart broken. But, now, I've written a totally different book. I wrote a book about how my heart was mended.

It's strange. I set out thinking I was going to write a different story, a story about two other people's hearts, but somewhere along the way, this story became about my heart. My heart and *his* heart. A man named Mike, who loves me just the way I am. Not prettier, not richer, not more famous, not anything else, but me: Pebecca. The girl with the sloping line that disappeared all those years ago, along with the father I never knew—two events that set my strange life in motion. But the thing that I'd once seen as a curse, I now see as a blessing. Otherwise, my life wouldn't have played out in the way it did, and I wouldn't have landed up right here. Right here, in this moment.

And this moment is where I'm meant to be. I know that with

every cell in my body. Because I've finally found a place where I belong. I've finally found my tribe. My family. My home, the place I've been searching for all my life. And, I suppose, I've found myself, too. I found myself somewhere in a strange town, filled with strange people, that sits on the back of an indecisive turtle, which, if you think about it, is really a rather perfect place to find yourself. And I didn't need to buy another rose quartz table and practice chakra breathing to do that, either; it just sort of happened, without me even noticing it was happening. Perhaps that's how it's meant to be. Perhaps, when you put too much effort into something, you try too damn hard to be something and think too much about it, it doesn't happen. It's when you let go of the reins that things seem to fall into place.

I'm still a highly flawed person, though—let's just get that straight. I still jump before I think, I still probably care a little too much about what others think about me, but I'm working on that. But those flaws also led me down this particular fork in the road, and, this time, it was the right fork to choose. Because it led me to find love.

Do you believe in love at first sight? That strange concept, where two people who know nothing about each other just fall. How can they just walk off the edge of the cliff like that, without knowing if there will be anyone there to catch them?

But I think the answer is simple: you cannot help but fall. Jump. Sail down the other side of the cliff into the unknown. Because, when you meet *that* person, you have no choice but to fall. Close your eyes and let it happen. Don't fight it. Because what is waiting on the other side might be better and greater and bigger than anything you've ever known before.

The book I wrote is about that fall. This story is about how I fell down a fence and fell in love with a man named Mike. This is *my* story. This story belongs to me and me alone, and I know that telling it is the right thing to do . . . And that story I told is the story that you've just read. The story of how I fell in love with the last man

I expected to fall in love with. And how it all started one day, in an elevator . . .

YOU, ME, FOREVER
Pebecca Thorne

* * *

One year later

I hadn't seen these women since that day in the elevator. Since that day that changed absolutely everything. I sat at the coffee shop and waited for them. I wondered if their lives had changed as much as mine had in this year. So many things had happened to me, so many magical, wonderful things.

I was living with Mike and Ash and Emelia now, in that big old house with all the memories. Mike and I are still so in love and I'm enjoying every second of it. Ash and Emelia have gotten married. A small, beautiful wedding in the old stables, which Mike and Ash have converted into a wedding venue. (Techno Tannie now DJs the receptions there, and always manages to slip in one of her new tracks.)

Can there be a more perfect place to get married to someone, though? A place that held a lifetime of love stories in its walls. We have the photo of Abe and Edith up there, in a frame. Abe died a few months after reading those letters, and his granddaughter posted them all back to us, along with the photo of the two of them during that hot, sticky summer. She thought they should all come home, to the place they belonged. Abe came home, too. His ashes arrived in an urn. It was his dying wish that his final resting place be under the willow tree where he and Edith had carved their promise to each other. Mike and I had to pull some serious criminal maneuvers to get him there. The painting of Abe is now also hanging in the town hall, for all to see. It hangs tall and proud over the stage, so that the story of Abe and Edith is not forgotten. So that their story is now officially a part of this town's history.

The library is still full of porn. I've joined the ladies' weekly book club and, let me tell you . . . I am getting such an education there. I am learning about things I never knew existed.

But some sad things happened this year, too. Petra passed away, and her son never reached out to her. We buried her in the graveyard on the hill and the whole town came to her funeral. She was very loved and cared for. She might not have had the love she wanted, but it was always all around her. I just hope she knew and felt it when she was alive . . .

I decided to phone my mother, after that funeral. I didn't want things to be left between us like Pierre and Petra had left things. She's fine. She's married to a man that she loves and she's happy. I'm happy, too. The call was short; I think too much has passed between us to have a typical mother–daughter relationship. But I do forgive her. I forgive her for what she did, because I think I understand it a little more now than I did as a child. After seeing what losing the love of your life can do to someone, I think I finally understand her pain and struggle. But it's okay if I don't have the family I was meant to have, a mother and a father, because I've found my own family—a perfect, unconventional one that I can call my own.

I looked up as I heard the door to the coffee shop open. I was expecting to hear that urgent click of heels, expecting to see that scraped-back hair and those puckered matt lips. But I didn't.

She had changed. Everything about her was totally different. She walked over to my table and sat down. We looked at each other for the longest time without saying a word. And then we smiled. The door made another sound and we both looked up at the same time again as the third person from the elevator walked through the door.

I looked at her forehead and the red scar by her hairline. She wore it like a badge of honor. And she also looked different. We all sat down at the table and looked at each other. They were both so changed. Altered in the most profound way, the kind of way that changes who you are, right down to the lines in your face and the look in your eyes. A change so deep that it's seeped into your blood and your flesh and your soul . . .

But, then again, I was completely changed, too.

"So?" I finally spoke, looking from one to the other.

Frankie leaned forward. She was the one that had walked into the elevator first, the one whose shoe had smacked me between the shoulder blades.

"Well," she said, smiling at me, "I don't know about you guys, but that day in the elevator changed my whole life . . ." And, then, she started telling us *her* story.

ACKNOWLEDGMENTS

Thanks to Zoe for being an amazing assistant, supportive reader and for giving feedback on this book! Again, as always, to my husband for helping me with it! Natasha, for encouraging me to write this story.

Don't miss Jo's glorious, laugh-out-loud standalone office rom-coms!

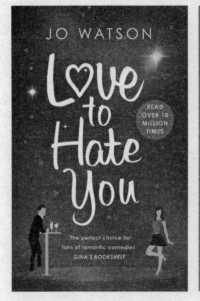

For laugh-out-loud, swoon-worthy hijinks, don't miss Jo's Destination Love series!

HEADLINE
ETERNAL

FIND YOUR HEART'S DESIRE...

VISIT OUR WEBSITE: www.headlineeternal.com
FIND US ON FACEBOOK: facebook.com/eternalromance
CONNECT WITH US ON TWITTER: @eternal_books
FOLLOW US ON INSTAGRAM: @headlineeternal
EMAIL US: eternalromance@headline.co.uk